PRAISE FOR *ONE MINUTE OUT*

"As always, Gentry is up to the task. Spy thriller fans will be enthralled."
—*Publishers Weekly* (starred review)

"It's satisfying to witness our larger-than-life protagonist put his combat skills to good use. . . . Great storytelling about the pursuit of extrajudicial justice."
—*Kirkus Reviews*

PRAISE FOR *MISSION CRITICAL*

"The latest in the Gray Man series continues to demonstrate why Greaney belongs in the upper echelon of special-ops thriller authors."
—*Booklist* (starred review)

"Greaney knows what military action fans want and delivers in spades."
—*Publishers Weekly*

"The action is almost nonstop, with nice twists right to the end. . . . This is good, Clancy-esque entertainment."
—*Kirkus Reviews*

"Mark Greaney continues his dominant run with *Mission Critical*, his most impressive novel yet and the clear-cut early favorite for best thriller of the year."
—The Real Book Spy

TITLES BY MARK GREANEY

THE GRAY MAN

ON TARGET

BALLISTIC

DEAD EYE

BACK BLAST

GUNMETAL GRAY

AGENT IN PLACE

MISSION CRITICAL

ONE MINUTE OUT

RED METAL

(with LtCol H. Ripley Rawlings IV,
USMC)

ONE MINUTE OUT

MARK
GREANEY

BERKLEY
NEW YORK

BERKLEY
An imprint of Penguin Random House LLC
penguinrandomhouse.com

Copyright © 2020 by Mark Greaney Books LLC
Penguin Random House supports copyright. Copyright fuels creativity, encourages diverse
voices, promotes free speech, and creates a vibrant culture. Thank you for buying an authorized
edition of this book and for complying with copyright laws by not reproducing, scanning, or
distributing any part of it in any form without permission. You are supporting writers and
allowing Penguin Random House to continue to publish books for every reader.

BERKLEY and the BERKLEY & B colophon are registered trademarks of
Penguin Random House LLC.

ISBN: 9780593098936

The Library of Congress has catalogued the Berkley hardcover edition of this book as follows:

Names: Greaney, Mark, author.
Title: One minute out / Mark Greaney.
Description: First edition. | New York : Berkley, 2020. | Series: The Gray Man
Identifiers: LCCN 2019045859 (print) | LCCN 2019045860 (ebook) |
ISBN 9780593098912 (hardcover) | ISBN 9780593098929 (ebook)
Subjects: GSAFD: Suspense fiction. | Spy stories.
Classification: LCC PS3607.R4285 O54 2020 (print) | LCC PS3607.R4285
(ebook) | DDC 813/.6—dc23
LC record available at https://lccn.loc.gov/2019045859
LC ebook record available at https://lccn.loc.gov/2019045860

Berkley hardcover edition / February 2020
Berkley trade paperback edition / August 2020

Printed in the United States of America
4th Printing

Cover photographs: image of man running © Mark Owen / Trevillion Images;
image of blurred cars by Paul Meneshian / EyeEm / Getty Images
Cover design by Steve Meditz
Interior art: black-and-white Paris map © Nicole Renna / Shutterstock.com

Dedicated to the men and women who fight
human trafficking around the globe.

ACKNOWLEDGMENTS

I would like to thank Joshua Hood (JoshuaHoodBooks.com), Rip Rawlings (RipRawlings.com), J.T. Patten (JTPattenBooks.com), Allison Wilson, Kristin Greaney, Larry Rice, Mystery Mike Bursaw, Simon Gervais (SimonGervaisBooks.com), Jon Harvey, James Yeager, Jay Gibson, the staff at Tactical Response, and the men and women on the *Aqua Cat*.

Also special thanks to my agent, Scott Miller, and everyone at Trident Media Group, and my editor, Tom Colgan, along with everyone at Berkley, especially Sareer Khader, Jeanne-Marie Hudson, Jin Yu, Loren Jaggers, Bridget O'Toole, Christine Ball, and Ivan Held.

Hell is empty, and all the devils are here.

—WILLIAM SHAKESPEARE, *THE TEMPEST*

CHARACTERS

COURTLAND GENTRY: Freelance assassin. Former CIA Special Activities Division (Ground Branch) paramilitary operations officer

LILIANA BRINZA: Moldovan citizen

RATKO BABIC: Former general, Bosnian Serb army

CAPTAIN NIKO VUKOVIC: Chief of police, Mostar, Bosnia and Herzegovina

TALYSSA CORBU: Europol criminal analyst

GIANCARLO RICCI: Security director of Alfonsi crime family, Italy

ROXANA VADUVA: Romanian university student

DR. CLAUDIA RIESLING: American psychologist

KOSTAS KOSTOPOULOS: Greek sex trafficker

KENNETH CAGE: Hollywood-based investment fund manager

SEAN HALL: Bodyguard to Ken Cage

JACO VERDOORN: Director of White Lion Security and Risk

ZACK HIGHTOWER: CIA contract employee. Former CIA Special Activities Division (Ground Branch) paramilitary operations officer

MATTHEW HANLEY: Deputy director for operations, CIA

SUZANNE BREWER: CIA officer

CHRIS TRAVERS: CIA Special Activities Center (Ground Branch) paramilitary operations officer

SHEP "PAPA" DUVALL: Former CIA, former JSOC (Delta Force) operative

RODNEY: U.S. Army veteran

KAREEM: U.S. Marine Corps veteran

A.J.: U.S. Army veteran

CARL: U.S. Army veteran

ONE MINUTE
OUT

ONE

GORNJI CRNAČ, BOSNIA AND HERZEGOVINA

The grandfather of six stood on his front porch, a cup of tea in hand as he looked out across the valley at the green hills, thinking of the old days.

They didn't seem so long ago, but still he often wondered where they had gone.

The warm afternoon tired him, and he considered a nap before dinner. It was something an old man would think to do, and this bothered him a little, because he didn't really consider himself old.

At seventy-five he was in robust health for his age, but back when he was young he had been truly strong and able physically, as well as a man of great power in his community.

But those days were long past. These days he lived here on this farm, never ever ventured off it, and he questioned if his labors in life had amounted to much of anything at all.

Money was no problem—he had more than he could ever spend—but he often pondered his purpose here on Earth. He'd most definitely had a purpose once, a cause he believed in, but now life amounted to little more than his easy work, his occasional pleasures, and the strict rules he'd adopted to live out his days in quiet and in peace.

Another day here, he told himself, reflecting on both the years and the decisions he'd made in life. Good decisions all, of this he was certain. He was not a man to harbor doubts about his actions.

But he was painfully aware that the decisions he'd made had come with a high cost.

The wet heat hanging in the still air tired him even more. He drank down the dregs of his tea, looking out over the lush green hills, contemplating his existence, and he made the final and resolute decision to go back inside the farmhouse to bed.

The old man's eyesight was not good, but even if he'd had the vision he'd enjoyed in his prime, he would not have been able to see the sniper across the valley, dressed in a green foliage ghillie suit and lying in thick brush 470 meters away, holding the illuminated reticle of his rifle's optic steady on the old man's chest.

The grandfather turned away from the vista before him, oblivious to the danger, and started back for the door to his large farmhouse. He put his hand on the latch, opened it, and stepped inside.

There was no gunshot; only the single crow of a rooster broke the quiet of the valley.

• • •

Dammit, Gentry, take the fucking shot already.

My finger comes off the trigger. My eye blinks and retracts from the scope. I thumb the safety, then lower my forehead down into the warm grass next to my weapon's buttstock.

Dude, you suck.

I get like this. Negative self-talk echoes through my brain when I don't do what I should do, what I've told myself I *must* do.

The voice is annoying, but the voice is right.

Why didn't I shoot that asshole when I had the chance? I've been lying in this sweltering, bug-infested overwatch for two days, my neck and upper back are killing me, and my mouth tastes like something crawled in there and died—a possibility I can't really rule out.

I've had my target in my twelve-power scope six times so far, and I could have taken him the first time, which would put me in Zagreb or Ljubljana or even Budapest by now. Shaved and fed and showered and safe.

Instead I am right here, caked in thick layers of grime and sweat, lying in the itchy grass, and bitching at myself.

I should be gone, and he should be dead.

Retired Serbian general Ratko Babic may look innocent enough now, living quietly on this farm in Bosnia and Herzegovina, just northwest of the town of Mostar. But I know who he is.

And I know what he did.

The old goat may be up to nothing more nefarious these days than harassing his chickens to lay more eggs, but twenty-five years ago, Ratko Babic was a household name, known the world over as one of the worst human beings on planet Earth.

And for the past quarter century he has paid exactly no price for his actions.

I don't like that shit.

He's a war criminal, the perpetrator of acts of genocide, and personally responsible for orchestrating the mass execution of eight thousand men and boys over three days in the summer of 1995.

I don't like that shit, either.

The UN wants him, NATO wants him, the International Criminal Court wants him, the families of his victims want him—and he's slipped by them all.

But now *I* want him, and that pretty much means Ratko's fucked.

Or else I'm fucked, because I can't make myself shoot him at standoff distance.

No, my dumb ass has to do this the hard way.

I'm not holding fire because of any second thoughts; no, this bastard richly needs to die—but if I pop him from here with a .300 Winchester Magnum round at 477 meters, then he's going to drop like a sack of wet sand and die quickly and unaware, and the thought of that has been driving me crazy since the moment I first saw him.

Eight thousand lives, plus. Torture. Rape. All because of that asshole on the other side of the valley.

Me simply flipping his lights off, sight unseen, from a quarter mile away . . . that's too good for him.

So instead I'm going in.

I'll penetrate his property after nightfall, breach his wires, and sneak past those protecting him. I'll make my way to wherever he sleeps, and then I'll appear out of the darkness and let him feel my hot breath on his face while I end him. Up close, personal, and so slow he will lose his head before I stop his heart.

That's the plan, anyway.

I've been doing this long enough to know that sometimes plans go sideways, and it's given me a healthy fear.

But not enough, clearly. There's still the voice in me that says, *You've got this, Gentry. Don't do what's easy. Do what's right. What's righteous.*

And that voice is in charge today, not the one that keeps telling me I'm an idiot.

I've been studying the sentries. They're pros, which actually surprises me. Six static, six mobile, with a second team that lives somewhere off property and rotates in every twenty-four hours. It's a lot more guns than I thought he'd have. Most other Balkan war criminals busted over the years were found to be lying low, with no more than two or three guys watching their backs, so I had figured on a lower profile for Babic, as well.

But Ratko's out here in the sticks with two dozen gun monkeys, and that seems strange to me.

They seem to be well trained, but my time in this overwatch has uncovered a serious compromise. The mobile guys are the toughest to anticipate, but at dinner they go static, same as the rest. A couple of sentries stay down on the road that leads into the property, another hangs out in the main house with the protectee, but the rest sit at tables in front of the bunkhouse a hundred meters away from Babic's farmhouse while three women bring dinner out to them.

Babic himself doesn't eat with the detail. He takes his meals inside the house.

So that's where I'm headed.

Tonight's going to be a bitch, if experience is any guide.

Whatever, I tell myself. *I'll adapt and overcome.*

Hopefully.

My principal trainer in the CIA's singleton operator school, the Autonomous Asset Development Program, was an old Agency shooter and Vietnam vet named Maurice. And Maurice had a saying that has stuck with me over the years, possibly because he screamed it into my ear something like half a million times.

"Hope is not a strategy."

Nearly two decades living downrange has me convinced that Maurice was right, yet still I plan on scooting down this hillside, climbing up the opposite hillside, and *hoping* like hell I can get in my target's face.

One last time that angry voice in my head implores me to stand down. *C'mon, Gentry. Just lie here and wait for Babic to walk his fat ass back in front of your optic again. Then you can smoke him and be gone: quick, clean, and safe.*

But no. I'm going in, and I know it.

I look up at the sky, see the sun lowering over the hills on the other side of the valley, and begin slowly stretching my tight and sore muscles, getting ready for the action to come.

I've got to load up the Jeep and position it for a fast getaway, and then I have to change into black, pull on a ski mask, and head out through the foliage towards my target.

This is a bad idea and I know it, but that bent and broken moral compass of mine is in the driver's seat, it's more powerful than the angry voice of reason, and it's telling me that a quick and painless end for Ratko Babic would be no justice at all.

TWO

The general woke in time for dinner, made his way down to the dining room in his large but simple farmhouse, and sat at the table alone. Often old friends dropped in, fellow officers from the war, men who had served their sentences and then returned to the area or who had somehow avoided being charged with crimes in the first place. Only once had he met with another Serbian wanted by the authorities for his actions, but this man had soon after been killed in a shootout in Sarajevo.

This evening Babic had no guests; it was just him, the hollow ticking of the grandfather clock in the main entryway, and the clanging of pots and pans in the kitchen as the cook and her two assistants prepared dinner.

One hundred meters away, most of his security boys from Belgrade would themselves be sitting down to dinner in front of the bunkhouse.

Ratko ate the same food as the men, a habit he'd picked up as a young officer in the Yugoslav army. The Hungarian wine he drank was better than the Žilavka, a Bosnian wine provided to the security team, but that was a small personal allowance to his wealth and his seniority, and none of the boys from Belgrade who watched over him judged him for saving the good stuff for himself.

He'd earned some perks for his lifelong dedication to the cause, and the men from Belgrade all knew it.

Babic put a napkin in his shirt as his chief protection agent leaned into the dining room. "You okay, boss?"

"Fine, Milanko. When I'm finished, I want to go spend time with the boys."

"Sounds good, sir." Milanko stepped back into the living room to return to the TV he'd been watching.

Tanja served the old man a steaming bowl of *podvarak*: sauerkraut casserole filled with bacon and bits of beef.

"*Hvala,*" he said. *Thank you.*

Tanja bowed a little and left the dining room.

She didn't like him; it was obvious to the general that she didn't approve of what he had done or what he did now, but she'd been sent from Belgrade along with the others and she did what she was told, and that was all an old officer like Babic expected out of anyone.

Petra came in next with a basket of bread and a plate of butter and put it to him with a nod and a little smile, and Babic reached out and grabbed the nineteen-year-old girl's ass as she walked away.

She didn't turn back or even adjust her stride. This was a nightly occurrence for her; she was past the point of caring.

"Cold little bitch," he said under his breath. Tanja and Milena were plain and middle-aged. Petra, on the other hand, was young and beautiful. But Babic didn't push it with Petra, because, like all the others here on the farm around him, she came from Belgrade, and Ratko knew he could do just about whatever the fuck he wanted till the day he died, as long as he didn't leave the farm, and as long as he didn't piss off the Branjevo Partizans—the Belgrade mob.

He watched her ass wiggle out of the room and then returned his attention to his food.

Behind him the window displayed only darkness, but if he'd bothered to turn his head and peer out, if he'd retained the vision of his younger days, and if he'd concentrated hard in just the right portion of the property, he might have been able to detect a brief flash of movement—fast, from right to left, from the fence line towards the back of the house.

But instead, he dug into his *podvarak* and sipped his wine, and his mind shifted again to the glorious past.

. . .

After dinner Babic and his protection agent Milanko headed over to the bunkhouse to chat and smoke with the crew still eating there.

He enjoyed his evening visits with the boys; they made him feel respected, important, vital. Long ago it was a sensation he'd known so fully and so well, but now it was a feeling that only came in passing.

As he and Milanko walked through the night, behind them the dogs began barking. The general sighed.

They never shut up.

. . .

Damn dogs. I mean . . . I love dogs, who doesn't, but not when they're compromising my op. I knew about the two massive black Belgian Malinois, but their kennels are behind the farmhouse, and I ingressed from the west side and was careful to stay out of the dogs' line of sight. But clearly they smell me here on the southern side of the building, because they're going *fucking* bonkers back there now.

As I squat here picking the lock on the door to a utility room in the darkness, I will myself to go faster and for the two big furry assholes around the corner of the house to shut the hell up.

I've used silver-lined body suits to hide my smell from dogs in the past, and they function as advertised, but it's July and hot as hell here, so if I *had* put a scent guard on under my ghillie suit I would have dropped dead in my overwatch from heat exhaustion.

With the way I reek right now, the dogs are probably barking out of disgust and not to alert their handlers, but no matter the reason, I have to get this door open, pronto. I've been defeating locks for twenty years, and I'm pretty good at it, but this isn't the movies. It takes time and concentration.

I hear footsteps approaching on the gravel drive at the front of the house, moving in my direction. Just one person; it must be a cook or a guard coming over to check on the Malinois in their kennels. Either way, I have a silenced Glock, a couple of knives, and a B&T ultracompact submachine gun. I can kill anyone in my way, but doing so while Ratko is on the other side of the property surrounded by seven or eight bodyguards would most definitely be the wrong move for me.

So . . . open the fucking door already, Gentry.

As the footsteps grow louder I rake the last tumbler into place and I hear the click as the latch gives—and I slip inside with only a few seconds to spare.

Outside the footsteps continue past the door towards the kennels, and I breathe a silent sigh of relief.

I'm in.

• • •

Ratko Babic sat smoking and drinking with the off-duty men from the Belgrade detail till after eleven, and then he made his way back over to the farmhouse with his bodyguard at his side.

This night was like any other on the farm. The rest of the protection team patrolled the grounds or sat in static positions. One was on the front porch, night vision goggles on his forehead, ready to pull down at the first sound of trouble. Two other men covered the driveway from a concrete pillbox mostly hidden in tall grass, and another from the roof of the bunkhouse, while another pair patrolled the fence line.

This security plan had kept Babic safe for the past several years, but the truth was, these men were not here to protect Ratko Babic himself.

They were here to protect the farm and, more specifically, what secrets the farm hid.

• • •

The seventy-five-year-old climbed the wooden stairs to the second floor with Milanko behind him. Babic would go to his room for a quick shower, take a pill . . . perhaps two, drink some more wine, and then he would enjoy a little recreation before bed. His nap had rested him, prepared him for what was to come, and if Milanko was aware of his boss's plans, he had the good manners to give no indication of it.

The old man felt the first little surge of excitement in his chest of the day, and this depressed him some. There wasn't much left to live for, he told himself. His service to his people was long ago; now he served other masters, and this work did not fill him with one one-hundredth of the same pride.

• • •

Once Milanko saw the general to his bedroom, he turned and walked back up the hall for the large wooden circular staircase. There was a chair at the top, and he'd sit here for a couple of hours, facing the lighted stairwell, to provide protection to the man behind him. He wasn't worried about Babic. The bastard had lived invisibly since the 1990s. First moving around Serbia, Bosnia, and Macedonia, and then settling here some ten years back. Now the general was nothing more than a caretaker and, Milanko had to admit, he was good at his job. He was efficient and organized and he led the people under him like the military officer he had once been. And, more importantly than anything, he had impressed his employers with his discretion and his willingness to do that which must be done.

So Milanko sat up here and kept him alive.

He glanced down at his watch and realized it was time for the radio check. Normally he initiated it, because he was leader of the detail, although sometimes he'd be otherwise occupied so one of his subordinates would make the initial call.

He grabbed the radio clipped to his belt and pressed the talk button. A wireless earpiece also contained a microphone so he didn't have to bring his handset to his mouth. "Station One, reporting in."

Instantly he heard Luka at the front gate guard station, where two men sat. "Station Two, reporting."

Then Pyotr on the second-floor window of the bunkhouse. "Station Three."

"Station Four," said Karlo on the front porch.

The patrolling men checked in next, and the radio fell silent again.

As soon as the radio checks were complete, Milanko heard a door open in the hall behind him. He didn't turn around because he was a professional, and he was discreet. It was the old man, heading off towards the rear spiral staircase. Normally a principal protection agent would put himself on the shoulder of his protectee, but Milanko knew where Babic was headed now, and he also knew the old man didn't want a bodyguard with him.

And Milanko was sure he would not want to witness what Babic was about to do. So he just sat there on the chair, began playing a game on his phone, and protected the empty hallway behind him, waiting for the general's return from the basement.

. . .

Put your war face on, I tell myself as I slowly push the latch down and crack open the door of the closet, just ten feet or so behind the chair positioned at the top of the stairs. The guard's back is to me, and I'd just gotten lucky; I'd only had to wait a couple of minutes for him to make his commo check with his team. Now, I have some time. I don't know how much, because I don't know their check-in schedule, but I'll make it work.

My confidence is increasing as I hit my waypoints, one by one.

The hallway is well lit. I reach to the black vest on my chest and pull a knife with a six-inch blade from its sheath, and I close for a silent kill.

. . .

Milanko had spent his entire adult life in the military, and then in various security postings, in both the Serbian government and the Serbian underworld. He had a sixth sense for his job; he could sense trouble, perceive danger before those around him.

And he'd learned to rely on these instincts, so when a sudden feeling of threat registered in his brain, he looked up from his game of Scrabble, then cocked his head to listen for a noise. Hearing nothing did not assuage his concern, so he rose quickly from his chair and turned to check back over his shoulder.

A man stood two paces away, head to toe in black, a balaclava covering the lower half of his face.

Before he could even shout in surprise, Milanko saw a black blade coming for him, and then he felt it buried in his throat.

The man holding the knife embraced him, pulled him over the chair, and then pushed him up against the wall.

Milanko felt no pain, just a sense of shock and confusion, and then, shortly before his world went black, he felt one more thing.

He felt like he'd failed.

THREE

I don't get off on this. But it's the job. The sentry needs to be silenced before he can alert either my target or the rest of his comrades, so I jam my knife into his throat, yank his weakening body up to the wall, and hold him there, waiting for the kicking and shaking to subside.

He barely makes a noise as he dies.

Nothing like a blade through the windpipe to shut you up and shut you down.

Snapping his radio onto my belt and putting his earpiece in my ear, I wipe my knife off on his pants leg and resheathe it. I draw my suppressed Glock and cover up the hallway, then spin to check down the stairs.

No threats, no noise.

I drag the body into the closet off the hallway where I'd been waiting, lay him there with blood all over him, then look down and see the red smears on my own filthy black clothing and tactical gear.

The sentry wasn't my target, but he also wasn't exactly collateral damage.

I myself have been the guy working close protection for some asshole, although I only did it in cover and on the job for some cause that I thought to be worthy. Unlike this guy in the closet, I don't work to keep the shit-heads of the world alive.

I pretty much do the opposite.

So while I might feel a twinge of regret acing some working stiff who made a bad career choice, I do it anyway.

Sorry, buddy. Slinging a gun for the bad guys can get you killed. If you didn't know that already, then I can't help you.

I open the door to Babic's room slowly, look around, and am surprised to find it empty. His bathroom is a dry hole, as well. I step back out into the hall, certain I heard the old man come this way minutes earlier, confused about where he's disappeared to. I hold the Glock high, scanning left and right, and I notice a covert door on the wall at the opposite end of the hallway. Opening it, I find a circular staircase that leads down.

It's dark as hell, ominous looking, but I guess I'm going down there.

I flip down my NOD, night observation device, and it pulls in and magnifies the ambient light, turning it into a dim green hue before me.

I begin my slow descent, with my weapon at the end of an extended arm.

I move as quickly as I can down the stairs, while still doing my best to remain as silent as possible. I'm working with an accelerated clock now because, sooner or later, someone is going to check in with the guy I just aced.

I descend one flight, which takes me back to the ground level of the house. Here I find a landing with another narrow door, just like upstairs, but I also see that the circular stairs continue down.

Did he go back to the main floor? Or did he go down into the cellar?

Something tells me to keep descending.

I arrive at the basement, satisfied that my climb down the metal staircase was as quiet as I could make it, but once here, I realize a little noise wouldn't have posed a problem. I hear music, some sort of pop shit that surprises me considering that this guy seems a bit old for that, but it does at least give me a hint there might be someone down here.

There is a narrow hallway with doors on either side and a door at the end, and enough illumination from a string of white Christmas lights staple-gunned to the ceiling for me to flip up my NOD. I adjust my B&T submachine gun so that it's hanging from its sling at the small of my back and begin moving with well-practiced footwork that keeps me damn near silent.

The music gets louder with each step forward; my pistol is trained on the door at the end of the hall because that seems to be the origin of the crappy tune, but as I arrive at the doors to the left and right, I know I have to clear the space behind them.

The door on the right opens with a slow turn of the latch; as soon as I crack it I see that the room beyond is pitch-black, so I quickly re-don my night vision equipment.

Dirty mattresses line the floor along with cigarette butts and soiled sheets.

What looks like dried blood stains the walls.

Shit.

Someone has been living in these horrible dark conditions, a prisoner here, no doubt, but I don't take the time to dig into how long ago they vacated.

I'm here for the general; thinking about anything else right now is just going to get in the way.

There are a tiny washbasin and a toilet in a small room beyond, but the area is clear, so I head back into the hall to check the second room.

I keep my NOD down over my eyes as I crack the door, but upon seeing red lighting in the room, I flip it up again quickly. I open the door and swing in with my pistol.

Two heads turn my way in surprise, and then in utter shock, because an armed man dressed in black with his face covered is an understandably distressing sight.

Illuminated by dim red light, a young woman sits on a bed; she's wearing a dirty button-down shirt sized for a man. It's open and her large breasts are exposed. Her hair is frazzled, she has an unkempt and tired appearance, and her face is a mask of horror now as she looks my way.

She has a black eye that looks fresh to me, even in the weird lighting.

And standing above her at the side of the bed is an older man with his shirt off, his girth hanging over his pants, his belt doubled in his hand as if he just removed it so he could use it to beat the woman.

I look the man over, but not for long.

Target . . . fucking . . . acquired.

"Evening, Ratko."

He says something in Serbian I don't understand, but fortunately he seems to be fluent in gun-in-the-face because when I raise the Glock towards him he shuts the fuck up. He shows confusion, as if he's wondering how the hell this lone gunman made it through all his boys above, but he's not showing much in the way of fear.

"No shoot," he says. "What do you want?"

And here we go. English. The international language of begging for one's life.

Before I can answer his question by drawing my knife and stabbing him through his intestines, the woman climbs off the bed, raising her hands in the air. This is a ballsy move in front of a guy waving around a 9-millimeter, but she seems to get that I'm not here for her.

The girl looks at me, then at the door. I nod, knowing that whatever was going on here wasn't consensual, and I doubt she's about to go running to the protection guys to be a tattletale.

The woman passes me, her hands still raised and her eyes never leaving mine, and she disappears out the door.

Now Ratko and I have our alone time.

"You are the assassin, yes?"

This dude's a fucking genius. "I am *an* assassin, yes."

"I tell you . . . I have no regrets."

"Yeah? Me, either. Especially not about this." I advance on him.

"You . . . you are the Gray Man."

I stop. He's right, unfortunately. Some people know of me by that ridiculous nickname. But how does *he* know who I am? I want to get on with it, but my own personal security concerns tell me to dig into his comment. "Why do you say that?"

"Belgrade send me their best men. They say, 'Only Gray Man can get you now, but Gray Man not real, so do not worry.' I listen to them. I do not worry."

I take another step forward; I'm almost in contact distance now. "No reason in worrying about things you can't change."

"They say . . . that you are a ghost."

"I get that a lot." Quickly I snap the suppressed pistol into the Kydex holster on my hip and draw the black, six-inch blade from the sheath on my chest.

The gun didn't faze him. I guess he's ready to die, but he clearly does *not* like the looks of the knife in my hand. His eyes fill with terror as he realizes I have plans for him, and this won't be a quick and painless end to his long, horrible life, after all.

I slip a gloved hand around his thick throat and push him up against the wall. The tanto blade of the Spyderco knife is pointed at his midsection, an inch away from drawing blood.

Quickly he says, "What does Gray Man want?"

I hold the blade up in front of his face. "For this to hurt."

I talk too much in times like this. I should've taken this guy out from a quarter mile away, forgotten about penetrating his compound, and there would have been no talking.

But I am done talking now, so I put the knife against his bare stomach. Before I even draw blood, though, he says something that makes me hold again.

"Girls! Girls here. You take. I give all to you. Perfect girls. The best in world."

At first I think he's talking about the young woman who just ran out of the room, but he definitely said "girls," so I next assume he means the three female cooks who I saw bringing the food out to the security guys. I'm not really looking to open a restaurant, so I don't answer. I recover again, then ready the knife to drag it across Babic's midsection.

"Twenty-three. No! Twenty-five. Twenty-five beautiful ladies. High class. For you! Yes!"

Wait. *What?* I ease up on the blade, but just a little.

"Twenty-five ladies, *here*? You're lying."

"I show you. You take. Make you happy."

Oh my God. Is this motherfucker a war criminal *and* a pimp?

"You were already going to die poorly, Ratko. If you give me reason to form an even lower opinion of your character, this might get even nastier."

He doesn't get what I'm saying. He responds, "Here. In cellar. Beautiful. All for you, friend."

I close my eyes. *Shit.* There's always something. Some fucking fly in the ointment.

The knife is poised; I am ready. I think about just killing him, ignoring the crazed rantings of a condemned man.

But no.

Because I am an expert in detecting deception, and I don't think this asshole's lying. There probably *are* some more women down here, and my educated guess is that they'd rather not be.

And, much as I'd like to, I just can't walk away from that. It's my fatal flaw: time after time my conscience gets me deeper into the shit.

"Show me."

"Yes, I show you."

I draw the Glock again, sheathe the knife, and push him back out into the hallway.

We move quickly to the door at the end of the corridor where the music is coming from, the tip of my suppressor six inches from the back of his neck. I don't know where the woman with the black eye has gone, but I assume she took the staircase up and is making a run for it.

In seconds Ratko and I arrive at the door; he taps a code into a keypad and turns the latch. Quickly I shove him inside, rush in behind him, and pull the door shut, because in the hall I was exposed to anyone who came down the stairs at the opposite end.

The room is so dark I reach for my NOD to pull it down over my eyes, but Ratko flips a light switch.

A low-wattage red bulb hanging from a cord from the ceiling gives an eerie dim scarlet glow over the room.

Before I can even focus on what's before me, my earpiece comes alive.

I don't speak Serbian, but it's clear: the security detail is performing a radio check.

But it barely registers. I am too fixated on what I see.

A room, about ten feet wide and twenty-five feet deep. Walls of bare earth and wooden beams. There are more dirty mattresses on the floor, more broken sofas around the perimeter. A row of three chemical toilets, essentially buckets with cracked plastic seats, sit exposed in the corner on my right.

And two dozen or so women, some may be girls, sitting, squatting, lying flat. Pressed close together and forming a single life-form in the red dim. Someone turns off the music and I hear coughing, crying.

I see chains, and realize they are all shackled by their ankles to eyebolts in the floor.

I smell bad food, cigarette smoke, sweat, shit, piss, and, above it all, absolute and utter despair.

No one speaks a word. They just stare at me with wide, fearful, imploring eyes.

What . . . the . . . fuck?

I've seen some things in my days. I've never seen this.

"I tell you," Ratko says while standing next to me. "Best in world for best in world. All for you, Gray Man."

I'm not the "best in world," and though the ex-general keeps saying it, these people are probably not "best in world" at *anything* in this condition. But that isn't for me to judge. They are all daughters or wives or sisters or mothers. And they are all human trafficking victims, it is plain to see.

I have no idea what they're doing here, why an old Bosnian general would have so many slaves with him on his farm, but whatever the reason, I know one thing for certain.

All these women and girls, all of them are human beings, and right now they are circling the drain of a sick fucking world.

I was mad before. Now I'm wild with rage.

I raise my Glock at Ratko with my right hand while looking back to the ladies. "Those of you who speak English, close your eyes, and translate that to the others."

That gets Ratko agitated, but some of the ladies do as instructed. Others just keep looking on, knowing exactly what is about to happen, but unafraid.

Babic speaks in a rush now. "There are more. Many more. In two weeks. You get them all. You come back. I give to you when they come."

I can't listen to another fucking word out of this piece of shit's mouth, my fury is so overpowering. My right hand clenches, not from the seething anger, but because I want to hear my gun go *bang*.

My gun goes *bang*.

I don't even look at the general as the hollow-point round slams into his fat bare belly. The suppressor, plus the fact that we're down in the basement, makes me feel confident I am still covert. He thumps to the floor, writhing and moaning. I glance his way briefly, and shoot him twice more.

His body jolts with the impact of the rounds, then stills.

The radio check continues in my ear. I hear the clipped cadence of different men as each calls in, with either a name or a location or something else in Serbo-Croatian that I can't understand.

I tune it out again and look at the large mass of women in the tight space in front of me. "Who speaks English?"

All eyes are open now, and one blonde stands up in the middle of the crowd.

"I do." Other women call out, as well.

"Listen carefully. There's an old bus behind the house. We're going to get on it and get out of here, but we have to work fast, and we have to work together."

The standing woman—she sounds like she could be Ukrainian to me—simply says, "No, sir."

I've turned to check down the hall, but my head spins back towards her. "What?"

"It is not possible. We stay. We must stay."

"Are you out of your mind? None of you look like you want to—"

But I hold a hand up, telling the women to wait a moment, because the earpiece I stole from the security guard upstairs just came alive again.

A man keeps repeating a word in a questioning tone. "Milanko? Milanko?"

I guess I now know the name of the dude I dumped in the closet.

The voice on the radio turns loud and authoritative, clearly telling someone, probably *everyone*, to get their asses to the farmhouse to see what happened to the guy at the top of the stairs.

Back to the crowd I say, "We have to get the hell out of here right—"

"Sir." The standing woman speaks up again. I can tell even through the grime on her face and the bad light of the basement that she is young and pretty. "We have family. Ukraine. Romania. Moldova, Chechnya, Kosovo, Bulgaria. We leave . . . someone back home kill our family." She shakes her head. "We no can leave."

For a moment I am frozen in place. I look at a busload of kidnapping victims who don't want to leave their hellish prison; I know that something like a dozen men and a pair of attack dogs are about to rain down on my position, and I don't have a clue what the fuck I'm supposed to do now.

FOUR

Five men rushed into the house from various stations, all with guns drawn and held at the low ready because, for all they knew at this point, Milanko's radio had failed or he'd dropped it in the toilet.

But when Karlo got to the top of the stairs he thought to open the closet just behind Milanko's chair, and when he did so, a very dead team leader flopped out onto the runner lining the floor.

He called it in immediately, and within seconds the dogs were brought from the kennels and let loose in the farmhouse.

• • •

I turn off the red light in this chamber of horrors, open the door to the cellar hallway, and notice that the Christmas lights running along the ceiling are plugged into an outlet within reach. I unplug them, casting the hallway into darkness, and I flip the NOD down over my eyes. Holstering the Glock, I heft my B&T MP9 machine pistol, extend the short stock, and bring the holographic sight up to eye level.

I see nothing, but I hear the careful footfalls of a single person descending the circular staircase past the open doorway thirty feet up the hall.

Then the footsteps stop.

To the ladies behind me I ask, "Is there another way out of here?"

One of them answers. "We no leave."

I'm over it by now, so I snap back at her. "I'm talking about me! You guys can do whatever the hell you want."

Can't help the helpless, I tell myself, and then I consider their situation. If I had someone special back at home, I wouldn't want them to pay a price for my noncompliance.

But I don't, so my ass is out of here.

A lady says, "Only the stairs. There is no other way."

I turn back to them quickly. "They will move you after this."

The blonde who spoke before says, "They move us anyway. This is just a stop. We go to Europe, America. They use us for as long as they can, then . . . who knows?"

Another woman says, "We are going to die."

She was immediately hushed by another English speaker.

The blonde's voice is grave. "They'll punish us, now. Because of you coming here."

I'm certain she's right. Anyone horrible enough to keep slaves for sex work is horrible enough to discipline the slaves for something that isn't their fault.

I find my feet rooted to the floor. I don't want to leave these girls, but my tactical brain can't find a solution to all this. "I'm sorry," I say. It's not enough. It's nothing, in fact, but I've got nothing else.

I don't ponder my words long, because almost instantly I'm racing up the dark hallway towards the staircase, leaving two dozen desperate women and girls behind me.

Nice work, Gentry.

It seems my footfalls make noise in the hall because I see the dude in the stairwell lean out with his rifle. I have my B&T on full auto, and I fire a pair of three-round bursts at him while at a dead sprint. One or more of the rounds hits his hand or arm, because he drops the weapon and tumbles to the floor.

I take the Swiss-made machine pistol in my left hand as I run, aim it high at the stairs, and as I leap over the wounded guard, I draw my Glock. I point it down between my legs and fire twice into the wounded sentry during my vault so he can't draw a backup weapon and shoot me from behind.

It's dirty, but people who offer quarter in a gunfight typically don't make good gunfighters.

I holster the pistol but sense new movement on the staircase now, which is why I've kept my machine pistol aimed there. As soon as I see a rifle and a man holding it, I fire a long burst. The sentry falls forward and rolls down the stairs, and I leap over his sliding body to begin my ascent.

Angling my B&T high and leaning out to cut the corners quicker than if I just kept running up the middle of the stairs, I catch the side of a descending man's head in my sights before he sees me. I fire four rounds at him, and down he goes, ass over teakettle, his weapon clanking along with the thuds and slaps of his body as he tumbles down the stairs. I round the landing below the ground floor and vault this guy like I did the one below.

Keep coming, assholes. I can do this all day.

I hear a volley of impossibly loud gunfire above me, and the plaster on the wall inches to my right is chewed into dust by pistol rounds, and this tells me I probably *can't* do this all day. I dive flat on the steps and return fire, almost blindly, nearly emptying my magazine, and then I roll tight against the wall, my head facing up as I reload.

Two men look over the side one story up, whipping short-barreled rifles down at me as they do so.

I slam the magazine in and rake them with outgoing fire, dumping two dozen rounds onto their position above. One man gets a single shot off before he flies back out of the view, and the second sentry spins away and falls onto the stairs above an instant later.

I'm up and moving again, bursting through the door on the ground floor, where I catch one man kneeling down, getting into a fighting position. He obviously heard the battle in the stairwell and wanted to be prepared in case I made it out of there.

I made it out of there, and he's not prepared, so I fire the last six rounds from the B&T at him, killing him where he lies, and then I drop the empty gun on its sling and pull my Glock again.

The house is dark, but I see a door open slowly on my right. I spin my weapon towards the movement, take up the give in the trigger safety on my weapon, then see the face of a middle-aged woman looking out at me. She isn't holding a weapon, so I keep going, but as I near her position, I shout, "Close your door!"

My ears are ringing from the gunfight in the stairwell, so if she says anything to me, I don't hear it. But at least she shuts the door.

I attempt a mental head count while I run. There were twelve security on the property when I came in; I knifed the dude upstairs, took down four in the stairwell, and another here.

Six left. Shit.

I open a door to find a bathroom with no window large enough to escape from. As I turn out of the space, I realize that I have not accounted for all the threats.

It's not just six sentries. It's also the dogs. Can't forget about the two—

I face the room again and see a massive black form flying through the air in the darkness right at me. One of the Belgian Malinois slams my pistol against my chest as he knocks me against the wall. We both fall to the floor, and his crazed teeth snatch my right hand. The hand is wearing a Kevlar-lined glove with the trigger finger cut out, so he doesn't rip it off immediately. Still, I know that with a simple shake or two he can snap my wrist.

With my left hand I punch the dog hard in the snout, and he lets go and recoils an instant, but I'd broken this hand a couple months back, and the pain from the punch prevents me from driving it harder into the canine's face.

The dog recovers quickly, then charges at me again.

He leaps, I duck, the eighty-pound animal flies into the bathroom, and I spin around and grab the door latch, yanking it closed in his snarling face.

Hefting my pistol, I stagger a few feet; the damn dog knocked the wind out of me, but soon I'm heading off again.

I don't shoot dogs. Ever. Still, my Glock is up, and I'm muttering to myself as if I'm talking to the barking dog in the bathroom. "Where's your buddy? Where's your buddy?"

I hear continuous voices in the earpiece, and I really wish I spoke Serbo-Croatian, because I could use some clarity on where the other half dozen assholes are right now. I make my way into the kitchen, scanning for threats as I advance, then pass a stairway on my right. Looking up with my pistol trained, I see two men rush past up there, but neither looks down in my direction, probably because they don't have night vision.

I don't fire; I continue through the kitchen towards a door, and then, through my ringing ears, I hear a sound behind me in the large living area I've just passed.

Paws beating on hardwood, getting louder and louder.

The other dog is running me down from behind.

"Shit!" Fresh panic wells in me, and I know I have to make it outside, because I don't shoot dogs.

I run as fast as I can, desperate to get out before the black monster rips me apart, but when I put my hand on the latch and pull, nothing happens.

I see two deadbolt locks, and both are engaged.

Behind me the beast keeps running; it snarls frantically as it races across the kitchen tile.

I'm in trouble, serious trouble, but I don't shoot dogs.

I turn one of the locks, then begin to reach for the other, but I can tell I'm not going to get out in time. He's only three huge bounds away from sinking his teeth into the back of my neck.

Fuck it. I'm shooting this dog.

Spinning around, I lift my pistol to line it up on the animal's fat face; he's ten feet away, just on the far side of the stairwell.

The Malinois launches himself at me just as a man appears, leaping into view from the stairs, obviously responding to my shout or the sound of movement down here in the kitchen.

He turns towards me, swinging his subgun, and the big canine slams into the man's back, knocking him facedown and causing the dog to roll and slide on the tile, crashing through chairs and a small wooden table.

I turn back to the door, open the second lock, and dive outside while pulling it shut behind me.

I'm in the well-lit drive; there could be four or five guns lining up on me right now, but I don't even scan for threats.

I run. I just . . . fucking . . . run.

. . .

Twenty-four-year-old Liliana Brinza raced through the woods down the hill, lost in the dark with no real concept of where she was or where she was going; all she knew for certain was that she had to get the hell away from the dungeon she'd been living in for the past week or so.

She'd arrived at night, and since then she'd lived in the room with the red light, only to be dragged out, away from the other women, once or twice a day to be raped.

The old man was the worst. He'd beaten her and raped her, and he'd been seconds away from doing it again when the man in black appeared. Liliana was no fool; she saw the opportunity and raced up the stairs, hid in a closet while she decided on her next move, listening to gunfire and the frantic shouts of men downstairs. Then she heard the dogs in the house and finally she took a chance and ran for the back door next to the empty kennels. She saw no one outside at all, so she raced across the back pasture to the woods, hid in some brush for a few minutes, and now she wanted to find a road or a town or another house with a phone or *anything* that could help her out of this desperate situation.

She ran on, her bare feet bleeding and thin branches whipping against her body, and she told herself she was in the clear, that no one was out here looking for her.

This horrific ordeal was over.

Just then a form spun in her direction from behind a tree, moved in front of her in the moonlight, took her by the mouth and covered it, and pulled her down to the ground.

He had her in a headlock, held her facing away from him as they sat in the grass, with his other hand still tight against her mouth.

She couldn't scream, but she could bite. So she did.

. . .

It's not my night. A dog bites my right hand, and now a woman bites my left. I pull away from her choppers before she sinks in deep enough to do damage, and I lean into her ear, stifling a scream of pain. With one arm wrapped around her neck and my hand still hovering over her mouth ready to stanch any noise, I say, "It's okay. It's okay." Guessing she might speak Russian, I say *"Nyet problem, nyet problem,"* which means "no problem," and is an admittedly asinine thing to tell a woman who just left her terror dungeon to find herself racing barefoot through an ink-black forest pursued by vicious dogs and men with guns.

Only to end up with some asshole holding her in a headlock telling her everything is cool.

I loosen my grip, and in both languages I say, "I'm here to help you."

Her breathing is almost out of control for several seconds. Finally she swallows, controls herself. In English she says, "You . . . you are man in black?"

She can't see me, I've got her held facing away, so it's a reasonable question.

"*Da*. I mean . . . yes."

In the distance I hear barking dogs, but they aren't close. I'd seen wild boar in the trees as I made it to the woods, so I wonder if the Malinois are off chasing the wrong fleeing prey.

"You are British?" she asks softly.

Why not? "Sure," I lie, but I don't bother to fake an accent.

"The other girls?"

"They would not leave."

To my surprise, she nods. "Yes. They have family, or they think they go somewhere better. I no have any family, and I know where they are going."

"Where are they going?"

She shrugs. "Sex work in Europe, I think. But they no make money. They will be slaves. Just products to be used."

"What's your name?" I ask.

"Liliana. What is your name?"

"Prince Harry." I'm British, might as well take advantage of it. She either doesn't get the joke or doesn't like the joke, but either way, she makes no response.

I ask, "Where are you from?"

"A village near Tiraspol. It is in Moldova." I know where Tiraspol is, I've been there, but I don't let on.

"Why you here?" she asks.

"I came for Babic."

"That is the old man?"

"Yes."

"You kill him?"

With a shrug I say, "I did."

"You Albanian mafia?"

What a strange question, I think, but I just say, "No. Someone else hired me."

But then I think about it. That someone is unknown to me. Hell, for all I know, I *am* working for the Albanians, though that would be a first. I used a broker in this industry, a shadowy guy on the dark web who I know to be reliable enough. After he established my bona fides, he'd offered me something like ten ops over a couple of months, all of which I turned down, until the day I opened an e-mail to see "General Ratko Babic" on the top of the target portfolio.

Yeah, I told myself at the time. *This one, I'll do.* The pay was one point one million, but I would have worked pro bono. A half mil has already been put in my account in good faith, and my return display of good faith was to shoot that worthless sack of shit and let him bleed out, which I just did.

Services rendered. Whoever the hell paid for this hit, be they sinner or saint, I expect them to be another satisfied customer.

"I don't know where to go," the girl says, and I realize I'm thinking the same thing. All those women and girls back in that chamber of horrors are still there. There are still armed men around them, and the victims still have the fear of retaliation to their families if they go against the wishes of those holding them.

"How long have you been here?" I ask.

"I don't know. Maybe one week."

"There are kids in there, aren't there?"

Liliana nodded, still facing away. "One is fourteen. Two are fifteen. Two are sixteen."

Christ. I loosen my hold on the woman, and she scoots away a little, but she doesn't get up and run. She just turns towards me. I still have my balaclava covering my face, so I let her do it.

I say, "I have a Jeep. I can take you to Mostar. It's not far. You can tell the police what happened. Maybe they can—"

I stop talking when her expression changes. She regards me like I'm nuts. Slowly she shakes her head.

"No police?" I ask.

"Police are bad, Harry."

"Mostar police?"

What sounds like a weak laugh comes from her, and she looks off to the sound of barking dogs, which now seem to be even farther away. "Mostar police. Belgrade police. Tiraspol police."

"Are you certain, or are you guessing?"

"Always police. Police from Mostar come to farm."

I say, "We have to help the girls."

"I want to help girls. But girls gone. Never see girls again."

"How do you know?"

She shrugs now, looks me hard in the eyes. "Because you came."

I feel that pain in the pit of my stomach that comes the moment I realize I fucked up. I went into this with the objective of making the world a better place by taking an evil man out of it, but in doing so, I just might have condemned many others to a horrific fate.

Gentry, what have you done now?

I stammer as I talk. "Someone down there told me they would all be beaten for what I did tonight. Is that . . . true?"

She nods assuredly. "It does not matter that they no responsible for what happen. The men . . . very bad. They punish for this."

Slowly I ask, "Will they kill them?"

She shakes her head now. "No. They no kill them. Women are money to them. Thousands of euros a day. The men never let them go while they can make money."

"Who are these people?"

"Serbian mafia. Local police, too. I think old man pays police for protection."

I change gears. "Would you recognize the policemen who you saw at the farm?"

"Recog-nize?"

"If you see them again, will you know them?"

She nods. "They rape me. I sex with them. Of *course* I see faces."

"Right." I want to drop this chick off in Mostar and put this entire clusterfuck in my rearview, but I know I can't do that. I'm responsible for those women now, for the simple reason that I showed up tonight and imperiled them even more than they already were. It may not make sense to others, but I accept it.

Their fate . . . simply put . . . is my fate.

I say, "Look. If I take you to Mostar, you can show me the policemen who came here."

Again, I get the "what's wrong with you" look from the young woman.

"If they see me, they kill me. Why I go to Mostar? I want go Moldova."

"I can protect you, then I will get you back home. I promise."

"How you protect me?"

"Sister, I just killed six . . . correction, seven men back there. Believe me, I can protect you."

Her eyes widen. I don't brag about killing as a rule, but I need her to know I'm deadly serious about this. Apparently, she isn't quite buying it yet because she asks, "Why? Why you care? No one care about the girls in the pipeline."

"The pipeline?"

"*Da*. The pipeline. Our countries, into Serbia, into Bosnia. From here I don't know. Someone say a boat, but I don't know where boat going."

"How many girls?"

She shrugs. "In Belgrade? Fifty in the apartment. Here? Twenty, twenty-five in the cellar."

"Where are the other girls? The girls you saw in Belgrade and Sarajevo?"

"I do not know. They take away. Do not return."

Jesus. "I can't help them, but maybe, if we're fast, we can help these women. Find out where they are going next. I have to do something."

Again, she asks me, "Why?"

"Because I came," is all I can say, parroting the reason she gave me that the women would be brutalized even beyond what they were already being subjected to.

"Come with me to Mostar. One day. Two, tops. We'll watch the police station, and you try to find one of the cops who came here."

I tell myself there might still be time to save all those trafficked humans I saw in the cellar. I don't know if it's true, but I have to believe. "Liliana, will you help me, please?"

"You get paid for killing old man?"

The question comes out of nowhere and it surprises me. I'm so surprised, I answer honestly. "Yeah. A lot."

She nods slowly, taking this in. Then, "Good. I am very hungry."

I nod and smile in the dark. I can work with this woman.

I help her to her feet. "We'll be in Mostar for breakfast."

With a sort of noncommittal shrug she says, "Okay, Harry. I go with you. I find policeman, but you cannot stop the pipeline."

I don't have to stop it, I just have to pull a few girls out of it so my conscience will leave me alone.

I'm no saint, I'm just a slave shackled to his principles, just like those women were shackled to one another.

We're all in this together now, like it or not.

FIVE

Five minutes after the gunfire ended upstairs, the women and girls sat huddled together in the cellar in darkness, because no one dared to get up, pull the slack in the chains on their ankles, fumble around the dead body by the open door, and flip the red light back on.

Already the smell of blood added to the closed room's stench.

Between the sniffs and coughs and sobs from the group, a new sound emerged. The prisoners heard frantic, angry voices on the stairs down the hall, and they shuddered as one.

Lights shone in the stairwell, then came closer, the shouting between three men continuing. These Serbian guards were known to all of the prisoners down here, and as one of them flicked the red light back on, the other two waved their guns at the group, causing a few fresh shrieks of terror.

One of the security men checked over the dead body on the floor, and then two of them carried him away with no small struggle while the third closed the door.

Only when the loud lock engaged did the women and girls begin talking among themselves about what they had just witnessed and what it all meant for them now.

Some worried they would be killed because of what they had seen, others that they would be beaten or otherwise brutalized, and every last one of them was certain nothing good would come of this event.

They hated the sick and cruel old man, but none of them were thankful that the masked man with the American accent had shown up and killed him.

The females were aged from fourteen to twenty-four, and they had traveled different paths to get here. Many had been duped, promised employment in casinos in Dubai or Italy, or jobs in fancy restaurants or five-star hotels where beautiful women were needed. These women were trafficked and smuggled from their home countries, and then told by dangerous gangsters that they would have to compensate the traffickers for their travel and housing, and the only way they had to earn the money to pay was via sex work.

Others had been recruited at nightclubs or outside Internet live-camera porn sites or even from brothels, told they could work as high-dollar prostitutes in the West, make a thousand euros a day entertaining wealthy gentlemen, and then, after a few weeks, they could go back home, their luggage stuffed with cash desperately needed for themselves and their families.

Some women believed this and went willingly, others had to be coerced over time, and still others felt certain it was some sort of a scam, but desperation at home forced them to hope for the best and go along with it.

And still others had been kidnapped outright, drugged in bars and pulled into taxis or vans and driven off into the night.

But now, after all these twenty-three women had been through, after all they'd heard from others about their experiences, after the passport confiscations and the locked doors and the sexual abuse many had been subjected to by the old man and the police here or by gangsters at the apartment building in suburban Belgrade, all along this underground railway of hell . . . now they *all* knew. Their decisions, well intentioned or not, were not important now.

They were slaves.

Some of the girls held on to the hope that once they worked off their debt, they would be allowed to return to their homes, to their families. But it wasn't much hope. Others, usually the older women in their twenties, insisted none of them would ever see their homes or families again.

And now this. They had no idea what the evil men holding them would do to them now.

The new, even deeper sense of hopelessness in the red room was god-awful.

And fresh sounds of men shouting at one another in Serbo-Croatian in the hall on the other side of the door only made it worse.

· · ·

A twenty-three-year-old woman sat in the back of the little room, leaning against a threadbare cushion propped against the back wall, her head in her trembling hands, and she thought of home.

The day she was kidnapped she had been given a new name, as had all the others, and they were ordered to never speak their given names again, not even to one another.

This woman had been called Maja by her captors, and it was her name now, as far as anyone in the room knew. Maja looked drawn and pale, with dark circles under her eyes that were evident even in the poor lighting. She hadn't worn makeup or taken a bath in days; she'd been shuttled from one dank room to another, or transported in a bus with armed guards and covered windows; and though she'd been fed regularly, the food was low quality and she'd been forced to eat with her filthy bare hands.

Her humanity had been taken from her along with her identity.

But she was one of the lucky few who had not yet been raped. She assumed it was only a matter of time, though, so she felt no great comfort in this fact.

The door clicked, then opened. One of the Serbians appeared, a rifle around his chest and blood smeared all over his T-shirt. He took in the scene, and Maja could tell he was still amped up from the fighting—he was angry and, she sensed, even scared.

The man spoke in Russian to the group. Only some of the girls spoke the language, but no one here spoke Serbo-Croat, so it was better than nothing.

Maja's mother spoke Russian fluently, and she'd learned enough as a child to follow the man's words.

"Your hero ran away, leaving you behind. He will be found, caught, and killed. More men are coming in now, and you . . . you *all* will be disciplined for what has happened here tonight."

The same blonde who had spoken to the masked gunman fifteen minutes earlier spoke up again, this time in Russian. "We had nothing to do with—"

She stopped talking when the man hefted his rifle and pointed it at her, then shined the tactical flashlight mounted on the rail into her eyes. She and the other girls recoiled at the brightest light any of them had seen in days.

"One more word and I paint this room with all of your blood!"

Two more gunmen appeared behind the first, and they all conferred quietly with one another. Finally, one began unlocking the women from their chains. The first man said, "We are all leaving now. Follow us, and if you try anything, we will shoot you." No one moved. After a few seconds he screamed, "Stand up!" The women and girls stood and moved huddled together out of the room, past the Serbians, and up the hall. Some cried when they saw the dead bodies of the guards lying unattended in the stairwell, and upstairs they struggled to pass two dog handlers whose snarling, snapping beasts chomped the air as they tried to get to the prisoners.

All the women were put on a bus; Maja thought this one was different from the one they'd arrived on, but just like the other bus, the windows on this vehicle had been blacked out with cardboard. They sat in silence save for some sobs of terror, and soon the engine came to life, armed Serbians filled the front seats, and the bus began rolling off.

None of the victims knew where they were going or what would happen to them when they got there, but that had been the case for Maja since the beginning of this ordeal.

The bus drove for an hour through tight mountain roads; the women were continuously admonished and threatened if they made any noise, so they did little more than look at the headrests of the seats in front of them and worry about both their short-term and long-term futures.

A few vomited, the undulating road and the terror both competing for attention in their stomachs.

Finally, the bus stopped, then began creeping forward. It stopped again, rolled a few meters forward again, and then stopped again. This continued for minutes, and Maja thought it likely they were at a border crossing. This meant they would be passing by police or border guards, but she didn't get excited with hopes of rescue. She'd been through other border crossings since she was taken over a week earlier, with other men guarding her, other vehicles transporting her.

They'd gone through checkpoints before, and they'd always been allowed to pass. She suspected that whoever was manning the checkpoints had been well aware of the nature of the cargo in the blacked-out bus, and they'd taken money to let it through.

Soon the big vehicle returned to its previous speed on the winding roads, and Maja felt certain they were now in another country.

After another fifteen minutes of driving through hills, the bus rolled to a slow stop. One of the Serbians stood; Maja noticed he had a bandage on his arm and another around his head, and he shouted to the vehicle for everyone to get out and line up single file.

When Maja stepped out of the bus and into the night, a fresh terror washed over her. She saw they were off the road in a gravel parking circle, surrounded by dense forest.

She'd expected a new dungeon. A farmhouse or a warehouse or some sort of out-of-the-way building. But they were out in the middle of nowhere.

No . . . this didn't look right at all.

Once all the girls were lined up by the bus, the man with the bloody wrapping around his head stepped in front of the group. He hadn't been the leader of the Serbian security men. No, that man was nowhere to be

seen now. *This* man, whatever his name was, had been just one of the junior guards before tonight.

She had no idea why he'd been promoted but wondered if that meant
all the men above him were dead.

Maja's Russian wasn't great, but she knew enough to understand.

"There is a price to be paid for attempting to leave our care."

Our care? Had Maja understood him correctly?

She fully expected the Ukrainian blonde to interject here, but when she
did not, Maja realized the bravest of the group was as unnerved by these
surroundings as she was.

The injured guard continued. "We have tried to treat you all with respect and kindness. And yet our kindness is rewarded with murder." He
repeated his assertion. "There is a price to be paid."

Girls began to sob; this new leader looked around to the four men with
him, motioned to a younger man with a thick black beard, and said something in their native language. The man handed his rifle off to a mate and
walked up to the line of girls, looking at each one closely with a flashlight.
He made a few sounds of disgust as he stepped from one to the next, but
on the sixth prisoner, a nineteen-year-old Maja knew as Stefana, he
stopped. With a violent motion he reached up and slapped her across the
face, and as she fell towards the graveled parking circle, he grabbed her by
the hair and began pulling her towards the trees.

She screamed, but this only caused him to pull her along more roughly.

A second guard and then a third grabbed girls from the line; these men
held on to their rifles as they dragged the women into the darkened forest.
The two Serbians watching the row of prisoners kept their weapons trained
on them while the sounds of violent rape echoed around the trees.

Girls still in the line fell to the ground in despair. Maja cried, but she
kept her feet.

The two remaining men talked while they guarded the group of
twenty; they seemed to have a short argument, but soon one of them—not
the new leader—slung his gun over his shoulder and walked forward. He

was older, well into his forties, and he looked over a couple of the hostages standing by the bus, but quickly his flashlight's beam centered on Maja herself.

He reached up and grabbed her by the arm and yanked her off-balance, began pulling her towards the woods.

"*Ne! Ne! Ne!*" *No* was one of the few words she knew in Serbo-Croatian, and she said it now, over and over, as panic threatened to overwhelm her.

But before the gangster could get her off the gravel and into the grass, the new leader of the group called out to him, and he stopped.

Maja could not understand, but whatever he said instigated an argument between the two. While the women in the woods continued to cry out, these last two men entered into a full-on shouting match.

But then it ended, and the man holding Maja's arm yanked her back to the bus, where she was ordered to sit down on the gravel with all the others.

Save one. The older guard walked down the line, shined his light on more faces, and then grabbed another young girl. Despite her cries and pleas, he pulled her off into the woods while Maja looked on, mouth agape.

She didn't understand. Why had she been spared?

She put her hands over her ears to drown out the pitiful cries from the trees, but a man in the forest shouted and she peered into the darkness. She saw a figure, a young Bulgarian girl of sixteen she knew as Diana, running off. She was naked other than socks, and she was sprinting, her long legs leaping over obstacles like a gazelle.

"No," Maja whispered. And then she shouted it. "No!"

A Serbian guard rose to his feet, pulled his pants up and cinched them, and then reached down to the forest floor and retrieved his rifle. Other men shouted at him, two of them taking off in pursuit of the girl, but the man with the rifle leveled it, aimed carefully, and fired a single round, just seconds before Diana would have disappeared into thick foliage.

The gunshot echoed off the trees and into the night.

Maja watched in horror as the sixteen-year-old tumbled to the ground and lay still.

"No!" the girls sitting by the bus croaked out now.

Maja began weeping heavily, for the senseless death of the young girl, for the brutal rapes that were happening before her eyes, and for the fact that she had been singled out and spared the fate of the others.

She didn't understand it, not *any* of it, but even though her brain was riddled with shock, that last part confused her most.

Maja vomited onto the gravel in front of her, over and over, while the mournful cries of the women around her resumed.

SIX

The balcony overlooking the azure water was lined with potted plants and trees, keeping the large space cool despite the warm morning sunshine. The tallest of these cast shade on the breakfast table with the seventy-two-year-old man seated at it, but they had been positioned so as not to obstruct his view of the sea.

Hvar was a resort town on an island off the coast of Croatia, so although it saw a lot of tourists in July, it would be absolutely filled to the brim with foreigners in August. For now, though, the man who owned the penthouse apartment above the rocky coastline enjoyed the relative calm of the streets below and the fact that although there were a number of pleasure craft offshore, they weren't choking out the beautiful bay and he could still see the crystal-green water.

He would leave in a few days, remain outside Croatia for the month of August, and this way he would avoid the highest of the high season.

Kostas Kostopoulos was not Croatian, although he kept a penthouse here. He was Greek, and his own nation would become even more crowded in August than Croatia, so he wouldn't bother with going home. No, he planned on heading to Venice for work, and then he would take another business trip to the United States. He'd remain in Los Angeles for the month, and only return to the Adriatic when the summer holiday season died down.

Kostopoulos didn't like crowded streets; he barely ventured out of his properties into the masses, and only did so when business forced him to.

The Greek oversaw the Southern European trafficking channels, from Turkey to the south and Ukraine to the north, all the way to the terminus of his territory on the eastern edge of Western Europe. He'd built an empire over decades: drugs, guns, sex trafficking, labor trafficking, illegal immigration. He had made hundreds of millions of euros in these endeavors. But the pipeline of women trafficked for sex work from Eastern Europe into the West was his most profitable revenue stream, and he was only a regional director of a much larger enterprise, known to those involved as the Consortium.

Kostas wondered how much the person who ran the operation earned from his European network, and he marveled at his best guess. He had no idea who this person was; he himself worked through the Consortium's Director of operations, a South African.

But whoever the Director of the Consortium was, Kostas was sure he or she was in possession of a spigot that poured pure gold.

As he sipped his coffee, the sliding glass door opened behind him, and a bearded man stepped through in a rush, passing two burly bodyguards. He stopped at the table.

In English Kostopoulos said, "Good morning, Stanislav. Hope you don't mind if I finish my breakfast. Sit, take a few breaths, calm down, then tell me what's so important."

The younger man did as instructed; he even took a sip of pineapple juice, already poured in crystal, when the older man motioned towards it. But he rushed through the act, spilled a little down his chin, then hurriedly put the glass back on the table. He spoke with a Serbian accent, but the Greek talked to Serbs daily, so it wasn't difficult for him to understand.

"There has been a disruption in the pipeline."

Kostas Kostopoulos showed his displeasure with slightly sagging shoulders but nothing more. "Where?"

"Mostar."

The Greek took a bite of yogurt, then said, "General Babic and his Belgrade men."

"Yes, sir."

"Details?"

"Attacked last night. Seven men dead, including Babic."

The Greek sighed now while he buttered his croissant. He displayed a subdued countenance, though this was highly distressing news, to be sure. Still, he wouldn't let the Serbian see him react with the shock he felt. "So who is interfering with my business interests *this* time? The Turks again?"

"Belgrade doesn't know who ordered it, but they think they know who carried out the operation itself, and they believe this was not an attack on the way station, but simply an attack on the general."

The older man looked up from his croissant and said, "Well? Who is responsible?"

A pause. "An individual known as the Gray Man."

Kostopoulos cocked his head. "An . . . *individual*?"

"We have no information that he was acting in concert with others."

"One man? One man killed seven, including the general, who has been hunted for a quarter century? That sounds like a tall tale."

Stanislav was a member of the Serbian mafia, the Branjevo Partizans, and he served as his organization's link to the Consortium that operated the pipeline. Kostopoulos was the only contact in the Consortium he had ever met, and that was by design.

He said, "Belgrade has interviewed both the surviving security force and the whores, sir. Everything points to it being one very skilled man. Belgrade seems to know him by his moniker, Gray Man. They said no one else could have done this."

Kostopoulos looked down to the water at the gorgeous summer morning. He didn't believe the lone-assassin theory and thought the Serbian mob was a bunch of fools for even suggesting it.

"The merchandise was undisturbed?"

"There were twenty-four items on site. One is missing."

"The missing item. What's her story?"

"Moldovan. The whores say Babic was fucking her himself in another room when the gunman appeared. Nothing special about her. They don't know where she is. Security men never saw her leave, but they were fighting it out with this killer at the time."

After a nod and a bite into his croissant, the Greek said, "Obviously you will close down that way station."

"Under way now, sir. The product is gone already, moved on to the next stop."

"They are early for the next stop. We aren't set to pick them up on the coast for three days. That could pose problems."

"I'm sorry, sir. But there is nowhere in our area of influence that we can put them."

"Banja Luka?"

"We are getting it ready now, but it won't be secure for a few more days. Moving the whores on west was the only thing we could do."

Kostas let a little frustration show now. "This will be costly. Time-consuming. Obstructive to our work. How, dear Stanislav, do we exact our revenge for this?"

"This Gray Man will be hard to find. He's probably already far from here."

Kostopoulos shrugged. "Assassins will come and go. Keep an ear out for him, and I'll tell the other directors in the pipeline to do the same.

"But he'll be long gone by now, so I'm not talking about him. I'm talking about revenge for the failures in your ranks." After a pause he added, "The local constabulary there in Mostar was involved in protecting the operation, is that correct?"

"Yes, sir. Our contact there is a police chief in Mostar. A man named Vukovic."

"I'd say he did a rather poor job. Do you agree?"

After a brief pause the Serbian replied, "Agreed."

"We will make an example of him. Something that will show the other pipeline way stations that we do not accept underperforming from those we compensate well to keep our systems functioning safely."

Stanislav looked uncomfortable for a moment.

The Greek picked up on this. "He's one of Belgrade's assets, and you don't want to kill him. Is that it?"

"He is well positioned. He has helped us with many—"

"I can move the pipeline out of Belgrade's area of influence. I can move the women via northern routes or south through the Mediterranean."

Stanislav said nothing.

"I want a pound of flesh for this debacle. You can either find yourself a new chief of police in the little shit town of Mostar, or you can find yourself another endeavor as profitable as what I offer you."

Stanislav sat up straighter. "I'm sorry, sir, but it's not *you* offering us the work. It's your masters in the Consortium."

Kostopoulos bristled at this but fought any show of anger or insult. Instead he said, "I rule this area, and my opinion holds weight with the Director of the Consortium."

Stanislav kept his defiant posture. "Then we ask you to contact him and request that he take no action on Vukovic. We have other needs for him in the area. If you are leaving Mostar anyway, why should you care if he's still working for us?"

Kostas let it go, but he had no plans to contact the Director, and no idea how to do so, even if he did want to.

The Serbian left the Greek alone on his luxurious balcony and stepped back inside to head to the elevator, pulling a phone from his pocket as he did so.

Kostas Kostopoulos did his best not to let his temper flare in this work. He always tried to retain a dispassionate approach. So many other traffickers were thugs, gangsters, criminals through and through. But the organization Kostopoulos worked for, though they used petty gangsters for their grunt work, was made up of businessmen and businesswomen, not thugs. They acquired, produced, transported, traded, and profited on a product, and the fact that the product they dealt in was human beings had been tamped down by years of incredibly positive balance sheets and a growth line unparalleled in any other legitimate industry since the dot-com boom twenty years earlier.

Nobody in any position of authority in the endeavor thought of their product as people. They were resources. Assets.

Merchandise.

But despite the Greek's desire to remain unemotional about what happened, he recognized that the shuttering of one of his pipeline way stations would hurt the monthly flow of product west, and this would ultimately reflect poorly on him.

Kostopoulos might have been a powerful regional director in one of the largest human trafficking organizations in the world, but he didn't call the shots, and his dispassion now was tempered by the fact that he knew that some extraordinarily powerful and dangerous individuals were going to be very unhappy with him when he told them of last night's events.

He'd have to make a call now, to obtain Consortium approval to send assassins after this Vukovic, because Kostas Kostopoulos didn't make these decisions on his own.

. . .

Jaco Verdoorn didn't like this part of his job, but it was not because he was squeamish or sensitive about murder.

He'd killed before, many times. He'd killed in combat, and he'd killed in security contract work, and he'd even killed once in a street fight in Pretoria.

But this? Tonight? This kind of killing, he felt, was far beneath him.

These weren't combatants. These were lambs at the slaughterhouse, he was the butcher, and there was no game in that.

Still he drove in the front passenger seat of the Mercedes G-Wagen as it motored north away from Los Angeles, through Calabasas, west of the hills of the San Fernando Valley, checking his phone idly and thinking about the old days, back in the nation of his birth, back in his time in South Africa's military and intelligence services.

Those had been interesting times.

So unlike tonight.

Tonight he would put bullets into the heads of two young women, dump their bodies in a ditch, and then turn around to head to Van Nuys airport for a flight to Europe.

The girls were all but unconscious in the backseat of the Mercedes. They'd been injected with heroin, not for the first time, and then they'd been helped out of the large property where they had been kept, folded into the SUV, and joined by Jaco Verdoorn and two of his men.

Their heads lolled in the back with the bouncing on the roads, and Verdoorn showed his boredom with a wide yawn.

This was just another day at the office.

The driver stopped beside a ravine that ran along Big Pines Highway. This wasn't a particularly out-of-the-way location, but it was the middle of the night now and there were no cars in sight and, anyway, this would just take a moment.

The young women—one was a nineteen-year-old brunette from Belarus, and the other a seventeen-year-old Indonesian—were barely aware of their surroundings as they were let out onto the street, over to the shoulder, and up to a low metal railing.

The two young women faced the ravine, both only now feeling a hint of confusion, because during their months of captivity, they'd never been out of the compound they were kept in, they'd never been in a car, and none of this felt exactly right.

The Belarusian muttered through a tongue slurred with the drug injected into her, "What is happening?"

The South African climbed out of the front passenger seat, pocketed his phone with a sigh, and then drew the SIG Sauer P220 pistol from the waistband of his khakis under his too-tight white polo shirt. As he leveled it at the back of the brunette's head he said, "The Director grew tired of you, like he always does. Time to make way for the next shipment."

A gunshot rang out on the quiet hillside, and the young woman pitched forward, disappearing from view before the echo of the pistol's report made its way back from the other side of the ravine.

The Indonesian, even in her drug-induced stupor, recoiled from the loud noise, and she started to turn around, but Jaco Verdoorn fired again, striking her in the left temple, and she, too, tumbled over the metal railing and down into the thick brush.

One of the other South Africans shined his tactical flashlight down the ravine. A cloud of dust rose, indicating the women had come to rest on the earthen floor.

Verdoorn had already holstered his pistol and sat back down in the SUV by the time the light clicked off and the two other men returned to the vehicle. This wasn't the first time Jaco had done this—this wasn't even the tenth time—and he expected in a couple of months, certainly no more than four or five, he'd be back, either here or on some other little lonely mountain road, and he'd be doing it all over again.

It was the job.

It wasn't the action he'd wanted, but the pay was good and, every once in a while, something interesting came up.

As the vehicle rolled off to the west to begin its journey back towards Van Nuys, the South African's phone rang and he answered it.

"Verdoorn."

He listened a moment, cocked his head, then said, "Kostas, that is, indeed, distressing news. I'm gonna have to go to the Director with it, and he will be bladdy well displeased."

The Greek spoke a moment more, but Jaco interrupted him.

"I don't give a *fuck* who did it, I just know that—"

The bald-headed man in the polo shirt hesitated suddenly. This story about an entire way station shot up, seven killed, a targeted assassination. Something about this triggered his brain. He changed his tune suddenly. "Who did it?"

Seconds later, it was plain to the other two in the Mercedes that Jaco Verdoorn very clearly *did* give a fuck who did it. "You're kidding me. How sure are they?" A pause. "*Of course* I bladdy well know who that is!"

He listened now as the Greek talked about a Bosnian police chief who he felt should be killed for allowing the hit to happen, and Jaco agreed, but he wasn't thinking about a police chief.

No, he was thinking about the Gray Man.

Courtland Gentry.

Finally he hung up, called a contact in the Serbian government in Banja Luka for confirmation, and then hung up from that call and looked down at his phone.

He thought about calling the Director immediately; the man did not like to be bothered during the night, but Jaco knew he'd have to get approval for the hit on the Bosnian cop. Still, as the wheels in the South African's mind turned, he realized he would need more information about the American assassin before going to his boss.

And he knew where to get it.

With a pounding heart that only came from the prospect of hunting the most dangerous prey in the world, the South African smiled now.

"What's up, boss?" asked the driver.

Verdoorn said, "Tryin' to not get my hopes up too high, Samuel, but we might have ourselves a spot of fun on the horizon."

The man in the back spoke with sarcasm. "What, more exciting than this?"

Verdoorn ignored him.

The driver saw the look in his boss's eye. "New target, sir?" Samuel knew there was only one thing that his boss considered fun.

Verdoorn brought the phone to his ear as he placed the call. To his driver he said, still through a smile, "New target."

SEVEN

I dream about the women in the cellar. I can't make out any faces clearly, but I see eyes shining red: desolate, fearful, despairing orbs that track me wherever I move. I am enveloped by the sights and sounds of their prison; I sense the inevitable bleakness of their futures and, more disheartening, I see that *they* sense that bleakness, as well.

And then, just before I wake up, I remember that this is all my mother-fucking fault.

Opening my eyes now, I realize that I am not in the red room, but I don't know where I am. I wake up in a different hotel or apartment or flophouse or bunk bed with staggering regularity, so I'm used to the sensation. My left hand hurts, and the muscles all over my body feel strained and knotted: also nothing out of the ordinary for me.

I've seen action, that much is clear by my aches and pains.

I'm on the floor of a closet with a gear bag under my head, which also tells me I'm operational. I always sleep in closets when I can for my own security, and I'm more comfortable here on the floor than alone in a comfortable bed.

You get like this when people make killing you their life's work.

I lie there, shake off the dream, and remember the reality that was last night. Babic, the women and girls, the dogs, the gunfire and shouting and running.

And then I remember Liliana.

Did she leave? I sit up quickly. When I lay down she had already fallen asleep in the bed, so my eyes go there.

I see only tousled bedsheets.

Shit.

But I scan to the right and find her in the little living room of the apartment, sitting at a table by the window, looking down at the street into the night.

I lie back down, pleased to see that at least one of us is working.

It all comes back quickly. I'm in the closet of a third-floor walk-up flat in Mostar, Bosnia, overlooking the main police station. I rented it this morning after feeding Liliana and myself, and buying both of us new clothes. I also remember something about a fuzzy plan I had to help the women I left behind in the cellar, and that's the only reason I'm not three hundred miles away by now in Zagreb, boarding a train to Prague for a flight back to America.

That was plan A. But Alpha is shot, and to be honest, I'm having trouble remembering a time where I actually executed a plan A.

I need to get back to the States, and I don't need to be over here, fifteen miles from where I fucked up a farmload of gunmen last night, playing house with a sex-trafficked Moldovan woman in an attempt to rescue an unknown number of victims from an unknown number of perpetrators who are I don't even know where.

Fuck. Plan Alpha is out the window, and so far plan Bravo isn't looking too hot, either.

I think again about returning to the States. The Babic hit was a free-lance assignment, but I also have a day job. Sort of. Contract work for the CIA. I used to be an actual employee, then they tried to kill me, and now we've patched some things up. They are still officially hunting me down, but the director of operations uses me as his own deniable asset, an off-book hitter in a blacker-than-black program called Poison Apple, so I have a little bit of pull and that keeps the American goons off my back, at least for now.

Yeah . . . everything about my relationship with the Agency is bonkers. They piss me off consistently, and I'm sure I am personally responsible for a sizable portion of antacid sales in the pharmacies in and around Langley. But I do help them out from time to time. Not sure what they do for me, really, but I guess I'm doing my civic duty or something by killing the enemies of America, and that's important.

Isn't it?

I could call my handler at the Agency, tell her what I saw here, and maybe enlist the assistance of the best intelligence service on Earth. But I decide against it. She'd probably just tell me to get my ass back to work, and the Agency would know in a heartbeat that I was the one who killed Babic.

And I don't need that.

I look over the little flat now. The girl just sits at the window in the low light, smoking cigarettes I bought her to help calm her, staring out to the street in silence. Even in the dim here I can see the hard look in her eyes, but I figure it's just what she's been through these past few weeks.

Then I ask myself, *What the hell am I doing here?* I should bail on all this. I should walk away before this goes deeper, because everything always seems to go deeper if I stick around long enough. Yeah, I should get out, get back to the United States, back to the Agency. I can't save those girls I saw at the farm. They're in the wind by now, I'm sure of it.

Soon I sit up again, knowing all this thinking is a waste of time. *Of course* I'm going to see this through. I *always* do. And I always will, until the day I go lights out as a result of catching a supersonic hunk of copper-jacketed lead with my forehead.

That day is coming, I'm as sure of this as I am that the sun will rise tomorrow morning.

A minute later I sit down next to Liliana with a couple of bottles of Velibitsko beer in my hand. "How are you?"

"Fine," she says, and she takes a beer, but she's not fine. She just gazes out the window down at the station.

"Anything so far?" I ask.

"No. Nothing." My camera sits on the table next to her, but I don't think she's even touched it. I look at my watch and see that it's nine p.m.

"You need to take a break. I can watch, take pictures, show you when you wake up."

"I don't sleep very much."

I imagine not, I think.

It's quiet in the room for a moment, and then I ask, "You were kidnapped in Tiraspol by this group?"

"By another group. They were locals, Moldovans. Then I was sold into the pipeline. Moved from east to west. Each time a different group, but I do not know who in charge."

"When they took you, what were you doing?"

She doesn't look away from the front door of the police station across the street. She answers matter-of-factly. "I was working girl."

She means a prostitute, and this surprises me. She doesn't look like a prostitute.

"How long have you been doing that?"

"I make cakes in bakery in small town. But I want to live big city. I want to be something. I go to Tiraspol when I twenty, and no work, so . . ."

She stops there, but I get it.

I don't ask her again how long she's been a working girl. She looks thirty to me, but taking into account her impossibly tough life, I figure she's about twenty-five.

Shit, with what she's been through, she could be even younger.

I don't know why I say the next words that come out of my mouth, but it's probably due to the crippling guilt I am feeling right now about my responsibility for the fate of those women in the red room. "What happened to you . . . it isn't your fault."

She waves a hand. "Other girls taken from nightclubs, from normal jobs, from other places. Other girls tricked into sex. I taken from brothel. I make sex for money. I am not victim."

Blowing out a sigh, I reply with, "After what has happened to you, only a true victim would say she was no victim."

But I see I'm not getting through to her. Talking isn't my strong suit; it's why I tend to shoot people in the face instead. But I try again. "If you help me help those girls, you can do some good."

She shakes her head. "You no help those girls. You hurt those girls when you came."

Yeah, I know.

She looks me over. "Why you kill old man?"

"He was a Serbian general in the war. A bad one. War crimes."

She rolls her eyes. "The war? You mean the war before I was born?"

"Yeah."

"Nobody care about that war. You come and kill him for it, and now the girls suffer."

I nod. "I get it."

She adds, "Girls are gone. Taken away, somewhere else." After a moment of silence she softens, sips her beer, and says, "Soon new girls taken from Moldova."

"This shit happens every day around the world, doesn't it?" I hadn't even been thinking about the larger picture of this. Only the women and girls I saw who, by my actions, were condemned to more brutality.

She shrugs. "I do not know the world. I know only Tiraspol, Belgrade, and here. But yes . . . every day some new girl has freedom taken away."

More to myself than to her, I say, "The shit I've seen in this life . . ." My voice trails off because the shit I've seen in this life is not really any of her business, but she surprises me with her response.

She takes a long swig of the beer and then she turns to face me again. "The shit you see. What it make you want to do?"

I think about the question. "It makes me want to kill people."

"Yes. I want kill people, too." She nods. "But that does not make everything better."

Maybe she's right. Maybe she's wrong. I see the shittiest parts of humanity, and it is a soul-sucking experience, but at least I have an outlet. I am an assassin.

A killer of men.

Someone like Liliana . . . a baker forced into prostitution by economic hardship, then kidnapped into slavery. What can she do but sit there and take the world as it comes at her like a monster reaching out from under her bed?

Neither of us speaks for over a minute. Finally I break the uncomfortable silence. "When you get home to Moldova, I wouldn't go back to Tiraspol."

She nods. "I go back to bakery. It is safe. No one steal baker for sex traffic."

She has the right idea, and I clink my beer bottle against hers. She starts to bring it back to her mouth while she keeps her eyes across the street, but she stops suddenly and points out the window. "There! That cop, getting out of the car."

It's a white SUV with the Mostar police logo in blue on the side. A driver climbs out and steps up to the sidewalk, opening the back door of the vehicle when he does so.

"You know him? From the farm?"

"Yes. He not in charge. But he always with man in charge."

The passenger side opens now, and almost as soon as the man steps out, Liliana recoils. "*He* man in charge."

A cop in his forties wearing a smart uniform takes off his cap, rubs his hand over his short gray stubble, and then replaces it.

"That asshole right there?"

"*Da. Da.*"

"You know his name?"

"I hear them call him Niko. That is all." She begins to cry suddenly, her hardened look evaporating in an instant.

Three men in total climb out of the vehicle, and another two emerge from a second, identical SUV. They all walk together up the steps to the front door of the police station. I take a few pictures, focusing on the one called Niko, then help Liliana out of her chair and lead her back over to the bed by her arm.

She is weeping still, and I sit her down. "You did great. You just made a difference. Get some rest. Tomorrow morning I'll take you to the train station and tell you how to get home."

"What about Niko?"

I smile a little in the dim light. "I'll be back for Niko."

She nods slowly; I start to stand to return to the window, but she holds me by the wrist.

"You are good man."

I'm not, but I say, "Thanks."

She pulls me closer, tries to lead me down onto the bed on top of her.

I attempt to break away without making a big deal out of it, but her grip is surprisingly strong. I say, "You aren't thinking straight, Liliana. You need to sleep."

There are fresh tears in her eyes now. "I know what you need. I give you what you need."

She's wrong. I don't need that. Not like this.

"No, you aren't thinking straight," I repeat.

I stop her advances as gently as I can, but gentle isn't exactly my strong suit. Within seconds I have her arms pinned over her head, and only then does she stop trying to pull me down.

She nods without emotion now. "This you like? You like rough?"

Shit. "No. No. I'm sorry," I say. "But I can't." I let go of her arms, but she doesn't move them.

She sniffs and looks at me quizzically. She doesn't seem offended, just surprised. "Assassin who is gay, or assassin with girlfriend?"

I marvel at the absurdity of this moment. "There is a girl."

Another dispassionate nod from Liliana. "British girl?"

The comment confuses me, but then I remember that I'm Prince Harry. Surprising myself, I don't lie when I answer her. "No. A Russian girl."

I get yet another look from her like she thinks I'm an idiot. With all the certainty in the world she replies, "Russian girl? She take your money."

"Not this one."

Then, "Russian girl drink too much."

To this I shrug. "You may be right about that."

She looks at me, then again says, "You are good man."

A good man? She's got me all wrong. For the third time I say, "You aren't thinking straight, Liliana. Get some rest."

EIGHT

It was an especially beautiful summer morning in the Hollywood Hills. Three kids—a ten-year-old boy and girls of twelve and sixteen—lounged around the infinity pool behind an Italian Renaissance Revival mansion, a woman in her forties looked gorgeous while sipping her coffee at a table on the expansive back patio, and landscapers and gardeners toiled around the steeply graded two-acre property. The skyline of LA was striking in the distance; the smoggy haze that usually blanketed the city was less pronounced than usual.

And all this filled fifty-four-year-old Kenneth Cage with a sense of peace.

His palatial home had been built in the 1940s for a Hollywood mogul, and an impressive list of actors and musicians had resided there over the years. Cage himself was attached to the world of entertainment via one of his businesses, but he had more money than any five of the movie stars or rock stars who'd ever lived at this Hollywood address.

And this home was but one of six he kept here in the United States. There was Steamboat Springs and Boston and New York and Jackson Hole and Lake Tahoe, and he had his eyes on a four-hundred-acre winery in Sonoma County.

All this wealth and property came with a cost, of course. Even now as he sat at his kitchen island, looking out the open patio door and enjoying his family while they enjoyed the fruit of his labors, in the distance he also counted three men patrolling the well-manicured grounds. There were three more somewhere around here he couldn't see, and the house was lined with cameras, all fed into a control center with yet another security officer monitoring them.

The leader of Ken Cage's security detail was an ex–Navy SEAL and LAPD SWAT officer named Sean Hall, and while the other men rotated in three shifts throughout the day, Hall lived in a detached two-thousand-square-foot pool house just off the patio, and he went *everywhere* his boss went from the hours of nine a.m. until Cage was tucked into bed at night.

Right now Sean was still in his pool house, because Cage had a strict rule: no work before nine. That meant no bodyguards inside the mansion, no phone calls or e-mails, no spreadsheets or PowerPoints or business-related visitors.

Cage traveled on business regularly, but he was a family man and, when he was home, he carved out time for Heather and the kids.

Cage always told others that he regarded the security precautions as one of the ancillary and necessary costs of success, but the truth was, he liked the feeling of significance it conveyed when he walked as the nucleus of a group of beefy ex-cops and military men. Heather didn't like the intrusion into her life brought on by the bodyguards, but Ken truly didn't mind, because it fed his massive ego.

He finished his breakfast on the marble kitchen counter, chatted briefly with his son about the Dodgers' win over the Twins the night before, and looked over some art made by his twelve-year-old daughter, pronouncing the watercolor to be magnificent.

Soon his three kids were swimming and splashing in the big infinity pool overlooking the city skyline. Heather would join them as soon as she changed into her bathing suit, but now she sat on the sofa with her husband in the living room, enjoying her coffee and his companionship before he retired into his home office for the workday.

They were in the middle of a discussion about colleges for their daughter; Cage had gone to Princeton and then Wharton while Heather had graduated from Harvard, but Charlotte wanted to go to UCLA and get a degree in fine arts. Heather was pushing for Ken to use his clout to try to get her into Harvard, and just as Ken tried to shift the conversation back to Princeton, his mobile rang and he glanced down at it, saw the number, and furrowed his brow.

"What's wrong?" asked Heather.

"It's eight fifty and this is work. On my cell." He rolled his eyes. "I don't punch in till nine when I'm home. Everybody knows this is my family time."

She smiled back at him. "You've been a good boy lately. I'll let you off the hook today."

Ken chuckled. "Nope. I'll get rid of him and go hang with the kids while you get your suit on."

Despite the work interruption, Cage answered the phone with a little smile on his face. He couldn't help it. Life was good. With a light and airy voice he said, "Hey there. I'll call you back in about fifteen—"

Ken Cage stopped talking. As he listened his smile faded, and he stood. To Heather he said, "Gotta take this. Sorry, babe."

He turned and headed for his study. When he closed himself in, he walked over to his antique walnut partner's desk, picked up a remote, and pressed a button. Instantly his office stereo system, a half-million-dollar Backes & Müller BM 100, began projecting the lifelike, warm, rich sounds of a thunderstorm throughout the room.

He sat down and spoke in a low and gruff voice utterly different than the one he had been using with his family. "We're going encrypted."

"Encrypted," came the confirmation from the man on the other end of the line, speaking with a heavy South African accent. Now Cage tapped some unmarked buttons at the bottom of his phone system. The sound over the line changed a little, as did the tonal qualities of the men's voices, but the two could hear each other without difficulty.

Cage opened with, "*Fuck*, Jaco. You know the rules. No calls till nine."

"Something's happened."

"I told you to send the two whores back home and then get over to Berlin. You need me to hold your hand for that?"

If Jaco Verdoorn felt chastened, he didn't show it in his voice. "Sorry, sir, but this isn't about the two items you asked me to deal with. A new situation warrants your attention."

"*What* situation?"

"Bosnia, sir."

"You know what? Stop. I don't have time for any drama right now. I've got to prepare for the trip next week to—"

"A hit man killed seven, including the man running the Mostar way station, a former Serb general named Babic."

Kenneth Cage, the Director of the Consortium, froze in place at his desk for a moment. Then he said, "Well . . . that's pretty dramatic. Who hired the hit man?"

"The Serbs think a Croatian concern was gunning for Babic due to his activities in the nineties, and when they found out where he was living, they outsourced the hit so they didn't start anything directly with either Serbia or Bosnia and Herzegovina."

Cage knew the name Ratko Babic, but he'd known nothing about Babic working for him. He'd not even known Mostar was a way station. He never concerned himself with the minutiae of his operation, considering himself above that level of work. He delegated power both to optimize efficiency and to keep his hands clean.

Cage wasn't ready to involve himself in these dirty affairs across the globe directly. "I can't believe I'm talking to you about this shit. You need to handle stuff like this before it makes its way up to me."

"Frankly, sir, we've never encountered anything like this."

With a sigh, the man in Hollywood said, "The regional director over there in Croatia . . . he's the Greek guy, right?"

"Kostas Kostopoulos, yes. I've been in contact with him."

"Tell him he's got carte blanche to find this asshole and terminate him. That's the word you guys use for this sort of shit, isn't it?"

"It's . . . it's one way of putting it, I suppose. But I'm not sure Kostas's people are the right men for the job."

"Why not?"

"They have limited range and no influence anywhere other than in the Balkans. This might be something I need to handle alone. I can find him, and I can eliminate him."

Cage looked down at his phone. "*You*? You've got better things to do running my day-to-day operations than going on a personal safari for some hit man."

"Respectfully, I think he could pose a threat to our interests, and I should also take steps to—"

"C'mon, Jaco," Cage said. "You aren't a man hunter anymore. You are helping me run a ten-billion-dollar-a-year business."

A pause from the other end, and then the South African responded with obvious disappointment. "Yes, sir. I'll tell the Greek to look for the assassin."

Cage hung up, then looked at the grandfather clock on the wall. It was after nine now, so he opened up an e-mail to check this month's numbers in Denmark.

As the Director of the Consortium, he was responsible for keeping his eyes on the bottom line.

But his attention didn't stay on work for long. This new situation in Bosnia, the removal of the two girls, a trip he had planned to Italy in just a few days, and the arrival of his next shipment of merchandise, including two new girls he'd taken a particular interest in . . .

There was a lot for Ken Cage to think about these days, a lot of balls in the air. He began poring through the Danish numbers, telling himself he'd spend the full day in his home office.

• • •

Police captain Niko Vukovic left his station at ten p.m., climbing into his SUV with his driver and his chief protection agent, both well-trained officers, with a chase vehicle rolling behind with two more cops. They drove north towards Vukovic's residence to the south of the urban center of Mostar, just on the east side of the small but swift Neretva River.

A gray Mercedes panel truck followed the two SUVs the entire way, but traffic was dense enough tonight, and none of the five cops picked up on the tail.

The two police vehicles pulled into a small quiet square three blocks from the river and stopped in front of an old gray building close to the street. The two bodyguards who weren't also drivers climbed out with the captain, then walked him into his residence.

A few minutes later the pair of guards exited the building, leaving Niko Vukovic alone inside.

Once the protectee was safely ensconced in his residence for the evening, the two SUVs rolled out of the square.

None of the four cops providing security for their chief noticed the gray van rolling slowly up a road on the far side of the square, finally coming to a standstill ten meters before the intersection.

Two individuals sat in the van now, but there were three in total in this team of Hungarian hit men. The third, the unit leader, was busy back at the hotel, preparing their escape route, poring over maps, circling areas of major congestion.

The Hungarians were all active-duty members of their own country's national police force, but they also worked a side job as enforcers for the Pitovci, an organized-crime entity based in Bratislava, Slovakia. Normally their duties for the Pitovci kept them in and around Budapest, where they lived and worked, just over the border from the Slovakian capital, but today they had been sent much farther abroad, all the way here in southern Bosnia.

The men had driven themselves down and checked into a local hotel with forged passports, but they had no plans to stay in town long. A night to reconnoiter and a night to act, and then they'd race back north.

These men had killed before, and they were confident they had it down.

The passenger in the van made a call on his mobile, waited a moment, then said, "He's home; his security has left for the night. No, they didn't even stay with him. I'll text you the address. Fifteen minutes from the hotel. Karoly and I can do it right now if you want."

"No," came the reply. "We have a plan. We are sticking to it. Tomorrow night, all three of us."

"*Oke*', boss. You want us to stay here?"

"For another hour. Just to make sure he doesn't have any visitors."

"*Mergertem.*" *I understand.* The Hungarian in the passenger seat ended the call, then looked to the driver. "Wouldn't be hard. Small-town Bosnian police chief. What's the big deal?"

"You know Zente. If he makes a plan, you are not going to change it."

"Yeah," the other man said. "He does like to be the boss, doesn't he?"

. . .

The road where the van sat had a good view to the building across the tiny square, but from the Hungarians' vantage point they were unable to see a darkened alcove in front of a small mosque to the right of the intersection in front of them. There, a lone woman stood in a black raincoat, and she kept her eyes on the same building as the men on her left, who she was also unable to see.

Talyssa Corbu was twenty-nine years old, thin, with small elvish facial features and short dyed red hair mostly hidden by the hood of her jacket. She was a foreigner here in Bosnia and, also like the men sitting thirty meters to her left in the van, she was associated with law enforcement.

This was Talyssa's second day in Mostar. On the first she'd staked out the police station for ten hours before seeing what she wanted to see, and then she had followed Niko Vukovic home. She'd come back this morning, saw him head in to work around ten a.m., and then tried breaking into the man's apartment building in broad daylight. But Vukovic had good locks and a better security system, and his building had several other units nearby. Moreover, he lived next door to a private day care that created a lot of come-and-go activity on the sidewalk out front during the daytime hours.

So she had abandoned this plan, and instead she spent the day here in the tiny little park at the center of the square a kilometer north of the Old Bridge, waiting for Vukovic to come home.

Now she waited for his light to switch off.

Minutes later it did, and then Talyssa Corbu wrote the time down and began walking away.

Tomorrow, she told herself. Tomorrow she'd get what she came for.

It was a good line for her to repeat through her head, but the truth was she had little real confidence in her plan.

Unlike the Hungarians, Corbu was not here on the job for anyone. No, this was personal, as personal as things got. She was in a foreign country planning on extracting information from a city police chief, and she had no training whatsoever to do so.

But she also had no choice.

She made her way back to her hotel a few minutes later, climbed the stairs to her room, all the while trying to come up with a better plan than the one she had now, because she worried that the one she had now would get her killed long before she found what she was looking for.

NINE

Liliana and I get up at five a.m. and drive to Sarajevo, arriving at the main train station at eight, right in the middle of the morning flow of commuters. Since she doesn't have a passport, I spend most of the drive from Mostar talking her through the tradecraft I employ to avoid immigration officials on trains, and as soon as we arrive I book her a long, circuitous trip that will take her north into Croatia, then northeast into Hungary, then south into Romania, then finally east to Moldova. With a little luck and the info I give her she'll make it home fine, and I also hand her five thousand euros in case she needs to drop some bribes along the way to ensure all goes smoothly, as well as to help her get started when she makes it back home.

This route will keep her out of Serbia, and I make her promise to get off the train in Moldova before she gets to Tiraspol, where she can take a local bus to her little town.

She'll be fine, I tell myself. At least in the short term.

Long term? I don't know what this experience has done to her, but I can take a guess.

I feel bad for Liliana, because even if this is over for her . . . it's not over for her.

The public address system announces the boarding of the train to Zagreb, and Liliana looks up at me without speaking.

"Take care of yourself" is all I can manage.

She hesitates, and I realize she's trying to think of something to say, as well. I figure she could just say *Thanks*, but I've got her all wrong.

"The other girls, Harry. They are not like me. They don't deserve what happened to them."

Jesus. This woman is so psychologically damaged I don't know if she'll ever recover. It's the most depressing thing I've seen in the past day. Not the violence, the murder, the kidnapping, the rape. It's the fucking with people's brains that is the end result of shit like this.

Like someone once fucked with mine.

This world. I swear to God. If there weren't just a few good people left in it I'd burn it down to the ground with me inside.

I wish I had a way to make her understand that what happened to her isn't her fault, but I'm not that guy. All I say is, "Go home. Be safe. Find out what makes you happy, and then do it. Everybody's got to do something that makes them happy." I give her a smile, or my version of one. It's stressed, tired, forced . . . but it's all I've got at a moment like this.

She nods and boards the train. I wonder about her, whether she'll go back to her village or whether she'll go back to Tiraspol to start turning tricks again. I have no idea.

I'm a gunfighter. Full stop. So much of the other stuff that happens around me is over my head.

I tell myself this so I don't think about it too much, but it doesn't really work.

I think about it all the time.

A minute later I'm in my Jeep, heading back to Mostar, ready to beat the holy fuck out of some piece-of-shit dirty cop because, just as I told Liliana, everybody's got to do something that makes them happy.

. . .

Shortly before ten p.m., the three Hungarian police officers working for the Slovakian mob stood in the shadows of a side street just twenty-five meters from the foyer to Vukovic's old building, smoking cigarettes and doing their best to control the adrenaline that had been rising in their bodies all day as the moment their target arrived home from work approached.

Their plan was straightforward, but it had worked for them in the past in similar situations. When his vehicles pulled up out front, they'd start walking along in that direction, just three men out for an evening stroll.

And then, when Vukovic and his two guards were close to them on the sidewalk, the three Hungarians would pull pistols. Two would shoot the three on foot, while the third man would empty his handgun into the driver-side windshields of the two SUVs on the curb.

Three men attacking five didn't sound like great odds, but the Hungarians knew they would have complete surprise on their side, and they were confident killers.

The leader of the group looked down at his phone. "Should be leaving the station about now. Probably another ten minutes till he's here."

Karoly replied, "We're ready."

And Florian said, "Quick and dirty. Like last year in Maribor."

Zente, the leader, nodded. "Just like Maribor."

. . .

While the Hungarians had chosen a closer position than the night before, Talyssa Corbu stood in the same darkened alcove she'd hidden in the previous evening. And also the same as the night before, she was unable to see the Hungarians because her sight line into their side street was obstructed by a corner building.

Unaware she wasn't the only person here right now with aims on the Mostar chief of police, Corbu had a plan of her own. She would wait for the police chief to be dropped off, and then, once the man was alone in his flat, Corbu would walk across the square and knock on his door. Using authentic credentials in her pocket but hoping to flash them so fast the cop didn't catch her name, Corbu would make her way inside and then pull out the little stainless steel pistol she'd bought on the street in Belgrade a few days earlier.

She'd demand answers from Vukovic, threaten him by waving both her gun and her credos, and just stay there and keep it up until she got what she wanted. That Corbu had never shot anyone, had never roughed anyone up for information, had never even been trained with handguns, was not lost on her. But with each passing day since she'd left her home, her limits had been challenged, broken, and thrown out the window.

She stood there in the alcove, checking the time on her phone and talking to herself over and over in a frantic whisper. "You can do this. You can do this."

. . .

I shift my eyes left and right as my brain tries to take in and process the scene in front of me. In the distance I see three men in the dark next to a gray van in an alley near the home of my target, and they definitely do *not* look like part of his security team. They've got the bearing of police officers, but they are plainclothed, and from their furtive looks to Vukovic's building and their nervous pacing around the alley, I think they've got some sort of mayhem in mind.

These guys are waiting for the chief of police of Mostar, and not to get his autograph.

My guess is they're here to kill him, and I can't let them do that. Not yet, anyway.

But the three men in the alley are just one part of the equation. Ahead and to my left, on the opposite side of the quiet little square, I see a lone man covered in a hooded raincoat doing his best to stay invisible next to a darkened mosque. A couple of vehicles have rolled through in the past five minutes, and both times I saw the figure in the edges of their headlights, and both times the man shuffled and bounced from one foot to the other with nervous tension.

Focusing on the black alcove helps me see him a little better now, even without the headlights. But I can't make out a face. *This guy is a lookout for the three in the alley?* It's the only thing that makes sense to me, but I can't be certain. Otherwise he's some sort of a solo act, just like me, because I don't see anyone else around.

I'm inside a real estate office opposite the alleyway where the three men are standing by the van, maybe forty meters away. I broke into this business half an hour ago, wanting a secure place to watch the square, just to get a feel for the rhythm of the scene. A few passing vehicles, one or two people walking dogs on cobblestoned streets on a warm night, lights on in many of the windows of apartment buildings.

But a manageable location for my plan.

Except for the three in the alley.

And the other guy.

I know I have to remove the three closest to the building from the picture before Vukovic arrives, which, if he leaves work at the same time every night, could be in the next ten minutes. Steeling myself for what's to come, I push the thoughts of the guy by the mosque out of my mind for the short term, put my hand on the latch of the door to the real estate agency, and take one deep breath. Then I step out onto the sidewalk and begin walking in the direction of the alley. I stroll past my target's building on my right and continue forward, closing on the three men smoking in the dim light. I don't look up at them; I just advance as if I'm planning on walking by.

I pass the building that shields me from the other man in the square, the bozo I take for the lookout for the muscle team, and then, when I'm just ten feet from the three men, I stop and turn their way. All three are looking at me; they drop their smokes onto the sidewalk.

"Hi, gents. Any chance you guys speak English?"

The man in the middle is the leader; this is clear in an instant. "What do you want?"

"I was just wondering what's going on."

"What?"

"C'mon. Three big dudes standing around a dark alleyway next to a rape van. What's the plan here, fellas?"

"Keep walking," says another of the three, and now I recognize the accent. These guys aren't local. They're Hungarian.

Scanning their clothing and their shoes as I speak, I say, "I think you guys need to call it a night. Go get a beer."

They look at one another in confusion now, and my eyes burrow into the folds of their jackets, their front pockets, the cuffs of their pants. I don't see any weapons printing there, but it's dark and these guys seem like pros, so just because I don't yet know where they are hiding their guns doesn't mean they *aren't* hiding guns.

The man in the middle takes a step closer, and the others do the same. "Who are you? You are not police. You are not from here. Why do you care where we stand?"

I don't answer immediately; I just stare the man down with a slight smile on my face. My actions are bizarre, true, but I have a plan. Right now I'm just talking to them, but I'm doing it in a way that ratchets up the heat slowly to the point where they will eventually realize that I am, in fact, a danger, and not just some oddball American tourist.

It's all to elicit the reaction I'm looking for out of them.

But so far, I'm not getting what I need.

Time to turn the ratchet some more.

Still looking the men over, I lower my voice from its light and airy tone, giving it some heft. I say, "I'm the guy who's going to stop you from doing your jobs tonight."

This, plainly, is a threat, and I begin to get what I seek from the Hungarians.

In my business, we call them grooming cues. A subconscious touching of the area where a weapon is hidden when an armed person feels a threat and is readying himself to draw.

They all do it within seconds of one another. The big man on my left crosses his hands in front of his waist and surreptitiously pats just above and to the right of his crotch. This tells me he's got a pistol in an appendix holster to the right of his belt buckle.

The man in the center unzips his coat and then, as he takes his hand away, brushes across the right side of his chest under his arm. From this I determine he's also carrying a handgun, but in a shoulder holster.

And the one on my right may have multiple weapons, but his left hand slips nonchalantly into his pants pocket, and I can see he's taken hold of something there. It's printing on the fabric now, and it looks like it could be a closed switchblade.

While this is happening, the leader of the group asks me again who I am and what I want with them. I can tell he is stalling for time, trying to figure out if I'm with Vukovic, if I'm some idiotic American mugger, or if I'm something else.

You got this, Gentry, I tell myself, psyching myself up for the violence that I know is mere seconds away. But while I do this I keep talking. "So if you guys just want to get back in that van and head home to Budapest, it would probably be for the best, because nothing good is going to come from—"

The man on my right takes a nonchalant step forward, but I read his intent. He's closing the space, getting into striking distance, and I know this means his knife is coming out.

I could go for my gun but I sure as shit am not going to fire it right outside the home of the man I'm planning on snatching in a couple of minutes; it would turn the dark square into a mob scene of onlookers before Vukovic even arrives. Instead I keep talking, angling my body towards Knife Man so I can get a foot up in his face fast when he goes for it.

He goes for it.

Just as I shift weight he turns into a flurry of movement, lunging forward while pulling a switchblade. It opens with a click that echoes in the alleyway, but before he can stab me I send one of my size ten-and-a-half leather Merrell boots up and into his nose, and I hear the bone snap as his head pitches back hard enough to give him whiplash.

With my right leg still coming down from the kick I throw myself forward to the man in the middle, who is now drawing from his shoulder under his jacket. I pin his hand there against his weapon before he can pull it, and then, as soon as my right leg lands, I launch my left foot out towards the guy on my left, short-circuiting his appendix draw by kicking his hand at his belt, breaking one of his fingers as his pistol clatters into the alleyway.

I head-butt the man in the center now, striking my forehead against the top of his nose while still controlling his gun hand against his body.

My ears ring and pain fires from my head into my spine, but he falls back towards the wall and slides to the pavement, and I can tell by the blood that his nose is broken, as well.

No gunfire so far, which is good news, but this hasn't exactly gone down quietly. All three of them made some sort of loud noise when I struck them, and the inevitable echo through the alley into the square makes me certain that the lookout in the alcove fifty meters away is aware his associates are in some sort of a melee.

I pull the gun out of the center man's shoulder holster as he falls onto the cobblestones, conscious but temporarily out of the fight because of his broken nose. The guy on the right also has a busted snot box, but he's pulling himself up by the back bumper of the gray van. From the looks of him I've got three seconds or so before he becomes dangerous again, so I turn back to the man on the far left.

Instantly I see that this dude still has a lot of fight left in him.

He's lost his pistol but he draws a hooked knife from a belt sheath at the small of his back under his jacket, and he slashes wildly with his uninjured hand as he lunges my way. I duck the blade, shift to his right, and use the pistol I just lifted from the leader of the group to bash him in the left temple as hard as I can.

His arms cartwheel, he drops the knife, and he hits the back of the van face-first.

I thank the Lord the van doesn't have a burglar alarm, because his impact shakes the vehicle on its shocks.

The Hungarian who had been on my right has pulled himself halfway back up to his feet, but by doing so he's put his head in a perfect position for me to drop-kick him in the chin. He probably already has whiplash, but this time I just about decapitate him.

He falls down on his back, unconscious like the man next to him.

I point the leader's gun in the leader's face as I kneel and speak softly but quickly, knowing Vukovic should be pulling up right now, so there is no more time to hang out in this alley in plain view of the entrance to his building behind me.

"Call your friend. Where's your radio?" I fish around in his jacket but don't find anything. "You're using your mobile phones for comms?"

The man's nose bleeds freely into his open mouth as he says, "What friend?"

"The lookout over by the mosque. The other—"

The headlights of two vehicles flash in the square behind me, reflecting off the glass of Vukovic's building, and I know that in seconds the occupants of both vehicles will see me. I'm sure it's the police chief and his security entourage, so I have to get out of their line of sight somehow. I hoist back my right hand and punch the leader in the jaw, knocking him out cold, same as his colleagues. Hurriedly I drag him behind the van, grab the second man by the arm, and pull him most of the way behind cover.

And then, just as a pair of Mostar Police vehicles turn onto the street that gives them a clear view straight ahead into my alley, I grab the third man, heave him up off the ground, shuffle one step back, and then fall with him onto the other two, mostly out of view behind the van.

But not totally out of view. My feet are sticking out from behind the van, as are those of the dude I've got in a bear hug. Looking down I see that the legs of the two men under me are protruding, as well. We're a big pile of bodies, and we'd be obvious to anyone looking right at us.

But we're twenty-five yards away, in a relatively dark alleyway, and I'm hoping like hell everybody in the two vehicles rolling to a stop now has their attention elsewhere.

Otherwise I have a shit-ton of explaining to do.

To my right the leader of the group moans softly and starts moving. I slam an elbow into his face, knocking the back of his head into the cobblestones, and the noise and movement stop.

Looking down between my legs, I see three men get out of the two vehicles. Vukovic is in the group, and they all head towards his building.

Nobody looks my way, which is good, but when the three go inside, the two vehicles roll off, which is bad.

Chief Vukovic has company tonight. A pair of bodyguards. It's too late to snatch him on the street, and breaching his house without getting into a gunfight in the center of town isn't looking too likely, either.

But just as I sit up and start trying to come up with a plan C, the man in my arms wakes up. He looks around slowly; clearly he's in no position to put up a fight. I lean into his ear.

"Take your pals and go home. Heal up. If you're ready in two weeks, come back for Vukovic. Kill him. But I need him alive right now."

I don't know if Niko Vukovic will be here in two weeks. He might be in jail, he might be in hiding, and he might be dead. But the Hungarians are my backup if I fail.

I climb to my feet, pushing the dazed man off me.

And then, just as I stand upright, I see the man in the black raincoat from the alcove step up onto the sidewalk, walking towards the police chief's house.

He starts to turn in my direction, and I freeze again, but this time it doesn't work. The man's eyes lock on mine.

And now I see that this is not a man.

A young woman stares at me, mouth agape. She stops walking and stands there in the middle of the street.

The lookout is a woman? Why not?

Assuming she has put together the fact that I just beat the shit out of her three cohorts, I expect her to draw on me if she's carrying a weapon. I've got my Glock in my waistband, and I begin to reach for it, but the lookout, standing twenty yards away, does something I don't expect.

She turns to her left and runs, disappearing around the corner of a building in an instant.

I take off as well, giving chase.

TEN

I turn and search the darkened little square for the lady in the black rain-coat. I don't see her, but I do see the elongating shadow of a figure running through one of the side streets to the east.

I leap onto and then over a bench and I race around little trees, up a steeply angled cobblestoned street. I cross a footbridge over the Neretva, passing where I saw the shadow, which I can no longer find, although I do catch a quick flash of movement ahead and on the left.

A car door shuts quickly. The driver fires the engine of the two-door hatchback. An instant later, headlights engulf me as the vehicle lurches in my direction.

I am not one hundred percent sure this is the black raincoat lady, but I like the odds. I definitely don't want to fire my pistol and alert the entire neighborhood, but I draw it anyway, hoping the lethal weapon in my hand will force the driver to stop the lethal weapon barreling down on me before it runs me over.

Like magic, the Glock 19 does the trick. The car skids to a halt feet away, with me standing in its path, my gun leveled at the driver's head through the windshield.

I move around to the passenger side and get in, still keeping the barrel trained on the driver. Only now do I see that this is, in fact, the woman in the black raincoat.

Her hair is covered by her hood, but wisps of dyed red hair poke out. Her skin is alabaster white, her eyes wide, heavily bloodshot and with gray half-moons under them.

And they are locked on the weapon pointed at her.

"You armed?" I ask it in English, because I don't speak Hungarian.

"What?"

"Gun! Do you have a gun?"

I can see in her eyes that she does. After a moment she gives a little nod and speaks through the heavy breath that came from her run through the square and across the bridge. "It's . . . in my . . . pocket." She has an accent, but it's faint. Her English is flawless.

I wait a few seconds, then say, "If you tell me *which* pocket, then I won't have to run my hands all over you. We just met, after all."

She looks scared shitless, and in a voice that confirms to me she is, in fact, scared shitless, she says, "My jacket. On the right."

I reach in and pull out a stainless semiauto that looks and feels like a piece of junk. I stick it in my back pocket, then say, "Anything else?"

She shakes her head emphatically, and I believe her. She's so tense I worry she might spontaneously combust, and quickly I realize that she doesn't have much of a background in this sort of thing.

Certainly not the way her three buddies obviously did.

Thinking for a moment, I decide I might be able to get some info off her about Niko Vukovic. The Hungarians probably know more about the man and his movements than I do, after all.

"Stay calm," I say. "Just drive."

The young woman stares at me, still breathing heavily from her run. Finally, she asks, "Drive where?"

"Let's find someplace quiet to go talk."

"I do not . . . I do not wish to go with you."

"I do not give a shit." Waving the pistol again, I say, "Drive!"

She doesn't say one word while she motors her way out of the hilly town, up a dark, steep road. Nor do I, as my own heart rate is still up after the alley fight and the mad sprint. I need to focus on breathing, but through her silence I can feel the terror emanating from her.

I do nothing to calm her; her fear is a tool I can employ to earn her compliance, and I won't give that up cheaply.

Nearly ten minutes later I direct her to park in a quiet hillside overlook, mostly out of sight of the road and with no other vehicles around. She does as ordered, and then, with the lights of Mostar down below us, I take the keys out of the ignition and put them in my pocket.

We are enshrouded in near darkness, but I can see her trembling hands well enough to know immediately if she reaches for a weapon, and my pistol is on my knee and ready for her.

I say, "Your friends will all live, but they're going to need a doctor. I want them out of town tonight."

"My . . . my friends?" She adopts a look of surprise and confusion. She puts on a good act, I'll give her that.

"Or," I continue, "you could just leave them and run home on your own. Looked like that was what you were doing. It's your call."

"I . . . I don't have any friends here. I just arrived in Bosnia two days ago. I live in the Netherlands."

"Wait . . . you aren't Hungarian?"

"Who said I was Hungarian? I am Romanian."

Now *I'm* confused, but I try not to let it show. "You're not with the three guys watching Vukovic's house?"

Now I see her first obvious lie.

"Who is Vukovic?"

Bullshit. Her mannerisms are all wrong for someone making a truthful statement. Whereas before her terrified eyes were locked to mine, now she glances down to the left and she brings one arm across her body, holding on to the steering wheel with it. These are tells I learned in my first day studying body language back at the CIA's Autonomous Asset Development Program in Harvey Point, North Carolina, and they are so obvious to me now I can often pick up on deception without making any effort to do so.

I say, "You were watching Vukovic's place, too. I don't need you lying to me right now, and you don't need me angry with you."

The woman looks out the windshield and nods. She looks exhausted. "Yes, I was watching the home of Chief Vukovic. I did not know others were doing this also."

"You didn't see the three big Hungarians?"

"No. I saw you, then I heard fighting in the alleyway. I didn't know what was going on. When I saw you I got scared and ran."

"You got . . . *scared*?" I get scared all the time, but I don't run into many people in the field who would admit this.

She nods. She's still scared. Her eyes show only mistrust and apprehension, all directed towards me. She says, "You are a gangster? You are part of the pipeline?"

Slowly I cock my head. I reach with my non–gun hand into her purse in the backseat, and I pull out a wallet. Flipping it open, I don't see a Romanian driver's license at first. Instead I see an official-looking identity badge.

And in my world, that's *never* good news.

> Talyssa Corbu. Junior Criminal Analyst.
> Economic Crime Division. European Union Agency
> for Law Enforcement Cooperation.
>   EUROPOL

Terrific. The last time I checked, Europol had published international warrants for me on about ten different charges, from Dublin to Tallinn, from Kiev to Stockholm.

Interpol, the world police organization, has a dozen more: from Hong Kong to Mexico City, and from Ho Chi Minh City to D.C. I've got a healthy fear of cops, because in their eyes I'm as bad a man as exists in this world.

But even though this woman works for an agency that would like to see me thrown into a windowless cell somewhere, she clearly doesn't know who I am, and she's clearly not here for me.

I say, "Europol coordinates with and supports law enforcement around the EU. Why would you be here, all by yourself, watching the home of a municipal police chief?"

She looks at me with even more suspicion now, but I guess I'd be suspicious, too, if some jackwad beat up three dudes, jumped in my car, stuck a gun in my face, and then took me to a darkened roadside turnoff.

"Is it any of your business?"

"I've got the gun, so my business is whatever I want to make it."

She belts out a nervy laugh. "You *are* a gangster."

"I'm *not* a gangster. Gangsters work for gangs. I don't. I'm self-employed."

She makes no reply, but I gather she doesn't believe me. Her terror continues, and it's absolutely palpable. Even in the poor light she appears almost ill to me.

Now I want to calm her down a little, because she's no good to me while she's this amped up, and I don't need her tossing her cookies in my lap. I say, "Relax, Ms. Corbu. It's possible you and I aren't enemies. I'm after Vukovic, too."

"Why?" she asks with genuine surprise.

"You first."

"I am . . . I am here looking for someone."

"Who?"

"I . . . I don't have to tell you."

I shake my head in disbelief. "You really have no idea how this whole 'being held at gunpoint' thing works, do you? I'm pretty sure that, in fact, you *do* have to tell me."

She doesn't speak for fifteen seconds, and then she starts to cry. I don't love making women cry, but I don't let off the pressure, because I don't know what the hell is going on here.

I shout now. "Who?"

And then, to my surprise, the meek little mouse shouts back at me. "My sister! I'm looking for my sister!"

I didn't see *that* coming.

"Your . . . your sister?"

Talyssa Corbu nods, tears dripping into her lap. She looks like a child again as she speaks through sobs. "Roxana. She disappeared nine days ago. Her flatmate said she went to a nightclub in Bucharest, where she lives, and then she never came home. I flew in the next day. Local police were no help, even to me, a Europol analyst. They said she probably ran off to Germany or Italy or France like all stupid girls. But Roxana would *never* do that. I did everything I could to find her, but then the police tried to stop me. I reached out to my office for assistance, but they just told me I needed to deal with family issues on my free time. I had to take a leave of absence to continue looking for her alone."

"That's harsh," I say.

"Then my mother received a phone call that I was later able to trace to Belgrade. She said the man had a Serbian accent, and this Serb said he found my mother's number in Roxana's phone. He wanted her to know he'd personally killed her daughter for meddling in the affairs of the Serbian mob."

I blow out a sigh. She's not looking for her sister. Whether she can admit it to herself or not, she's looking for her sister's body.

She keeps talking, wiping her eyes with her sleeve.

"The man on the phone said he shot her in Belgrade and then threw her into the river. Her body hasn't been recovered." She looks at me, and her sad and exhausted eyes fill with hope for an instant. "Maybe . . . maybe she isn't dead."

It's not my place to force her to face the facts. Instead, I say, "What did . . . what *does* your sister do for a living?"

"She is a student at the University of Bucharest."

"That's all?"

"Well . . . she is an actress, too."

With an incredulous look I repeat her words. "An actress."

"Yes. Some TV commercials. Some plays. Nothing that paid the bills."

"But why was she in Belgrade? And why would she be involved with the Serbian mob?"

The young woman looks down at her hands. "I have no idea."

She knows. Or at least she knows more than she's letting on. But I let it go for now. "So what did you do?"

"I drove to Belgrade. I had this crazy idea I could get local authorities to help me because of my position, but Europol has no jurisdiction in Serbia. The cops there were okay at first. They searched the banks of the Danube River, said they'd make inquiries into the underworld. But after I kept coming back, kept pressing, they threatened to have me deported. In the end I used resources at Europol to trace the call my mother received. The caller was using software to prevent a trace, but I had a friend in the technical division find the origin of the number. It was the phone of the wife of a man who has been on a European criminal organization watchlist. He is a member of the Branjevo Partizans, the most dangerous mafia group in Serbia."

"And . . . let me guess, you went, alone, to go spy on him."

"I went outside his place of business, a pool hall in the Branjevo neighborhood. I was too scared to go in."

Fear can be a healthy thing. "Keep going," I say.

"When he left, I followed him to a bar, and from there he went with other men to a building near the river. I had downloaded hundreds of faces from the database of Serbian gang members, and I started matching them up. There were a lot of known gangsters from the database right in front of me.

"Doing research on the faces I saw, I realized some of them were involved in human smuggling. The local police had records of this, and I had access to the records."

"Via Europol."

"Yes. My work involves tracking the proceeds of organized crime, and the sexual slavery market is the third-largest criminal enterprise on Earth, behind drugs and counterfeiting, and ahead of weapons, so I do know quite a bit about that world."

"The world your sister got herself involved in."

Talyssa looks out the window for a moment. With a little anger in her voice, the first emotion I've heard other than fear, she says, "She wasn't involved in that world. She was just a college student. A kid."

I let it go. "Your work at Europol. You're not a cop. You're a bean counter?"

"I am a forensic accountant. A data analyst."

"A bean counter," I repeat. "And yet, there you were, following mobsters through a foreign city. Alone. Very brave." I want to say it's braver than she appears now, but I catch myself. I *did* just see her preparing to attempt a solo entry on the home of an armed police officer with two bodyguards, so I realize I should probably give her more credit.

She dismisses my comment with a wave.

"I was able to ID most of the men there, but there were a few not in the database. I took pictures of them, ran them through facial recognition, and discovered the identity of one of them."

"Niko Vukovic, Mostar Police."

She corrects me. "*Captain* Niko Vukovic, *chief* of the Mostar Police." She wipes away the last of her tears. Either she is comforted to talk about this with someone, or else she is fully absorbed crafting a make-believe story for me.

"The next day Vukovic was back there, with a bus and some other men in cars. The bus had plates from Bosnia and Herzegovina. They all drove off on the highway to the west. I began to think maybe Roxana had been kidnapped by the smugglers and not killed. I thought that if this was about smuggling women, Bosnia is the next country to the west of Serbia. Perhaps this policeman was involved in whatever happened to my sister, and she was on the bus."

With only half the doubt I'm feeling in my voice, I say, "You . . . a woman who didn't see three big Hungarian hit men standing thirty meters from her. You . . . an accountant, no less, personally and single-handedly followed a convoy of vehicles all the way across two countries, for four hundred kilometers."

"Of course not. I didn't follow them. Instead I flew directly to Mostar and waited for Vukovic to show up back to work, which he did two days later."

"Why did you do that if you didn't know what was in the bus?"

A long pause now, then, "There were women in the bus."

"You saw them?"

She looks away. It's tough to tell if her distrust in me is what's leading her delays in answering, or if she's just making this shit up as she goes along.

"Yes. Just a few girls getting into the vehicle. They looked scared, exhausted. But I'm sure there were others in that bus."

"Why do you think that—"

"Because the windows were blacked out with paper. They were hiding something. Why a bus if they weren't hiding people?"

"How big was the vehicle?"

"A commercial Daewoo. I looked it up. It has seating for thirty."

She may not have a mind for tradecraft on the streets, but she *does* have a hell of a mind. Both Ratko Babic and Liliana Brinza had said there were about twenty-five girls at the Mostar farmhouse, and while I didn't take the time to count heads, I estimated roughly that number myself. Twenty-five women and girls, along with a few guards, would just fit in a bus of that size so, for the first time, a part of her story checks out with my own knowledge.

She says, "I knew I would lose the girls if I followed Vukovic, but I thought I could make him tell me where they were taken." Her head droops, and I wonder if she's about to cry again.

"And you brought a gun."

"I bought it on the street in Belgrade. I don't even know if it works. I'm afraid to test it."

"Your plan was to . . . to do what, exactly?"

"I wanted to get into his house. Wave the gun in his face. Intimidate him."

I don't want to insult her by telling her she wouldn't intimidate me if she waved a flamethrower in my face, so instead I say, "Your plan is dangerous. He's got security around him, day and night, apparently."

"Yes."

"So your idea won't work."

She looks up at me now. "Apparently not, because I've been kidnapped by a gangster."

"Kidnapped?" I ask in surprise, then consider the fact that I have a Glock 19 pistol on my knee, pointed vaguely in her direction. I holster it but say, "I haven't searched you, so if you make any sudden moves, we're going to have a problem. But otherwise . . . I have no intentions of hurting you. Looks like you've been through enough already. And I'm *not* a damn gangster."

Holstering the gun seems to calm her down, but I can tell she still sees me as a potential enemy.

I drum my fingers on my leg a moment, then say, "Here's my problem with your story, Talyssa. You can lie about what you've been doing for the last week, you can fake your entire timeline, but you can't fake the smell of terror that is pouring off you right now. You look like you haven't slept in a week. How am I supposed to believe you took on the Belgrade mob all by yourself, and you're in the middle of a one-woman op against the head of the police here, a man who has armed bodyguards and a man who, you say, is tied to the mob? How the hell are you able to—"

"Because of Roxana! Because she's my sister! Because I'm all she has!" Talyssa screams it. "She is either dead, or she's their prisoner. But either way, I have to find her, or find out who killed her." She begins weeping again. "I *have* to."

If this part of her story is an act, it's a damn good one.

Through sobs she asks, "What is your name?"

"Harry."

"Harry *what*?"

"Just Harry."

"Let me ask you, Harry, whoever you are. Have you ever lost a loved one? Someone you cared about more than anyone in the world?"

Yes, I have, more or less, but I don't answer her. Still . . . I think about this, think about the anguish I felt back then, and I dial back my skepticism about her story. "Okay. There's more to you than meets the eye. I can believe that."

Sniffing back more tears, she nods. "But you're right. Pointing a gun at the captain will probably just get me killed."

"And even if it doesn't, with that crazy bright red hair of yours, it won't be long before the opposition IDs you, realizes you're following them, and then they *will* grab you."

"They've . . . they've already identified me. In Belgrade."

I was wondering how a girl like this was able to tail mobsters without getting made. Apparently, she wasn't.

"As the bus was leaving, I tried to get the license plate number, so I stepped out in the street. They had a truck following the bus. I didn't know."

"A chase car," I say. "Pretty standard stuff."

"Yes, it chased after me, but I managed to get on a streetcar and get away. I don't know if they told others what I looked like and what I was doing, but—"

"Trust me, they did." I look at her hair. "Let me guess. After you were blown, you dyed your hair thinking it would throw them off."

"Yes."

I want to laugh, but this shit isn't funny. "And to make sure you would blend in with the crowd, you chose candy-apple red. Is that it?"

She runs a hand through her hair self-consciously. "It . . . I didn't know it would look like this. I've never dyed my hair before."

I let it go. It is a damn miracle this girl is still alive with her nonexistent tradecraft, but she is. Beginner's luck is a thing, but in my experience it's nothing to bet your life on.

I say, "You are blown. You are absolutely and positively compromised to the enemy."

"But I have to—"

"No. Trust me, you are done with fieldwork. But . . . but there is another way forward."

"What do you mean?"

"I haven't been compromised. Not yet, anyway. I can snatch Vukovic instead of you."

"Snatch? Is that like capture?"

"Yep."

"But you are a one-man operation, as well. Correct?"

"Yes, but . . . this is kind of what I do. No offense, Talyssa, but I'm guessing you're a first-timer."

She looks at me for a moment, and I hate it when people look at me. Finally she says, "For what purpose do you want Captain Vukovic?"

"I want to know where the women are."

She looks up at me. "One of them . . . she is close to you?"

I shake my head. "I have a reason, but that's not it."

"And when you have Vukovic, you will interrogate him?"

I think, *Sure, that's one word for it.* "Exactly," I say out loud, knowing well that she and I probably have wildly divergent definitions of the word "interrogate."

Corbu gazes out the car windshield down at the city a moment, and then she finally nods. "I help you. I know about the sex trafficking business. I know how the industry operates, how the money is moved. It is my job. I can help with the interrogation."

"All right, then, let's do this together," I say, and I wonder suddenly if she is going to have the stomach for what will happen next.

ELEVEN

Kostas Kostopoulos looked out over the Adriatic Sea as the first hues of dawn cast flickers on the gently breaking waves. He'd only been up a few minutes, hadn't yet bothered his cook to bring him his first coffee of the morning. He was awake now, earlier than usual, because he was waiting to hear news from Mostar.

He'd spent the previous day on the phone arranging the hit on the chief of police and having the area searched for the Gray Man. The seventy-two-year-old Greek did not like dissatisfying his superiors with bad news that came out of events taking place in his territory.

Kostopoulos knew his place; he was king of the Consortium here in the Balkans, but he wasn't one of the Consortium's top leadership, and just as he'd sent Hungarians to take out the police captain, the Consortium could always send assets from all around the globe to come after him if they chose to do so.

Not that he expected them to. No, Kostopoulos was certain that once Vukovic was dead, the way station was completely sanitized, and a new way station, already under development in Banja Luka, opened for business, the matter would be forgotten.

But first things first. He needed to know that the three Hungarians had completed their mission, and so far, he'd heard nothing.

Just then, the phone rang on the tiled table in front of him. Looking at it, he saw it was his contact with the Pitovci mafia, the Slovakian organization that provided the Hungarian assassins.

Kostopoulos answered. "It's done?"

The man said, "I just got a call from them. The team failed. All three men were injured and they are fleeing right now."

The Greek shouted into the phone, all pretense of control lost. "Imbeciles!"

"They claim they were attacked by someone unrelated to Vukovic. He was an American. Alone."

Just like at the way station, Kostopoulos thought.

The Slovakian added, "They say the man had incredible skill."

Just like at the way station.

Slowly a panic began welling inside him, and he lashed out at the man on the other end of the phone. "*Of course* they would say that if he beat their asses, wouldn't they?" He sat there for a moment, took control of his anger, and suppressed his new fear about the fallout from above from all this. Finally, he asked, "What happened?"

"I only know what I told you. We are already sending another team. Eight men. They'll be in Mostar late tonight. They'll take out Vukovic at the first opportunity, and they know to keep an eye out for this American."

Kostopoulos hung up and thought about the assassin. Belgrade assumed he'd come to kill Babic, but Babic was dead, and now the man was still there in the area, targeting the men who were there to kill Vukovic. What on earth for?

The Greek sex trafficker looked out over the Adriatic again and found it suddenly less beautiful. More ominous. A vessel would arrive here in Hvar the day after tomorrow. He would board and then they would head down the coast, where they would pick up the merchandise. Then he, along with the merchandise, would continue to the next stop in the pipeline, where most of the items would be sold off to other groups.

Everything was still functioning in the system, but Kostopoulos couldn't shake the worry that this American, whoever the fuck he was, would show up again.

He reached for his phone and dialed the number for his contact with the Consortium. It was a call he didn't want to make, but it was also a call he knew better than to avoid. "Jaco? It's Kostas. I'm afraid we've more bad news."

. . .

It was six a.m. when Talyssa Corbu sat down at the little table in the apartment and lifted the *dzezva*, a small copper pitcher. She poured thick Bosnian coffee into a chipped ceramic vessel the size of an espresso cup. She would have liked some cream and sugar with it, but she'd only found the coffee setup and an old bag of ground roasted beans in a cabinet, along with three cups and a pair of spoons.

She was glad to find these, actually, as the nearly barren cupboards in the tiny flat didn't offer up many more options.

As she poured from the *dzezva* she noticed that her hands were trembling, and she thought it to be less the immediate fear and more the intense anxiety she had been feeling every waking moment for the past week and a half.

Her quest for answers about what happened to her sister was taking a toll on her body; this much was clear to her. And last night, with the plan to confront an evil man, then her subsequent abduction, and then the gun in her face . . . these events hadn't helped her get over her anxiety, either.

She placed a second small cup on the table, and she looked back over her shoulder to see if she should fill it now with coffee or wait on the American to wake first. She saw him there in the darkness, lying curled up in a closet hardly designed to accommodate a full-sized man.

What a strange individual.

If she knew who he was it would help her trust him, but if she simply knew what he wanted, what his aim was in all this, then she would at least breathe a little easier. Talyssa had not known many good men in her life, and certainly none that were simultaneously as dangerous as this one.

No . . . nothing in her brain lined up right now. She looked at Harry again, watching him sleep. He'd been up most of the night while she rested, and then a couple hours earlier when she woke he told her he'd grab some rest. He'd taken her weapon with him into the closet, along with her phone; he'd left the door open so he could see her, and she had no doubt he was an incredibly light sleeper.

It was odd to her, as scared as she was and as unsure about this man as she felt, that she had no desire to run. She'd been in over her head coming here to Bosnia in the first place, and she also knew in the back of her mind that it was simply a matter of time before one of the evil men involved with Roxana's abduction would spot her, and then it would be all over for her, too.

She was scared of this Harry, and she certainly didn't trust him.

But she knew she needed him. He could go places she could not, and he most definitely could do things she could not.

Talyssa wasn't above using a bad man to help her navigate her way through bad men.

She'd do *anything* to resolve this situation. Which is why the evening before she had told the American a series of lies about what had happened.

Harry simply *couldn't* learn the truth, because if he *did* know, then she worried he'd be no help to her at all.

. . .

I wake up in the closet again in my Mostar flat, and see that dawn is just now breaking outside. A soft rain falls outside the window. The events of the evening before rush back into my mind like a flood, and I turn to look for Talyssa Corbu. I find her sitting in the living area, in the same chair and at the same little wooden table where Liliana and I sat the day before yesterday. She's wearing jeans and a dark blue pullover, just staring out the window at the weather, or at the police station across the street, I can't tell which.

She still looks like a little girl to me. Freshly dyed red hair and small mousy features. Pale skin and tired but fearful eyes.

But she's got balls of steel coming here alone to find out who killed her sister, I'll give her that much.

I smell coffee, and this is a surprise, because I didn't know I had any coffee.

I close my eyes and ask myself what I'm going to do. I'd spent a couple hours before falling asleep trying to figure out the best way to grab Vukovic without a rolling gun battle through the middle of town.

My plan to take him late at night after he got home from work had been a good one; so good, apparently, that four other people had been planning on trying it themselves, but the nighttime kidnapping option is off the table now. I don't want to stick around Mostar all day to wait for him to come back home. The Hungarians will have already reported in to their leadership, so there might well be another vanload of assholes already on the highway heading down here.

Nope, I've got to do this today, at the first opportunity.

And I don't think Corbu will be much help. She's a bean counter, not a cop.

And that means I'll have to do this shit alone. *Why should today be any different?* I think.

I shake off my moodiness, climb up to my feet, and walk over to the Romanian. She pours me a cup from a little copper pitcher she must have found in a cupboard in the kitchen. I sit down and sip the hot coffee and it's strong and good, better than I could have made. I'm no aficionado but to me it tastes like Turkish coffee, something I'm very familiar with.

Her first words of the day to me are, "You sleep in closets?"

I shrug. "I'm weird."

She doesn't reply. I know she's still trying to get some kind of a fix on me. Her analytical brain hasn't put me together yet, and it's twisting her in knots.

After sitting together in silence for a moment, I say, "I'm going to roll him up during the day today."

"Roll him up?"

"Capture."

Corbu is surprised. "While he is working? While he is armed?"

"Everybody I meet is armed."

"I'm not armed. You took my gun."

I sigh. "Every *bad guy* I meet is armed."

The woman seemed to marvel at what I was planning on doing. Then, "How can I help you do it?"

"You won't be there, not when it happens, anyway. But I need a place to take him. Somewhere outside the center of town. You can help me find a suitable location."

"The place in the hills where we parked last night?"

"Not there, exactly, too close to the road. But up in the hills, for sure. Go back in the woods on the other side of the street from the overlook, see if you can find a building or a clearing or some barn. I need it to be well hidden."

"So you can question him?"

And now we've come to the moment of truth. Clearing my throat, I say, "Talyssa . . . your idea of an interrogation probably differs from mine. I know men like this Vukovic, and I know what he will be able to resist. I also know what he'll respond to. We're going to have to do this my way to get anything out of him."

Talyssa cocks her head. "You are saying . . . you are saying you are going to torture him?"

"There's a good chance he won't tell us anything if we ask nicely, which means this is going to get ugly. If you don't want to be around to see it, I get it. I'll ask him questions about your sister's murder if you want me to."

"Her disappearance," she corrects.

"That's what I meant."

I can hear fresh nerves in her voice now. "Are you going to kill him when you have the information?" She thinks I'm a bad man, and she thinks I'm nuts. Yet still she seems all too eager to receive my help.

"I'm not going to kill him," I say, but I know I might be lying. There are a lot of ways that this can go down. It will be a violent encounter when I take him, and if that son of a bitch draws on me, I'm going to put a couple of rounds through his heart and end him. But I'm doing my best to keep Talyssa on board, because I need her help.

Her continued suspicion is evident. "I still don't know who you are, Harry."

"I'm the guy here to screw with the people who run the pipeline."

"But *why*? Why do you care? Did they kill your sister, too?" She says it sarcastically, but I can tell she needs to know something.

"No." I think about making up a story, but decide against it. This girl is being straight with me, more or less. Not completely, I know there is a missing piece to her narrative, but I haven't pushed her about it yet. Still, she deserves some truth. "Two nights ago I went to a farm thirty kilometers from here. I was doing a . . . a thing, but I discovered a room full of sex trafficking victims. They wouldn't leave with me, afraid of what would happen to their families back home.

"I think there is a chance the women will be . . . will be punished for me showing up there. And I can't just walk away from that. I need to try to help them somehow."

She seems astonished by what I just told her. "The way station? You found the way station here? You saw the women?"

"I did."

Corbu reaches quickly across the table to where her jacket lies over a chair and shoves her hand into a side pocket. Startled by the rapid movement, I rise to my feet, spin towards her, and go for the pistol inside my waistband on my right hip, all in one motion. I draw faster than her hand comes out. "Don't pull it!" I say with authority. I don't know what "it" is, but she's going for something obviously, and I'm trained to do whatever's necessary to avoid surprises.

She freezes solid, and the poor girl looks like she's about to wet herself. In a stuttering voice she says, "It's . . . it's just a picture. I want to show you a picture."

"A picture? Bring it out slowly."

The hand comes out, there is a palm-sized photo in it, and I holster the gun. As Corbu offers it to me she eyes my Glock, now back on my hip. She asks, "What kind of *thing* were you doing at that farm?"

"The kind of thing you really don't want to ask about."

"You were trying to rescue the women?"

I shake my head. She looks me in the eyes and registers my intensity, and she doesn't ask me for any more details.

As I take the picture from her, she says, "My sister, Roxana." Corbu's voice turns hopeful now. "Did you see her there? Anyone who looked like her? She doesn't usually wear so much makeup, but this is the most recent photo I have. A cousin's wedding in Timisoara in May."

Before I even look I say, "The Serbian told your mother she was dead."

I watch pain in her face reappear, clouding over her new excitement. "Yes. I guess I am just holding out a little hope that—"

"I get it." Hope isn't a strategy, as my mentor Maurice used to say, but it *does* go a long way in helping us deny the awful truth.

I look down at the image now. Two women stand at a party in flowing dresses, a flute of champagne in each one's hand. At first I don't recognize Talyssa on the left. She has longer dishwater-blond hair in the photo, and now her hair is dyed red and cut shoulder length. And she's wearing makeup, while now her face is unadorned. She's by no means unattractive, but she's relatively plain, her features all but nondescript.

Kind of like me, I guess.

Plus, it takes me a moment to associate the dressed-up, confident, happy woman in the picture with the buttoned-up, terrified, exhausted woman seated in front of me.

But next to her in the photo I see another woman. She is stunning. Beyond stunning. She doesn't even look real.

Talyssa says, "I know what you are thinking. We don't look like sisters."

"I wasn't thinking that," I say, but in truth, that's *exactly* what I'm thinking.

Roxana's features are all soft, her eyes large, her lips full. Where Talyssa has blond hair, this woman is a brunette, and she is easily four inches taller than Talyssa.

"We have different fathers. And she's six years younger than me."

Looking over the photo, I feel sure I've never seen Roxana before in my life. I'd remember someone who looked like that, I'm certain.

But I keep staring in silence for a few seconds. I really don't remember any of the faces I saw in the cellar. I only remember Liliana; she is Moldovan, and she looks nothing like the girl in this photo.

"I'm sorry. I didn't see her . . . but it was dark, and there were a lot of girls in the—"

"Never mind. She's dead. I know she's dead. I keep telling myself not to think about finding her alive." She pauses. "The only thing I can realistically hope to find are her killers. Maybe they will lead me to her body." She looks at me with suddenly fierce eyes. "I'll find you a place to take Vukovic. It will be far from the road, far from people, and covered." With a cold smile she adds, "He can scream all he wants . . . and nobody will come to save him."

I raise my eyebrows. "You're starting to get the hang of this."

TWELVE

Captain Niko Vukovic ran the police force in Mostar, but that wasn't where he made his money. He was paid by the Serbian mafia in Belgrade for a number of things, but his main income came from assisting with the flow of trafficked humans from the East, on their way to the West, the Middle East, and even Asia.

Vukovic didn't know the scope of the operation in which he played a part. No, he was a big fish in a small pond, and his pond was Mostar. Here, as far as he was concerned, he was in command. Not that old general who'd run the way station until the night before last, but the police captain who had kept the pipeline open through the territory for the past several years.

After Babic's obviously politically motivated assassination, Vukovic worried that those involved in the pipeline would hold him accountable, even though his job was not to provide physical security for the general but rather safe passage of the women on the roads to and from the way station, and police coordination if something went wrong. Still, the first thing he did when he heard about the attack on the farm was to assign himself four of his best officers to act as a security detail.

The four all took money from the Branjevo Partizans, the Belgrade mob, same as Vukovic. He figured they could be trusted to watch over him, both during his regular police work and when escorting him to a restaurant frequented by one of his Serbian mob contacts on the second floor of a small hotel on Stari Pazar Street.

The hotel was in the hilly Old Town at a cobblestoned intersection a block from the swiftly flowing Neretva River. It was luxurious by local standards, and the neat lobby was nearly empty. He walked up the stairs with his entourage to the restaurant and found it all but deserted, as well. It was late for lunch but early for dinner, his preferred meeting time with his contact.

He saw a heavyset silver-maned man alone in a back booth on his phone with a bottle of Serbian liquor in front of him.

Vukovic nodded. Always here by four. Just like clockwork.

The police chief entered with his four officers. He directed them to stay by the front door of the restaurant while he headed to the back.

"*Zdravo, Filip.*" *Hello, Filip,* Vukovic said as he sat down. "Haven't heard from you. Time for a quick chat?"

The Serbian mobster gave him a half nod, then finished his call and poured Vukovic a drink.

They toasted without much emotion, then drank down their shots in silence.

Another round was poured and drunk, and then a third poured into the little glasses. But instead of picking it up and downing it, Vukovic said, "I'm sure your people in Belgrade have spoken to someone in the Consortium."

Filip just nodded.

"What do they say?"

"What you'd expect. The Consortium is mad at us, mad at Babic, and mad at you."

The police chief did expect this, but he also knew he had to push back against it. "You told them I didn't have men providing security at the way station, didn't you? That was not my role."

"Yeah. I told them. Look, this will blow over, but they are moving the way station. It's already closed."

"Shit," Vukovic said, but he wasn't really surprised.

The man from Belgrade added, "The whores were taken to Dubrovnik. They are going to filter the next batch of product from Sarajevo to Banja Luka."

"Banja Luka? That's out of my territory."

"What can I say? The Consortium makes those decisions."

"What about me?"

The man with the silver hair shrugged. "What *about* you?" After a moment he said, "Look, we've got other jobs around here, we're not cutting you off."

"Are those other jobs going to pay as much as I was getting from the pipeline?"

The mob official shook his head. "You were getting Western money for that. Sorry, Niko, but that gold mine is shut down now. Be glad the Consortium didn't tell us to terminate you."

In a raised voice he said, "*Terminate* me? It wasn't my fucking fault. They know that, right?"

Another shrug from Filip; he didn't seem to care. Then he softened. "Look, Niko. You've been good for us here. Belgrade does not blame you for this; we aren't going to hold it against you. But the Consortium, they demand everything run perfectly, all the time."

"Your people aren't going to come after me. But what about someone else?"

The Serbian mobster nodded to the four cops at the front of the restaurant. "Just keep those boys close for a few weeks. I'm sure things will settle down by then."

Vukovic shut his eyes, squeezed his glass hard, and downed the rest of his drink. Banging the empty vessel back on the table, he said, "I have more to say. Don't go anywhere. I'm going to take a piss."

Filip nodded and grabbed his phone to make another call. Vukovic stood and waved over one of his men, and together they ambled to the stairs to go to the toilets on the ground floor of the hotel.

The police officer entered the restroom before his chief, his hand on the

CZ pistol he wore on his utility belt while he checked the area. The first three stalls were empty, but he pushed on the door to the last one and found it locked. In Serbo-Croatian he said, "Police business. I need you out of here."

Soon the toilet flushed, and behind the cop, Niko Vukovic stood in the doorway.

The cop cautioned him with a raised hand. "One second, sir." Wanting to check the hotel guest who had been using the toilet, the cop kept his right hand on his pistol and his left hand up, signaling his boss to wait.

The stall door flew open, and before the cop could react, he registered a black semiauto pistol a foot from his nose. A man in a ski mask came out quickly and pointed a second weapon at the chief.

Niko Vukovic did not move, other than to raise his hands slowly.

• • •

I rush out of the stall with my weapon pointed at the cop, then train the stainless steel semiauto on Niko standing at the door. When I can tell neither man is going to go for his weapons, I shove my Glock in my waistband and yank the Czech-made pistol out of the cop's holster, racking the slide against my belt buckle to make sure the guy had a round chambered. A bullet ejects and falls to the floor, and then I point the cop's own gun back at him.

Both men are frozen in place, and this makes me happy.

I know what I'm doing. Speed, surprise, and violence of action will win most violent encounters without the need to fire a shot.

To the cop I shout through the fabric of my mask: "Drop your radio and phone on the floor, and pull out your handcuffs. Lock yourself to the shitter."

The guy doesn't speak English, apparently, and he just stares at me. I look to Vukovic, motion for him to enter the bathroom all the way and to close the door behind him. When he does this I tell him, "If you don't speak my language, you've got five seconds to learn it before I shoot you both."

Instantly the chief answers in a heavy accent. "What you want?"

"For you to tell him what I just told him."

He speaks to his subordinate, nods as if to give him permission. I move out of the way of the john and the cop reluctantly enters the stall, then handcuffs himself to the pipe going into the cistern. I kick his radio and phone across the bathroom, and they come to rest under the sink. Then I order Vukovic to remove his own radio, but let him keep his phone. He does so, I check the cop kneeling over the toilet and see that he has clasped the handcuffs as instructed, and all the while I keep Corbu's little pistol pointed at the police chief. When the cop is secure I put the crappy gun in my back pocket and shift the CZ to Vukovic.

"Turn around."

As the chief turns he says, "Are you from the Consortium?"

I have no idea what he's talking about, but he doesn't need to know that, so I don't answer.

He follows that with, "Whoever you are, this is *my* territory. Not yours. You throwing your life away today."

I close on him fast, spin him around, take him by the back of the neck, and jab the pistol in his kidney. I kick open the door, then start hustling the Mostar chief of police quickly through the ground floor of the hotel.

There's not much activity around, but the few people in the lobby see me instantly. Everyone freezes in shock, and I scan each person I see to evaluate if they're a threat. A hotel security man slowly starts to open his coat, but I train the gun on him and he raises his hands.

In fifteen seconds we are out the employee-only utility door that I used to enter the hotel, and on a quiet Old Town side street. I shove Vukovic into the front passenger seat of my Jeep, then rush around to the other side and leap in.

I'm driving as soon as I get behind the wheel, my gun on the Bosnian Serb next to me. I don't make it fifty feet before I glance into the rearview and see two of his bodyguards racing out the front entrance to the hotel, heading directly for their SUV. I slashed the tires on the police vehicle parked on the side street near me but didn't do anything to the police vehicle sitting out front, because I couldn't chance being spotted by any of the hotel staff standing around the entrance.

They call me the Gray Man, but this shit's not magic.

I'm low profile . . . I'm *not* invisible.

The police vehicle lights up and sirens wail, and it falls into hot pursuit behind me.

. . .

Vukovic looks in the passenger-side mirror now and sees his men behind us.

"You let me go, and you keep running. They will not chase you."

I speed through the center of the hilly town with no idea where I'm heading. It's tough holding a gun on a passenger while driving one-handed, and I clip the mirror off a parked panel truck during a left turn.

I look to Vukovic, then tap the cell phone on his belt with the barrel of the 9-millimeter.

"Call them! Tell them to back off, or you're gonna get shot!" It's nearly impossible controlling the Jeep at these speeds, and I know the cops behind me are already radioing to others with instructions to cut me off ahead. My only chance is to get Vukovic's help in having them end the chase, and then get out of town before all the other police of Mostar rain down on me.

But Vukovic doesn't move. He looks at me without fear and speaks calmly, because he knows I'm after information, and I won't kill him. He says, "You are going to die."

I move the gun from his temple to his knee, and press it there. "Maybe. But first, you are going to limp."

"What?"

"I need information from you. I can still get it from a one-legged man."

Vukovic looks at the weapon, taking stock of his predicament now, and I see a slight crack in his visage. The first real hint of concern.

He pulls out his phone, hits a button, and brings it to his ear.

I speak fair Russian, better Spanish, a little German and French, and some Portuguese, and I've picked up a dozen phrases in Serbo-Croatian, but I can't understand a word of what this guy's saying now. I look at him while he talks, hoping to give him the false impression I have a clue, but it makes racing through these tight narrow streets even more dicey.

He starts yelling into the phone, and I tag another parked vehicle, side-swiping the little two-door with my left rear quarter panel. My tires scrape a curb on a turn as he ends the call.

Looking in the rearview I'm relieved to see the police vehicle behind me slowing down. It turns off down a deeply sloped side street a moment later.

With the barrel still on Vukovic's knee, I ask, "Can they track your phone?"

"No."

It's impossible for me to tell for certain if he is being truthful or not, so I take his phone and throw it out the window anyway.

In times like this, it pays to be a dick.

"What do you want?" he asks, but we have some more housekeeping to attend to before we get down to all that.

I move the gun off his knee. "Put your handcuffs on. Behind your back."

In response he just says, "You are the man who shot Babic. The Branjevo Partizans are going to kill you for that. You need to be running for your life, not talking to me."

I move the CZ back to his temple now, and with a sigh designed to show me he's a tough guy who isn't scared, he pulls out his cuffs and puts them on. I break the keychain off his belt and toss it out the window so he can't unlock himself, and I let him stew silently in the fear hidden behind his false bravado as I drive up and into the hills.

THIRTEEN

We make it out of the city without any more problems, and Talyssa Corbu calls and directs me to the place she found for the interrogation. After driving around a bit more to make damn sure no one is on my tail, I follow her directions. When I get there I muscle the Jeep into deep foliage off the road till it's hidden, then park it and pull out my prisoner.

I'd put a black hood over Niko's head as soon as we were out of the city, and this, along with his hands cuffed behind his back, makes him utterly compliant.

It's work getting up this hill through these trees, which means Talyssa has done a good job finding an out-of-the-way spot. I get lost for a minute, but the young Romanian woman calls me and talks me back on track, and ten minutes after climbing out of the Jeep with the chief, I see the location. It's a concrete bunker from the Bosnian civil war, mostly covered in vines and brush, pockmarked with bullet holes and RPG strikes. Still, the structure is remarkably intact.

I shove Vukovic inside. Rain drips through blast holes in the concrete above my head, openings that give some light to the otherwise dark space.

The walls are covered with graffiti. The words "Red Star," the name of a soccer team, are emblazoned in red. "Tito" is written in spray paint all over the place, which surprises me, because he was president of Yugoslavia a long time ago, he's been dead forty years, and he was an asshole back when he was alive.

Weird that kids around here take the time to tag bunkers with his name.

Talyssa Corbu stands in the middle of the dim space in her raincoat, the hood over her red hair and a scarf tied over the lower half of her face, just as I'd instructed her.

I pull a spare handcuff key from where it's stitched behind my belt loop at the back of my pants—kept there just in case—and I unlock my prisoner, then resecure his hands over his head, attached to bent rebar sticking through one of the mortar holes. I leave him there, the bag still over his head, while Corbu and I step outside the bunker and speak in whispers.

"This place will work fine."

I see now in the outside light that her eyes are filled with terror and concern, and she speaks in a voice tinged with trepidation. "Any problems?"

I know what she is asking by this. "Nobody got killed."

Obvious relief washes over her, but I see her lower lip continue to tremble. "What now?"

"Now is the ugly part. I won't know how ugly till I get started. You want to wait out here?"

"Of course not. I need to be in there listening to what he says. But . . . please do not torture him first. Give him an opportunity to tell the truth."

She's so out of her element right now. It speaks volumes about her relationship with her sister that she's doing all this, but I worry about bumping up against her limits soon, perhaps in the next five minutes.

"I'll start gentle. But what's gentle for me probably won't be considered gentle by you. I will use something called the presumptive. It means that although we don't know everything, we're going to come at him like we do. I'll lead. I'll tell him we know he's with the pipeline, and the Consortium."

"The Consortium?"

"In the hotel he asked me if I was sent by the Consortium. Does that mean anything to you?"

She shakes her head and looks back at the entrance to the bunker. "What about me? What do you want me to do?"

"You just whisper in my ear if you have something to say."

She nods her assent, although she remains incredibly reluctant about all this. I return to my captive and hear him muttering something in Serbo-Croatian. I don't know what the hell he's saying, but I don't like it. I smack him on the side of the head, and he shuts up.

Talyssa gasps in surprise behind me.

"You better speak English, Niko, otherwise the only language we can communicate in is pain."

He switches to English, and again he says, "You the man that kill Babic, yes?" After a little chuckle he says, "Some bad people looking for you."

"Where are the women?"

"Who are you? What do you want?"

I didn't go through all this shit to get interviewed, so I don't answer. Instead, I repeat, "Where are the women?"

Now he replies with "What women?" and I punch him in the jaw. I know it hurts, because I've gotten my own face bashed in a time or two.

Talyssa gasps again.

Vukovic grunts, and his head shakes inside the hood. After a moment it begins to hang. He's not unconscious, he's just showing signs of defeat, coming to the frightening realization that his future depends on me. It gives me some slim hope that I won't have to pound on him all day.

"The women and girls who were locked in the cellar of Ratko Babic's house. Where were they taken?"

He spits inside the bag, and bloody phlegm drips out of it, down onto the tunic of his uniform.

I ask with more authority in my voice. "Where . . . were . . . they . . . taken?"

"They gone. I don't know where. I don't know what happens before Mostar, I don't know what happens after Mostar."

Talyssa Corbu surprises me by stepping forward and shouting now. "Liar! I saw you in Belgrade with the Branjevo Partizans. You picked up the girls, brought them to the farm near Mostar."

His head cocks to the side; perhaps he's surprised to hear a woman's voice, but he makes no reply.

I lean closer to his face. "Oh, shit, Niko. You're lying to me? I guess it's time to knock your block off." I punch him again. It's not a particularly hard blow, but I am pacing myself. Still, my right hand throbs with pain and I think I'm going to have to look around for something else to bang against his face if this goes on much longer.

More blood and spit drip out of the bag. Corbu has stepped back against the graffiti-covered wall, apparently surprising even herself with her outburst.

I say, "Okay . . . if you know about Belgrade, the previous stop in the pipeline, then I bet you know about the next stop."

His head shakes hard. "They tell me nothing. Belgrade is Serb mafia, like here. That's why I go there. I work with them. The next stop . . . it is different group."

"*What* group?"

"I don't know."

"Where does the pipeline lead?"

Niko just shrugs. "I do not know. The men who run it . . . they are somewhere else. I do not know. Not mob." The bag stops moving, and it appears he is thinking for a moment. Then he says, "I don't think mob. Not Serbian. All I know. It is business. Only business."

"Only business?" I say with growing rage, and I realize I have to smack this asshole again, but this time, Corbu beats me to the punch. Literally. She appears on my left, charging forward, and she throws a crazy haymaker at Vukovic's head.

The Romanian woman hits the Serb in the cheekbone, and I can tell by the sound of the impact that Talyssa Corbu is going to feel the strike a lot longer than Niko Vukovic.

She clutches her hand in pain, and I'm certain she's regretting the first and only punch she's ever thrown in her life. I pull her back a few feet. "Let me handle the rough stuff."

Ignoring her injury, she says, "My sister." She pulls out the photo and gives it to me with her uninjured hand.

I return to the police chief again. "I need you to look at a picture of a girl, and I need you to tell me, truthfully, if you have seen her."

He snorts a laugh. "One of the whores? That's what you want? One of the whores?"

"She's not a whore!" Talyssa shouts, and she rushes forward again, swinging the same fist as before. I catch it before she makes contact, not for the prisoner's benefit but for hers, and I spin her around and walk her back to the corner.

"Allow me," I say, and I walk forward now and hammer Vukovic's face with a left jab.

Speaking to Talyssa, he says, "They are all whores. Like you . . . whore."

I slug him harder now, connect with his right cheekbone. His head pops back and I know he's going to feel that all the way down his spine, because I feel it all the way up to my shoulder.

As his head hangs again I say, "I'm going to show you a picture."

"Who cares? Who cares about this woman?"

"I do. Which means you'd better care, too."

I put my balaclava back on and yank off his hood. He looks at the picture without any emotion as blood runs from his nose and mouth. "Never seen her," he says.

I can't tell if he's being truthful, but I push him. "You're lying again, and you are trying my patience."

He shakes his head once more. "No. I don't have time to look at all the property."

I bet he takes time to do more than that with the prisoners. I ball up a fist but calm myself and hold it back, deciding to try another tactic. Taking the picture from him, I say, "You are worried about what I will do to you now, but maybe you should worry about whoever it was who sent the Hungarians after you."

He looks at me with confusion, his nose and mouth dripping blood. "Hungarians?"

"Three assassins were outside your building last night. I stopped them before they got to you." When he says nothing I add, "You're welcome."

"Lie," he says. "I have no problems with Hungarians."

"I could be wrong," I say, "but I'm guessing someone high above you in all this wants to send a message to other little people in the pipeline about the price of failure. They brought these guys in from another gang."

Niko does not respond for a long time. Finally, he whispers, "Pitovci."

Talyssa leans into my ear and whispers, "Slovakian mafia. From up north in Bratislava."

"How do you know this?"

"When I worked for the Romanian federal prosecutor's office we dealt with them. They are active in Bucharest."

To Vukovic I say, "But the Slovakian mafia didn't order the hit on you, did they? Somebody else is pulling their strings."

He doesn't respond.

"It was the Consortium, wasn't it?" I don't know what the hell the Consortium is but, again, I'm doing a presumptive interrogation approach, and sometimes it requires taking a chance.

His eyes rise to mine, and I know I've struck gold.

I'm completely improvising now. "They aren't happy with you after what went down at the general's farm. You are being made an example of, and then, after you've been brushed aside, you will be replaced." He looks away, sniffing bloody air, but I press him. "Time is short, Niko. The Slovakians will send more killers, and I won't be there to beat them up for you. Somebody wants you dead, Chief, and it's the exact same people you've been serving."

I'm inside his head now, I can see it.

"What are you going to do to me?" he asks.

"You have three choices. I can kill you right here, I can take you back home to where the next hitters from the Pitovci are probably already waiting, or I can just leave you here alive. Number one and number two both sound like more fun to me, but I'll do number three if you give me something valuable to help us find those girls."

Blood bubbles on his lips as he thinks. "I know one thing. *Only* one thing. I tell you, I tell you the truth, all the truth I know . . . and you will leave me here? Alive?"

I lean into his ear and speak softly. "I'm a man of my word. If you believe I'll kill you because I said I will, you should believe I'll let you go if I say I will."

He hangs there and bleeds a moment while he weighs his options. He nods a little and starts to speak. I interrupt with, "Remember, it better be really fucking helpful."

Finally he just says, "Dubrovnik."

I cock my head. "Dubrovnik?"

"It's a city in Croatia."

"I know *that*, dipshit. What about it?"

"From Mostar, the whores go to Dubrovnik."

"How do you know?"

"My men escort the trucks that come, then lead them to the Croatian border. They take the southern route, through the mountains . . . it goes to Dubrovnik."

"Where in Dubrovnik?"

"I don't know."

"Not *that* helpful, slick."

He shouts now, fear and anger in equal measures in his tone. "It's all I know! It's everything I have!"

Talyssa speaks up again. "That's not a small town. How are we supposed to find them there?"

Vukovic's head hangs again. "I have no answers. I don't work in the pipeline, I just protect it here."

I say, "And you've done one hell of a fine job, haven't you?"

He looks up at my masked face, but not in anger. It's more a look of resignation. I wonder if he knows he's a dead man no matter if I spare him right now or not. This fact seriously hampers my ability to extract any more intel from him, but I have to try. "Tell me about the Consortium."

With his head still low, he gives it up. "They run pipeline. They deal with Branjevo Partizans. Partizans deal with me. That it. That everything."

He seems like he's telling the truth, and I walk back to Talyssa. "How's the hand?"

"It's fine."

She's rubbing it still; it isn't fine.

I say, "This is all we're going to get out of this guy."

"What happens to him now?" There are nerves in her voice, and I take that to mean she's worried I'm going to just shoot my prisoner in the head and leave him hanging here like a piece of meat at the butcher shop.

Honestly, I like the imagery, but I need Talyssa, and I need her with her wits about her.

"We're leaving him here. Alive. We'll take your vehicle; mine's been compromised."

"But . . . how will we find the women?"

"We'll discuss that on the way."

We leave Niko Vukovic with his arms over his head. I don't hand him the key. I do, however, pull my Jeep back down to the street and leave it there alongside the road.

His people will find him soon enough, and they will release him. Then, judging from the look on his face when he realized the Consortium had targeted him, I assume the Consortium's people will find him, and then they will murder him.

And I, for one, won't miss him.

• • •

We head south from Mostar, the terrified young Romanian criminal investigator looking for information about her sister's disappearance, and me, an assassin on a poorly-thought-out quest to make up for my mistakes.

We're a strange pair, to be sure, but for now, anyway, we have the same goal.

It's quiet; a fresh gentle rain falls from the low gray summer sky. I look over to Talyssa; she's rubbing her hand. I don't see the woman who threw the punch in the bunker. I see the scared young accountant.

"How did you start working for Europol?"

She looks out the window as she talks. "I received an advanced degree in forensic accounting. I started working in economic crimes for the state prosecutor in Bucharest. After a few years I applied to Europol. Now I live in The Hague and work in money-laundering crime in the European Union."

"And sex trafficking."

"At the prosecutor's office in Romania, following the money from the international criminal enterprises to the local gangs was a big part of my work. Hundreds . . . thousands of young women disappear every year in my country. They are trafficked and smuggled abroad, forced into prostitution, used as slaves, dehumanized. We could see the money making its way into the gangsters' accounts, but it was laundered somehow, and we could never see where it came from. I moved to Europol thinking I could make a difference on a bigger level, but my office is not so interested in human trafficking. It's seen as a law enforcement problem, not a forensic-accounting problem. They are wrong, of course, but I am still very junior, and no one listens to me."

"I'll listen. I want to understand what the Consortium is."

"I have never heard the term when related to trafficking, but a consortium is just an association of organizations."

"How does all this work, typically? Where are the victims taken?"

"They are taken to anyplace where the economy can support a large commercial sex industry. The developed nations. Europe, America, wealthier parts of the Middle East and Asia."

"How are they taken?"

"Many different ways, but victimization is all about vulnerability. Statistics say ninety percent of sex trafficking victims suffer some kind of abuse before they are recruited. Sexual abuse, physical abuse, dire economic hardship. Often, all three."

"What do you mean by 'recruited'?"

"An unfair term, I agree, but that's the term. It encompasses all the ways they are brought into the trafficking system. First, there are recruiters. These are usually women, and they make initial contact with the intended victim. Typically, this is called the grooming period. The recruiter uses money, flattery, and the like to get the victim pulled in. They make connections with them to earn their trust. And then, when they are more susceptible, transporters are brought in."

To this I just say, "The pipeline."

"Exactly. Vukovic said the Serbs pass them off. I imagine whoever they pass them off to passes them off again. Finally, they will be sold into slavery."

"Do they ever escape?"

"Sometimes. Not terribly often. But if they escape their captors in a foreign country they are treated like illegal immigrants by the local governments. They have no rights, they are just shipped home. There is no witness protection, so if they say anything to the cops, the traffickers will know.

"The sad part is that many who escape return home to the same hardships they were drawn away from. Women and girls are often revictimized, time and again."

I think of Liliana Brinza, and I hope this doesn't happen to her again.

"Christ," I say.

"The people running the pipelines and other systems like it have this down to an art. The way stations are hellholes, but they are also refuges. Food, music, the bonds made between the captors and women, the drugs administered to them. It's all part of the plan. These young women and girls go into a system that has been honed for hundreds of years. Thousands of years."

And here I am, getting in the middle of all this.

She sighs loudly now, then asks, "How can we possibly locate them in a city the size of Dubrovnik?"

"I have an idea. But you may not like it."

"Anything. I'll do *anything* to find out who is responsible."

"I was hoping you might say that." I breathe out a long sigh, knowing this idea isn't great, but it's all I have. "We use you as bait."

She looks up at me slowly as I drive. "Bait?"

"Look, the cops have been tainted at each stop on the pipeline. Not just here in Mostar, but in the other locations, as well."

"Yes." I can tell she gets it. "So . . . so you are saying I go to the police in Dubrovnik and start asking questions?"

"Exactly."

"About my sister?"

"I wouldn't do that. If there is one chance in one hundred she could still be alive, you will endanger her by letting the opposition know you are looking for her. She just may become too incriminating for them to keep around."

Talyssa thinks about this for a long time. "I can't do that. I think she is gone . . . but without a body, I do not know for sure. So . . . what do I say?"

"Tell them you know about the pipeline, and you know about the Consortium."

"But . . . what do I know about the Consortium?"

"Nothing, really, beyond the name. Throw that out there. Ad-lib. Like I did back there with Niko."

"And *then* what?"

"Then return to your hotel and let me take over. They'll come for you, I'll get you out before they take you, and then I'll be there to see who they are and where they go."

She sits in silence a moment. I start to waffle. I even consider telling her we'll think of something else because this is too dangerous. But I know there is nothing else.

She knows this, too. "Yes. That is the best idea."

"Not sure it's the *best* idea, Talyssa, but it's pretty much the only idea I have."

"When do we leave for Dubrovnik?"

I've turned on the highway through high hills towards mountains in the south. "We'll be there in a few hours."

She nods and we drive on.

I've made it out to her like our plan will be much easier than I envision things, because if Dubrovnik is, in fact, the next stop along the pipeline, the people who run this thing are going to be looking for us there. The same guy—me—shot up one of their way stations and then snatched one of their police conspirators, so it's no great leap to assume I'll turn up again at the next stop in the line.

If they normally had five guys with guns around the girls, now they will have fifteen. If they would normally send two guys to pick up Talyssa when they realize she's on to them, now they will send six.

My involvement in this whole thing has made it more difficult for everyone—victim, friend, and foe alike.

Nice work, Gentry.

This is going to get complicated, and it's just me and the accountant with the missing sister against an opposition we haven't even identified yet.

Yeah, any way you look at it . . . this blows.

FOURTEEN

Kenneth Cage sat in a plastic chair, staring at the girl dancing in front of him. She moved with grace, but with a look of intensity on her face that would tip off an expert that she was struggling to remember her moves.

She stopped and bowed, and the crowd clapped politely.

Ken Cage, on the other hand, stood up and cheered.

Juliet was his twelve-year-old daughter, after all, and as far as he was concerned, she was magnificent.

Soon he sat back down and watched the next girl at his daughter's ballet recital take the stage.

He knew he'd be stuck here for another hour, but just as he steeled himself to endure the rest of the damn dancing, his phone vibrated in his pocket. Heather glared at him as he looked down to it, but when he saw who was calling, he turned away from her and left the room.

His bodyguard moved into position behind him, radioing the driver of the Mercedes outside that the principal was moving.

But Cage didn't go to the G-Wagen. Out in front of the Hollywood dance studio, he moved over to a bench and answered the phone in an angry tone, while his bodyguard remained a few feet behind.

"Not the best time, Jaco."

"Sir, I need this encrypted."

The American sighed, tapped a couple of keys that encrypted the call on his end, and said, "What's up now?"

"It's about the Balkans."

"I told you to handle that."

"I need someone who can make a decision, sir."

Cage sat on a bench by the parking lot, his head sagged. "Dammit," he said, while looking around to make certain no one was in earshot. "What's the fucking problem now?"

Jaco's voice was its usual businesslike tone. "It was thought the killings in Bosnia were associated with an assassination attempt on the man running the way station. Something unrelated to the pipeline."

"Some uber assassin, right?"

"Yes, sir. But if that were the case, we'd expect that man to be long gone from the area where the killings happened, and we'd also expect him to pose no more threat to the pipeline."

"But?"

"But by all reports, the man who killed Babic the other day also kidnapped the Mostar police chief this afternoon, local time."

The American replied with, "And why does that interest me in the slightest?"

"Because Chief Niko Vukovic worked for the pipeline."

Cage felt hot anger welling within him. "So . . . you are saying someone is fucking with my operation."

"It seems that way, sir. The entire police force in the Mostar area is looking for their chief, of course, so I hope to have news before long. If he's recovered alive, then—"

"He's been grabbed by an assassin. Finding him alive doesn't sound very likely, now, does it?"

"No, sir. But even if he *isn't* recovered alive, we can hope for clues. Obviously, the cops will turn the area upside down looking for the assassin whether he keeps Vukovic or kills him and dumps the body."

Cage said, "Is this something Kostopoulos can handle?"

"No, sir. I know a lot about this mysterious Gray Man. He's just too good."

"What is it you want from me?"

"I want to get my team together. Fly into Dubrovnik, the next stop in the pipeline. It will take some time; my men are spread out all over the world right now. But we'll get in there and protect the shipment, keep an eye out for this American bastard."

Cage waved a hand in the air. "Approved. If the Greek and his Albanians can't get it done, then it's up to you and your boys. I'll be at the market in Venice in two days. I sure as hell don't want this maniac showing up there. This gets dealt with now, and it gets dealt with hard! Got it?"

The pause was short, and the reply bore all the deference of a military man serving his master. "Yes, sir. I'll get the boys together."

Kenneth Cage hung up his phone, shaking his head in disgust. He wasn't worried about his overall operation in the slightest. It was strong and secure, and the men, women, and organizations under him in the Consortium would do what needed to be done. No, he was bothered by the fact that his day had been sullied with talk of hit men and kidnappings.

Cage didn't consider himself a criminal. Just one hell of a good businessman.

A partner in a Hollywood production company valued north of eight hundred million dollars, he was also senior partner in a hedge fund with assets under management seven times that.

With a business degree from Wharton, he'd gone into banking in the eighties and computer programming in the nineties, he had been at the vanguard of virtually all the advances that technology had brought to the finance industry in the past three decades, and he'd made a name for himself—and a fortune along with it—exploiting the markets with the latest electronic tools.

He created and managed a hedge fund at the height of the dot-com bubble, but with the bust his fortunes evaporated overnight. This hit him hard, not because his investors lost mightily but because he'd grown accustomed to both the lifestyle and the sense of personal power that came along with his riches. After a single lean year he decided, without a moment's guilt or indecision, that he would regain his stature by any means necessary.

Cage used his vast skill set in computers and finance to begin laundering money. First for the doctors and lawyers who were his hard-hit fund's clients, helping them protect endangered assets from their wives, their business partners, and Uncle Sam. But soon he developed both tactics and processes that could clean dirty money on a much larger scale.

By the stock market crash of '07 he found himself recession proof, because he was hard at work for drug cartels, third-world dictators, high-end corporate and government embezzlers, even revolutionary and terrorist organizations, along with a host of other shady clients.

Through his efforts, aircraft and even cargo ships full of palletized cash were turned into sound, legal assets, and though he'd gone to great lengths to keep himself safe and out of the eyes of police, those in the underworld knew that there was a shadowy man in the United States who could get their massive amounts of currency turned into heavy balances held in untraceable offshore accounts or into hard assets like property, luxury cars, and jewelry.

Cage had the brains, the know-how, and the sheer creativity necessary for his work, and he loved it as passionately as he loved Heather and his three kids.

For the first several years that he worked in illegal finance, he was more than satisfied to play the exciting shell game of money laundering, and play it better than anyone else.

And though he was a dedicated family man while at home, he began to enjoy his role on the periphery of the underworld when away. This wasn't hard for him, as his work introduced him to the top criminal industries on Earth: drug trafficking, weapons trafficking, and human trafficking.

An organization out of the Middle East that trafficked women from all over Asia and Eastern Europe into Western Europe employed his creative financial services, and on a trip to Marseilles Cage had been offered a taste of their wares. Cage enjoyed the power he saw in himself while subjugating and abusing the young women; it made him feel virile and potent, and soon he tweaked his illicit business model to cater specifically to this industry so he could be more involved with human bondage.

He didn't traffic drugs or weapons himself, not because he had any moral aversion to doing so, but rather because that was not where his interests lay. He was a businessman, obsessed with the allure of expanding his realm, but though he might have made more money with drugs and weapons, he never ran the numbers to find out.

It didn't matter, because Ken Cage's heart and soul were in sex slavery.

Within a few years he led a large organization without a name; it was referred to among the players as simply "the Consortium." He'd made arrangements with over two dozen other regional organizations around the globe: mafia groups from Turkey, Slovakia, Serbia, Greece, Italy, Belarus, and Ukraine, and criminal gangs in Germany, France, the UK, Belgium, Spain, and the United States.

He also developed, along with advice of the experts in the target regions, systems for finding and bringing the best product to market: Albanian, Belarusian, and Ukrainian "recruiters" who snatched or coerced women and sold them into the pipeline.

The American mastermind saw himself as an overseer of a process and the inventor of a brilliant, efficient, well-oiled machine. Together the organizations and assets of his Consortium now accounted, by his money cruncher's recent estimations, for roughly six percent of the world's 150-billion-dollar annual human trafficking revenue.

Ten billion dollars a year filtered into the Consortium's component parts, and the cash and the Consortium's share of the world's supply of slaves was growing in double digits. It was real money; men and women would kill to get it and to protect it from any threat to the Consortium, and men and women had killed to do just that.

Whether through assassinations, turf wars, or executions of slaves who either could not work or would not hold their tongues about the pipeline, the violence associated with the organization was truly staggering. And this was in addition to the rape, the humiliation and subjugation of human beings, and the theft of liberty and labor that took place as a matter of course in the day-to-day operations of the Consortium.

Police had been bought off; high government functionaries in developing nations had been corrupted.

Ken Cage had started it all, retained ultimate control over much of the oversight, but just as he had a rule that his involvement was hidden behind dozens of shell companies, he also had a rule that he would never, *ever* sully himself with violence. He had others to do that for him. Not only in the form of his security force—Jaco Verdoorn's small but specialized unit of well-trained Afrikaner shock troops—but every single organization that assisted along the pipeline had their own killers and captors, corruptors, and enforcers.

MS-13, 'Ndrangheta, the Gulf Cartel, the Pitovci, the Branjevo Partizans: the names of the gangs and cartels and the other criminal concerns had meant nothing but news headlines to Cage before he started his process, but now they were integral to his own success.

The American in the Hollywood Hills was a supervillain masquerading as an everyman, albeit an outrageously wealthy one, and no one who saw him on the streets of LA would ever have a clue that the short and bald middle-aged man had almost single-handedly created a massive worldwide organization of abject misery.

That was by design. Cage compartmentalized his criminal behavior and his home life, and nothing was more vital to him than keeping those two worlds apart.

He took trips every four months or so to different source locations to personally pick out his own stable of girls and had them recruited by any means necessary and brought over to a large property owned by one of his offshores north of LA, where he would travel to sample the best of the best of his product.

He'd expanded the ranch into a compound of sorts, had it staffed with attendants for the women—prison guards, essentially—as well as a robust security team, and he'd invited his close friends and business associates to use the facility, and the product stored there, as they wished. Hollywood moguls, investment bankers, shipping magnates, the CEO of an airline: "the Ranch" became their own personal Disneyland of debauchery.

Over the previous winter Cage had traveled to Vilnius, Lithuania, spending time with his entourage in nightclubs. Jaco Verdoorn and his men ran his personal security detail. Cage and his associates chose six women over their week there, then returned home.

Recruiters took the women and placed them into the northern pipeline, and in a matter of weeks the girls were in California, standing before Cage.

But as was always the case, after a few months he grew tired of the new lot and wanted some fresh supply.

So six weeks earlier he'd gone to Bucharest, a return trip because his last time there had been fruitful. On this visit he picked out three women, including a stunning young brunette who chatted with him at length in a nightclub. The young brunette was half a head taller than him, and she possessed the highest cheekbones, the softest lips, and the most piercing eyes he'd ever seen.

He'd grow tired of her once she was his, but for now the anticipation of having her subjected to all manner of humiliation for his pleasure in his nest filled his brain with an impossibly rich mixture of "feel good" chemicals.

Cage lived for this shit.

He'd left Bucharest with instructions for his local recruiters to get that girl in the pipeline and over to him as soon as possible, by any means necessary.

And then he'd returned home to the world of a multimillionaire father, to baseball practice and dinners with friends in outdoor cafés on Rodeo Drive and evenings in the hot tub talking over family matters with his wife.

. . .

Ken Cage pocketed his phone, then started back towards the door to the studio, but he stopped himself. Turning to his bodyguard, he said, "Fuck it, Sean. Juliet's done her bit. Heather's already pissed at me for leaving. Might as well call it a day."

"Back to the house, sir?"

Cage shook his head and began walking towards the Mercedes. Hall stayed with him. "Where Heather can yell at me? Hell no. We're going to the Ranch."

"Right, sir."

FIFTEEN

Maja stared out at the ocean and the late-afternoon sun hanging over it, and she wondered where the hell she was. Her view was partially obstructed by the ruined wall of the large, old, bombed-out warehouse, but enough of the coast was visible that she could tell she was somewhere beautiful.

But it did not make her happy. Her predicament had not changed, only her view.

The last two days and all of this morning she and the others from Mostar had sat in the blacked-out bus, parked in an underground garage. They'd been fed fast food, and a pair of buckets had been placed in the back for the women to use as a toilet, but no one was allowed to leave or to make a sound. It was a miserable two days, and Maja's back ached and her bleary eyes burned from crying and lack of sleep.

Then the girls from Mostar had been brought inside the ruined building during the daylight this afternoon, which surprised her because this was the only time she'd seen the sun since the night she was taken.

Now she and the others, minus Diana, the poor girl who had been shot while trying to flee through the woods, were kept in a large open room with blown-out windows and trash all around. There was a view of a large body of water outside, but a fifteen-meter drop straight down onto broken masonry and concrete, sharp bent rebar and shattered glass meant no one here was going to jump out the window, run to the beach, and swim away. Bombs or tanks had attacked this building, but long ago, as Maja could see full-sized trees growing through the rubble below.

She hadn't paid attention in history class in school, but of course she knew about the war in Bosnia and Croatia and Kosovo and all those other places in the Balkans. This had to be Croatia, she felt almost certain, and the water in front of her the Adriatic Sea.

When they'd climbed off the bus she'd been surprised to see that the Serbians were gone, and other men were watching over them now. Maja did not know what that meant. The one who ordered the women and girls about spoke English, and they were all darker-complected men. She couldn't tell if they were Turkish or Albanian or perhaps even Greek, but they seemed more organized and professional than the group of gangsters who held them before.

She had no clue if this was good news or bad.

There was no door to this room, and no furniture, either, so the women and girls sat on the concrete floor. Any possible escape to the stairwell and then freedom was cut off by a group of five men who stood and sat near the open doorway.

She had not been raped in the past two days, and she had not been raped in Bucharest or in Belgrade or in the cellar of the farmhouse. As far as she could tell, she was very much in the minority here in that regard. She didn't know what this meant, only thought it could be because she kept her head down and avoided any eye contact with anyone, even with the other hostages.

Just as she thought this, the leader of the new set of guards stepped closer to the group, and he spoke in English with an accent Maja, not a native speaker of English, could not identify.

"We heard about the killing the other night. That wasn't us. That was the Serbs." He said "Serbs" like it sickened him to do so. "We wish you no harm, but if you try to leave our care, we will be forced to recover you, and then to punish you and everyone else for your misbehavior. Do not try to leave, and you will be treated with respect."

Respect? Did he really say "respect"? Maja wanted to laugh at this, but she kept her eyes averted and her mouth closed.

The man continued. "I suspect you all have been wondering why you are here and where you are going. I can only tell you this. You arrived early, due to the attack in Bosnia the other day. We were not ready to accept you, so we have put you here. Normally your quarters would be better, but we did the best with the time we had. Right now we are waiting on a boat, and it will arrive tomorrow night, and when it does arrive, you will all be taken to it and moved on to your next destination."

No one spoke still, but he answered the question everyone had. "You want to know where you are going, yes? I do not know. My men and I are here to keep you safe, and to put each and every last one of you on the boat. That is *all* we know."

He paused, as if waiting for questions, but no one dared. Finally he said, "I've heard all about this American who tried to rescue you, and then committed another attack on the process in Bosnia."

Maja didn't know anything of another attack.

"Just be aware. My men are nothing like the Serbian hoodlums you've been surrounded by. My men are trained. Skilled. We will remain vigilant, but we are unafraid of this masked man.

"Now," he continued, "we will be here for the rest of today and all day tomorrow. I suggest you rest, eat when the food arrives, and relax. I know the Serbians do not allow talking. That is not us. Talk to each other if you wish, but do so softly, or you will all lose privileges."

The leader turned away and left the room, leaving four more armed men standing around or sitting on broken windowsills.

Maja sat quietly, her long dark hair hanging in her eyes, until a woman scooted over to her and sat close.

"Do you speak Russian?" the woman asked in Russian.

Maja did speak some, but she didn't feel like talking. *"Nyet."*

"English?"

Maja hesitated. She was afraid to speak but was certain this woman had heard her speaking English back in Belgrade. There was no denying it now. "Yes."

"My name is—"

Maja interrupted. "No. You know the rules. Don't say your real name."

"No one can hear us if we speak softly."

Maja looked at the floor. "I don't want to know your real name."

The woman leaned closer to Maja. "Fine. They call me Anke here. Where are you from?"

"Romania," Maja said.

"I am from Kiev. Ukraine."

"Okay."

"I wanted to tell you, because you look older than many of the others." Maja had just turned twenty-three, and this did put her as one of the older women in the group.

"Tell me what?"

"I have learned that one of us is a spy."

Now Maja looked up in surprise. "A *what*?"

"A Serbian guard told me when we were getting off the bus. He likes me, I guess, and before they left he whispered that I should watch what I say to the others because one of the girls was put in here to inform on the rest of us."

Maja looked around in the dim. "That . . . that sounds crazy. Nobody is here because they want to be."

Another woman, Maja knew her to be Moldovan, leaned into the conversation.

"Maybe it's crazy," the Moldovan said, looking at Maja. "Or maybe it's you." Louder she said, "Maybe *you* are the informant."

"I . . . I am not an informant."

Others tucked closer on the floor, listening in as the Moldovan girl continued. "I have been watching you. I have been raped twice. Once in

Belgrade, and once last night in the forest. Most of the other girls have been raped, as well."

All of the girls within earshot nodded.

"Others have been beaten. But you? I haven't seen them lay a finger on you."

Another young woman, also one of the Ukrainians, said, "I saw her touched. In the woods the other night. One of the men selected her, dragged her a few feet. But then he put her back in line when the other man yelled at him." She eyed Maja now. "It was like you were being protected for some reason. Why?"

"I . . . I don't know. I swear I don't understand what is happen—"

The first woman hissed at her. "Liar. You are working with them."

She tried to protest, but the rest of the group moved away from her, leaving her alone on the floor in the middle of the room.

With everything that had happened so far, Maja didn't think she had any more tears left in her, but she began to cry again.

• • •

Talyssa Corbu and I find ourselves sitting a couple blocks away from the main police station in Dubrovnik, Croatia, on a hilly residential side street off Ante Starcevica. It's pouring rain; Talyssa has her coat on and an umbrella in her hand, but she's not worried about the weather at present. Instead she's trying to psych herself up to walk straight into the police station and reveal to some possibly very bad people that she is here to unmask their very bad actions.

I sure as shit wouldn't want to do it, so I can understand her reluctance.

I'm trying to psych her up, too, but I can see that accomplishing her task this afternoon is going to take reserves of strength I have no confidence this young woman possesses.

But she's all we've got right now, so I'm sending her in.

Together we decide she will identify herself as a Europol criminal analyst, and say that she is investigating rumors of a sex trafficking pipeline run by an international consortium, a pipeline that leads from far in the East to right here in Dubrovnik. The local police will be able to check out Talyssa's credentials easily enough, and when they do, they will speak to her superiors, who will quickly tell them she has taken a leave of absence from work—work that involves coordinating with European law enforcement agencies on money laundering and other financial fraud.

At this point Talyssa's story of her hunt for the ringleaders of a human trafficking network will unravel, and it will be obvious to the local cops that she has gone rogue for some reason and has no sanction for her work here. Then—we hope, anyway—the crooked cops and whatever gang is working with the pipeline in Dubrovnik will determine that the woman and her questions are at once dangerous *and* easy to silence, so they will pay her a visit, either to kill her or to scare her into giving up her hunt for answers about the Consortium.

We are lucky that Talyssa and her half sister have different surnames, as they were born to different fathers. We know Talyssa won't be able to talk to the police without producing some sort of identification, and I have no way of obtaining quality forged documents for her in the time we have available to us, so on the off chance Roxana is still alive, she won't be endangered by this fact.

The women and girls I saw in the basement in Mostar, if they are reachable at all, will soon be distributed all over the world, dispersed into the wind where I will never be able to help them. For this reason we hope our thin backstory holds, because we've no time to craft a better one.

Hope isn't a strategy, I know, but we need a break.

We arrived in town last night and I rented two rooms. One was a top-floor pension in the walled Old Town, and the second a larger apartment, also in the Old Town, but in a basement several blocks from the first.

The first room is Talyssa's: high on the hill on the southern side, backing up to the medieval outer wall that separates the Old Town from the ocean. Here she will wait for whoever the Consortium sends after her. I chose the location carefully after walking the neighborhood and the staircases of the building. I've checked her window to make sure it opens, and

I've looked at the roof and the courtyard out front, deciding on several courses of action depending on our enemy's tactics. I've picked a place in the large pedestrian-only Old Town so the opposition can't just roll up in a convoy of vans and snatch her out of her bed and race away without me having time to stop them. No, with the location I've chosen, they will have to come on foot, climbing flight after flight of outdoor cobblestone stairs through narrow alleyways. I will be lying in wait and able to see and hear them coming by any route available to them long before they get to her building, much less through the courtyard, into the entrance, and up the three flights of stairs to her room.

And I won't just be trusting my eyes. In my pack of gear brought along for the hit on Ratko Babic, I brought a half dozen small remote cameras, all of which connect to an app on my phone. I hid two of these in planters in the courtyard and entryway of the building where Talyssa will be waiting, and two more cover angles around the outside that I won't be able to see from my vantage point.

The tiny basement apartment I rented nearby can be converted into a torture chamber on the fly if I happen to get my hands on one of the men sent to silence the pesky Europol woman here on an unsanctioned mission to get intelligence on their operation.

We don't move our belongings into either location. All my possessions I have in my backpack in the backseat, and all of Talyssa's are either in her purse or in her roll-aboard in the trunk. Additionally, during the day I went shopping at a camping store on the eastern edge of the city, purchasing items I anticipate needing. I also bought a burner phone and a prepaid card at a gift shop.

I wish like hell I were on an Agency op, where I'd have access to intel and labor and gadgetry and the like, but I'm performing with limited resources and no support, so I have to make the best of it.

The rain beats down on the roof of the little Vauxhall Corsa four-door. "You've got this," I tell her. "You'll be great." I say these lines with conviction, at least I think I do, and she gives me a little bob of her head in acknowledgment. But neither of us believes this plan of mine has much chance of going smoothly. *I* know it, and she lets me know she knows it when she articulates just exactly what I am fearing.

"But what if they just take me into custody while they check out my story?"

I'm ready with an answer, because I've been pondering this all day. "Tell them you are working with others. If they act like they aren't going to let you out of there, call my burner phone and give me the names of the people you are talking to."

"Right."

"Once they check you out they'll know you're full of shit, but making that call will probably keep them from detaining you until they're certain you're a rogue." I have no idea if this will work, but it sounds good, anyway.

She nods again distractedly, looks out at the rain in the direction of the station. Her facial features are pinched tight with worry, and the bangs of her short red hair hang over her eyebrows. "I better go."

"I'll be parked right here when you're done."

"Sure," she says, and I worry she's not going to be able to go through with it.

"Look. You can do this."

I still can't work out exactly how someone so petrified of the danger can manage to push forward the way she has done. I understand her sister is either dead or in desperate peril, and I understand she doesn't trust local authorities to help . . . but I have never seen *anyone* this physically sickened by terror able to soldier on through the danger.

I want to just respect her for it and move on, but I am certain there is another part to her story that I haven't explored yet.

My thoughts drift away from this, because I see her staring catatonically out the windshield. She's thinking about something, her trembling lip has returned, and she's on the verge of becoming unhinged right before my eyes.

I quickly say, "Listen. If something bad happens in there, if something goes wrong. If they take you in . . . I *will* get you out."

She turns to me with bloodshot eyes that are as imploring as her words. "Please, Harry. Whatever happens to me. You have to find out what happened to Roxana." She sighs now, and adds, "Don't worry about me. Worry about her. You *can't* just come in shooting people in a police station."

That isn't my plan, simply because it won't work. I'm not the Terminator. "I promise that won't happen. Just keep calm, play your role, and if I have to, I'll play mine. Together we'll find out about Roxana once this part is done."

This seems to help to some degree. Talyssa fixes her gaze in resolution and then, without another word, she climbs out of the little car and walks off in the rain.

I watch her go, and I find myself picking holes in the parts of her story that don't add up, and filling in the pieces with my own ideas of what might really be going on here.

SIXTEEN

At five p.m. Talyssa Corbu stepped through the doors of the main police headquarters, showed her credos at the front desk, and asked to speak to the highest-ranking person in the building. A smiling middle-aged and heavyset woman appeared and shook her hand, then ushered her into an office.

Even though the Romanian couldn't read the citations on the wall, she got a pretty good idea that this lady was, in fact, the top cop here in town.

This meant that either someone lower on the totem pole was involved with the trafficking ring, no one in the police department here was involved in the pipeline, or this middle-aged female with an easy smile was, herself, involved in ferrying female sex slaves from the East to the West.

Talyssa didn't see much likelihood in the last option at all.

In English the captain asked, "How can I help you, Miss Corbu?"

"Thank you for seeing me. I'm here in town looking into allegations that women are being trafficked through Dubrovnik for the purposes of sexual slavery."

The woman blinked, but this gave away nothing to Talyssa, because Talyssa had no training to hunt for facial cues or body language that would tip her off as to whether the person she was speaking with was attempting to deceive her.

"This is an investigation being overseen by Europol?"

"Correct."

The captain looked again at Corbu's credentials. "It says you are involved in economic crimes."

"That is true. I'm following the money, and it leads to traffickers, and it has led me, ultimately, to Dubrovnik."

"I haven't heard anything about this investigation. Who are you working with on the ground here? Our federal authorities?"

"I am here in advance of a formal investigation in Croatia. This is preliminary, more of a fact-finding mission."

"You aren't coordinating with anyone? That's unusual, isn't it?"

"Unusual, yes. Unprecedented, no."

"May I see some of your evidence?"

Talyssa had been expecting this. She rubbed her sweaty palms together between her knees, out of the captain's view, and she measured her breathing as well as possible. "The police chief in Mostar was kidnapped yesterday. I'm sure you heard about it."

The chief replied, "Yes. Terrible, terrible thing." And then she said, "His body was found in his home just a few hours ago."

Talyssa Corbu was poleaxed by this news, and she did a poor job of hiding her shock now. "Oh . . . I . . . I just understood he was missing."

The police chief regarded the Europol analyst curiously. "Europol is not terribly well informed, then."

"I . . . I've been working, haven't checked in with the office in several hours."

"Well, let me bring you up to date. Apparently, Captain Vukovic was recovered alive yesterday, but then was killed sometime overnight along with two other police officers staying in his flat with him."

"I see," Corbu said.

"I'm sorry, what does this have to do with us down here in Dubrovnik?"

Talyssa struggled to keep her voice as dispassionate as possible. "We . . . we have reason to believe Captain Vukovic was involved in the trafficking concern. There was a home where girls were kept, it was in his jurisdiction, and our investigations indicate Dubrovnik was the next stop along the pipeline."

"The *pipeline*?"

"This is the name we are hearing. It begins as far east as Moldova or even Ukraine. Who knows? Russia, perhaps. And it leads as far west as Dubrovnik. After that . . . we don't know. We'd appreciate any help you could provide about the movement of exploited women through this area."

The captain wasn't smiling any longer. "You think the chief of police of Mostar, our neighbor, was tainted by this crime? Is it really help you want from me, or did you come to question me as a suspect?"

"I am making no allegations at all. I am an analyst, not an investigator. I am merely asking for help from your office, Captain."

The older woman leaned back in her chair and waved a hand. "Well . . . I for one know nothing of the matter. Of course, we've broken up rings of traffickers in the past. Albanians, mostly. Some Turks. Horrible people, horrible crimes. But nothing recently, and nothing that came through Bosnia. I've never even met Captain Vukovic personally, but he was well regarded, as I understand."

Talyssa felt her trembling mouth, pinched it shut quickly, then asked, "Have you heard of something referred to as the Consortium?"

Again, the police chief blinked, but Talyssa didn't register the gesture as significant.

"In what context? I mean, there are all sorts of consortiums, aren't there? It simply means a group of people or organizations affiliated to perform some sort of transaction or business."

With this last sentence Talyssa Corbu began to notice a definite defensiveness in the police captain. She raised an eyebrow. "I'm sorry. I thought I was being clear. I am speaking in the context of the trafficking of human beings."

The woman just stared at Corbu now, then looked back down at her credentials. "Again, as you said, you are a criminal analyst. And clearly quite junior. Help me, please, because I don't understand your interest or your mandate."

This was just the suspicion Talyssa and the American hoped to elicit from the captain. Still, she swallowed hard, fear welling within her.

"You can check it out with The Hague. I'm on a fact-finding trip. Very preliminary."

"Yes. I *will* be checking this out." She looked up at Corbu. "Are you alone here in our city?"

The Romanian's heart began to pound even harder, and she squeezed the armrests of the chair. Harry had warned her not to oversell her power, because in order to serve as bait, she had to appear vulnerable.

She answered, "I'm in contact with colleagues back at the office, but I came alone."

"Where are you from?" the captain asked.

"I live in the Netherlands."

The policewoman leaned her forearms on her desk, her eyes narrowing. "Not what I meant. Where were you born?"

There was a faint air of menace in the woman's voice now.

"I . . . I am Romanian. But I am here in my capacity as a Europol—"

"These trafficked girls. Any of them coming from Romania?"

Corbu fought the urge to leap to her feet and run out of the room. The captain was sensing something, picking her story apart before even checking with anyone back in The Hague. This was a dangerous dance, because the Romanian woman couldn't appear like she really did have the pipeline figured out; that would mean Europol would have this information, too. No, she needed to give the police here the impression she was doing this on her own, but she also needed to cast enough uncertainty on this that they would let her leave the building to give them time to sort her story out.

Corbu said, "I would imagine that women have been trafficked from Romania. They have a lot of missing-person cases. Young, impressionable girls. Girls who, quite simply, have vanished from our streets."

"So . . . this is personal to you in some way, isn't it?"

There was no empathy in the captain's words, no concern about trafficked women or the investigator claiming to be looking for them. No, she was darkening by the minute, reaching a tone and demeanor that conveyed outright malevolence.

Talyssa Corbu looked into the woman's eyes and felt certain now this Croatian knew all about the pipeline, and she saw Corbu as a potential threat.

The Romanian kept control of her voice. "It's my job, Captain. Just as keeping people safe here in Dubrovnik is yours." She took a pen and a notepad from her purse and jotted down the address of her room, well aware of a tremor in her hand. "Here is where I'm staying. I'll be here for several days, I imagine."

The captain looked at the paper, then back up at her foreign guest. "This location. A small third-floor pension in the Old Town? Are things so tight at Europol that they send you to a backpacker's residence?"

Harry had told her that her accommodations would cause suspicion with the police. This was by design, although it was yet another gamble that might cause her to be held in the station while her dubious story was checked out. She fought tears of dread, controlled her voice as best she could, forced a smile, and said, "It's fine. Fewer questions on the monthly expense report if I keep costs down."

"I won't hear of it. Let me put you in one of our better hotels. A single call and I can have you in a room at the Marriott. Close by."

Corbu felt herself losing it. The captain was already trying to take control of her, to put her somewhere she or men involved in the pipeline could easily access her.

"No . . . thank you very much, but my accommodations are of no concern to me. I'll just stay where I am."

She stood now, as did the captain.

The middle-aged Croatian said, "One more question. I have to ask. Were you, in any way, involved with what happened to Chief Vukovic?"

Talyssa was quick to answer—perhaps, she recognized after the fact, too quick. "No. Of course not. I was on my way to speak with him when he disappeared." She held out her hand for her credentials. Once they were returned, she thanked the captain and left the police station, all the while terrified someone behind her would call her name and ask her to step into some side room, where her liberty would be stripped from her.

• • •

I sit against the wall of a bank, the car in view up a street to my right, the front door of the police station ahead on my left. I know I told Talyssa I'd be waiting for her in the car, but I haven't survived this long by sending an agent into the enemy's hands possessing knowledge of my exact location. No, I got out just after she disappeared from my view, and now I'm waiting for her, careful to do my best to keep myself low profile and out of sight of any cameras.

At this point I'm so worried about the girl that I'm fantasizing my way through an intricate one-man attack on the police station to rescue her, Terminator style. But even in my imagination, it doesn't go as well for me as it did for Arnold Schwarzenegger.

Probably because I'm no cyborg.

No, if they *do* keep Corbu for questioning, then there is nothing I can do but hope like hell they release her in one piece, and not in many pieces tossed into the Adriatic Sea.

I lean back against the wall of the bank, my eyes shifting regularly to the front door of the police station in the distance. The rain has stopped, but the low clouds and mist are hastening the onset of darkness. I check my watch and see that Corbu has been inside less than thirty minutes, although it seems quadruple that.

Then the door of the police station opens for the dozenth time since Talyssa entered, but this time is different, because I see what I've been praying for. The young redhead in the black raincoat is alone, moving at an assured pace back in the direction of the car. She seems okay, so I begin looking behind her, curious if anyone follows her from the station.

No one exits the building while I watch, which is very good news.

A few minutes later I meet her back at the Vauxhall, and she is agitated.

"Where the hell were you?"

"Making sure you weren't followed." I climb behind the wheel. "Get in."

She heaves her chest, annoyed by me, but she does as I ask.

I fire up the little car and I drive off without saying another word.

SEVENTEEN

It's only when I'm deep into the late-afternoon traffic and I've scanned all my mirrors and convinced myself there is no tail that I begin talking to her.

"Well, they let you out, so that's a win. You okay?"

I can feel the tension in her and I worry she's about to cry, but she takes a few breaths and answers me. "I'm okay. I was very scared."

"You were very brave."

"Just desperate."

The comment means something, but I'm not going to pursue it now. I ask, "Do you think they found you suspicious enough to check out your story?"

She looks down at her hands. I can see them shaking. "Suspicious enough? The police chief didn't believe a word out of my mouth."

"Good."

"She's a woman. And I'm sure she's involved."

"What makes you so sure?"

"Just . . . just the way she acted. We are fellow law enforcement professionals. There should have been a courtesy extended. I mean . . . there was, at first. But then I mentioned the pipeline and the Consortium, and she turned to ice before my eyes. She showed no respect for the trafficked women. She dehumanized them, as is often the case with those who exploit them."

I find myself wishing I had been in the room to evaluate the chief for signs of deception. Still . . . Talyssa seems to know what she's talking about, so I take her word for it. It's not enough proof to snatch this police chief and pump her for info like we did Vukovic, but it's good information nonetheless.

I ask, "Does it surprise you that women can be just as terrible as men?"

"No . . . I guess not. But in this type of crime? It's just extra horrible that it is someone of the same sex doing the exploitation. Isn't it?"

"It's pretty bad."

"What now?" she asks after a moment more collecting her thoughts.

"You gave them the address of your flat?"

"I did."

"Then what comes next depends on your level of commitment."

I'm watching the road while I drive in the direction of the Old Town, but when Talyssa doesn't answer, I look to her. She is staring me down with anger, and I realize I just said the wrong thing. Quickly I add, "I didn't mean to question your commitment to your sister. I just mean that the more risk you take tonight, the larger the chance that the opposition will take the bait."

"What sort of risk?"

"Well, we can do this a couple of different ways. I can take you someplace where they won't find you, and then I can haul ass back to overwatch your room. If they come for you tonight, I'll be able to photograph them and, hopefully, identify them. Maybe even follow them back to somewhere associated with the crimes, or grab one of them tomorrow."

"That sounds like a good plan. No?"

"It's the safest for you, but there's a way we can increase the odds they'll make their move."

"How do we do that?"

"We walk you through the city, with me trailing you. We make it obvious you're here alone, and I look for someone tailing you. Then, tonight, we put you in your flat, just where you told them you'll be."

"And then they come to kidnap me?"

"Exactly. If the police have watchers or informants around your hotel, we'll make it look so easy for them, they'll have no reservations about snatching you."

She bites her lower lip and closes her eyes as if she's just willing this to all go away. "Are you making it *too* easy for them?"

"If you do as I say, I won't let them get you."

She replies, "If someone comes, how will you know it's someone from the Consortium?"

"Let's just say I have pretty good asshole radar." This doesn't translate well to Romanian, apparently, because I get no response. I add, "Trust me. I'll know."

"You ask for a lot of trust as a man who has told me little about himself."

"That's fair. What do you want to know?"

"What is your background?"

"Meaning?"

"Are you a member or former member of the U.S. military, American law enforcement, or an American intelligence agency?"

"I can't answer that. Sorry."

"Okay, you won't tell me about your distant past. Tell me about your recent past. You assassinated General Babic, saw the women being held there, and then left them behind, running away to save yourself. Am I correct so far?"

"Not very charitable, but also not wrong."

"And you kill for money, yes?"

She's drawing conclusions here, but she happens to be right. I think about giving her a non-answer, but I need us to keep up this relationship if I'm going to recover the women. I say, "Sometimes, yes. Sometimes, no."

"You are a hit man, then."

This lady's not going to be president of my fan club any time soon, I can see that plainly. "I operate. I'll leave it there. Not all jobs are like the Babic op."

I turn into a parking garage right outside the pedestrian-only Old Town along the coast. As I look for a place to park, Talyssa says, "These women. What is it about them that is making you do this? I mean . . . why are you even here?"

It's a variation of a question I ask myself over and over. "They were in a bad situation, and I might have put them in a worse situation. I feel responsible. If I can help . . . I want to do that." I add, "And I also want to help you find answers about what happened to Roxana."

"But *why*?"

"Because sometimes I have to do what's right."

"But you are a killer."

"I said 'sometimes.'" I park the car while she thinks. When she doesn't speak, I say, "I only kill bad people."

She chuckles mirthlessly, showing me she thinks I'm joking. I don't reply, but she adds, "Is it maybe that you aren't so interested in saving people, but are more interested in the action? The danger? The killing? I mean, why else would someone do what you do for a living?"

Damn, she's hitting close to home, and I don't like it. I say, "I didn't choose this life. Let's leave it there."

"But you are here now, when you could go anywhere else and do anything else. Do you like to kill? You don't seem like a psychopath."

This is her first compliment. "Thanks," I reply. "This is what I do now. I'm good at it, even though it's a shitty thing. I figure I might as well use it for good."

"You kill people for 'good'?"

We're sitting in the still car, looking at each other. "You know what Ratko Babic did, don't you?"

"Of course. I was a baby then, I guess, but I've heard the stories. Still . . . that was a long time ago. What is the point in killing an old man now?"

"I like the thought of terrible people hiding out, running scared, because even though they were bad a long time ago, they know that there is someone dangerous out there who hasn't forgotten about what they did. If there is one chance in a million that the bogeyman is going to come for them to make them pay for their past sins in the present, it will terrorize them. Even if I can't get to everybody out there who deserves a visit from me, I can give a lot of assholes sleepless nights, and that's better than nothing."

"You are a strange man."

Also fair.

I reach into my backpack and pull an earpiece out of a charging cradle and hand it to her. I pull a second, identical unit out of the cradle and put it in my ear, then cover it with my brown hair, which is plenty long enough to hide it. I say, "Put it in and let your hair cover it. It can transmit and receive, and the charge will last at least sixteen hours. The silicone cap will keep it in place. You could fall off a bridge and it won't come out. I've got another set to switch to if necessary."

"So I just talk and—"

"And I'll hear you, so don't say anything bad about me." I'm joking, but she's not in the mood. I can see her stiffening up some, knowing she's about to become live bait in waters where predators are lurking.

She puts in the earpiece and adjusts her short red hair, slings her purse over her shoulder.

"Wherever you go," I say, "I'll be watching."

"Just don't kill anyone." She turns and starts walking out of the garage.

"No promises," I mutter to myself, and I wonder if she'll be singing a different tune before this evening is over.

Quickly I reach into my backpack, pull out a black T-shirt and a gray long-sleeved shirt, and reach for a ball cap, but decide against it. Nobody around here is wearing a ball cap, other than the occasional American tourist, so it won't do a thing to help me blend in. Instead I grab a pair of eyeglasses with uncorrected lenses, and I put my pack over a shoulder. Before Talyssa disappears onto the street I am moving into position behind her.

She eats a leisurely dinner in an outdoor café, and then strolls the length of Stradun, the main street of the Old Town, where I almost lose her in the heavy crowd of tourists. But I have the benefit of being in comms with her, so I ask her to slow, and soon I'm back in position.

My eyes scan the scene robotically. I'm not looking for people watching her; that would be impossible in such a crowd. Instead my brain is taking in data quickly, only the information relevant to my work, and weeding out anything extraneous. As I shift my eyes to the left and right, I search for likely places for surveillance personnel to position themselves, and then I look at the clothes and hair and age and sex of the people in those places. I can narrow down ninety percent of the public in just a few seconds, and then my eyes lock onto anyone filling out a general threat profile.

The watchers, if there are any, could be either male or female, but they will probably be male, between twenty-five and fifty-five, wearing some sort of clothing a local would wear, and an overgarment or outer garment that covers their waist so they can hide communications gear and/or a weapon.

I pay special attention to those with facial hair, but also those with military-length haircuts, not because I think the Croatian military would be involved in this, but rather because those involved might be regular police, and they often have specific grooming standards that must be maintained.

Even if they are working for some mob element.

If someone fits all the criteria, then I'll look at their attire, their shoes, their fitness level, and, if they're wearing them, their sunglasses and their watch.

Trust me, it doesn't matter where they are from, from Brazil to Hong Kong, there is a look to those in the game.

Not me; I'm careful. I'm not wearing anything tacti-cool and I'm not built up like a linebacker. And, unlike others who do this sort of thing, I keep my eyes moving, but my head doesn't swivel left and right like I'm guarding the damn president.

But I'm on the lookout for those who do.

It's exhausting work. My eyes and my brain tire, but I've been doing it for so many years I know I can keep it up as long as I have to.

As Talyssa turns off Stradun to head south, I don't see a tail, but I do see two men who might be interested in her. They aren't walking behind, but are instead leaning against the wall of the old bell tower between a pair of arched passages that lead directly to the Old Port, a marina just outside the walls of the Old Town. Both are in their thirties; they are thick, tough-looking guys with close-cropped hair, jeans, and tracksuit tops. They're just smoking and talking, but my eyes lock onto them because of their appearance, and once Talyssa passes their position, I see them turn their heads her way and focus on her exclusively.

Got 'em, I think, but I quickly check my enthusiasm. These guys look like cops, and I'm on the lookout for dirty cops, but these could just as easily be clean cops unaligned with and unaware of the pipeline, ordered by their superiors to find Corbu in the Old Town to make certain she is, indeed, alone.

I want to tail or capture dirty cops, and I don't know if these two are bad guys or just two dudes on the job for what they assume to be legit reasons.

The men do not follow the girl, but I see one of them speak into a mobile phone, and I imagine he's notified someone else ahead of Talyssa so that person can pick up the surveillance.

I normally wouldn't walk right past two guys who are either opposition assholes or else doing the bidding of opposition assholes, but I don't have time to take this slow, because for all I know they've radioed ahead to a snatch team, and their aim is to roll up my agent before she even arrives at her room.

That would be ballsy on their part; it's only nine p.m., the sky has cleared, and there's still some light out, and the narrow passages of the Old

Town are full of shoppers and diners and tourists. But they *could* try it, and I can't let them succeed if they do.

I slip past the two men; they are still watching Talyssa as she disappears in a crowd up a passage leading to a long and high stairwell to the south in the direction of her hotel.

The men take no notice of me at all.

A minute later I'm heading up the stairs behind the Europol analyst, and I see a second pair of men, so identical to the first it's almost laughable. These two are also static, and as she passes their position, I see one of them reach for his phone, then begin speaking into it.

I'd lay money on the fact that there is at least one more set of goons up closer to her flat, and this guy in front of me is in comms with them now.

Again, I can't be certain their job isn't to pick up the Romanian criminal analyst, but I can't imagine why, if they were ready to detain her now, they would let her walk past four cops not far from the exits of the pedestrian and walled-in Old Town, only to be detained by more guys hundreds of stair steps higher and farther away from the exits.

It would serve no purpose, I tell myself, and then I rethink things and pick up my pace even more, because the third group could potentially be hitters. Assassins. And if this *is* the case, they'd have every reason to kill Talyssa Corbu far from the heavy pedestrian traffic of Stradun.

I continue up the stairs, and I check in with the girl.

"You doing okay?"

Softly she answers; I can hear the labor of her climbing the stairs in her voice. "You should know how I'm doing. You said you would be watching me."

"I *am* watching you. No, don't turn around, just trust me."

"Trust again," she mumbles. Then, "I don't see anyone following me or paying me any attention. I've been stealing glances in windows and such."

I roll my eyes as I move in her direction. "Leave that part to me, please. Just walk."

"Trust you, you mean." There is a mocking tone in her voice.

I consider telling her about the surveillance I saw, but I don't want to scare her. Instead I just say, "Don't go straight to your flat. Make your next right, follow that alley for a couple of minutes, give me time to get ahead of you and look at the area up there."

"You think they are waiting for me there?" she asks, a little nervously.

The answer is an almost definite yes, but I say, "Let me find out first."

EIGHTEEN

I head straight for the address Talyssa gave the police captain, and when I get there a couple minutes later, I see a tiny children's playground, no larger than half a basketball court, across the narrow cobblestone passage from Talyssa's building.

Three grown men are in the playground. One of the three is on his phone, standing by the gate in the park, twenty feet away from the other two. He's lean and wiry, but with the same almost military-style short hair worn by the two other pairs of men I saw a few minutes back. And it's apparent to me now that the opposition is pretty sure Talyssa is acting alone, outside the bounds of her duties for Europol, because the other two tough-looking goofballs maintaining this watch are sitting on opposite ends of a children's seesaw in the middle of the little playground. One of them has his back to the building where Talyssa's flat is located, but the other is facing it directly, and they're idly chatting in Serbo-Croat as if they don't have a care in the world.

For a second I wonder if these three might not be involved in all this, so relaxed is their posture here, but then as I walk past I see the dude on the phone look up, check me out, then turn to flash his eyes quickly on the stone steps up to the building across the passageway.

It's obvious to me that he's here on a job, and the job involves looking for people and monitoring a location.

He's oppo, they *all* are . . . no question about it.

I sit down on a bench on the cobblestones one hundred feet away from them, and I check the cameras I have stationed all around.

Seeing no one else who appears threatening, I speak softly so that only Talyssa can hear me. "You cool?"

"I'm fine, Harry. What is the situation up there?"

"Well, it's pretty obvious you did a good job selling your story back at the police station. There are some men here waiting around for you, but I don't think they've come to pick you up. They're just here to see if you are going where you said you were going."

Nervously she asks, "What . . . what do you want me to do?"

"Come up to your building, don't pay any attention to the three guys in the playground, and go up to your room."

"But . . . but what if you're wrong? What if they just shoot me?"

"Nobody's shooting anybody." I amend this. "Unless it's me shooting them."

She whispers more softly now, as if to herself, but I can hear her. "Oh my God."

"Trust me," I say, probably for the tenth time. "It will be fine."

I spend the next couple of minutes pretending to look at my phone, until finally Corbu walks past me. She sneaks a glance my way but I glance down, willing her to just play cool. She strolls along next to the low stone wall of the playground, ignoring the men there, all three of whom I'm now watching carefully. Their eyes are on her, but they do a pretty good job of looking disinterested. Cops, for sure. I am guessing they're all probably detectives.

Like the men in the more touristy part of the Old Town, I don't know if these guys really are part of the pipeline, or if they've just been sent here as lookouts by the brass on the take from the traffickers. I'd hate to have to shoot them without more knowledge of their intentions, but my right hand is inches from the Glock on my hip and I am certain I can have it out and on target faster than any of these big goobers can get their hands on the grips of their weapons.

Talyssa disappears up the steps into the stone courtyard of her building, heading towards a staircase at the back that will take her up to her room. I look back down at my phone and soon hear the three men talking softly. Stealing a quick glance, I see the guy who'd been on his phone walking away, leaving the two men on the seesaw.

In my earpiece I hear Talyssa. "Did everything go okay?"

"Yes. I count a total of seven men tailing you."

"*Seven?*" There is a fresh shock in her voice.

"Yeah, but they are just watchers. These aren't the troublemakers."

"The troublemakers . . . they are coming later?"

"They're probably coming later, yeah." I hope this to be the case, but I don't say that to the scared woman in her room. Instead I say, "Just stay where you are, keep your bag nearby. I'm going to get on the roof of your building so I'll be able to cover all the stairwells they can climb when they come for you."

"When they come . . . how will you get me out of here?"

I have a plan for this, but I don't want to tell her about it yet, because I don't want her to freak out. I say, "Don't worry. That part is easy." And this is true, as long as she doesn't freak out.

Pushing concern for this out of my mind, I rise from the bench and head off in the opposite direction of the park, with plans to double back behind Talyssa's building and climb through a window so I can make my way inside the courtyard.

· · ·

Jaco Verdoorn dozed in the cabin of the Gulfstream jet, sitting in the middle of a team of nine men, most of whom were also asleep. It was only ten p.m., but this brief rest between jobs was likely all this team was going to get for a while, so the men were taking advantage of it.

In Verdoorn's lap was an open dossier on his target in the Balkans. Courtland Gentry, former CIA officer, now on the run from the Agency.

His information came from the SSA, the State Security Agency of South Africa, his former employer. SSA had the file because the Americans had shared it years ago, when they first deemed their former employee a threat and issued a "shoot on sight" sanction against him.

Verdoorn had spent nine years in the intelligence realm and had been involved in his nation's hunt for the infamous Gray Man, to no effect, but to great and lasting frustration to the forty-one-year-old. He knew the dossier in his lap from back to front, had all but memorized it.

But now he was back in the game, hunting the Gray Man again, and he couldn't have been happier about it.

Verdoorn had left his nation's intelligence services four years ago to found White Lion, a private security concern registered on the island of Crete. White Lion had paperwork to show a robust list of clients, but in truth they only worked for one organization now, the Consortium, and one man, Kenneth Cage.

All the shell companies that acted as White Lion's official clients served some sort of purpose in the Consortium, and White Lion billed them for work such as convoy operations in Nigeria, personal protection in Ukraine, and professional risk-management consulting in Germany.

Verdoorn had a staff of dozens, all hard men well aware of the organization they serviced and the industry in which it did business, but tonight he flew south towards Croatia with only his nine best assets. These were all former South African military officers, all highly trained with weapons and tactics, but beyond this, each and every one of them had learned the art of invisibility.

It was Verdoorn's own fascination with and study of the Gray Man, years ago when he was put on the hunt, that made him mandate to his assets that they dress, behave, and operate in the field not as members of an intelligence service or a military unit but as regular members of the public. To this end they made dozens of adjustments to normal operating procedure regarding dress, communications, equipment, tactics, and the like.

They didn't work in teams of two or three, an instantaneous tip-off to some watchers. No, Verdoorn's assets each operated alone when on surveillance missions, while remaining in covert communications with one another.

These nine men, plus Verdoorn, were elite specialists in the tradecraft of remaining clandestine, and Jaco Verdoorn had employed this team on dozens of operations for the Consortium around the world.

The Gulfstream hit some turbulence, and this woke Verdoorn up. He looked out the portal at the night sky—he imagined they were somewhere over Austria about now—and he thought about going to the galley for a bottle of water.

Just as he was about to release his seat belt, the phone next to Jaco Verdoorn flashed. He scooped it up. "Yeah?"

It was the cockpit. The first officer was a White Lion pilot who, previous to joining the security firm, flew Saab Gripen fighters for the South African air force. "Call for you, sir."

"Send it through, Jimmy."

And for the next ten minutes, the president of White Lion corporate security and the director of operations of the Consortium spoke with Kostas Kostopoulos, the regional director of the Consortium in the Balkan states.

. . .

The Gulfstream only had seating for nine in the cabin, but there was a belted seat in the aft lavatory, and here Rodger Loots slept, only somewhat annoyed to be assigned to the lav seat because he'd worked in conditions a hell of a lot more austere than a sleek corporate jet, even considering the fact he was sitting in the shitter.

Loots stirred with the buffeting turbulence, then looked at his watch. It was twenty-two fifteen, and he figured they must be somewhere over Austria by now.

Just then the PA in the lav chirped, and he heard his boss's commanding voice. "Rodge . . . front and center, yeah?"

Seconds later Loots squatted down next to Verdoorn in the center of the cabin. "What's up, boss?"

"We have a new target."

"Damn. Was hoping we'd get a shot at the Gray Man."

"We still might, actually. A woman who works for Europol is down in Dubrovnik asking questions about the Consortium."

"By name?"

"By name."

"Shit."

"She went straight to the local cops, who we have in our pocket, and said she was part of an investigation into trafficking involving the pipeline and the Consortium."

"Shit," Loots repeated.

"Shit is right, but the police chief, who is with us, checked her story out with The Hague." Verdoorn looked down at his notepad, now sitting on top of the Gentry dossier. Reading the notes he'd jotted down while talking to Kostas, he said, "Talyssa Corbu is an economic crimes analyst from Romania, she's got nothing to do with trafficking, and, according to her employers, she is currently on a personal hiatus at work due to some sort of a family emergency back home in Bucharest."

"What the hell is she doing in Dubrovnik, then?"

"The Hague thinks she's trying to crack some case open to get advancement. Something about money laundering. Sounds like she's bloody bonkers."

"So . . . she's workin' off book?"

"Totally. Swingin' in the bloody wind. I looked at the names of the merchandise in the pipeline now and don't see any relation to her. This seems like it is, in fact, her bid for a pat on the back and a shot at advancement."

"So since she's on her own, we need to remove her."

"Bladdy right. The fact that she knows about the Consortium means she's a dead woman. She's staying in Dubrovnik. The cops have followed her and confirmed she's alone, but the timing with the Gray Man activity over the border in Bosnia is too convenient for my taste. She's workin' with ole Gentry, I'm sure of it. She's the face and he's the brawn in whatever little scheme the two have cooked up."

"What's our role, boss?"

"The police chief in Dubrovnik wants this woman picked up tonight and disposed of. The Greek is sending a team of Albanians to take her from her pension and put a knife in her, then splash her in the Adriatic. But Kostopoulos has agreed to order them to hold her at a safe house till I get there. I want to question her before they put her on ice."

"We should grab her off the street ourselves. You know how it is with the Albanians. They've got the will . . . good hard heads for this sort of thing, decent shooters. But they're not the sharpest tacks, are they?"

Verdoorn shrugged. "No, they're not. But taking the woman off the playing field at the first opportunity is the right call. Whatever intel she has, it's a danger having it out there in public. I'll go to the safe house and interrogate her myself, see what she knows about Gentry and who else she's talked to. I'll squeeze her hard, pass her back to the Albanians for disposal, and then we'll go after our man."

"Sounds good."

"Only problem is this. There is a shipment in Dubrovnik right now, sped up due to the Gray Man hit in Mostar. They're waiting on transport, which isn't coming till early tomorrow morning." He added, "It's a VIP shipment, and one of the items is tagged for special handling."

"Unlucky," Loots said. He knew a VIP shipment meant the women being shipped had been picked out at other way stations and evaluated as being of especially high quality. This stock was sold in a special quarterly market, where criminal organizations around Europe and the Middle East could bid on merchandise that had the potential to earn them millions of euros throughout their admittedly short life cycle. These items could generate a dozen times what the average woman being sold into sexual slavery by the Consortium could produce.

The special-handling item Verdoorn referred to meant a woman who was to be protected at all costs because of the destination she was heading to and the men who had ordered her taken. One of these special-handling captives was worth a dozen or more of the other VIP whores, and after a brutal indoctrination period of travel through the pipeline, these women were then treated with kid gloves. Their mental and physical health was improved through a time-honed process to make them ready for their du-ties ahead.

Loots knew he was being told the shipment that was now passing through the area where the American assassin was causing trouble for the Consortium was a shipment that must be protected at all costs, only rais-ing the stakes of this operation.

He whistled softly. "The VIPs we can't do much about other than to help the Albanians watch over them till they make it onto the boat. But why don't we at least take the special-handling item out of theater? Get it out of danger and on to its destination?"

"I've run into this before," Jaco said. "Protocol mandates that merchan-dise, special handling or not, goes through the pipeline to the end. It's part of the psychological reeducation."

"Makes things difficult."

"It's a process that's been refined for years, and it's working well. You, me, the rest of the shock troops: we'll all have to shoulder the burden of finding this killer and protecting the merchandise all the way to market."

Loots said, "So you are saying we've a full plate. We'll need to do this discreetly, too."

"That's it, mate. We land at two hundred hours. Let's wake the boys and tell them what they're in for."

. . .

Moments later Verdoorn stood at the bulkhead and addressed the team, who were all now quite awake and interested. "We have to keep the pipe-line secure for the current shipment and for future shipments. A situation has arisen in Dubrovnik, and we're goin' in to sort it out."

"Who's the target?" a bearded man named Van Straaten asked.

"We have a woman to interrogate, but she isn't our ultimate target. The *real* target is an American. Courtland Gentry. Ex–CIA Ground Branch. A tier-one para, all the way."

"Military?"

"No military or law enforcement service. I have no clue how he found his way into Ground Branch; it's not in the file I've got, but we do believe he's here working alone, or perhaps with limited support from some rogue law enforcement."

"The task, sir?"

Verdoorn's answer was succinct. "E.E."

Men nodded impassively, but they were all pleased. They knew that "extrajudicial execution" was a euphemism for assassination, and they knew their target would be in possession of great skill. When White Lion killed, their targets were usually hoodlums involved in the pipeline who'd gone astray. A "weapons-free" order against a former CIA Ground Branch paramilitary was a thrill to each and every one of Jaco's troops.

Someone asked, "Where do we start?"

"We talk to the woman he's working with, and then we'll go hunting. Trust me, you'll have to be switched on tonight. He'll be ready to look for men like you."

He surveyed his team now. "Jonker. Lose those pants. Too new. Klerk, your watch . . . what tourist wears a Luminox? Van Straaten . . . the necklace. Put it in your kit bag and buy something local from a street vendor."

"Sir."

"Liebenberg . . . every bladdy item you're wearing has to go."

"Right, sir."

He went through the rest of the team, looking them over one by one with a discriminating eye, trying to pick out the most subtle clues that they were involved with this sort of work. He found things wrong with the attire or gear of Bakkes, Duiker, and Boyle, but Loots, his second-in-command, was perfectly clean of incriminating telltales.

"Let's break out the maps and get to work. Three hours till landing."

NINETEEN

The Old Town is a ghost town in the middle of the night when the tourists leave, and it's so quiet I find myself on the verge of dozing as I sit here on the slanted slate roof of the apartment building, tucked behind a small satellite dish that breaks up my silhouette to anyone looking from a distance.

But I fight sleep, check my camera feeds every couple of minutes, and try to push worry from my mind.

I have a rope already attached to an iron bar affixing the water tank to the roof. I'm wearing leather gloves, and my backpack is secured on my back. I'm in the black T-shirt and jeans, the brown Merrell hiking shoes, and I have a black balaclava over my hair like a watch cap, ready to pull down over my face if necessary.

The Glock 19 is hidden inside my waistband on the right with an extra magazine and a quick-utilization tourniquet; my Spyderco matte black Paramilitary 2 folding knife is in my back-left pocket next to my SureFire Tactician tactical flashlight. I have medical gear, more clothing, rope, cash, and ammo in my pack.

This is me rolling light, but I'm in the middle of the city, and that mandates the absence of body armor, a long gun, and other gear that would make me less comfortable, but more comforted, considering I might have to put myself up against a half dozen assholes tonight.

I also have Talyssa's pistol in a side pocket of the backpack, but I'd fire every round on my person out of my Glock before I went for her little gun.

Around one a.m. I hear the sound of movement over my earpiece. Talyssa is stirring in her bed. I'm surprised that she's been able to sleep, and wonder if she might have been doing so only because she was finally granting me the nearly blind trust I've been asking from her for the past two days.

Her soft voice comes through a second later. "Harry?"

I'm on the roof directly above her window, but she doesn't know my exact location. "I'm here. Everything is fine."

"Everything is not fine," she replies.

"What do you—"

"I have something I need to tell you."

Yes, she does. I know she is lying about parts of her story. I've worked out a theory about some of it, and I do want to hear it all from her at some point.

But not now. Now I need her focused on the operation, not on what led her to everything that has happened.

"Listen, Talyssa, whatever it is, it will keep until we—"

"No. I need to tell you, I need to tell *someone*, because I don't know if I will still be alive when the sun comes up."

There goes my theory that she was giving me blind trust. She doesn't even know if I can keep her alive for the next few hours.

"Two things," I say. "You aren't going to die, and I already know what you are going to tell me."

"No, you don't."

With a tired sigh I say, "Okay. Stop me when I'm wrong."

"What?"

I should ease into this, but sometimes I don't filter myself well. "You say you got involved in all this when your sister was kidnapped. But that's not what happened, is it? Your sister got involved in all this when you used her to help you investigate the Consortium."

I can hear her on the verge of crying when she answers. "Yes. Yes. This is all my fault."

I sigh again. She's going to tell me about it. She *needs* to tell me about it, so all I can do is stay vigilant while we talk.

Talyssa says, "I spent two years digging into the ways transnational crime launders money through European banks. I worked with police organizations around the EU and, with the help of some friends in Liechtenstein, in Switzerland, and in Portugal, I began to put together a picture of something massive. Different shadowy companies I was finding in my research, companies that didn't seem to have any connection between one another, all seemed to be following the same set of practices. Their offshore corporations were set up the same, their capital purchases, their investments—the ones I could see, anyway—were nearly identical."

I scan my cameras, then the alleys below. "Sorry, Talyssa . . . you're losing me."

She sniffs hard. "We dug into a corporation registered in the Cayman Islands that made large deposits into an account in Germany. I find out the corporation has investments around the world, small percentages of above-board companies. Restaurants, shipping, computer applications, whatever. But then I find another corporation making deposits into another account at the same bank, this one registered in Singapore, and it has virtually the same holdings. A third and a fourth concern, these with transactions into and out of other accounts, do exactly the same. Over time I started looking for little tip-offs, and I was able to identify over one hundred forty concerns, all around the world, acting in concert."

She's forgotten that I knock heads for a living. "So . . . what are you saying?"

"It's simple, Harry. If one organization purchases a million dollars' worth of common stock in Siemens, the other one hundred thirty-nine do the same. There are some variances, but there is a definite pattern."

"Okay, I'm tracking, but I don't know the relevance of it."

"It means there is a process in place, and there is someone overseeing the financial end of a massive amount of shell corporations."

"Right . . . like a consortium."

"Exactly like a consortium. A collection of concerns, each individually worth something below the threshold of an amount that would generate much interest from banking investigators. But together they value billions of dollars."

I'm with her now. "And whatever they were doing, you think it was illicit."

"Clearly. I presented my theory to my employers but was told I was venturing out of bounds of my mandate. They told me to get back to doing what I was being paid to do. Instead I began researching this consortium alone. Six weeks ago I tracked an airplane owned by a company tied to the group to Bucharest, my hometown. I thought that, just maybe, this would be the break I was looking for. I didn't tell a soul in my office, I only contacted local immigration officials there. I found that the men on board the plane were in town for a week of meetings with a hotel and restaurant chain."

"Who were they?"

"I didn't know any names. Corporations and individuals can shield that easily. The flight itself originated in Budapest, but that doesn't mean anything. The businessmen could have been having meetings there. It landed in London and Barcelona, as well. Whoever was on board, all I knew was that they managed money illegitimately. I took them for white-collar criminals. Boring illicit finance and tax evasion, maybe some associations to accountants who worked more directly with organized crime. I didn't think these people were dangerous. I mean . . . I just assumed they were wealthy bankers laundering money."

I look down over the narrow passageways to the north below me as I say, "Rich people can be assholes, too."

"I know." She hesitates a moment. Then, "Roxana . . . you've seen the picture. She was . . . is . . . beautiful. She's also charming, irresistible to men. I used to be so jealous of her growing up; even with our age difference she always got all the attention." She's crying again, but keeping it together. "You know what my mother said to us?"

"What's that?"

"She would tell her friends, in front of us, 'Talyssa is the smart one. Roxana is the pretty one.' It used to upset us both."

"I get it." I'm sensing Talyssa wasn't just jealous of her sister growing up, but she retains some of that jealousy even now. I wonder if the sister felt the same way, but jealous of Talyssa's intellect.

But it's time to get to the hard stuff. I say, "So . . . how did Roxana get involved in all this?"

Through tears she says, "The best, most exclusive nightclub in the city is owned by the hotel group the bankers were flying in to meet with. It's in a factory building near where they were staying, and it was no big leap to assume those rich bankers on the flight would go there. The afternoon the plane landed I called Roxana from The Hague, told her I was working on an investigation with Europol, and I asked her to go to the club to help me."

"And she just did it?"

Talyssa sighs. "Roxana looked up to me. She would do anything I asked. I knew that when I called her."

"So you two were close?"

Another pause, and I can feel the weight behind it. She says, "No. We weren't. We've had a strained relationship for a long time. I could tell she agreed to go spy on the bankers only because it was her sister who asked her to do so. She wanted to impress me. To please me. And I knew she would react that way."

"So she went to the nightclub?"

"That evening. And, just like I'd hoped, she met a group of wealthy men who'd flown in that day; they said they were looking to buy hotels and restaurants around Bucharest."

"Where were they from?"

She replies immediately. "The head of the group, the one in charge . . . he was American. He told her his name was Tom, and he had her sit next to him at his table. He came on to Roxana that night, but she played cool, rejected his advances. She called me at four a.m., said she'd agreed to meet him the next night at a restaurant with a girlfriend of hers. She didn't know if she should go; she worried about how far this could lead." A pause. "But I encouraged her. I wanted names, specifics."

I point out the obvious now. "She was your agent. You were her handler."

Talyssa sounds like she's about to break down now. "Exactly."

This was bad. Worse than I'd expected. "Keep going."

"The second night after dinner they went to a club again, and again he tried to get her to come back to his room. She resisted, although she admitted he was very charming. She also told me Tom met with gangsters from a local group known as the Clanu, or Clan. She said she'd seen them around in discos before, so she knew who they were. She was worried about this, *and* about the fact that Tom had gotten more aggressive with her, but I talked her into seeing him one more time.

"Everything she told me he said . . . none of it helped me pinpoint anything tangible. A few details about his home and family is all. I knew this man was from the West Coast, that he had a family, and that he worked with the local mafia in Romania in some capacity. I needed photographs, names, I needed *something* to help the case I was working on.

"So Roxana did what I asked, and she met him the third night in his hotel room."

I put my head in my hands on the darkened roof. Clearly Talyssa's drive in all this, despite her lack of experience and her abject terror about what she is doing, stems from deep unwavering guilt about all but handing her sister over to some powerful and evil men.

She seems to sense what I am thinking, and she only confirms it when she says, "I don't know how to run an agent. I don't know how to do any type of criminal investigation that doesn't involve spreadsheets. I sent her into danger, over and over. But I didn't know it was dangerous. I swear to you, I didn't know."

She feels bad enough, so I don't draw the connection that she's probably gotten her sister killed.

But she's been thinking it, thinking about nothing else. That much has been clear all along.

I let her sob a moment without replying. Finally, I say, "And you still didn't find out who he was?"

"No. She didn't get me any pictures for facial recognition; she said his bodyguard was always close and always looking. She wasn't trained for this either, it's not her fault, but I was hard on her. I knew how much my approval meant to her, and I used that to my advantage.

"She didn't sleep with him, even after three nights, and he became more aggressive. She sensed a growing anger welling in him."

"What did this guy look like?"

"About forty-five or fifty years old. Tom was bald, short, very sure of himself. She liked him at first. Found herself being sucked in by his personality."

"He sounds like a douche."

"A . . . a what?"

"Never mind. What about others with him?"

"She told me about two men who were always by Tom's side. One was American; late thirties. He was the bodyguard, and she heard Tom call him Sean. She thought he was nice, and she thought Tom treated him badly."

I'm picturing an ex-military man being ordered around by a rich and bossy little runt.

"But the one who scared her most, much more than Tom, was a South African. They called him John; I don't know if that is a real name or not. She said he looked at her with eyes of pure evil."

"But still . . . you told her to go back and see them again."

"No. Not after the third night. It was getting too much, even for me. The gangsters, the aggressive behavior of Tom, the unease Roxana felt from John. On that fourth day I recognized this wasn't just about bankers with ties to organized crime. I began to suspect that this American who called himself Tom was the leader of an organized-crime concern himself. But even then, I had no clue whatsoever that they were sex traffickers."

She cries a moment. "Roxana decided to go back on her own. By now I guess she felt bad she hadn't given me what I asked for, so she took the risk."

"What happened when she went back?"

After a heavy, wet sniff, she says, "She told me he tried to rape her in his hotel room, but she got away, raced past his bodyguard outside the door, and made it through the lobby. I flew to Bucharest that afternoon. Her face and arms were bruised, and she was terrified. I went personally to the police, but they did nothing. I went to the hotel, but the American had left.

"Roxana didn't want anything else to do with me or my investigation, and I couldn't blame her. She wouldn't talk to me."

"And then she disappeared."

"Four weeks later she went out to a club, a different club, with some girlfriends. They said she started acting strange, very tired, like she was drugged. They put her in a cab to send her back to her flat, but she never arrived. The cab was found burning under a bridge. There was no one inside."

"Jesus Christ," I mutter.

"Harry, either she is still alive, which means I can't rest until I find her . . . or she is not alive, which means it doesn't matter what I do."

"Of course it does. You want to bring her killers to justice, right?"

"Yes," she says, but it's not very convincing.

"What is it?"

"This is my fault. If she is dead . . . I will die, too."

She isn't speaking metaphorically; I can hear that in her voice.

I say, "I don't need a partner with a death wish."

The sobs continue for a time, and then she says, "I understand. I am okay. I must see this through."

I think a moment about my own actions, then say, "I've learned something in my years doing what I do. If you don't feel guilt, then you can't change. Guilt can be a driving force for good, for doing what's right. Or it can be a limiting force. Something that causes you to throw away right and wrong, to justify yourself. That's the weak way to deal with your conscience. The determining factor in whether guilt locks you into evil or spurs you on towards good is your own inner strength. Your own moral compass."

"What are you saying?"

"I'm saying you fucked up. Bad. But you've come all this way because you are strong enough to admit it, and strong enough to try to rectify your mistake. That's all anyone can ask of you now."

I add, "I've fucked up before. I've gotten people killed. People who didn't deserve it. It never goes away, but I tell myself the only thing I can do is to help others."

"That's why you are here?"

"I guess you and I have similar motivations."

She sobs yet again, but her voice regains some strength. "I am okay, Harry. I will do this."

I understand so much now. What I saw as an almost childlike fear in Talyssa was, in part, at least, an incredible dread about what she would find.

A scared young woman who simultaneously wants to pay penance for what she's done. And I see her for what she is now.

Dangerous.

. . .

Minutes later, I sense fresh trouble. Movement in the dark, down a long passage that runs up from the center of the Old Town, hundreds of ancient stone steps, past dozens and dozens of doorways leading to private residences, raised porches lined with potted plants.

At first I can only tell I'm observing a group of individuals, but as they pass into one of the too-sparsely-placed streetlights, the orange glow reveals a half dozen men, dressed differently than the ones I saw earlier. Whereas the other men looked more tactical in nature, this group looks like a tiny gang of soccer hooligans.

I see dark clothing, facial hair on some, longer hair on others.

Again I use the app on my phone to check the cameras I've hidden in stairwells and passages I can't see from here. Everything seems quiet other than the men moving straight up the middle.

But even though I don't see others on my cams, I wonder if there are more around.

The men close on my position with confidence, climbing stairs through the night as one. They are cohesive, an organized unit, each man comfortable that the other has his back.

The men's hands are empty, but that means nothing. They'll have weapons.

I work with just a few operating principles, but one of them is ironclad: every motherfucker I come in contact with has a weapon.

I speak softly, careful to not show any anxiety now, though I'm feeling a ton of it. "Talyssa?"

I guess I failed, because her own voice changes suddenly; apparently, she can sense the change of gravity in mine. "Yes. Yes, I'm here. What's wrong?"

"It's showtime. I've got men approaching, and they fit the mold. They're about two minutes from us at their current pace."

"Oh my God . . . what do I do?" Her voice cracks as she speaks.

"First, stay calm. I've got everything under control." This is a lie; I'd only *really* have control of this situation if I were up here on the roof in a sand-bagged position with an M60 belt-fed machine gun. But I tell myself that showing confidence I don't have is for her own good. Quickly I move in a low crouch along the angled tile roof to the west side of the building, out of the view of the men approaching from the north. While doing so I say, "I need you to go to your window and open it."

I grab the rope and step up on the ledge. Rappelling down quickly, I arrive at her window in just seconds. She is just now opening it, her purse and a backpack over her shoulder.

Our comms channel is still open, but we are five feet away so she can hear me through her earpiece and in person. "Come to me. Grab me around the neck."

She moves closer, but she looks down and then backs up a little. It's only about thirty feet to the cobblestones, which isn't that far, but it's plenty far enough to kill her if she fell.

I urge her on. "You're fine. Come on."

She comes closer again, but she doesn't put her foot up on the window-sill, and it's going to be impossible for me to haul her out while holding the rope.

"Work with me, Talyssa."

"I . . . I *can't*. I'm—"

"Really bad dudes will be coming through that door behind you in one minute. You want to take your chances with me, or with them?"

She looks back to the door, makes no move towards me, and she's just out of reach. I'm straining on the rope as it is.

I try a joke. "You're hurting my feelings."

But she looks at me, then back at the door. She has a fear of heights, which is not unreasonable, but I also sense that she has a fear of me.

I get that, too, I guess.

She's nearly panic-stricken now. "I . . . I can't do this. I'll meet you downstairs. I'll find a back way out. I'll hurry."

"There's no time for that. Trust me. Just step up and—"

But she's already turning away and rushing to the door of her room.

Son of a bitch.

I quickly rappel down towards the passageway on the west side of her building, and while doing so I try to come up with a new plan. I've got to work with the situation before me, because my original scheme is up in smoke. Fortunately, I have a rich history of shit going wrong for me to fall back on.

I speak softly for the mic in the earpiece, not wanting my words to carry in the narrow passage. "Run down the stairs to the ground floor and find a window, as far away from the main entrance as possible. Do *not* go out into the courtyard because you'll walk right into them if you do." I don't know for sure that they won't send men around the back or sides of the building. *I* would. But I *do* know for sure they'll send men straight up the middle, because I saw them advancing up the stairs without any defensive tactical posture.

I could see it in their walk, in the way they moved—these guys aren't worried about shit.

"Okay," she says.

"I'll come around back to meet you."

"Yes," she says again, and I hear nothing but stress in her voice.

Once on the ground I release the line, pull off my gloves, and jam them in my pack. I start moving towards the rear of the building, and I keep trying to calm her.

"You're fine, just get out of there."

"I'm in the kitchen. The window opens. I can climb out."

"Okay, keep quiet."

I near the building's edge at a silent run, my hand brushing the stone of the wall as I slow to look around. I haven't drawn my weapon and hope I don't have to; a single gunshot in these narrow stone corridors would bring every bad guy down on me in seconds. And even though I have a silencer in my pack, the report of suppressed Glock 19 fire is still louder than a snare drum at a heavy metal concert.

I want to maintain stealth, but how the next few minutes go down is not up to me. Instead it's up to the Romanian woman I've tied myself to in this op, and the assholes coming to get her.

Just before I peer around the corner, I hear noise in the back passageway. The scuffle of footsteps on stone. I whisper, "Move quietly. I can hear you running from here."

But Talyssa's reply in my ear causes me to stop in my tracks. "Just climbing out the window now."

And this is bad news, because it tells me there is someone else running behind the building.

"Wait," I say, but I can hear the sounds of her climbing out the window, both over my earpiece and through the echoing of her movements along the passages.

I look around the corner and see two men in black tracksuits running on the cobblestones, and they see Talyssa as she finishes climbing out of the window. They charge towards her before she even turns to face them.

I pull my pistol and whisper for the transmitter in my ear. "Run to your left. Go, go, go."

But the men are on her in seconds; she screams as they tackle her to the stones, her voice simultaneously loud in my ear and echoing all around me.

I am only fifty feet away, but I don't have a shot from here because I can't be sure my 9-millimeter rounds won't overpenetrate the bad guys and hit the woman. I decide to remain stealthy, to try to get to them before they see me so I can stick my knife into their ribs, but to my right I hear racing footsteps running in my direction along the western wall of the building.

Shit. The men holding Talyssa down pull her up to her feet; they clearly are not about to assassinate her, so I turn away from the Europol analyst and her captors and climb a narrow stairwell that leads up to a locked metal gate in the wall surrounding the entire Old Town.

Kneeling in the darkness I see two men run past, in the direction of Talyssa, and I know that the opposition—whoever the hell they are—has her now.

Softly I speak to her through our communications link.

"Stay calm, Talyssa. Don't say a word. I'll get you back. Try to keep your hair over your earpiece so they don't see it."

In my gut I feel wrenching pain as I realize that the girl I used for bait is now in mortal danger and, just like with the women in the cellar, it's all my motherfucking fault.

TWENTY

Talyssa Corbu was yanked to her feet by the two men, and two more arrived a few seconds later. She tried to scream for help but a hand slammed over her mouth and nose. A man with a thick accent leaned into her ear. "We kill you if you make sound. Understand?"

Tears rained from her eyes as she nodded, and the hand came away. All four had hold of her body now; her arms were gripped tightly, a man behind grabbed the collar of her raincoat, and a fourth person manhandled her while ripping off the backpack and her shoulder bag, and feeling into every pocket of her clothing.

She heard Harry speak to her softly, and she turned around to look for him, but all she saw were two more men arriving at her position and helping the others. All the goons had dark hair, most had beards, and they wore dark clothing. One spoke into his mobile phone but he stepped away from her to do so, and she couldn't make out the language.

There were smiles among the men, so proud they were that they'd captured her.

Soon they began pushing her forward, turning away from the wall at the eastern side of the Old Town and heading on foot down the first of many long stone staircase passageways that led down to the Stradun.

Talyssa was in the middle of the group, and though she mostly kept her head down out of abject terror, she did look to her left and right and regard the faces around her. These were cold, hard men. They weren't police.

They were gangsters; she took them for Turks or perhaps Albanians, but she had no way of knowing until she heard them speak again. As a Romanian, she knew a few Albanians and a few Turks, and although she couldn't speak either language, she could quickly identify it.

Her mind began racing. She came to the quick conclusion that there was no way the Consortium would have sent Albanians or Turks to kidnap her out of her hotel room in Croatia unless they had something awful in store for her. She wasn't going to be driven to the edge of town and given a warning.

She was certain they were taking her someplace to torture her for information, and then to kill her.

And wherever the hell Harry had run to, his promises to protect her rang hollow now. Still, she didn't blame him. She'd panicked at the window: a lifelong fear of heights, a fear of most everything that had to do with danger, was to blame. If she'd just trusted the American, she wouldn't be moments away from death now.

Her teeth chattered and her mind raced, and she fought a wave of nausea as she continued down the steps.

. . .

I'm hauling ass two blocks and two passageways to the left of and parallel to where Talyssa and the men in black are descending. I had to wait for them to pass my position before running here to the east, behind Talyssa's building, past the window she climbed out of, and then I turned to my right to begin my own descent. Now I'm thirty or forty seconds behind the group, but I feel sure I'm making up for it with my speed.

As I run I speak again to Talyssa, still softly, because this medieval neighborhood feels like one damn echo chamber. "Walk as slowly as you can. You *have* to slow them down."

I hear her speak to the men around her in English, her voice halting. "Please. Slow down. I can't walk this fast."

A man snaps at her in a heavy accent. "No talking. Walk faster."

"I . . . I hurt my ankle when you knocked me down."

I can hear frustration in the man's voice now as he speaks to the others in a foreign tongue that I think may be Albanian. When Talyssa says, "Thank you," I know they are complying with her request and slowing.

I run faster. At each little narrow intersection I glance to my right, hoping to see the group so I know I am getting in front of them. I'm having a hard time coming up with a cogent plan, but I'm definitely preparing for a confrontation. Taking on eight goons at the same time in an outdoor stone stairwell barely eight feet across seems like a bad course of action, but I don't know that I have any choice.

I consider letting them just take her and then following them to see where they go, but I see the flaw in that plan. If I lose Talyssa, then she's dead. If the Consortium runs the chief of police of this town, if they have the juice to get a bevy of cops for a surveillance operation, then I don't see why they would pull the cops and send in an Albanian gang to grab the woman if they plan on simply interrogating and intimidating her.

No. They could have used dirty cops for that. The fact that they didn't kill her immediately tells me they need to take her to a secondary location, perhaps with plans to torture information out of her, and the fact that they brought in a foreign criminal gang to snatch her tells me they then plan on killing her.

Either way, right now I'm Talyssa Corbu's only hope.

. . .

Just as I sprint through the next intersection, doing my best to stay as far from the streetlamps as possible, I gaze to my right again, expecting another narrow east-west street. But instead I see I've run out into the northwestern edge of a large triangle-shaped open-air area, two blocks wide. The entourage is just entering the square on the southeastern side, and though I'm forty yards away, in low light, and in front of them, there is no way they can miss a man running at top speed.

I hear immediate shouts, both echoing around me and through my earpiece from Talyssa's microphone and, just as I disappear from their view, I see two of the eight men peel off and come my way. They are a minute out if they move along the square at a careful pace, but less than half that if they run.

I figure they'll run, because they won't know for sure I'm with Talyssa and won't immediately move in a defensive posture. They find me curious enough to send a couple guys to check, and I'm sure someone has told them to be on the lookout for a lone male operator in all this, but they aren't going to just open fire.

I don't think.

And I won't open fire on them. I have no qualms about killing a couple of kidnappers, but I want to avoid a direct confrontation, if possible, while there are so many guns around the girl. At the same time, however, I don't want to go into full retreat, where I'll likely lose my chance to get her back.

Looking towards the sky as I run to the north, I make my decision.

I'm going up.

To my left a copper drain spout climbs the side of the three-story building, all the way to the roof. I adjust my backpack and start heading up, moving as quickly as possible, hoping like hell I can get over the lip of the tiled roof before the two Albanians make it onto my little stairway passage. For a brief moment I consider pulling my pistol and firing a couple of rounds into the cobblestones to slow their approach, but instead I just concentrate on climbing as fast as I can.

My knuckles scrape against the ancient walls behind the drainpipe as I struggle for handholds, and the toes of my boots dig for purchase as I climb. Quickly I realize I'm not going to make it all the way before the men arrive below me, but I chose a pipe out of the illumination of the streetlamps, so I do have another way to remain undetected. On the second floor I swing away from the pipe and step onto the ledge of a darkened window. I squat down, positioning my body totally within the window's frame, next to a planter with a small orange tree in it, and then I freeze.

Below me two men run into view, pistols swinging low in their hands, and they continue down the eight-foot-wide staircase towards the main street of the Old Town, still several blocks away.

Since I'm in my black clothing and squatting in front of the black window, twenty feet above their heads and in dim light, they don't see me. Once they travel another block down, I reach back out to the drainpipe, carefully take hold, and swing my body off the window ledge. Quickly I continue my ascent up to the roof.

Getting up the overhang is tricky, but the drainpipe helps as I dangle off it and climb out, hand over hand, until I can pull myself up onto the tiles.

The building I've chosen is on the opposite side of the street from Talyssa and her captors, and this puts me farther away from her, with two narrow north-south passages between us. I run along the angled roof and see that there is one more connected building before the next east-west street, so I leap down to it, its roof a few feet lower than the one I climbed onto.

Rushing again through the dark, I tell myself I can make the leap across the narrow alley to the next roof, one story lower because it's farther down the hill that descends to the center of the Old Town. I pick up my pace, pull my backpack off my back, and swing it in my arm as hard as I can. I let it go, and it flies through the air in front of me over the street. While it sails on, I time my footfalls so my last one will land right at the roof's edge, and then I leap, giving it everything I have.

I sail over clotheslines full of drying laundry, my feet and arms flailing.

I make it over the narrow street and land tumbling onto the roof, using my forward momentum to keep from rolling off the steep tiles. The Glock on my hip bites into me when I bang it on the hard surface, but I'm up on my feet with the momentum of my roll and I lean down and snatch my pack as I climb, sliding it over my shoulders.

I'm well behind Talyssa and the others now, still two blocks west of me, and I don't yet have a plan as to what I'll do if I manage to catch up.

But I keep going. If I don't reach her before they get her piled into a van and out of here, or I don't get to my vehicle to tail them, then I won't get another chance.

Almost out of breath, I speak softly for Talyssa's earpiece as I run on. "Slow them down. You *have* to slow them down."

. . .

Talyssa heard the transmission from the American; she could tell from the desperate tone of his voice and the exertion that she hears along with it that he was doing his best to get to her, and she was certain she would die if he did not. Already she could see a large square that ended at the main street of the Old Town, just a few blocks below her, and the gate that led out the eastern side of the walled pedestrian-only space was just to the right on the far side. She imagined there would be a car waiting out there for her, and she'd be in it in a couple of minutes unless she did something to slow them down more until the American could arrive.

The two men who had ventured off to check out the man running a couple of blocks over were still gone, but the other six men surrounded her, and they jostled her when she tried to slow again.

She knew she needed to do something, so she tried the only thing she could think of. On her next step down, she purposefully turned her ankle and fell onto the cobblestones, shouting in pain.

"My leg!"

She spoke for Harry's benefit, letting him know that she was trying to delay her kidnappers. She didn't know if it would be enough, but it was all she could think of.

One of the men grabbed her, pulled her upright while shouting at her in his native tongue. She knew almost instantly he was Albanian. He then switched to English. "Walk!"

She took a step and then started to collapse again, as if she really had injured herself, but two of the men lifted her off the ground and began all but carrying her with their hands under her shoulders.

"Put me down. Let go!" she shouted, this time to let Harry know her plan had bought her a little time, as the men carrying her would be forced to move slower now, and the others surrounding her would be forced to wait for them.

. . .

I hear Talyssa while I'm in midair, making the desperate kicking leap over the first of the two north-south staired passageways between me and her. I land on the roof to the west, my hands and my feet striking the tile, and then I climb up, running diagonally along the pitched surface so that I am still heading in the right direction to get to the woman, or even to get back in front of her.

A few seconds later I make the crest of the roof, then run down the other side, picking up speed, and I launch myself off again, then land again, one block over. Unless the Albanians have changed direction, they should be three stories down on the other side of the roof I'm now on, so I move more quietly. At the peak I lower to my butt and crab-walk down towards the edge, then look over the side.

A group of six men surround the Europol analyst directly below me, and they are only twenty-five yards away from entering the large square with the fountain where I first saw the police surveilling Talyssa earlier in the evening. They are moving at a reasonable pace, but I can tell the girl is making things difficult for them.

Still, they will be through the square and out the eastern gate in under two minutes at their current speed, so there's no time for me to focus on hashing out a brilliant plan. I start to reach for my pistol but stop when I recognize it will be too dangerous for Talyssa if I fire into the group from here.

Nope, I've got to get my ass down on top of them, where I can take them on up close.

I see multiple sets of clotheslines on the building outside the windows on the other side of the passage, one floor down from my position. Towels and clothing hang from them, and the line is about fifteen feet long before it loops into a pulley and then doubles back, making it thirty feet in all. An idea forms quickly, and I turn and head higher on the roof, yanking on gloves as I go. I then turn around, facing the passage.

I say, "Talyssa, count silently to five, then pull away from the men and run. Scream and shout while you do it. You *have* to do this for me in five seconds."

I don't expect a response from her; I can only pray she complies.

After a quick breath to ready myself, I begin running down the roof as fast as I can, counting as I go.

I leap off the building, kicking my legs as I drop down, and I cover the entire passageway with my bound. I hear Talyssa scream below and to my left just as I crash into the clotheslines affixed to the metal bars and pulley system, running alongside two second-story windows. As I hit, both of my gloved hands grab on to a towel hanging there and the line under it and, as expected, the clothesline absorbs the majority of my momentum, but my weight causes the pulley system to snap off the wall behind me. Hanging on with both hands now, I begin swinging down, alongside the building towards the backs of the seven people dead ahead, knowing good and well there isn't enough clothesline to get me all the way down to the stairs, and the other pulley bar is going to snap right off once I swing down and it's forced to endure my momentum and body weight.

I'm along for the ride now, but soon I'll be flying on my own.

I wrap the line around my right hand so I don't fall; the towel and gloves keep it from ripping my hand to shreds, but even hanging on as tightly as I can, I feel the towel slide down, and I know I won't be able to hang on for long.

I am making noise, the pulleys sticking out from the wall above bend and creak, and my backpack scuffs the stone wall before I swing out farther away from the building. But everyone below me is shouting as one as they lunge for their prisoner, who herself is screaming and shouting.

She doesn't manage to get very far before they grab her, but she *does* manage to cause an excellent distraction.

And if these motherfuckers think *she* is distracting, just wait till they get a load of me.

As the line whips me down to the lowest point I unwrap my hand, still ten or twelve feet in the air and arcing through the dark, and I shoot forward with all the momentum of my long swing. Landing on the cobblestones or steps would be painful at best, but I have no plans to hit the ground.

I'm instead aiming for that cluster of people right in front of me.

I fly out of the night air towards the backs of the tight group, and I slam into them from behind like they are bowling pins. I know Talyssa is in this crowd, and I'm sure I'm knocking her stupid like the others, but when you are fighting six versus one, a little collateral damage is difficult to avoid.

Everyone falls hard, slamming into one another and then hitting the ground, bodies tumbling out into the northern edge of the square. Talyssa ends up on the bottom of the pile, but I manage to roll over it all and am propelled up to my feet beyond the rest of them. I spin back around while drawing my weapon, and I aim at the first target I see: an Albanian in a black tracksuit on his knees right in front of me.

I fire twice into his chest at eight feet, shift aim, then fire once into the face of a man still on his back ten feet beyond. The noise from the shots pounds off stone all around us. A third man, this one also up to his knees, pulls his pistol and spins towards the fire, but I shoot him twice center mass, then shift my weapon to the left to drop another man, who has risen to a crouch and is just now reaching for his waistband.

But before I can press the trigger, another shooter opens up to my left, the boom of a pistol is close, and a shower of sparks blasts off the awning of a café just behind me. Whoever is firing is the larger threat now, so I drop to one knee and aim up the east-west street where the noise is coming from, scanning for a target.

I'm sure it's the two men who peeled off from the group to come after me, but they must be behind some cover because I can't see them anywhere.

While this is going on I know the men closer to me—the three still alive—are all pulling their guns, so I spin around to the window of the café and dive through. Glass shatters and I crash to the ground inside, roll behind the wall, and reload my weapon.

Fresh incoming fire breaks out the rest of the glass in my window as well as other windows to my right, and from the sounds I can tell there are four or five guns targeting my position now. All I can do is hunker down and try to ride this out.

After ten seconds the gunfire stops. I chance a look out the lower corner of the window, and I see two men dragging Talyssa towards the Ploce Gate on the eastern side of the Old Town. But when I lean out with my weapon to aim at them, I immediately catch fire from two or three positions.

I fall flat to the floor underneath the window as dust, bits of stone, and shards of glass fall over me.

I'm pinned down here so I can't go forward, but I sure as shit can run out the back of this café, and from there I can head to the west. That will, eventually, get me out through the western Pile Gate of the Old Town, near where my car is parked.

It means losing sight of Talyssa, but at this point, that's going to happen anyway.

I climb to my feet and run through the restaurant and, as I do, I shout over a barrage of gunfire from out in the square, hoping she can still hear me in her earpiece. "I'm going for the car. You need to find a way to tell me about the vehicle they put you in. Be clever, Talyssa, or else they'll figure out you're tipping someone off."

I hear her speak a single word in a tearful voice—"Please"—but I don't know if that was for me or for them. I feel helpless right now as I run in the opposite direction, but I tell myself I'm going to get this shit back under control on the road.

TWENTY-ONE

I'm still a minute away from my car, my right knee and right elbow are throbbing for some reason, and my lungs are screaming from the all-out exertion of my sprint, when I hear the side door of a van slide open through my commo link. Breathlessly I say, "It's a van. I hear that. I just need to know the color. Then I need to know which direction you're traveling. Do it carefully."

I hear no reply, only the sounds of Talyssa being placed in the vehicle roughly, men all around her speaking in a foreign language, and then the sound of the van door sliding shut. The engine was already running, obviously, because screeching tires come next.

I'm climbing into the Vauxhall when I finally hear Talyssa's voice. "I . . . who are you people? I see your black hair, your black beards. Are you Turkish? Moroccan?"

A black van. I nod and softly say, "Black van, got it. Good job. Now, be subtle . . . tell me the direction."

"Where are we going?" she asks.

"Be quiet!" a man shouts in English.

"To the Hilton? I see the Hilton. Are we going to the—"

"Be quiet!"

I look down at my phone's GPS, move the map around, and find the Hilton hotel just west of Old Town.

This is good news, as I am to the west of her, or at least I was when her van began moving. They could be right on top of me by now, since a minute or two has passed since then.

I launch the four-door out of the parking lot, jack the wheel hard to the left, and drive off, slowing only as I pass oncoming police vehicles responding to the sound of gunfire in the Old Town. They pay no attention to me, and soon I'm flooring it again, scanning each intersection to my left and right, desperately trying to find a black van.

And it doesn't take long. Other than the oncoming first responders there is little traffic out this time of night, so when I turn onto Anice Boskovic I see headlights behind me, approaching fast. I slow to match the speed limit, and soon a black van rushes by me on my left, then makes a left turn at an intersection. I continue straight, not wanting to get too close behind it, and then I one-hand my steering wheel while I hold the phone up to check the GPS, unsure how to link back up with my target vehicle. All the while I keep speaking softly into Talyssa's ear. "I see you. I'm right here with you. Don't worry."

There's a lot to worry about—I'm worried as shit, as a matter of fact—but keeping her as calm as possible seems like a good idea to me right now.

I see the van a minute later, one block south of me and still heading to the west, along the Adriatic coast and farther from the Old Town. It is speeding, almost recklessly, which tells me that long gone are the Albanians' mission discipline and the swagger I saw in their demeanor when they approached Talyssa's building.

The fact that several of their number are now lying dead on the cobblestones a couple of kilometers behind us has caused them to doubt themselves, so while shooting those guys thinned out the herd and was the right call for me to make, the assholes remaining are only going to be more dangerous to the woman from Europol.

I'm still forming a plan as I turn to head towards the road they're on, and *still* working on it when I fall in to follow them, a couple hundred yards behind. Traffic is light at two something in the morning, and I realize I may have a tough time remaining covert if they start driving around on random streets, trying to see if they've picked up a tail.

I also realize I may not get a better opportunity than I have now.

By my count there were eight men involved with Talyssa's capture. At least three are dead or wounded, and I don't think the two who engaged me from the east-west street would have had time to make it to the van before it drove off, so they are somewhere behind us, probably securing transportation for themselves. Assuming the snatch team left a driver in the van, which would have been the prudent move, then there are probably four men around Talyssa now up ahead of me.

That's bad, but it could be worse. And it will probably get worse, because, wherever the hell they are going, one thing's for sure.

There won't be fewer than four around her when they get there.

Plus, now I have them close together. They are close to Talyssa, as well, which is suboptimal, but I'm a guy who takes the best shot possible and doesn't wait for the perfect shot.

I floor the Vauxhall as soon as I decide on a plan. I'm going to take this van down and all the opposition in it.

Now, before they get to their destination.

It takes me a full minute to arrive to within two car lengths behind them, and now we are on a winding road heading northwest, with the moonlit sea off to our left. I cinch my seat belt tighter, put my hand on the gun on my hip for reassurance, and then speak to Talyssa.

"I'm right behind you. I need you to hold on to something, *anything*. I'm going to wreck the vehicle you're in, and it's going to be bad, but I *have* to do it."

She immediately replies to me, right in front of the Albanians, with utter dread in her voice. "*What?* No . . . no . . . *please*, no."

"Stop talking!" a man shouts, and then she screams in surprise and pain as if she's just been struck.

I say, "It's your best chance, Talyssa. You *have* to trust me. When the vehicle loses control, I want you to put your head in your lap and keep holding on till it comes to a stop. When it does, lie perfectly still, covering your head as best you can. I'll get you out of the van, don't worry. Just ride out the crash and this will all be over."

"Oh, God, no. *Please*," she says, and I imagine the Albanians are starting to wonder who the hell she's talking to.

Flooring it now, I say, "C'mon, Gentry. You got this."

I'm going to attempt a PIT maneuver, a Pursuit Intervention Technique, a standard tactic used by law enforcement around the globe to stop a vehicle, much better than shooting out tires or some bullshit like that.

That said, despite my comforting words to my Romanian partner, I imagine this is going to suck for everyone involved. Me, the Albanians, *and* Talyssa.

PITing is a pretty safe trick if done correctly, but PITing a van, even if executed perfectly, is almost always a terrible idea, because the high center of gravity of the van almost ensures it will end up tipping, or worse, flipping. But the threshold of what I think is acceptable risk for Talyssa is rising by the minute as she gets closer and closer to the moment I lose her and the bad guys have her all to themselves.

Flipping this van might break some bones in the Europol analyst, but I tell myself that if I were her, I'd rather suffer a violent car crash than torture followed by a point-blank gunshot to the back of the head.

It's all relative, I guess.

There is a counter to the PIT maneuver the targeted driver can implement, but I'm doubting this Albanian gangster will be well versed in high-level defensive driving. But even if he does, there is also a counter-*counter* PIT maneuver that not many people know. I know it because the CIA taught me everything they could about hurting people and breaking things, and I've picked up even more on the subject since officially leaving the Agency.

The CIA taught me everything they knew then, but they didn't teach me everything I know now.

If the Albanian driver tries to counter my PIT, he'll fail, and he'll wreck out just the same.

"C'mon, Gentry," I repeat. "You got this."

I can hear the Albanians shouting at one another through the earpiece; they are anxious and frantic, probably because they now notice that the car trailing behind them is coming up their ass. On the right side of me, a row of large houses is all but hidden behind stone walls and heavy foliage, and on the left it's mostly just trees, with the sea beyond. There's a wide sidewalk running along next to the road here, making the space for me to work in a little bit larger than just a two-lane road.

This isn't the perfect place for a PIT, but it's the best I'm going to get. I decide to go for it, and I move into the left lane as if I'm about to pass.

The driver isn't an idiot; he knows the headlights that came racing up from behind at two thirty a.m. are attached to a vehicle that poses a threat. He jerks his wheel violently to the left, squeezing me out.

Shit.

I slow a little, fake an attempt to approach on the right, and the van bites on this. He pulls hard to the right, and I think I've got an opportunity to get back to his left, but right then gunfire booms out of the van's rear window, and instantly my windshield spiderwebs.

These fuckers aren't messing around.

"Put your head down now, Talyssa, and keep it there!"

I've got to make this happen before one of their rounds hits me in the fucking forehead, so I accelerate till the nose of my four-door is just past the left rear bumper of the van.

Then I carefully turn the wheel to the right, nudging in.

I make contact; it's not much, but it's sufficient, because it pops the rear end of the van to the right just enough to cause the tires to lose traction and the driver to lose control of the vehicle. The nose of the van veers sharply to the left, and I keep my rightward steer going, even after I've broken contact, so I can get out of the way of what's about to happen.

What happens is a lot more violent than I'd hoped for, considering my aim here was to protect one of the people inside the van. The big top-heavy vehicle turns ninety degrees to the road on squealing and smoking tires, and immediately tips over at speed. As I slam on my brakes I look in my driver-side mirror and see the black van crash onto its right side. The rear door flies open with the impact, and a body ejects onto the street.

I can't tell if it's male or female.

Poor Talyssa, I think. First, I came slamming down from the sky, knocking her to the cobblestones in a pile of men, and now I've wrecked her out in a brutal crash.

I'm leaping out of the Vauxhall before the last of the debris from the crash has even rained back to Earth. Drawing my pistol, I actuate my weapon light under the barrel, shining it on the scene.

The person ejected is a man; he doesn't look as badly injured as I expected him to be, but I fix that immediately by firing twice into his right side as he tries to rise to his feet.

He spins away from me and ends up dead on his back in the street, arms and legs splayed.

I move around to the front of the vehicle, look through the cracked windshield, and see the driver and the man in the front passenger seat lying on top of each other. They are moving, but I don't fire, because I can't see Talyssa. She might be on the wall of the van behind them, so I run around to the back, crouch down, and enter there.

My light reflects off the dust and smoke in the air, but through it all I see an arm wildly waving a stainless semiauto pistol my way. The gun snaps, earth-shattering in the small space, and I return fire into the face of the figure holding it, unsure whether I've been shot. I don't feel any impact, but I keep firing till the stainless steel pistol falls away. Only when it does so do I see that this is one of the bearded men; he's lying on top of Talyssa in the second row. She is screaming bloody murder, thank God, and now that I know where she is I move into the van and put my hand on her head to hold her down against the closed sliding door resting on the street. When she's out of my line of fire I open up on the men in the front seat, dumping a dozen rounds from my Glock into them.

"Are you hurt?" I shout now as I reload, because my ears are ringing from the gunfire in the closed-in space, and I know the Romanian woman's virgin ears will be faring much worse.

She shouts back at me. "I . . . I don't know! This man is on top of me and—"

"Hang on."

I pull on Talyssa because I can't get over the seat to get the dead guy off her. It's hard work getting her turned around and over the seat back, but finally she is able to crawl out under her own power.

Her face is scratched and bruised, and her eyes show mild shock, but she could be a hell of a lot worse, so I count my blessings.

We stand amid the wreckage under a streetlamp; I feel all over my body to double-check that I didn't catch a bullet. I can't find anything but sore spots, and painful bruising is a lot better than being ventilated by gunfire.

Another car has stopped behind us and I hear barking dogs and shouting humans in the yards of the homes on our right. I've holstered my weapon under my T-shirt; I'm covered with cuts and scrapes and filth from all the scrambling and fighting I've been doing over the past half hour, so to the people here I look just like another car crash victim.

But we can't play this off like a simple traffic accident, since no one for a quarter mile in any direction could have missed the sound of all the shooting.

I help Talyssa along, ignoring the young man who climbs out of the tiny Nissan behind us. Then we get into the Vauxhall. Seconds later I've reversed direction and am heading back to the east, moving at a reasonable speed. Flashing lights approach, so I pull into a driveway, as the bullet holes in my windshield are easy to see, even at night.

Once the first responders have continued on to the west, I'm back on the road, and my right hand reaches out to feel over Talyssa's body. It's called a blood sweep, a quick way to find an injury on someone who may not even be aware they are injured because of the effects of adrenaline. You have to put your hand everywhere to be sure, and I do this without thinking.

It's a common practice in my world, but to the uninitiated I imagine it feels a little off.

Instantly she recoils and smacks my hand away. "What . . . what are you doing?"

I pull my hand back to the steering wheel. "Sorry, it's a thing we do."

"What? Who does that? No one does that!"

I let it go. "Check yourself, are you bleeding? Are you hurt?"

Coming out of her anger and shock, she does as I ask. After a moment she says, "I . . . I don't think I am badly injured, but I hit my head when we crashed." Rubbing her upper arm she says, "My shoulder hurts, but I think I'm okay."

I know from experience that if her head and shoulder hurt now, they're going to be killing her in about twelve hours, but I don't mention this. I have to find out if she learned anything at all in the few minutes she was in captivity. I don't expect to find out much, but I have no idea how else to continue my pursuit of the kidnapped women without some sort of new intelligence.

But before I can speak she turns to me. "Thank . . . thank you."

This I don't expect. "Uh . . . sure. I thought you'd be pissed."

"Pissed? I haven't been drinking. Have you?"

"Mad. Angry," I clarify, knowing she probably learned British English, so she thought I was telling her I thought she was drunk when I pulled her out of the van.

"Why would I be mad?" she asks now.

"I don't know. I guess because I used you as bait and almost got you killed."

She shook her head. "You saved my life. I put yours in danger by not trusting you on the rope, and still you came for me. Thank you."

I say, "I think you *are* drunk."

She looks me over a moment. "Maybe you didn't do it for me. Maybe you did it for the women you are trying to save. But still . . . thank you." She reaches out and squeezes my forearm, then retracts her hand and puts it back in her lap.

I ask, "Did the men say where they were taking you?"

"Not to me, no. But they did say something."

"What do you mean?"

"Romanian is a Romance language. Albanian is not. But both are from the Balkan *sprachbund*."

She's a smart woman. I'm lost already.

And she sees it in my face, apparently. "I can't speak Albanian, not at all, but I can understand some words and phrases."

"And they spoke openly in front of you?"

"Yeah."

"Not very professional of them," I say. "In fact, we can't trust it. It could have been disinformation."

She picks some grit from the car crash out of the back of her arm, wipes a little blood off her hand onto her jeans. "They were very agitated after you showed up, for good reason. I don't think they were thinking about being professional or trying to deceive me when we left the Old Town. They were all screaming at one another. At me, too."

"Yeah, I heard. What did they say?"

"I heard the driver say something about a boat."

"A boat?"

"Yes. He definitely said a boat, and then he said something strange. He said, very clearly, 'next to the president.'"

"The *president*?"

"Yes. I am sure of it."

"The president of Croatia?"

"I have no idea what he was referring to."

I pull hard to the side of the road and slam on the brakes.

Talyssa grabs the dashboard to keep from being propelled forward. "Why are we stopping?"

I don't answer; instead I lift my phone and look at the GPS, move the map back farther west, in the direction the van was headed. After a few seconds I find what I'm looking for. "The Valamar Dubrovnik President Hotel. On the tip of the peninsula. Fifteen minutes from here."

Talyssa looks out the window at the darkness, then back to me. "That *must* be it. Let's go, then."

I grab my pack out of the backseat, then fish through it a moment. Pulling out her phone and her pistol, I hand both items back to her.

"What . . . what is happening?"

"I'm going on alone. We will stay in communication with each other. We're lucky you survived tonight. I'm not pushing it again."

"But . . . my sister."

"You can do more to help your sister by supporting me than you can running around with me."

"You are just trying to get rid of me."

She's right, but I don't admit it. "Not at all. If I find that boat they're talking about, I'm going to need to follow it. I'm also going to need to know about the owner of it, where it might be going, that sort of thing."

After a moment she nods. "I . . . I can help with that."

"I know you can. Keep that phone on; I've got the number programmed into an app on mine that will keep me untraceable, but you will be able to reach me when you need to."

"Okay." She seems unsure, but right now I just want her out of danger.

I add, "Also, you may not know it yet, but you are going to be very sore tomorrow."

"I'll be fine."

"Not tomorrow, you won't."

She climbs out of the car and I follow her, then walk over to a pair of scooters parked along the street. Both are locked, but I pull my pick set and quickly free them both.

One is a Gilera Stalker, a little 50cc two-person two-wheeler. And the other is a Derbi Boulevard, a more powerful scooter with a 150cc engine.

"Where do I go?"

I don't really have an answer for this. "Just get out of town. Find a little suburb, sit tight, wait for instructions from me."

"That's it?"

I shrug. "Pick up some ice, painkillers, bandages, and antibiotic ointment." I add, "Trust me."

It takes me a few minutes to hot-wire both scooters, and soon she is heading east, and I'm heading west, looking for a boat next to the President Hotel.

It's not much to go on, but it's all I've salvaged out of one hell of a shitty night, so I do my best to think positively as the aches and pains from all my activity continue to make their presence known across my body.

TWENTY-TWO

Maja was well into her second night in the bombed-out warehouse with the rest of the women and girls. It was a warm evening, but the breeze off the water coming through the blast holes in the walls and the blown-in windows made it bearable. Bedding had been brought in by the guards, and there was plenty of room to lie down on the dusty concrete floor.

Maja now lay with her head on a little pillow, her eyes tired and bleary from the stress, and she looked around the room, which was difficult with the intermittent moonlight. The female captives around her lay on blankets and mats; most slept, but a few, like Maja herself, tossed and turned.

She heard a vehicle pull up and come to a stop outside, and then she heard car doors opening and closing. The three Albanian guards sitting around the room stiffened up and then the scuffle of what sounded like a dozen pairs of shoes echoed up the ruined staircase.

She sat up, as did many of the girls around her.

She couldn't make out the faces of the men who appeared out of the stairwell. Some seemed to be more of the group who had taken over from the Serbians, and they all carried rifles over their shoulders. But there were also four or five silhouettes that didn't match any of the men she'd remembered seeing since arriving here.

A tall and fit man with short hair and a clean-shaven face passed through a shaft of moonlight, looking over the women, but Maja didn't get a good look at him before he moved on towards a back wall. Others followed behind him, and she could see white faces, serious eyes, and well-made but casual clothing. She saw no weapons, but the men moved across the big dark space with true authority.

These guys were in charge, not the guards.

Maja wondered if this meant they would be leaving again soon.

She knew she was being smuggled and trafficked for the purposes of sex, but she had no idea where she was going or who she would be made to serve when she got there.

Not that it mattered. Her life was over; she held no hope for rescue or escape.

Maja looked over the new arrivals and focused again on the tall bald man, now in a darkened corner.

The light was insufficient to reveal any of his facial features, but something about his gait, his posture, and perhaps even his dark aura reminded her of someone she had met before.

. . .

Jaco Verdoorn stood in the darkness of the open third story of the ruined building, inspecting the condition of the women here.

Normally he didn't come personally to any of the safe houses in the pipeline. But this warehouse was the closest point to Old Town Dubrovnik where the Albanians could take their prisoner, so when he was told upon landing that a team had picked up the Europol woman and was bringing her back here, Jaco and his nine men came directly.

He would interrogate her to find out where she gained her intel on the Consortium and, more importantly to him, he'd find out where Court Gentry was, and what he was doing. Once he had this information, he would leave, the Albanians would take the prisoner and kill her, and then they would help guard the merchandise until five a.m., when the shipment would be moved to their transport to market.

Looking around, Verdoorn realized this wasn't the right location for an interrogation, but he was not surprised the Albanians didn't know any better. He wasn't going to beat and torture the woman in front of the merchandise; that would be bad for morale. And even if he took her down to another floor of the building, or did it outside in the back of a car, the sound of her screams would carry in these cavernous spaces and along the wide-open shoreline.

He was still thinking of this, trying to figure out where he could relocate the woman for a proper grilling, when the leader of the Albanian cell took a call on the other side of the room. The South African couldn't understand the words, but the tone made clear the Albanian was concerned, then confused, then angry.

Then scared.

Verdoorn just watched him, his hands on his hips, and he wondered how fucking bad this news could possibly be.

The cell leader ended his call and put his phone in his pocket, then walked over to Verdoorn. The two stepped farther away from the captives so they weren't in earshot, and Jaco prepared himself to receive this obviously bad news.

"What's happened?"

"There has been an attack. In the Old Town, then again on the road. Fifteen minutes east of here. My men are dead, and the woman escaped."

Verdoorn leaned back against the wall. This was bad news for the pipeline and for the Consortium, but he couldn't help but marvel at his target's ability to eliminate anyone in the way of his objective. "Gentry," he said, and the Albanian took it as a question.

"I do not know. No witnesses."

Verdoorn was already pulling his phone to make a call, but he lowered it as he spoke to the leader of the gangsters watching over the women.

"Get these *chots* ready to go. I'm taking 'em right now."

The Albanian didn't know the South African slang word for "whore," but he understood its use in context. He shook his head. "We have to make the transfer at five a.m. It's when the police in the neighborhood switch shifts, and the new cops work for the pipeline. It's only three a.m. now. The cops patrolling the neighborhood out there aren't under our control."

"Are you *dof*? You've lost . . . how many tonight?"

"Seven."

"Yeah. Obviously, mate, your men don't have the skills to deal with this adversary, do they?"

The bearded man shook his head adamantly. "No. It's *not* one man. Your intelligence is wrong. It *can't* be one man."

"It *is* one man doin' the killin', and he is the best there is. You . . . you lot?" Verdoorn looked around the room at the gaggle of armed men. "Not the best. We're doing the fuckin' transfer now. If the cops get in the way, kill 'em." He tapped a button on his phone and broadcast into the earpieces of all nine of his men positioned around the property. "Lion Actual to all Lions. Our target is still out there, and still active. Last seen fifteen minutes east of this poz. I'm callin' the boat to have the tender brought in now, will probably take ten to twenty minutes. I want two long rifles on the roof, scanning east and west; I want two men down at the dock, eyes open on the water. Four more men spread out on the east side of the property watching the hill. Loots and I will escort the women down, eight at a time, but only when the tender shows up ready to take them.

"I'll have this local crew spread out farther on the property, but don't leave security up to them. You know the operator we're up against. We don't know what his game is, but if he is aware of this location, you can bet he will be here. Be ready."

Verdoorn tapped his phone and placed another call, then said, "It's Lion. We've got to move up the delivery." A pause. "Right *bladdy* now! I want that Zodiac in the water and that throttle opened up! Be at the dock in ten minutes."

Dropping his phone in his pocket, the South African pulled his SIG Sauer P226 from its holster under his jacket, thumbed off the safety, and jammed it back into place on his hip. He stepped to an open window and looked out at the night. The water was off to his right, and in front of him was the glow of the Valamar Dubrovnik President Hotel, at the bottom of a hill near the coastline and brightly lit, even at three in the morning. But between the hotel grounds and his position, also near the bottom of the hill, was roughly fifty meters of broken building foundations mostly hidden in tall sea grasses, and well enshrouded in darkness. And higher on the hill, above the hotel, was another resort property, full of green spaces, a roof with a good vantage point on this ruined building, and a road in front of it lined with parked cars. Next to this was an apartment building still under construction, and farther up the hill were more apartments, well-lit but with a good line of sight on this poorly located safe house the Albanians chose.

There were one thousand places in sight for a man of great skill to hide himself in an overwatch position, and Verdoorn couldn't help the prickly sensation that came with the worry that the Gray Man had eyes on him right now.

He turned away from the view, facing the women and girls. In a calm voice, certainly calmer than he felt, he said, "We will all be leavin' in fifteen minutes. You be good girls, and this will go smoothly." His voice lowered, turning ominous. "But if you try anything . . . run, scream, fight, resist. If you try . . . *anything* . . . I'll punish you myself, then I'll feed you to the sharks."

. . .

Maja sat in the middle of the room, staring at the silhouette of the man who was obviously in charge here, and her heart pounded. Not because of the threat the South African had just made, not because of his dark tone, and not because of the gun he'd just revealed and then put away.

These reasons were not why her lower back seized with terror, the hairs on her arms stood up, and she thought she might be sick.

She felt the tremors of terror because, even though she could not see the man's face, she knew exactly who he was.

She recognized his voice, and suddenly things began to fall into place in her mind.

But no comfort came with this newfound understanding. On the contrary, now she was even more certain she'd never, *ever* go home again.

The girl the captors had been calling Maja since the day she was taken was actually named Roxana Vaduva. She was Romanian, twenty-three years old, and a university student in Bucharest, majoring in the performing arts.

But none of that, not even her name, applied to her anymore, now that she'd heard the South African speak. She was certain she'd never be called Roxana again, she'd never go home to Romania again, she'd never live till her next birthday, and of course she would never go back to school.

She knew what was happening now. It all made perfect sense.

Roxana had recognized the big South African the instant she heard his voice in the dark, bomb-shattered warehouse in Dubrovnik, because she had first met him in a nightclub a few weeks earlier, when her sister, an investigator from Europol, sent her in to meet some rich bankers in order to help her with a case. The South African had been called John, had been at the American Tom's side each of the four times she met with him during the week he was in Bucharest. John had never conversed with Roxana directly, but he sat close by, spoke often with Tom's bodyguard, local mob guys, and the employees of the nightclub. Roxana had asked Tom what John's role was, shouting the question into his ear during especially loud techno music, but Tom had simply explained that the man was a subordinate from South Africa, and they were on the business trip together. Roxana had wondered about the man after this.

The bodyguard had been introduced as Sean; he was American, also. He seemed laid-back, especially compared to the bald South African. She'd even caught him drinking a couple of shots of vodka when his boss wasn't looking.

But Tom was the most charming of them all. The minute she'd approached his table, he asked her to sit next to him; he'd poured her Dom Perignon and regaled her with stories about his homes in exotic locations around the world.

She'd been cool and standoffish with the American, despite his instant, obvious fascination with her; Roxana was both a talented actress as well as a confident flirt who knew how to attract men. She didn't sleep around but wasn't above getting a guy to buy her a drink in a bar by flashing a couple of glances his way. She knew how to play a role. She'd performed in theater in Bucharest and Timisoara since grade school, and had even done some commercial work for everything from bottled water to makeup to the Romanian car manufacturer Dacia.

She knew how to sell herself, and she laid the push-pull on thick with Tom, because she saw this as an opportunity to gain the respect of her older, aloof, and dismissive sister.

Then, on their fourth meeting together, Tom had tried to rape her. Roxana had run away, knowing she'd failed to gain anything useful for her sister, but glad the affair was behind her.

Until the previous week, when she was drugged while out with friends and kidnapped by a cabdriver, then taken to a cellar somewhere in Bucharest.

Since that evening she'd felt the panic and desperation, but only tonight did she know, without reservation, that she would not survive.

She'd been cruel to Tom, he'd gotten angrier and angrier each night that she'd spurned his sexual advances, and then she'd fought with him when he tried to overpower her.

Her sister had insisted he was just some kind of a banker, but if he *was*, in fact, involved in this human trafficking ring, she had no doubts that he could now easily get his revenge.

These were incredibly powerful men in charge of this entire operation, and they could make a young Romanian college student disappear with no effort at all.

Her mind weighed her options, and she considered killing herself. All she had to do was stand up and throw herself out of the huge paneless window ten meters to her left. Just leap over the little broken wall and fall to her death. Quick and easy.

But she didn't.

She didn't understand what was holding her back at this point. The desolation she felt knowing that the life she loved was over, to be replaced by a life in hell, was absolute.

But the truth was that she did not want to die.

Not until she took some of these bastards with her.

Roxana Vaduva told herself in that moment that although she was going down, she wasn't going down without a fight.

. . .

Scanning with my binos, I eye the Dubrovnik President Hotel, which looks pretty swanky, but to the right of it I see a large patch of empty darkness by the water. As I do my best to adapt to the low light, forms in the dark begin to take shape.

A concrete pad that looks like it could be used as a little dock juts a few meters out into the bay, and then the hill rising from the water is covered in tall grasses and brush. An unlit three-story building rests halfway up the hill to the road, and although it is standing and appears structurally sound, the window glass is gone and there are several gaping holes in the stone walls. Clearly the building was damaged in the war fought here nearly thirty years ago and has been left unattended since.

It's like this all over the Balkans. Chic tourist areas abut bleak, overgrown warscapes. I saw it in Mostar, and I see it here. The war kicked the shit out of these countries and, even though it ended in the 1990s, there is rubble all around still, evidence of the mayhem from long ago.

I'm flat on my belly on the second floor of an apartment building that's being built higher on the hill and next to a well-lit and new-looking complex of apartment buildings with views to the bay. Through my twelve-power binoculars I see several SUVs parked near one of the buildings, along with a telltale faint light in a doorway: a sentry checking his phone, perhaps.

Scanning around for a minute more, I identify more men, all armed, kneeling in the brush or prone on the roof of the building. But it's hard to see in the dark, even with the binos. If I had an infrared scanner, I imagine I would find a few more jokers down there in the sea grass.

Checking the ones in view again, I recognize an intensity in their posture, an especially alert pace to their head swivels, a weight to their bearing that's hard for sentries to maintain for long.

These assholes are looking for something. Not *something*; me. The asshole who keeps screwing with their business.

I breathe slowly, carefully, trying to minimize any movement at all. If any of these dudes have night vision gear I can only remain covert if I don't move a muscle and keep my body from being exposed to their lenses.

This is obviously the place where the Albanians were heading before I ended them, but I'm surprised by the number of personnel around. If the objective had been to just grab the Europol lady and take her offshore to a waiting boat, as Talyssa suspected, then why are there so many people standing around here looking for trouble?

I'm still pondering this minutes later when I see a brief flash of light out in the bay. A few seconds later it flashes again. The sliver of moon above is hidden by clouds at the moment, and I can't make out anything, but then I see a third flash, and realize this one came not from the water, but from the concrete dock below the large building.

I focus on the area and see a man standing there with a gun and a light. He flashes it again, signaling out to sea.

I can't hear the sound of a motor from here, but I feel certain some small craft is approaching.

Wanting to take advantage of the temporary moonlight, I shift my focus back to the right towards the hillside, and I make out fresh movement in the dark. A cluster of figures moves away from me, down the hill and towards the water from the darkened building in the direction of the concrete dock.

I widen my eyes and zoom in on the group.

Instantly fresh adrenaline begins rushing through me. There are women in the cluster, seven or eight of them, and they are all bracketed by men carrying rifles. Someone in front of the pack is using a weak flashlight beam to help everyone navigate the way through the foliage on the hillside, and to safely get around the grown-over broken concrete strewn all around the hill, wreckage given off by the building when bombs were dropped on it during Croatia's war with the Bosnian Muslims.

The women and girls aren't tied or being held at gunpoint, they're just walking along. Around them armed men continue shepherding them towards the water.

These *have* to be women from the farmhouse in Mostar. No . . . of course they don't have to be, but I really *want* them to be. But why are there only eight women here, if I saw something like twenty-five in the cellar? I ask myself this question, but the answer comes quickly when I see a rigid-hull inflatable Zodiac boat motor up to the platform and a man on board throw a line to the individual with the flashlight.

The Zodiac is larger than a dinghy, but only big enough for ten or so.

I understand what is happening. The Albanians are bringing the women down to the shore in groups so that a tender can take them out to a mother ship before returning again to shore for the next batch.

These are the kidnap victims from Mostar, I feel certain of it now. I'm happy I found the prisoners, happier still that they are alive, but I don't really know what I can do for them right now.

I count something like ten men in view dotted over the dark hillside and imagine there are more I can't see.

I, on the other hand? I've got a dirty pistol with a couple of magazines, a knife, a beaten-up and exhausted body, and a bad attitude.

And that's not going to be enough.

No . . . I can't save the women now, and in this low moment I wonder if I came all this way just to watch them sail off into oblivion.

Shaking the thought from my head, I tell myself that my objective tonight is to find out what boat they board and which direction they sail. I'll figure out the next stage of my operation after that.

I scan back out to sea, look over every vessel I can find. A tanker is darkened a mile or so out; several fishing trawlers are closer to shore, moored or anchored in the bay here.

There is a well-lit yacht just outside the mouth of the bay, partially hidden from my vantage point by a tiny island a couple hundred yards offshore. I can't even tell how big the vessel is because it's hard to judge distance and size over water, especially at night, but from here it looks massive.

I've heard of human smuggling taking place in this part of the world, and the stories often include speedboats that race immigrants across the narrow Adriatic Sea to some town on the eastern coast of Italy, Bari or San Marino being the largest.

But this big motor yacht hardly looks sufficiently inconspicuous to traffic sex slaves to the West.

Scanning back around the overgrown property while the Zodiac loads up, I focus on the blown-out windows of the building in the center. There are multiple points of light on the top floor now. I take them for flashlights, as the intensity increases and decreases randomly, presumably as the devices are moved around.

The remaining women could be held there, but it doesn't really matter, because there's not a damn thing I can do from up here.

The first group is placed in the tender along with two of the armed men, and they begin motoring out into the bay. After just a couple of minutes the clouds cover the moon again, and the tender disappears from view, right before it rounds the little island.

Much to my surprise, I'm pretty sure now it's heading for the yacht.

I back up on the floor of the new construction until I know I'm out of sight of anyone down the hill, and then I grab my gear, sling it all onto my back, and begin running for the staircase.

I've got to get a better look at that yacht, and I can only do so by finding another position to the north of here.

TWENTY-THREE

Roxana Vaduva sat on the inflatable sidewall of the tender, feeling it bounce gently while it motored through the early-morning darkness. She peered ahead, looking for some sort of clue as to where she was being taken, but she couldn't see any obvious destination.

She'd been in the second of three groups of women taken down to the shore and placed on the inflatable boat. Her placement had not been arbitrary; on the third floor of the bombed-out warehouse, a man with what Roxana took to be a South African accent walked up to her, shined a light on her face, and told her she was to move with the second group.

The other women and girls took her continued special treatment to mean she was the insider that one of the women claimed to have been warned about by the Serbian guard. Roxana wasn't a plant, and of course she knew this. But she also realized tonight, for the first time in this ordeal, that she wasn't just another one of the girls. She had a feeling she understood exactly why she was receiving special treatment.

It was only when they rounded the little island and she looked out to the southwest, nearly a kilometer in the distance, that she saw the yacht, well lit and dead ahead. The island had shielded her view before, but now she found the vessel before her magnificent.

As they approached the stern, she caught a glimpse of the name of the boat she was being delivered to. *La Primarosa*.

The tender pulled up alongside the yacht and a ladder was lowered, a line was tossed up to a man on deck, and the women were offloaded. Roxana was still climbing onto the main deck behind the others as the little boat with the inflatable hull turned away and began heading back to shore.

When the eight women in the group stood on the deck, they found themselves temporarily dazzled by the lights, and they squinted and held their hands to their eyes.

Roxana fought through the glare and looked around. It was a stunning vessel, unlike anything she'd ever seen. A teak deck polished to a soft glow. Glistening wood and brass, high-end electronics in the main saloon, and eight or so smartly dressed deck crew and interior staff members standing shoulder to shoulder near the entrance to the saloon. Several more men, all young, bearded, and wearing black polos and gray trousers, stood along the deck railing facing the saloon. Most had rifles around their necks.

These were the guards, Roxana knew, but to her this group looked different than the Albanians, and even more different than the South Africans she'd seen in the warehouse. They were all dark complected and tan, and her first impression was that they might be Greek.

The men looked straight ahead, which surprised Roxana. All the men along this pipeline she had seen had looked the girls up and down as if they were property, but these guards didn't leer at all. She recognized that this crew was more professional than the Romanians, Serbians, and Albanians she had encountered in the past week.

Through the window into the saloon, Roxana saw an attractive woman in her forties wearing a black pantsuit rising confidently out of the spiral staircase to the main deck. She then walked out of the saloon and over to the new arrivals. She spoke to the group in English with what Maja took for an American accent. "Ladies. Welcome. My name is Claudia. We understand the first part of your journey was arduous, but we hope to make your time on board with us unforgettable. Now, if you'll follow me, I'll show you to your quarters."

The stunned women followed Claudia back down the spiral staircase into the belly of the large vessel. In a corridor wide enough for two to move abreast, they passed another pair of suited men in their twenties with submachine guns on their chests.

As they continued down the corridor, Claudia stopped at two open doors facing each other. To the right, Roxana looked in and saw the first group of eight already packed into a stateroom. They sat on the king-sized bed, in the two chairs in the little sitting area, or on the carpeted floor. In the second room, across from the first, she saw an identical stateroom, although this one was empty.

"Ladies," the American said. "These will be your quarters. Step in and make yourselves comfortable. Once we get everyone on board, food and drinks will be provided, and then everyone can get washed up."

The confused women and girls began filing into the room, but as Roxana passed Claudia in the hallway, the American put her hand on the twenty-three-year-old's shoulder. "Not you, Maja. You will be staying somewhere else. Follow me."

The others looked at Roxana with malevolence as she followed Claudia farther down the corridor to the stateroom at the end of the hall. It was the same size as the other two, although it was empty.

The older woman turned around and smiled. "This will be your room."

"*My* room?" She stepped inside slowly and saw a pair of designer jeans, a black turtleneck, and conservative underwear, all laid out for her on the bed. On a rolling hanger next to the bathroom were several zipped-up garment bags, and boxes of shoes were stacked in the corner.

"Yes, dear. You won't be kept with the others."

"But why not?" she asked, though she worried that she already knew.

"You'll find out soon enough," said the woman. "I'll have food sent in. You should take a shower. I'll be back to speak with you before long."

The American turned away and walked back up the hall; Roxana watched her go, then looked down at herself. She was filthy, wearing threadbare cotton pants and a shirt gray with grime given to her in Belgrade. Her long brown hair was tied up, but oily.

Here in the pristine surroundings of the stateroom she was so much more aware of her messy appearance than she'd been in the past week. She was exhausted; her body ached from pervasive stress, hard floors, and cramped conditions; but right now all she wanted to do was get clean. She closed the door to the stateroom—the two men halfway up the hallway never even looked her way—then stepped into the bathroom.

. . .

When I finally do get a view out into the mouth of the bay, it's been twenty minutes since I've seen the yacht. I'd expected it to be right where I last saw it, but as I arrive at the far bank of the island I slow, my eyes locked to the distance. After a few moments I stop, fight to get my binos out of my pack, then bring them quickly to my eyes.

The yacht is there, but much farther out than before. It's sailing to sea with a northwesterly heading, and it's already too far away for me to make out any features, even with my binos.

"Son of a bitch."

I am dejected and exhausted all at once, but then an idea strikes me. I pull out my phone, zoom in as far as I can, and take several pictures of the distant vessel.

And then I call Talyssa.

"Harry?"

"It's me."

Her voice instantly turns hopeful. "What did you find out at the President hotel?"

"I saw the girls."

"Did you see . . . did you see Roxana?"

"I couldn't make out any faces. I'm sorry, I was too far away. They were taken to a yacht offshore."

"A *yacht*?"

"A big one. Where are you now?"

"According to my GPS, I'm in a little town called Stikovica. It's on the coast just fifteen minutes north of Dubrovnik. I ran out of gas. I left the scooter in the woods and am sitting at a train station, waiting for morning so I can rent a car or get on a train or . . . or . . . I don't exactly know *what* I'm doing."

I look to the GPS and see exactly where she is. The yacht will probably motor past her location within minutes, but it will likely be well out to sea, and she doesn't have binoculars that would allow her a chance to get the name off it.

But she might still be able to help.

"If I send you a couple of images, can you lighten them so we can read the name of the vessel on the stern?"

"No problem. I can Bluetooth it to my laptop and do it from here."

"Good." I text her the pictures, then glance up at the lights of the distant boat, barely more than a pinprick now. I know the girls from the red room in Bosnia are on board, and I feel so utterly helpless watching them go.

She says, "I've got the images. This will take me a few minutes."

That yacht is headed north, so even though I don't know its name, who owns it, or where the hell it's going, I'm going to haul ass to the north to be in position to intercept it.

I consider stealing a boat to go after it, but decide against it. A yacht that size probably cruises along at around fifteen to twenty knots; I can steal a car onshore and move three times that speed in the same direction.

Thirty minutes later I've boosted a Volkswagen Golf from a lot next to an apartment complex up the hill, and I'm negotiating my way out of Dubrovnik, being very careful to avoid any roads near where I tipped the van earlier, because there is no doubt they will be full of cops.

And I do my best to avoid cops, even when they *aren't* also evil sex traffickers.

My phone rings, finally, and I snatch it up. "I thought you forgot about me."

Talyssa says, "No . . . I just needed some time to—"

"Save it. I'm picking you up."

"What?"

"I'm ten minutes from Stikovica. Tell me exactly where you are."

She does so. I hang up and stomp the pedal down to the floor.

. . .

Talyssa Corbu is right where she said she'd be, standing near the train station. She climbs in with her pack, and then I floor it back onto the highway as the first hues of dawn appear to the east.

Before she says anything, she puts a couple of candy bars and a bag of chips in my lap and opens a bottled water for me. "The stores were still closed, but I found vending machines outside the station. I thought you might—"

I've already ripped into a chocolate bar and am wolfing it down. I put the water between my knees and unscrew the cap.

She finishes her sentence while staring at me. "—be a little hungry."

Between bites I say, "I thought you said it would just take a few minutes to get the images lightened."

"What? Oh . . . it didn't take long at all."

"You found the name of the vessel?"

"I found more than that." For the first time since I met her, Talyssa is speaking with authority in her voice. "The ship is *La Primarosa*. I went to Vesselfinder.com, which is a website that displays a map with real-time marine traffic, along with other voyage information, using data uploaded from the vessels' transponders to the AIS, the—"

I interrupt, because I know what AIS is. "The Automatic Identification Service."

"Actually, it's the Automatic Identification *System*."

"Right," I say. "But boats and ships turn off their transponders all the time. There is no way in hell a boat full of sex trafficking victims would be broadcasting their location—"

She interrupts me. "It is mandatory for vessels over three hundred tons, but they are allowed to turn it off in certain circumstances. Security threats being one of them. Sometimes wealthy people use their status to fly under the radar, so to speak, citing a safety issue to the passengers. If you have money, all you have to do is say you are worried about piracy, and they give you some latitude to turn it off."

"So, like I said, the *Primarosa* is not reporting to AIS, is it?"

"No. It's not. Not right now. But since I know the name and the general size, I was able to go into Vesselfinder's database of boats and ships and find a listing for it, along with a photograph taken off the coast of Santorini two years ago."

"Primarosa is a girl's name. I've heard it in Spain. Is it a Spanish boat?"

She shakes her head. "It's registered in Denmark to a company based in Cyprus. It's a shell. It only exists on paper to serve as the ownership of the yacht."

"You can't tell who actually owns the company?"

"That's what makes it a shell."

"So . . . a dead end?"

"It would be, except for one thing." She has confidence and energy in her now that I haven't seen before.

"What's that?"

"Me. Maybe I can't intimidate people or shoot people or anything else you do, but forensic accounting and banking is what I did all day, every day, until I came to the Balkans. If you keep driving north, I can work on digging into this yacht and its history. I will find us *something* that might help."

"Okay. North of us is Croatia, and northwest of us is Italy. There is nowhere else in the Adriatic to go, unless they turn around and head south, so I am assuming the yacht is going to Italy."

"Why?" she asks.

"I don't know why it would leave Croatia only to return back to Croatia up the coast."

"Right," she says, but she doesn't seem sold on my theory.

"It will take us six hours to get to the Italian border; I'll need to know something before then about where it's headed."

"I can do this," she says, then she pulls her laptop out of her bag and retrieves her phone. She sets up a Wi-Fi hotspot while I drive, and soon she's pulled up a map and is furiously clicking keys next to me.

. . .

Twenty-seven nautical miles away, the *Primarosa* motored northwest through the warm predawn light at fifteen knots. Standing on the bow and looking out to sea, South African Jaco Verdoorn stood alone. His men did not come aboard with him; with twenty-three women, fifteen crew, and nine Greek mafioso on board, there simply was not enough room on the vessel for nine more men.

Verdoorn sent Loots and the rest of his shock troops north by air to scout out the security situation up there. The *Primarosa* had one more stop to make before its final destination on this journey, just to take on a few more pieces of merchandise, but Verdoorn wasn't worried about Gentry showing up there. The rest of the girls would be locked up on board the yacht; the Greeks had a dozen guns on board. Kostopoulos and his men had maintained the pipeline in the Balkans for years without incident, and the South African had at least enough confidence in them that they could watch over the merchandise while in transit on open water. If the Gray Man was working alone, or virtually alone, there was little chance he was going to attack a forty-five-meter yacht that was out to sea and on the move.

He was legendary, but still, he was human.

No, if Gentry came, it would be at the final destination of this trip, so that was where Verdoorn sent his men.

As Jaco fantasized about getting Courtland Gentry's forehead on the other side of the front sight of his pistol, he heard footsteps behind him on the foredeck. Looking back over his shoulder, he recognized the small stature and gait of Kostas Kostopoulos.

He turned away and returned his gaze to the sea.

Verdoorn relied on the old Greek and his organization, but he didn't much care for the man, personally. He felt Kostopoulos had delusions of his own importance, was pompous and superior acting, and talked back to Verdoorn more than any of the other regionals in the Consortium. Kostopoulos knew that Verdoorn took orders from the Director, so the Greek treated the South African as a glorified errand boy.

Verdoorn would have loved to slit the old bastard's throat right then and toss him over the side of his own luxury yacht for the fish, but Kostopoulos was right about one thing: Jaco Verdoorn did not make decisions autonomously. While he ran this operation fully, he was beholden to the little American in California, the Director.

Kostopoulos said, "They tell me you are berthing in the equipment locker. Unacceptable! I'll gladly give you my stateroom and move some product out of one of the lower-deck cabins for myself."

Verdoorn knew Kostopoulos wouldn't "gladly" do anything of the sort. The foppish old man would be loath to give up his massive quarters on the upper deck. He'd do it, begrudgingly, but he'd martyr himself in the process, and the South African didn't want to be tempted to toss the Consortium's head of Balkan operations over the side because he was tired of hearing him talk.

And anyway, Verdoorn had lived for weeks at a time in the Namibian bush, months at a time in un-air-conditioned sandbagged emplacements in Afghanistan, years at a time in one-room apartments in a poor neighborhood in Johannesburg.

Even though he now earned millions a year for his work, he enjoyed rigor and self-denial. He felt it gave him his edge.

Denying himself luxuries from time to time helped keep strict discipline and order in his mind.

And there was something else Jaco did that he thought kept him sharp. He never sampled the merchandise. Never. He saw his job as that of an enforcer, felt he needed to be detached from the emotions of sex. Depriving himself of his sexual needs, he felt, made him a beast, made him loathe the product paraded before him, and it helped him do what he needed to do to keep strict discipline and order.

Yes, the equipment locker wasn't as posh as Verdoorn's condo in Venice Beach or his ranch outside Pretoria. But it was a hell of a lot better than the shitty Jo'burg flat where he grew up.

He waved the Greek's comment away, but the old man continued.

"If I had known before you boarded that you would be joining us, I would have made proper arrangements for you."

"Last-minute change of plans, Kostas. Since your regional network couldn't end the threat to the shipment, I'm forced to escort it to market personally."

The Greek let out a laugh. "Everyone . . . the Serbs, the Hungarians, the Albanians . . . *everyone* has taken casualties from this."

Verdoorn turned to him. "I don't give two shits about your casualties. I care about this shipment, and I care about the security of the pipeline. If you can't handle either responsibility, I can—"

"You know this man, don't you?"

Verdoorn took a breath, then turned back out to sea. "I know *of* him."

Another brief chortle from the Greek. "Yes, well, I am guessing you have a very healthy respect for his abilities, and that is why you are here now. You can insinuate that my people should have done better with him . . . but you know what they were up against."

Verdoorn let it go. The Greek was absolutely right; it was absurd to insinuate that Serbian and Albanian gangsters who had been trained as simple street thugs and knew nothing of the Gray Man should have been ready to deal with him, but the South African wasn't going to give the Greek the pleasure of admitting this.

Instead Verdoorn turned and leaned against the railing. Looking out over the lavish opulence around him, he found something new to complain about. "I never liked the idea of using this bladdy boat. Too fuckin' showy for a smuggling operation."

Kostopoulos was quick to counter him here, as well. "Showy? Certainly so. But not conspicuous. This vessel sails up and down the Adriatic all the time. Navies and coastal patrol craft know it, customs and immigration know it, the other traffic out here knows it. The ports we visit are used to seeing it, and no one gives it a second glance.

"But if we just threw the merchandise in a couple of low-profile, high-performance speedboats and ran them without lights, then they would be spotted and considered suspicious. The Italians or the Croatian navy would board them, and we'd lose our precious cargo."

Verdoorn made no reply, but the Greek continued his explanation.

"Ever since the migration crisis in the area began, the coastal patrol and navies all over the European Mediterranean have stepped up their interdiction efforts. Boats are getting seized and captains are getting arrested for smuggling every day. But this method of ours is working, and it's working well. We've been boarded a couple of times, but the compartments have never been thoroughly searched."

The South African kept his gaze over the water. "I don't like it. Toss the merchandise in a fuckin' freighter and ship them off to their final destinations."

"We *do* toss the items into freighters. All the time. But those items are destined to work as simple street whores in London or Germany or Holland. Lisbon, Stockholm, and Dublin. Class B or Class C material. But the products we transfer on *La Primarosa*, the Director has estimated, will generate roughly five million euros each through their life cycle. Twenty-three items on board now, another six boarding tomorrow night. That means we are transferring one hundred fifty million euros of product for ourselves and our clients. But this revenue will only be realized if they make it safely to market in good condition. The two days on the water now will improve the selling price of every single one of those items below. What we will do for them here on board, both physically and psychologically, cannot possibly be done in the hull of an ocean freighter."

Verdoorn let it go. Instead he said, "Two of the items are not for sale. You've been told this, correct?"

"I've been told. One is on board now. The one called Maja, who we've stored in cabin four. We pick up the other nonrevenue item tomorrow up the coast. They are calling her Sofia, and she can share Maja's cabin."

The South African looked back out to the morning gloom, the Gray Man at the forefront of his thoughts. He'd have to call Cage soon, give him the bad news. The head of the Consortium was due to come in person to the market in Venice, and this worried Verdoorn even more.

He made the determination to call Sean Hall, Cage's bodyguard, and recommend they not make the trip. The boss wouldn't like it, but Verdoorn deemed it the right move considering the threat.

While he looked out to sea thinking of the difficult phone calls to come, the Greek said, "Interesting. Very interesting. The unflappable Jaco Verdoorn is nervous. Can't say I've seen this out of you before. You really view this American as that much of a concern?"

Verdoorn clutched the railing tightly with both hands and looked to Kostopoulos now. "To me and my boys? No . . . I don't. But to all the other chattel marchin' around with a gun workin' for the pipeline? Yeah . . . yeah . . . he could take them all."

The Greek sniffed out a laugh, but Verdoorn only turned away and headed back up the deck towards his makeshift quarters.

TWENTY-FOUR

Roxana had showered and changed and now she sat on the comfortable bed, her eyes on the door in front of her. The American woman had said she would return, and though the Romanian could see the first hint of morning outside the portal, she had no doubt that her night was not yet over.

And she was correct. The door opened and Claudia entered, followed by one of the ship's smartly uniformed interior crew, who carried a bottle of Bollinger champagne in a bucket, along with two crystal flutes.

What the hell is this? Roxana thought.

While the male crew member set the items down and began removing the foil from the cork, Claudia said, "It must feel glorious to take a nice hot shower after all you've been through."

Roxana made no reply, so the American continued. "The other girls are taking their showers now. Don't worry about them. They will be fed and clothed and attended to, same as you. Well . . . not the same as you, but more than adequately." Claudia smiled. "Certainly more than what they are used to back home. You, too, right?"

"I had no complaint about my home."

"Of course not, dear. Everyone says that at first. Then they see what they've been missing, what is available to them in this world, and they come around." She put her hand on Roxana's knee. "I promise you, you'll come around, and you'll never look back." There was a comfort and an assuredness in the woman's voice; it seemed to Roxana to be practiced, like one of her professors in college who'd been teaching the same class year after year.

She wondered how many girls had sat here on this bed looking at the American woman with bewilderment, just like she was doing now.

Roxana asked, "Who are you?"

"My name is Dr. Claudia. We don't do last names here."

"A doctor of what?"

"I am a psychologist." The cork popped, jolting Roxana, but Claudia just laughed. The champagne was poured by the crew member as the ladies looked on.

The man soon left the cabin, closing the door behind him. As soon as it shut, the Romanian asked, "Why is there a psychologist on board?"

"I provide services as needed," the American said as she handed the younger woman a flute of champagne. "Every one of the ladies on board is unique and important, and they are all getting special treatment. But you and one other young lady who will be joining us tomorrow are the absolute cream of the crop."

"What is so special about us?"

The doctor's teeth were white and straight; she bared them easily with her smile. "So much is special about you. So much, indeed. But you're getting the star treatment, darling, because of where you are going."

Roxana felt a tightening in the pit of her stomach. "Where . . . where am I going?"

"You have been personally selected by my employer." Claudia kept up her smile. "The director of our entire global organization, in fact."

"Selected?" she said, but the woman did not address what she meant.

But Roxana knew, and she was pretty sure Claudia knew that she knew.

Claudia said, "You seem like a smart girl, so you know who he is. The two of you have already met."

Roxana looked down at the Bollinger in her hand, as yet untouched.

"Yes. I know what this is all about. The American. Tom. I met him in Bucharest."

The doctor replied, "I don't know what name he gave you, but we call him the Director. He is our leader, but the man who runs day-to-day operations is here on board, and he is who I report to. He rarely comes on these voyages, so it's a very special night for us."

"You are talking about the South African. What is his name?"

The older woman cocked her head in surprise. "You are very inquisitive, aren't you?"

"Aren't most girls? How many have sat right here like I have?"

After a pause, the answer came. "Quite a few. You'll meet some of them where you are going, I'm sure."

"You do this all the time, don't you?"

"We make these journeys regularly, yes." Claudia straightened up and took a slow sip of champagne. "Let's talk about what you want in life, Maja."

"I want to be called by my real name. My name is—"

"No. We don't use real names. It's for your own security, and I'm sure you've already been told this at all the other stops on the pipeline."

Roxana said nothing, and the American placed a hand on top of hers and squeezed. "I understand this is all . . . new, and more than a little stressful. I'm going to help you with that part of this. Believe me, I'm only here for your benefit."

"Why are you being nice to me? Do you think I'm just going to go along with this because you hand me expensive clothes and give me a glass of champagne and squeeze my hand?" Roxana pulled her hand out from under the doctor's.

"Maja, we all have bitter pills we need to swallow in life, to get us to where we want to be. A lot will be asked of you in the next few weeks and months, but so much more will be offered to you. You will be treated well, like a princess, in fact, if only you do your part."

"And my part is, is *what*? To submit to rape?"

Claudia's smile seemed forced now, but it persevered. "It's not rape if you want it, and you *will* want it. We decided you would be a perfect fit for the Director. He agreed, of course, and he wanted no expense spared in bringing you to him."

"If I am so fucking special, why was I kept in dungeons, why was I chained, why was I forced to go to the toilet in buckets?"

"The pipeline is mandatory for all of our girls. As in life, you must experience true hardships to appreciate true comforts. This is part of the process. But your difficult time is over, dear. Now it is time to see what is possible for you if you only play your part. I was brought in years ago to refine this process, to make the experience more pleasurable for both the women and the men. My focus is on helping you see the opportunities before you, and not focus on the negative aspects of your new life.

"We like to think of the pipeline as something they have in the American military called boot camp. Just like in the military, new recruits go through a difficult but crucial indoctrination period.

"But unlike those in the military, you and the other girls will be making a lot of money, living in surroundings you could only have imagined in your wildest dreams."

"People choose to join the military. We did not—"

"Conscripts don't choose. Look. You were drafted into this; I won't pretend you were not. But I promise you it's the best thing that ever happened to you.

"Look at this beautiful superyacht, for example. Have you ever been on anything so magnificent in your life?"

"The girls down the hall are staying eight to a room."

Claudia shrugged. "Boot camp never looked so good to any young soldier, I promise you that."

Roxana shook her head in utter disgust. "But . . . you are a doctor? How can you live with yourself?"

She saw the American's placid demeanor falter and the tone of her voice darken slightly. "I live very well, dear, thank you for asking." Claudia stood, headed for the door, and opened it. Right outside an armed guard leaned against the wall, a young man with a dark crew cut and a thick monobrow low over his dark eyes.

The doctor said, "Enjoy as much champagne as you want, dear. This door will remain open as long as the glassware is in the room. We want to make sure you don't accidentally break the flute or the bottle and injure yourself." She added, "From experience we've learned that the first night on board is the most challenging for the girls."

Roxana's stomach twisted, because she took this to mean that someone sitting where she now sat had used shattered glass to end her life.

Dr. Claudia flashed her teeth again and lightened her tone. "I'll pay you another visit this afternoon. Get some sleep, you'll feel better then." She turned and headed up the passageway towards the other rooms.

Maja drank down the Bollinger with a trembling hand.

· · ·

I dream of the women in the red room again. Of imploring eyes, dread, and heartbreak. I try to open the door to the room to free them, but it won't move, no matter how hard I pull.

And I can't get out, either.

I'm helpless. As helpless as they are.

And it's all my fault.

My head falls, then lurches back up. I'm holding on to a steering wheel on a highway, driving at one hundred kilometers per hour, and veering off the road. In front of me to the left is a concrete retaining wall, and I'm feet away.

I correct, steering to the right, jolting upright fully after being startled so completely from a dead sleep. The sky is filled with daylight, so I'm lucky the highway around me is all but empty.

Suddenly I remember where I am. The drive up the coast of Croatia, the hunt for the yacht somewhere out to sea.

I survived two gunfights and one fistfight in the past three days, but I almost got smoked driving into a retaining wall.

My passenger is next to me. "Be careful," she admonishes, unaware that I just dozed behind the wheel because her face is still in her laptop screen.

I say nothing.

After a few moments she looks up at me. "If this yacht is part of something known as the pipeline, can we assume it goes the same direction every time?"

I rub my eyes. "Not really, no."

"Why not? A pipeline doesn't move. They are pipes. Fixed in place."

"I think your analytical brain is looking at this too literally."

She deflates a little, and she's back to looking like a scared, helpless kid in an instant.

But not for long.

"What if it was all we had to go on? What if we just assumed that the yacht with these women on it has picked up other women and taken them to the same place?"

"What are you getting at?"

"I researched the vessel all the way back to when and where it was built, then followed the ownership until now. Three months ago it was sold from one corporation to another, the shell that owns it now. But I researched the previous shell, and see a similar pattern in behavior to the new one."

"Meaning they both incorporated in the same way, bank in the same place, that kind of thing."

"You are oversimplifying, but that's essentially what I mean."

"So whoever really operates the *Primarosa* also operated it before three months ago. How does that help us find it?"

"Both before and after the transfer it broadcast its transponder in some areas in the northern Adriatic."

"I thought you said it didn't use its transponder because rich assholes don't have to."

"Normally the *Primarosa* sails dark, but certain ports mandate that the transponder be turned on before allowing vessels to anchor offshore, for the safety of ship traffic coming and going. I was able to do research on the yacht's history, and I found several ports where it has appeared multiple times."

"Which ports?"

"Athens, Santorini, Naxos, and Mikonos, all in Greece. Istanbul, Turkey. Bari, Naples, and Venice, in Italy. Dubrovnik and Pula, in Croatia."

"I don't know where that last place is."

"The Istrian peninsula. Three hours north of here. I think that's where they are headed now."

"Why not Venice? That's north of here, too."

She shrugs. "Looking over the dates, I see some stops in Pula before Venice. Maybe they will do that, maybe they'll go somewhere different." She added, "Pula is on the way to Italy, anyway, so we might as well try there."

I prefer intelligence a hell of a lot more solid than this, but sometimes you have to take what you get.

I type the destination in my GPS and see that we can be there by a little after noon. I ask her to look up the cruising speed of the yacht, and from this we do the math. The *Primarosa*, if it is in fact going to this port in northern Croatia, will not arrive before nine thirty p.m. tonight.

That gives Talyssa and me an entire afternoon and evening to prepare to greet it. It's a gamble to commit to one location without being certain, but the Europol analyst seems like she knows what she's talking about. I haven't slept in almost a day and I'm beat, but if Talyssa can do some of the logistical work while I drive, we can both catch a few hours' sleep once we get to Pula.

"All right," I say. "Let's go there. We don't know if they are coming ashore or not, so I'm going to have to be ready to board the yacht."

"By yourself?"

I laugh a little. "You offering to tag along?"

She just shakes her head. "I'd be in your way." She's right, of course. "No chance we can just go to the police, is there?"

I shake my head. "The yacht goes to that port town because they have some influence over the police there. That's been their MO everywhere else."

"So what *can* I do?"

"We need a room near the port, ready for us when we arrive."

She nods. "I'll book something. What else?"

"I'll need a speedboat and some diving gear. You can make some calls before we get there."

She nods, types a note in her laptop, then looks back up at me. "I don't know who you are, and I don't know what you are capable of. But there is no way you can rescue all those girls."

"That's not my plan. My plan is, I'm going to get onto that boat to wrap my hands around somebody in charge. And if I have to kill any goons that get in my way, I'll do that, too."

To her credit, Talyssa has become dramatically more accepting of my dirty work since we met. She doesn't blanch at the prospect of me killing again. But she says, "You don't seriously think the head of the operation is on board that yacht, do you?"

I shrug. "There's *somebody* on there who can give us some answers. I'm going to beat the shit out of them till they talk."

She just stares at me a few seconds, and I know what's coming.

She says, "That is literally the only strategy you know, isn't it?"

I laugh again. I'm so tired I'm getting goofy. "Like I have a strategy. It should be pretty obvious that I make this shit up as I go."

"Wonderful," she mutters sarcastically, and then she looks back down at her screen to begin searching for an apartment to rent.

. . .

Just after noon we arrive in Pula, park the stolen car at a bus station, and then take a cab to a rental car office on the other side of town. We get a two-door Honda using my fake passport and credit card, and only after leaving a large deposit. Then we head for the marina, stopping along the way to drink espressos and eat a small lunch in a café.

At the marina I drop her off after reminding her of exactly what I need, and then I drive to a nearby scuba shop.

Here I buy a complete scuba rig along with fins, a mask, and a wetsuit. Fully equipped, I next drive to a marine-supply business, and I buy several items I think I might need to board the ship from its mooring line tonight, and several more "just in case" odds and ends.

I also stop at a hardware store and a pharmacy, and then, with the car laden down, I return to the marina two hours after I left Talyssa. I find her standing on board an eight-meter-long Mano Marine speedboat with a 350 horsepower Mercury Verado engine. I'd told her I needed at least 180 horsepower, so she has greatly exceeded her mandate.

My plan is simply to motor out a few hundred yards away from *La Primarosa* when it moors here later this evening, and I don't need a particularly muscular boat to do this, but when it comes to gear, I do subscribe to the mantra that more is more.

I'd been worried about her renting anything too ostentatious and conspicuous, but the boat she found for us has a simple, unassuming white hull and hardly looks like the powerful machine that it is.

"Nice," I say. "Any problems with the paperwork?"

"Had to sign my life away, basically."

"I'll try to return it in one piece."

She takes this as a joke and lets it slide with an eye roll, and I begin hauling gear out of the car to place in the little hold belowdecks.

. . .

An hour later we are locked in our rented flat within sight of the marina, and we treat our various cuts and bruises with first-aid items I bought from the pharmacy. Talyssa is in pain, her shoulder is killing her, and I doubt the pills I bought over the counter will do much more than blunt the sensation, but she takes them anyway.

Then I begin preparing equipment. I've bought a small utility anchor and fifty feet of ultralight braided anchor line, and I attach these, then pull a can of spray-on rubber coating out of the bag from the hardware store. I apply this all over the four-pound anchor, using the entire can and covering it completely with the quick-drying black rubber compound.

I put the line and the anchor in a black backpack and stage it by the door.

I also assemble my scuba equipment, clean my pistol, and take care of other small details.

Then Talyssa and I both set the alarms on our phones to go off in four hours. The plan is to wake up at eight p.m., and to be down at the speedboat ready to go by nine.

Talyssa lies down fully clothed on one of the twin beds, while I pull a pillow and a comforter off the other and toss it in the bathroom, then lie down, unholster my Glock, and place it on the floor next to me.

I pray for sleep, but I also pray that I won't dream of the red room yet again.

TWENTY-FIVE

The clouds over Los Angeles hung low in the morning, trapping the air and the exhaust of four million morning commuters. Street-level Hollywood was smogging up a couple hours after dawn, but high in the Hollywood Hills, the air was somewhat cleaner and markedly cooler.

Ken Cage wore a Harvard sweatshirt and an LA Kings ball cap to ward off the slight chill, and he sat at a canopied glass table near the deep end of his infinity pool, sipping coffee with his sandaled feet up on the table. Before him his landscaped and manicured two acres cascaded down a steep slope. Beyond that, Hollywood was splayed out flat and wide, and in the distance the skyline of downtown LA seemed to lord over the entire scene.

While he sipped coffee and gazed out at the view, all three of Cage's kids lounged around the pool, having just finished breakfast. This was family time, before Dad started his workday, but all of Cage's kids stared into screens held in their hands.

His wife, Heather, sat next to him, and she also held a tablet computer in her lap. She read aloud an article about a museum exhibit one of her friends had recently curated, but Ken Cage barely heard her.

As he gazed out at the view, his mind wasn't focused on his family, on his property, or on his work; it was focused on the next shipment of girls to Rancho Esmerelda. Two would be arriving from Asia in less than a week. Two more he'd see in Venice on his upcoming trip there, and then they would be flown back to America with Jaco in a jet owned by one of the Consortium's shells.

There would be other new girls coming, but these four he'd chosen by hand, and he was looking forward to enjoying them all.

His most anticipated, without question, was the snotty Romanian bitch who'd spurned his advances but drunk his champagne, had come to his hotel suite but refused to sleep with him, had slapped him hard across the face when he tried to overpower her, like he'd done so many times before with so many of his conquests.

The night he'd met the drop-dead-gorgeous brunette, she'd been all too ready to talk to him and to drink his booze, but she'd also seemed a little standoffish and dismissive. And when, on the third night in a row they'd seen each other, she told him he was too old for her, he'd leaned over to Jaco and demanded she be delivered on a platter to him in the USA, no matter the cost. Jaco had protested; he claimed to sense a rebelliousness in her that would be more trouble than she'd be worth, but Cage liked this trait. In fact, her defiance ranked just below her beauty in reasons why the American ordered the young woman be rolled up and placed in the pipeline for delivery.

He wasn't worried about rebelliousness, about defiance. At the moment, Cage knew, the girl sat aboard Kostas Kostopoulos's yacht, getting mind-fucked by Dr. Claudia Riesling. He knew Riesling would rid her of part of her rebelliousness, and he'd rid her of the balance of it himself when she got here.

So now the girl was on her way. He didn't remember what she told him her name was—there were so many women he met on his recruiting trips, after all—but he'd been told Riesling was calling her Maja. She, the Thai, the Indonesian, and the Hungarian would be the newest members of Rancho Esmerelda, just seventy minutes north of the Hollywood Hills, and he and his protection detail would make the drive up there whenever he could get away from his duties at home and at work.

His thoughts returned to his present surroundings, but only until he saw his personal protection agent, Sean Hall, step out of the two-thousand-square-foot pool house tucked deep into lush landscaping on the other side of the patio. The wiry and tan blond made his way purposefully along a small fieldstone footpath, past a pair of koi ponds, and towards the family he protected. He had iPhone EarPods in his ears, and his gesticulations as he walked suggested to Cage that the ex–Navy SEAL was fully engaged in conversation.

Ken looked down at his watch and saw it was not yet eight. Hall didn't normally report in till nine thirty.

The two men made eye contact and Hall ended his call, pulled out the EarPods, and stepped onto the patio.

Charlotte, Ken's sixteen-year-old daughter, sat on a lounge chair by the pool away from her parents. "Hey, Sean. You been surfing?"

He kept walking, but smiled as he replied. "As much as I can. You've been practicing on your board?"

"A little bit," she said unconvincingly.

"Waves have been up at Zuma Beach. We're still going next Wednesday morning, right?"

"Yeah, I'm down," she replied, and then Charlotte returned her attention to her phone.

Sean passed and high-fived twelve-year-old Juliet, also on her phone on a lounge chair, and waved across the pool to ten-year-old Justin, who sat watching a YouTube video on his iPad.

Ken Cage's head of security stepped up to his table, and Heather finally took her eyes off her tablet. "You're early. Want me to get Isabella to bring you out some coffee so you can join us?"

The forty-year-old shook his head. "I'm good, but thanks. I just need to talk to the boss here a second."

"Then you both are starting work early this morning, I guess." She said it with an admonishing tone, but it was clearly focused on Ken and not Sean.

Cage saw a serious look on his bodyguard's face, so when Heather's eyes drifted back down to her device, Ken jerked his head towards the house.

Hall nodded, indicating that whatever he had to say did, in fact, need to be said in private.

Cage finished the last of his coffee in a swig as he stood. "Just give me a couple minutes. I'll be right back."

His wife replied, "Ask Isabella if she can bring me a refill."

"Will do, honey."

The fifty-four-year-old entered his home office a minute later, followed by his security chief. As soon as he made it to his desk, Cage glanced down at his computer screens, getting his first look of the day at the international markets. While taking in the data, he said, "Heather kicks me in the nuts when I work before nine, Sean. Make it quick."

Hall shut the door to the office. "Can we get the white noise?"

Without looking, Cage reached for the remote next to him and tapped a button, and the ambient noise on the high-end entertainment system came on. Still looking over the markets, he said, "What's got you so fired up this morning?"

Hall said, "I spoke with Verdoorn a few minutes ago."

"That'll do it."

"He's . . . he's concerned about this clown who has been attacking points along the pipeline."

Distractedly, Cage said, "Believe me. I've been made aware."

"Right. Sir, in light of all the information he's provided me . . . I'm going to go ahead and suggest we cancel your trip to Italy tonight."

Cage swiveled his gaze away from his monitors quickly. "You've got to be kidding me."

"Jaco has filled me in on some of this threat's career exploits. He's the real deal. The Albanians didn't stop him in Croatia, the danger to the pipeline seems to be ongoing, and until White Lion puts a lid on it, I feel like it's in our best interests to curb your travel into that theater of operations."

Cage rolled his eyes. "Theater of operations? It's a fucking tourist trap where we're going."

"For tourists, it is. But for you, sir, it's an unnecessary security risk."

Cage sighed like a child, then sat down at his massive desk and swiveled his chair so he could face his phone. "We're calling Jaco right now." He punched numbers, then waited. He neither knew nor cared what time it was over in wherever the hell Jaco was.

He put the call on speaker and the two men listened to it ring in silence.

After a click and a pause, they heard, "Verdoorn."

"Encrypted," Cage said, and Verdoorn replied.

"Confirming encrypted. Hello, sir."

"You've got Sean here saying he wants me to cancel my trip."

The South African had clearly been expecting the call. He replied, "I think that would be best."

Cage sighed again, louder, slower, and more dramatically this time. "So some asshole running around in Croatia has control over my itinerary now? Telling me where I can and cannot go? Is that it?"

Verdoorn replied patiently. "He's not just some asshole, sir. He—"

"Are you telling me you don't have this situation under control?"

"Yes, sir. I am telling you that, exactly. And until we do, I need you to stay away from this area. If it were anyone else, he'd already be dead and in the dirt. But he's the Gray Man."

Now Cage shouted with rage. "I don't give a shit what *color* that motherfucker is! No one is going to get in the way of my business interests. I run this show! *I* do!"

It was silent for several seconds, and then Verdoorn's disembodied voice resumed. "Hall? I believe this is where you chime in."

Sean Hall was clearly more intimidated by his boss than Verdoorn was. He nodded to the phone, then looked to Cage. "Sir, sorry for pointing this out. But the fact is, your business doesn't have anything to do with why you want to go to Venice. The market would continue with or without you. I understand you want to meet with some of the players, but at the end of the day this is a personal vacation, and I don't see why we should risk—"

Cage interrupted. "I don't believe what I'm hearing from you two chickenshits."

Hall said, "Sir . . . it's not fear, it's risk management. We take threats seriously. I understand you want to retain free movement, despite the—"

Cage waved his hand in the air wildly. "I'm going to Italy. This asshole doesn't know who I am, or that I even exist. Verdoorn, you and your shit-hot South African badasses will take care of the Gray Man, and Hall, you and your shit-hot American badasses will protect me while I'm there if Verdoorn doesn't do his job. Am I understood by you both?"

Hall made no reply, but Verdoorn had some fight left in him on the matter. "The merchandise going to market in Venice. You've examined the best of the lot. We can have it over to you in just a couple of days. Stay home this time, boss."

The short bald man launched to his feet now. "Jesus Christ, I'm surrounded by pussies!" Though he was four full inches shorter than Hall, he jabbed a finger in the man's muscular chest as he spoke, his words meant for both the man in front of him and the man on the phone. "You two need to grow some fucking balls and do your jobs!"

Verdoorn remained eerily calm. "We *are* doing our jobs. It's our job to give you our fair assessment. I am in charge of overseas operations, and Mr. Hall is in charge of your personal security."

Cage shouted at the speakerphone. "Who's in charge of signing your fucking *checks*?"

The door to the office opened, and Cage and Hall spun towards the movement. Heather Cage leaned in with a worried look. "Everything all right, hon?"

Verdoorn began to speak, but Cage muted the phone. "Sure, babe. Just work."

She looked back and forth between the two men. "Sean, you look like you just ate a rotten peach."

Hall put on a quick smile. "Ha. No, ma'am. We're just working out details of the trip to Switzerland. Your husband wants to run around faster than we can keep up, but we'll take good care of him."

She gave a pout, then eyed her husband. "Sean knows what's best, Ken."

"Of course he does," he replied, and she left the room.

The conversation between the three of them continued for a minute more, but Cage managed to keep his voice down. Neither the South African former soldier and intelligence officer nor the American former Naval Special Warfare chief petty officer pushed back again on their boss's impending travel plans.

Together Hall and Verdoorn spit out a reluctant "Yes, sir," and the matter was resolved.

After Cage took a few calming breaths, he sat back down at his desk. In a softer tone, he said, "All right. Jaco . . . what do you need?"

"You have declined my one request, so I will proceed as follows: My men are already in Venice, where they are performing an advance reconnaissance of the market. I am on board the vessel with the shipment from Dubrovnik. We will moor off Croatia tonight to accept delivery of items traveling the northern route, and then head to Italy tomorrow morning. My men and I will provide an outer cordon for the market's security, and if the Gray Man should arrive, we will deal with him."

"There's nothing else you need?"

"I have all the resources I require at this time," Verdoorn said in a clipped tone.

Cage turned his attention to his bodyguard. "Sean . . . anything I can do for you short of locking myself in my office and hiding under my desk?"

"No, sir." He looked utterly defeated, and Cage liked this look on the normally easygoing and self-assured man.

"You gonna keep me safe?"

"Of course, sir," he said with a nod. And then, "Absolutely. I'll coordinate with Jaco offline and we'll take care of things."

. . .

Fifteen minutes later Hall was back in his pool house apartment, an icy 1.5-liter bottle of Grey Goose from the freezer in his hand and his EarPods in his ears. He was on another encrypted call, for the third time today, with Jaco Verdoorn, while he drank his fourth shot of vodka of the day.

Hall said, "Cage is a prick. But he fuckin' pays like no one else."

Verdoorn said, "We'll earn our money on this one. We have to plan on the Gray Man being there, in Venice."

"How can he possibly know—"

"He seems to be getting his intel on the fly. He learned something at the Mostar way station that led him to Vukovic. He learned something from Vukovic that led him to Dubrovnik. I think it's possible that he learned something in Dubrovnik that will lead him to Venice."

"Aren't you stopping to pick up more girls before Venice?"

"Yes, but we've moved the location. He won't find us there."

"All right," Hall said. "I can put guns and guys on my protectee, but I can't go out there and whack your assassin for you."

Verdoorn replied, "I suggest you bring Cage into Venice normally, the way you always do. Assuming we don't get Gentry before tomorrow night, we will attempt to acquire our target as he closes on his target."

Hall stared at his phone, then swigged more icy vodka straight from the bottle. "So you are saying my principal will be in the center of a manhunt. Like . . . like *bait*."

"It's a big world, mate. We can only find Gentry if we draw him to us. I have no bloody clue if the Gray Man knows about Cage, or the market, or even if he knows about Italy. I just know it's better to respect your enemy's capabilities. Something I learned along the way, and something they didn't teach our employer in business school, apparently."

"Christ, Jaco. That's a hell of a risk for the Director."

"That's right, it is. But I told Cage to stay home. He refused, so I'm gonna make the best of it and use him to bag my prey. And that means you and your men better be on bloody point, because this bastard's got the skill to take out your principal if you let your guard down for an instant."

"We'll be ready," Hall said.

Verdoorn hesitated a moment, then said, "I can hear it in your voice. You're drunk."

"I'm not drunk." Hall swigged another sip. "But I'm drinking. The boss is covered, why not?"

The South African snapped back, "Keep your fuckin' head, Hall! I see any evidence you aren't one hundred percent in Italy, and I'll tell the Director about your little problem with the bottle."

If Verdoorn expected Hall to melt in fear of this threat, Hall surprised him by saying, "I can hear it in *your* voice, Jaco."

"Hear what?"

"I can tell that you are excited by the prospect of going after this Gentry. Just make sure you don't put my principal in unnecessary danger to draw him out."

"Your principal, my employer, put *himself* in unnecessary danger. You and I will untangle him from it. It's what we do as professionals, Hall. You're the shield, I'm the sword. We'll both do our jobs."

"Yeah, right," replied the American. "I'll talk to you tomorrow."

TWENTY-SIX

Roxana slept fitfully for a few hours, but after waking and eating the best meal she'd had in years, she was told she needed to dress for a meeting with Dr. Claudia.

She didn't have a clock, but through the portal she could see that the sun was high in the sky, so she assumed it was early afternoon when the American entered, the woman's light but not altogether trustworthy smile on full display.

For an hour Claudia asked questions of the young Romanian woman, about her life, her education, her hopes, and her dreams. Roxana kept her answers short, clipped, and often noncommittal; sometimes she outright lied. In between, she asked questions of her own about the pipeline, none of which were answered by the psychologist.

Then the older woman began talking about money and glamour, told her how excited she was that Roxana—she called her Maja, of course—would soon be taken in by a powerful and successful man who would shower her with attention and adoration.

Roxana just stared back at her. "Are you trying to brainwash me?"

Claudia's smile faded a little. "I don't look at it like that. I'm here to appeal to you, to get you to understand how lucky you are."

"I am being forced into sexual bondage. The other women on board are going to be sold into sexual bondage. *You* understand *that*, right?"

With a frustrated sigh, the American responded with, "You need to see this as your liberation."

"My *liberation*?"

"Of course. You will come to America, live like a princess, and experience things you never would have had the chance to experience without this opportunity."

"Like rape? I'm sure I could get that at home."

Claudia frowned. It was clear to Roxana that this line of reasoning from the doctor had worked before, and the older woman was frustrated by Roxana's reluctance.

The doctor said, "We will need to spend quite a lot of time together, you and I. I promise, by the time you reach your destination, you will be so happy about everything that has happened to you, and thankful to me for helping you digest it all and appreciate it." She smiled broadly. "You have to be at least a little excited that you're getting to come to America?"

"What makes you think I want to come to America?"

"Every little girl's dream where you come from."

Roxana cocked her head. "Maybe my mother's. Not mine. Romania is actually a very nice country now."

"I'm certain it is, dear." It was the most disingenuous-sounding thing Dr. Claudia had said so far. "But the West Coast is magical, you will see."

"Does every American think that the rest of the world is just dying to immigrate? I'm not. I was in school; I come from a good family. I didn't *want* to be kidnapped."

The American woman sighed. "It is so crucial that we make progress. There are eyes upon us."

"What does that mean?"

"It means, if you come along in this process with a more positive attitude, then it will only help you."

"So . . . I should play a role in my own abduction?"

Claudia looked to the ceiling, obviously frustrated. She said, "Good things are in store for you, young lady." Then she darkened considerably. "But, please, for your own good, listen to one piece of advice from me."

"Which is?"

"The South African. John. Do what he says, when he says it. He is *not* a gentle man. He would fall in great disfavor with the Director if anything happened to you, but the Director would forgive him in time, and John knows it. The organization needs him to keep the operation running smoothly, so that won't protect you. Trust me, John is the cruelest person I've ever met and, frankly, dear, in this organization, that is saying something."

She added, "I am here to help you along your path, but this path will have some bumps along the way. John, and the Greek who owns the yacht, they are the bumps you'll have to contend with before I get you to your final destination."

Maja didn't know what the doctor meant by any of this, but she knew it was nothing good.

• • •

I sleep like the dead until my alarm goes off—no dreams about the girls, but they are the first thing I think about when I wake. I feel the aches and pains of the fight in Dubrovnik, the fatigue of the days of little rest, but at least I'm doing better than I was when I got to town.

I stumble into the bathroom and toss water on my face, then go check on Talyssa. I find her awake, but lying in the fetal position on the bed.

"You okay?"

"Everything hurts. My neck, my shoulder, my arm, my back. I can barely move."

"Some asshole must have flipped your van over last night."

She smiles a little at this and makes herself sit up. We both take anti-inflammatories, drinking them down with bottled water, and then she brews coffee in the pot in the kitchen, which we consume quickly, purely for the caffeine.

At nine p.m. we head out the door, our arms full of gear.

At nine thirty we are standing by the speedboat bobbing in its slip at the marina. I have a perfect view of the south from here, so I'm scanning the night with my binos. There are a number of vessels on the water, but my eyes fix on an especially bright light that grows by the minute. It's a couple of miles out in the sea lane, and while I don't know it's *La Primarosa*, the general size looks about right. It's a very large vessel, but smaller than a cruise ship or one of the big ferries that deliver people and cargo up and down the coast.

Each minute the vessel nears I become more and more certain I am looking at my target, and I know that if it is planning on coming to port here at Pula, it will change course to put it on a northeasterly heading, and then begin slowing.

But the vessel just keeps heading to the north, making no correction to bring it closer to Pula.

When it is still a mile or so to the south without any noticeable change in course, I can see well enough to recognize the outline of the yacht I saw last night.

I say, "She's the right boat, but she should be turning this way, and she's not. Wherever they're heading, it's not here."

Talyssa is crestfallen that her theory is incorrect. "What are we going to do?"

I look at her, then at the boat below me. "No chance you know how to drive one of these, is there?"

She shakes her head in bewilderment. "Me? No."

I heft my gear bags on my shoulder. "No problem. You're about to get one hell of a kick-ass lesson."

"You want me to go out there? On the water? And drive the boat?"

I climb aboard and take her hand without replying. She comes along, but reluctantly.

"Yeah," I reply. "It'll be fun."

I fire the engines and we head off through the marina, slowly and inconspicuously at first, but soon I'm pushing the throttle forward and we pick up speed.

The tiny forested island of Brijuni sits at the mouth of Pula Bay, and I decide to try to shoot between it and the shore in hopes of getting ahead of my target. Passing a superyacht in a speedboat wouldn't necessarily be suspicious in itself, but I don't know how alert those on board will be, so I don't take any chances.

I'm going to follow them from the front, because my boat can turn a hell of a lot faster than theirs, and if they do go into port somewhere up the coast, I'll have no trouble turning around and keeping up the pursuit.

Soon we're making twenty, then thirty, then nearly forty knots, while the yacht, now on the other side of the island off to our left, is probably doing about fifteen.

The water is choppier here between the two land masses, and the faster we go, the harder we slam back down on the surface. It's a rough ride, and our aching bodies protest every single moment of it, but once I'm clear of the island I find myself slightly north and about two miles east of the vessel. It's open water now, so I throttle up even further and head slightly west, converging slowly on the yacht's current heading.

I begin coaching Talyssa on how to operate the twenty-four-foot speedboat. I save a little time in my tutorial by skipping the safety features, because what I have in mind tonight is so fucking unsafe I'm not terribly concerned about her burning her hand on the outboard or slipping on the wet deck. Instead, I just give her the basics.

Soon I'm confident she can pull off the simple task I have for her, and she sits there and stares at the megayacht. She's holding on for dear life and looking sicker by the minute as we bounce along the slowly undulating sea, but I can tell she's still thinking about her sister.

I figure it's a hell of a thing to not know if your sibling is alive or dead, but to know, either way, that you were the one who put your sibling in peril . . .

But then I remember that I know *exactly* what that feels like.

I have skeletons in *my* closet, too.

. . .

Dr. Claudia Riesling entered the main-deck saloon of the *Primarosa* and sat down next to Jaco Verdoorn. The South African was finishing a dinner of pork tenderloin, and while he ate he communicated to his men, already at the yacht's final destination in Venice. She heard him talk about the American man who had been causing difficulties to the pipeline, and their efforts to lay traps for him around the Venice market the next evening.

She planned on remaining on the yacht during the market, as she did most trips. It would give her more time to work with Maja, who would not be going ashore because she was one of two items on the boat that were not for sale.

Maja needed a lot of work still. Riesling had just left her small berth after another frustrating session, and this was the reason she wanted to speak with Verdoorn.

Riesling waited for the security chief to end his call, then waited a little longer for him to give her his attention.

Riesling was a psychologist, but she knew she didn't have to be a psychologist to pick up on the fact that Verdoorn hated women. She'd seen him brutalize, heard of him killing, and listened to him while he gave orders that ensured the roughest treatment of the women around him. She didn't think he ever even had sex, which he easily could have done as much as he wanted considering his power in the Consortium along with his unfettered access to the merchandise.

Riesling realized quickly after meeting the South African that she was completely afraid of him, and she reasoned it to be a healthy fear.

Finally, he looked her way. "What is it?"

She said, "This Maja . . . she's a difficult case. She's utterly defiant."

He nodded impassively. She saw that he was unsurprised. "The recruiter said her family unit was strong. She was intelligent, no drug use, no sexual abuse in her past. These are the tough cases, but that's why you're here."

"I've been working with her all day. If anything, she's only become *more* recalcitrant."

Jaco shrugged, as if the conversation bored him. "The Director likes her stubbornness. He's looking forward to draining that out of her." When Riesling made no reply, he cocked his head. "But you are saying something else, aren't you?"

The doctor nodded. "Even the most obstinate ones respond to my tactics. I am beginning to think this one is here to make trouble."

"But . . ." Jaco was confused. "We took her, she didn't just show up. Saying she is here to cause trouble would indicate she willfully came along with some sort of plan."

"I'm not saying that. I am saying she is not like any of the other recruits. She understands this better than she should be able to. That or she's just incredibly wily, but I'm worried about this one."

Verdoorn said, "If you think the Director will just change his mind about seeing her in Venice, or about bringing her to Rancho Esmerelda, you can forget it. He is a hell of a lot more headstrong than this stupid whore we're transporting below."

Riesling sighed. "I know. It's up to us to have her ready for him."

"Are you making some sort of a request?"

"I think some additional . . . *intervention* is warranted."

The South African said, "You want her beaten? I can do it, but the boss won't like it. He'll want her healthy for his visit tomorrow."

The American woman shook her head. "No. Not beaten. I need to create some sort of a bond with her quickly, so it might help if we could initiate some trauma of a . . . of a more personal nature. This will help her look at me as something of a lifeline, a kindred female. Right now I'm just another of her captors as far as she sees things."

Verdoorn nodded as he ate his pork. "You want her sexually defiled, and then you want to come to her side to tell her you had nothing to do with it but can help her cope with what has happened."

"That's it exactly."

"The Director won't like that, either."

"I can give him my professional opinion that this was the prudent move."

Verdoorn thought this over, then nodded. "He will defer to your expertise." After a sip of beer, he said, "I can send one of the Greeks into her cabin tonight."

Riesling thought it telling that Verdoorn immediately said he could beat her, if necessary, but when it came to sex, he suggested someone else.

"I think that might prove extremely effective in cooling the fires of resistance in her. I suggest Kostopoulos himself. I know how he is with the girls. She will need a lot of help in her recovery after a night with him, and it will only make my job easier."

Verdoorn agreed. "I'll talk to him. No doubt he'll be happy to do his duty for the cause."

"If he does it tonight, by tomorrow when we get to Italy, I can all but assure you Maja will be more obedient and ready for the Director's visit."

"That's what we pay you for," Jaco said, then his attention returned to his meal.

TWENTY-SEVEN

Thirty minutes after Talyssa Corbu and I climbed into the speedboat, the Romanian woman has vomited twice, and I've almost thrown up a half dozen times. I came the closest when she didn't quite make it to the side and puked all over the deck, but I managed to hold my lunch in, and now *La Primarosa* is at least two miles behind us: still heading north, still a little off our port quarter, with its brilliant lights perfectly visible in the clear night.

I've been monitoring my fuel gauge, knowing I'm burning a lot of gas, and now see I'm down below half a tank. Over the sounds of the engine and the waves, I say, "We're not going to be able to lead them all the way up the coast. We have about thirty minutes of fuel left." I think it over for several seconds, then spend a few more seconds trying to talk myself out of the plan I'd devised while motoring along.

But the voice of reason can't break through and put an end to this insanity.

I hold the wheel with one hand while I bring the binos to my eyes, looking to see if there is evidence of anyone standing on the deck of *La Primarosa*. From this distance, while bouncing up and down on the water, it's impossible to tell.

With a sigh, I say, "Looks like I'm going to have to try a bottom-up under way."

"A *what*?"

"Raiding a ship from the waterline while it's on the move."

"That sounds difficult."

I laugh. "It's a little challenging, yeah. I've done it before, but not without a lot of equipment, and not alone."

"How will you—"

She stops talking when I throttle back hard, putting the Mano Marine speedboat in neutral. It slows violently, knocking Talyssa and me both forward.

I could have warned her, but I hear the ticking clock in my head telling me I have to act fast. The time to hold her hand has passed. I tell her, "You're going to have to drive the boat."

After the ceaseless full-throttle engine rumble and the noise of the boat beating against the waves, the relative silence now is shocking. Talyssa stares at me in disbelief and dread, and I know what she's going to say.

"Look. You showed me some things . . . but . . . but I've never done this before. I still don't know how."

"Do you know how to raid a vessel from the waterline while it's moving at fifteen knots?" She doesn't answer me, likely because she's tired of my smartass comments. I add, "Trust me, you've got the easy part in all this."

Talyssa leans over the side and vomits again. I just barely manage to suppress my own desire to hurl while I hold the wheel and focus on the approaching boat. I need to position myself nearly perfectly in the water to have any chance of pulling this off, and to get closer to the vessel's path, I turn slightly to the west and add a little power.

It doesn't take me long before I throttle back yet again, and we bob there in the darkness. The yacht is less than a mile and a half away, and closing steadily.

Talyssa sits there, staring at me, and I can feel the trepidation pouring off her.

"How are we going to do this?" she finally asks.

"I'm getting in the water, and you are going to pilot the boat in the direction of those lights on the coastline. Go slowly, one-third power. Make your way about halfway between me and the shore, maybe one mile out, and then throttle back to neutral. After *La Primarosa* passes by, keep your eyes out to sea, right here. If you see a light waving around in the water, that's me, and I wasn't able to get on board. Come and pick me up. If you don't see anything for five minutes, head for land. You should be able to beach it easily, but be sure to pick an area where the shoreline isn't too rocky."

"I don't know if I can do this," she says.

"I can't do it without you, and if I miss that boat and you *don't* come for me, then I'm dead."

"Don't put me in that position!"

"Look around you! We're *in* that position! We can go home and forget this, or we can go forward. The *only* way forward is for me to try to hit that boat, right now, while it's on the move."

Her meek voice has returned. "I'm just . . . scared."

My voice isn't meek at all, but I share her sentiments. "Yeah, me, too. Trust me, it doesn't go away, but after a while, you get used to it." I pull a bag of equipment up on the deck, retrieve my wetsuit, fins, mask, and snorkel. I leave my tank and the rest of my scuba gear because, as much as I'd love the ability to breathe underwater, there is no way I can pull myself aboard a swiftly moving boat with fifty pounds of shit on my back.

I also retrieve the small backpack that is holding the rubber-coated utility anchor attached to the braided line, and I stuff my pistol and suppressor in it, along with my knife, a flashlight, and a small red light to use underwater.

While Talyssa watches the approaching yacht, I strip down to my underwear and wrestle into the 7-millimeter wetsuit, pull the hood over my head, and slip on my fins.

She starts to say something to me, maybe to protest again that she has no training to pilot a powerful motorboat on the open sea, alone, at night, but she registers the intense look on my face and realizes I am not a man to be reasoned with right now.

I put the mask on, adjust the snorkel, and sit on the gunwale of the speedboat, facing in. Crossing my legs in front of me, I say, "You've got this, and so do I." Before she can reply, I pinch my nose and put my hand on my mask. I roll backwards off the gunwale, entering the water with the back of my head first, then doing a reverse somersault under the waves before resurfacing.

With my head back above the waterline, I get her to hand me the backpack, and I put it on my chest with the straps over my shoulders.

"Go," I say. "I'll call you when it's done."

Five minutes later I am bobbing alone in the dark water, making little corrections with my fins as a very mild current tries to pull me offline from the oncoming vessel.

My plan is as simple as it is crazy, but as I told Talyssa, I've done something similar before. When the boat comes level with me I will fin as hard as I can towards it, then throw the grappling hook at the metal railings alongside the sea stairs at the rear. I'll be lashed to the line, and then I'll use it to pull myself through the yacht's wake to the stairs.

That's the plan, anyway. But it will only work *if* I can get close enough to throw, and *if* I can get high enough in the water to throw, and *if* I snag the hook on the rail, and *if* there isn't anyone standing right there to stop me.

Easy day, Gentry. You got this.

If there is anyone down on the lower deck by the sea stairs, this plan won't work at all. I'm not shooting someone from the water and then just climbing on board and fighting it out, as cool as that would be, so this plan of mine is conditional on what I see in a one- or two-second look at the stern, as well as the execution of my throw.

Getting into position will be tough. I can't be right in front of *La Primarosa* when it passes or it will either run me down or suck me down. Instead I try to plant myself about fifty feet east of where it will pass.

One thing's for sure: I'll only get one chance at this, and failure means those women sail off to Italy or Slovenia or somewhere else in Croatia, while Talyssa and I motor back to shore, miles from town, with no earthly idea what to do next.

But I can't think about the prospect of failure because *La Primarosa* is just a few hundred yards away now. I commit myself to my objective, put all my energy and focus into it, and prepare to move.

The freediving fins I'm wearing have more than twice the surface area of regular swim fins, and this, along with decades improving my finning technique, allows me to move like a torpedo through the water. I dive just a few feet, then begin working my legs as hard as I can, and I close on the path of the vessel.

I can't see anything below the waves without my light, but using it now would tie up a hand I need for something else, so I just have to estimate how far away I am by my speed in the water and the loud humming noise coming from the one-hundred-fifty-foot-long vessel.

I surface, blow out my snorkel, and look up. The bow of the *Primarosa* is more or less where I'd hoped to find it, fifty feet in front of me to the west. The speed of the vessel up close is frightening, and the white caps of the bow wake along the hull are intimidating, because I'll be swimming right through that in seconds.

I don't dive this time, I just lower my head, breathe through my snorkel, and kick like my life depends on it. My heart pumps wildly, thanks to the adrenaline and epinephrine and cortisone from the fear, excitement, exertion, and desperation.

And as I kick, I have the weird presence of mind to realize something in this moment.

I fucking hate to admit it, but I live for this shit.

Just then I feel the wake hit me, knocking me back to the left as the vessel churns the sea, heading to my right.

Six seconds later I arch my back and my head surfaces; I kick as hard as I can while vertical, lifting my upper torso out of the water. The stern of the boat is close enough but already past me, and I realize I should have surfaced a couple seconds earlier for an easier throw.

From my imperfect view I see no one on the lower deck by the sea stairs so, while still kicking to keep my arms above the water and fighting the incredible wake, I swing my right hand over my head, hurling the four-pound metal utility anchor up and over the stern railing. The rubber coating I sprayed on the tongs masks any metal-on-metal noise, and I'm hoping the sound of the engine hides the clunking of the instrument when it hits the deck and again when it catches on the rail.

I quickly wrap my wrist and forearm in the rope and hope like hell that I am yanked along in the water.

I'm violently jerked and towed behind the yacht. I pull myself hand over hand up the rope through the foamy wake, using all the strength in my arms, legs, and back to do so. The mask is ripped off my eyes by the force of the water, but it slides down onto my neck and not over my head. I gulp a mouthful of seawater and fight the incredible drag of the small pack on my chest trying to haul me under the surface.

This? This is *not* the shit I live for.

But I keep pulling, and soon I take a hand off the rope and reach up to the sea stairs, looking for something to grab on to. I'm weakening by the second from exhaustion and the need to suck in a breath of air, impossible in the heavy wake of the megayacht.

A small tie-down is positioned just to the right of the water entry of the sea stairs, and my fingers take it in a death grip. I let go of the rope with my left hand now, wrap it over my clenched right hand, and, like I'm free-climbing a sheer wall, I pull myself out of the water and onto the lower stairs.

I fight the urge to vomit and to cough up a large volume of the Adriatic Sea and to collapse down onto the deck, because I haven't cleared the area around me yet. Barely able to function, I pull the suppressed G19, rise onto my knees, and, still with the massive fins on my feet, I scan the rear portion of the lower deck over the top of the stairs.

The area is clear.

I drop back onto the lower stairs, out of view from the deck, and take a few seconds to recover from the exhausting swim. I gag out seawater for a few seconds, and this makes me feel a lot better. Finally, I remove my fins and fold them till they fit in the pack. Taking off my mask and snorkel, I shove these in, as well.

I'm head to toe in a hooded black wetsuit, with black neoprene boots and a black pack on my chest, which I shift around to my back after retrieving my knife from it.

The blade and the pistol go in the utility pocket on my right thigh, and then I begin climbing the sea stairs again. I only make it a couple of feet before I drop back down, because a man in a short-sleeved black shirt is walking by from my right to my left. Luckily, I saw him before he saw me, but I nevertheless draw my blade and prepare to launch myself up the three remaining steps to shove it into his windpipe if he comes over here and peers down on me.

Thirty seconds later I chance another glance and find the deck clear of hostiles, so I move up the stairs towards the rear door to the saloon.

My objective is the master stateroom, at the top of a staircase out of the saloon on the bridge deck and then down a hall, aft. I don't know who is in this room, but I'm certain that whoever the big cheese on board is, they are going to get the best cabin.

I make it up to the windows into the saloon and then duck down, crawling behind a little rear-deck bar area to get a view into the well-lit room. Right across from me is the diving deck. Several scuba tanks, buoyancy control vests, hoses, and other equipment are fixed by bungee cord to racks along the bulkhead.

I rise up on my knees but lower back down out of view as a slight list to port becomes apparent. It takes me only an instant to realize the boat is turning to starboard. Seconds later it begins to slow.

Are we heading in to land? Pulling my phone out of my pack, I take it from its waterproof case and turn on the GPS. It takes a minute to catch the satellite, but when it does it shows that I'm a couple miles off the coast of the Croatian city of Rovinj.

Shit, I think. Talyssa wasn't exactly right, but she was close. *La Primarosa* was coming to northern Croatia, but to a smaller port than Pula for some reason, probably because I spooked them into changing their plans.

Thinking over my next move, I decide to take advantage of the opportunity the nearby diving deck affords me. I shoot across the aft portion of the lower deck crawling on my hands and knees under the windows to the saloon, and I grab the first scuba tank in the rack. Working in the dark I strap a vestlike buoyancy control device to it, and then I attach the regulator and BCD inflator hose to the tank itself.

I grab a few kilos of lead weights and drop them in pockets in the vest to help me sink below the surface.

Now I open the tank valve and check to make sure it's full, test the regulator and emergency regulator by sucking air from them both, and then screw the valve shut again. I move the entire rig into the corner and throw a towel over it.

I crawl back over behind the little bar, knowing that's the best hiding place here on the aft deck, unless, of course, some jackass decides to come out to make piña coladas.

But as I rise, I check the saloon again and see a man moving up the circular staircase on the far side, thirty feet or so from me. He's wearing a black polo and carrying a small submachine gun on his chest.

I duck back down to cover but keep my eyes looking through the glass.

Right behind the armed man I see a woman. She is young with short blond hair. I don't know who she is, but when she is followed by more women and girls, and they, in turn, are followed by a second armed man, I know *exactly* who they are.

A total of eight sex trafficking victims walk across the saloon and towards the port-side hatch to the main deck. The lighting in the saloon is good, so I'm able to look over the faces, but of the eight women I see, I don't see anyone who looks even remotely like the picture I saw of Talyssa's sister.

They are dressed in warm-up pants and yoga pants and T-shirts and sweatshirts; it appears their captors are treating them a lot better here than they'd been treated in Mostar.

At first I can't figure out where they are going, but the mystery about where the women are headed is solved thirty seconds later when I hear voices and then footsteps across the aft deck on the other side of the little bar. The women round the stern of the vessel, then head on to the starboard side, where they disappear, moving along together towards the bow.

When the entourage comes back around a second time a couple of minutes later, I understand. The women are being walked around up here for some air and exercise.

I wait for them to pass a third time, but before a fourth trip around the deck I see the girls walked back into the saloon and led back down the stairs belowdecks.

I like my hiding place, but it's not going to get me anything I need, unless some guy who looks like a sex-smuggling mastermind happens to walk by alone on the aft deck. I decide again I have to go for the master stateroom, which means the staircase that runs up the brightly lit saloon thirty feet away, but before I can move, I see motion through the window again. Another group of women, seven this time, are brought up and walked through the port-side hatch.

These girls are being escorted around the deck, just like the first group, obviously as a form of exercise.

Shit. I can't go anywhere right now.

Eventually these ladies are taken back belowdecks, and six more come up. They travel the same slow, monotonous route around the deck.

I've looked at every single woman, and none of them look like Roxana.

After the last group goes down, the engines of *La Primarosa* begin to slow more, then it sounds as if they are being powered back to neutral. Boat crew and armed men in suits walk around in the saloon, so I'm still stuck where I am.

Soon I hear the voices of crew members over a walkie-talkie at the stern, and I imagine men standing back there, lowering the tender into the water.

Almost on cue, the tender's outboards start up and I hear it rumble around to the port side.

I worry that they are going to start loading up the women to take them to shore, but instead I see a tall bald-headed Caucasian man in dark clothing coming down the stairs, with three armed men at his heels. All three head out the port-side saloon hatch.

A minute later I hear the tender leaving the yacht, and then the quiet returns.

The women have been given exercise and then they were taken back below, so the only thing I can assume is that the men who boarded the tender are heading to land to pick up supplies, or perhaps even more women.

I decide to wait here another few minutes, and then to make my way for the stairs.

TWENTY-EIGHT

Kostas Kostopoulos had readied his quarters, showered and dressed himself, taken his pills, and sprayed on copious amounts of cologne.

He put on a red silk robe, leaving it open enough to reveal a hairy chest and a thin gold chain. He fingered the rings he kept on six of his fingers, and he slicked back his thin silver mane.

And when he heard the tender rumble away from the port side of his megayacht, he looked in the mirror and pronounced himself ready.

He walked over to the little built-in nightstand next to his king-sized bed and pressed a button on a console, and the lock in the door to the upper-deck passageway clicked open. He called out to his bodyguard.

"Anton. Come."

A muscular, bearded Greek stepped up to the open doorway from where he'd been positioned at the top of the stairs. "Sir?"

"The product being held alone in VIP stateroom number four. Bring it to me."

The younger man masked a smile. "Right away, sir."

Now the seventy-two-year-old reached into a drawer and retrieved a fistful of silk scarves of different colors. He tossed them around on the bed and on the floor haphazardly, then picked a few back up and placed them more methodically around the room.

Jaco Verdoorn had told Kostopoulos that Riesling wanted him to take one of the women from below into his bed. He did this with regularity—it was the only reason he traveled personally with the merchandise to market—but tonight was the first time he'd been asked to defile one of the special-handling items.

Kostas was reluctant at first; he knew the Director himself would be on the yacht in just hours, and he did not want to do anything to bring on the powerful man's ire. But when Verdoorn explained they'd been having trouble with Maja, and the psychologist on board felt she'd get through to her more easily if she managed to form a bond with her after helping her cope with true trauma, then the Greek saw this as his one opportunity to sample the wares going directly to the man in charge of the entire Consortium himself.

And even though the past several days had been some of the most difficult in the Balkan pipeline with the attacks by the American assassin known as the Gray Man, now that he was out on the water, away from the Balkans, Kostopoulos felt a reversal of fortunes coming his way. As he waited in his master stateroom for the most beautiful and desirable woman in this or perhaps any other shipment to come up and fulfill all his prurient desires, he found himself amazed that he'd managed to get so fucking lucky in life.

. . .

I stretch my hamstrings and then my IT bands behind the bar. The cold of the water, even with my wetsuit on, tightens my muscles and lessens my ability for explosive movement, but the stretching helps me counter this somewhat.

And it's not like I have much else to do. I've been back here for a half hour now; the tender motored off ten minutes ago, and even though it is a thousand yards or so to the marina in Rovinj, I can't be sure the rigid-hulled rubber inflatable boat won't return soon.

I tell myself I've got to get on with it.

But as I prepare to move, I see yet another figure in the saloon. This time it's a muscular, bald-headed man with a beard, wearing a polo and a Brügger and Thomet submachine gun over his shoulder, descending the circular stairs. He arrives on the main deck and immediately continues down to the lower deck.

Something tells me to wait, and I do, but only for a minute. Then I see a woman ascend from below, followed by the bearded man, who holds a hand on her shoulder from behind.

As she continues up the stairs, I focus on her carefully, curious as to why this one, who is being treated like a captive, is being escorted alone.

I get a good look at her face as she steps onto the main deck before turning on the staircase to go up to the upper decks.

Oh my God.

It's Roxana.

Talyssa's sister is very much alive.

My heart begins pounding now. I count my blessings she isn't being held with the others, and I realize there just may be a chance I can get her out of here. It will probably mean killing at least one guard and maybe more and then a fast getaway, but considering what these assholes are up to, I see that as a feature of this plan, not a glitch.

They climb to the upper deck, disappearing from my view. I want to follow them now, but the sound of a walkie-talkie nearby holds me in my hiding place tucked behind the little bar.

. . .

Roxana had been told to dress for dinner earlier in the evening, and fine clothes were brought to her by the staff. She dressed in white slacks and a sleeveless black top, expecting that she and Dr. Claudia would be having another session.

She was led from her cabin, past a pair of armed guards in the foyer, up the stairs, and all the way to the upper deck. Here she could see an open door to the bridge, and an open door to a large stateroom.

The guard directed her aft towards the stateroom, and then he all but pushed her inside before closing the door.

Here an older man, wearing a red robe and leaning against a chair in a sitting area just a couple steps away from her, smiled and beckoned her to come closer.

His tan, hairy chest was exposed, and Roxana thought she might be sick.

"Good evening," he said in English.

She looked around and saw several silk scarves lying around the room. On the bed, on the floor in front of it, on the two chairs. She did not know what they were for, and she did not know why she was here.

"Who are you?" she asked warily.

The man said, "Call me Kostas." He reached out to shake her hand, and when she reluctantly offered hers, he grabbed her roughly by her wrist and yanked her off-balance. As she screamed in surprise, he shoved her down onto the bed with a confidence in his eyes that told her this was nothing new for him.

When she found herself on her back, the man said, "I find it's best for everyone if we get right to it, don't you?"

Her heart felt like it would tear out of her chest now. "No!"

Roxana began to hyperventilate, but through the fear she felt rage.

The older man said, "I hear you are quite a brat, but I will take responsibility for teaching you how to behave going forward." With that he reached and grabbed one of her legs, yanked it to the end of the bed, and began wrapping a silk scarf around her bare ankle. She saw him tie the other end of the scarf to the low bedpost, and she fought to pull her leg away.

The older man was surprisingly strong, and she could not break free.

Right before he cinched the knot tight, however, Roxana used her other leg to kick him in the side of the head.

The man in the red robe tumbled sideways to the floor, halfway to the lavatory, and Roxana scooted backwards along the bed until she had her back pressed against the headboard.

"Stay away!"

The man who called himself Kostas climbed back to his feet slowly; she could tell he was stunned and embarrassed but not especially injured. His silver hair hung over his eyes, so he shook off the impact to his head, then smoothed it back into place.

"You," he said with a grin. "The rumors are right about you. You *are* one disobedient little bitch."

He moved forward confidently, but when she kicked out at him again, he took a step back to rethink his plan. He stepped over to a small writing desk in the corner of the room, then reached into a drawer and pulled out a large knife. It was in a sheath, but he waved it in the air in front of him. "Now. You don't want to fight with me, dear. Nothing good will come of it."

Roxana stayed where she was, eyes locked on the knife.

"No?" he said after a few seconds. "Maybe you would like me to bring some friends. That will make this a *very* special night for you."

She said nothing.

"Yes . . . one of my roughest men holding you down, with he and I passing you back and forth." He smiled. "Won't that be fun?"

He stepped around to the left of the bed. Roxana scooted to the other side, but he didn't leap for her or come at her with the knife at first. Instead he pressed the button on his end table. She heard a loud *click* and realized he had just unlocked the door.

The Greek called out now. "Anton? Come in."

Roxana said, "I swear I will kill you if you touch me again."

Kostas just laughed and crawled onto the bed in front of her, and unsheathed his knife. She backed away as much as she could, pressing herself tight against the headboard. When he moved closer she slid off the bed but found herself in the corner by the other nightstand, with nowhere to go.

Kostas lunged at her, forcing another scream out of Roxana. He crawled all the way over the bed and landed on the floor on the other side, all but pinning the young Romanian girl between the bulkhead and the side of the bed, with the nightstand and the wall behind her.

He waved the shiny blade back and forth in front of his face, then moved forward again. This time she clawed at his face, scratching at him.

He swung the knife towards her reflexively. It missed her face by inches, but only because she fell backwards on the nightstand and then down to the floor.

Roxana was on her knees in front of the Greek in the red robe now; she couldn't see who came through the door behind him, but she heard it open, then close and lock.

The old man had all the advantages here: he had the knife, he had another man to help him, while she had her back to the wall and nowhere to maneuver.

The young Romanian woman readied herself for his move down onto her; her plan was to try to take the hand with the knife and jerk the man off balance, then disarm him and slit his throat.

She knew the guard behind him would only shoot her for doing this, but she told herself she would rather die than submit.

She reached up and clawed again, and her nails raked across the old man's right cheek.

The man rubbed a hand over his face, then looked down at the blood on it. He screamed now. "Jaco was right about you! You aren't worth the trouble! Better I just cut your bitch throat and toss you overboard. I'll tell the Director you committed suicide, and no one will ever talk."

He moved at her with the knife poised to strike.

And then, without warning, Roxana watched as his scratched and wrinkled face turned from pale gray to bright red in an instant. Roxana couldn't tell what she was looking at, but quickly she realized she *wasn't*, in fact, looking at his face. It was a red silk scarf being brought down over his head, finally continuing down lower to wrap around his throat.

And there it cinched tight.

The old man's eyes went wide with shock. He tried to swing back with the knife, but Roxana watched while a gloved hand at the end of an arm in black deftly disarmed him, and then the old man in the red robe was lifted up into the air, his arms and legs flailing just feet from the Romanian in the corner on her knees.

She stood up, pushed herself tighter into the corner, and she could see the new person in the room now. He wore a wetsuit and a hood over his head, but she saw enough of his face to register a short beard and intense eyes. He dragged the man over the top of the bed, finally heaving him back and into the middle of the stateroom, his bare feet dangling over the carpet as he was hanged by the silk scarf.

Behind him, just this side of the door to the hall, the bald-headed guard in the black polo lay crumpled, his eyes open in death.

The diver must have dragged in the body before shutting the door.

The man in black spoke now, right into the Greek's right ear. In a soft, low voice that was strained with the effort of holding the man in the air by the throat, he said, "You like it rough, buddy? I'll show you rough."

The old man's eyes locked on Roxana's, and then they slowly rolled back in his head.

She held her hands in front of her mouth as tears ran down her face.

The man in the wetsuit lowered the dead body down to the floor, then stood back up and looked her way.

Roxana wanted to scream, but instead she held her breath, terrified of what would happen to her now.

The killer moved a few steps closer to the end of the bed, looking to her. He jerked his head towards the body in the red robe. "Who's he?"

Roxana cocked her head in bafflement.

TWENTY-NINE

The girl doesn't appear hurt and, from the look in her eyes as I put my makeshift garrote around the old dude's head, she's a fighter. She was prepared to die in combat rather than yield to her attacker, and I have nothing but respect for that.

Maybe I shouldn't have killed him, but the logistics of getting him off this boat along with Roxana didn't compute. I figure I can swim out of here with one person, and I'd *much* rather that person was going along willingly. The moment I saw Roxana I decided she would get the other ticket off this boat. She could tell me where they were heading and who was who in this organization.

She spends five seconds staring me down, before replying in a halting voice. "He was . . . I don't know who he was. How is it *you* don't know?"

I don't answer her. Instead I ask another question. "Are you hurt?"

She replies by saying, "There are many men with guns on this boat."

"Tell me about it." I ask again, "Are you hurt?"

She looks me up and down, and then at the two bodies on the floor. "How can you kill two men and then just have a normal conversation?"

I don't agree this is a normal conversation, but I take her point. I look down to the two bodies. "They're bad guys, right?"

She nods. "Very bad."

I shrug. "Fuck 'em." And then I ask a third time, "Are . . . you . . . hurt?"

"I . . . I am okay." The shock of the moment seems to have her in its grip, but her eyes soon clear and she looks into mine. "It's you . . . you were the man in the red room. The one who killed the Serbian?"

"You were there?"

She nods, looks to a point on the wall. "I was there."

I want to ask her about what happened after I left the farm, but I have more pressing matters at the moment.

"What's your name?" I ask, although I know the answer. What I *don't* know, however, is her state of mind. I need to find out if any bonds have developed during her captivity that will make her a threat to me or my mission.

"My name is Ma . . . it's Maja."

This is pretty standard in kidnapping situations. They've got her using a different name, both for operational security and as part of her reeducation process. But I know, without a doubt, that this is the girl from the picture with Talyssa.

Nobody looks like this.

I shake my head. "No, it's not Maja. You are Roxana Vaduva."

Her eyes shut and tears cascade down her cheeks. She sits down on the bed roughly and sobs softly with her face in her hands. "How do you know who I am?"

"Because Talyssa sent me."

Tears flow, she collapses on the bed crying, and I look down at my watch.

I sit next to her, my pistol drawn and pointed towards the locked door. "Why are you up here with this old dude?"

She lifts her head, and with a hint of anger, she replies, "Why do you think? I was brought up to be raped. I haven't been behaving, I guess, and this is how they punish you around here."

"You've been held with the others?"

She shakes her head now. "I am getting VIP treatment, I have been told, because I am now the property of the head of the Consortium."

This has me momentarily confused. "The head of the entire organization?"

"Yes."

"No shit? Who is he?"

"I don't know. He told me his name was Tom, but that might be a lie. I met him in Romania."

"At the nightclub in Bucharest."

"Yes."

It's clearly the man from the airplane that Talyssa had been tracking. This confirms Roxana's sister's suspicions, but we still don't have any idea who this prick is.

I look over at the old dead guy in the robe. To myself I say, "Shit. I bet *he* knew the guy's name." Looking at the girl again, I say, "Anyone else on board in charge?"

"There was a South African man. He was making decisions. He calls himself John, but the man lying dead on the floor there talked about someone named Jaco. I don't know if that's John's real name or not."

"And this Jaco guy knows who Tom is?"

She nods adamantly and sniffs away wet tears. "He was there, in Bucharest. They were traveling together. Along with a bodyguard named Sean. There were some other bodyguards and some Romanian gangsters there with them, too."

My attention is on this South African, because I'm astonished someone obviously so high up in the organization is here. Getting hold of this guy might be worth the added risk. "What does he look like?"

She describes him, and my hopes are dashed. This is the dude who left with the Greek goons on the tender.

"He's off the boat now."

She raises a finger. "There is someone else. A woman on board. An American psychologist called Dr. Claudia. The entire pipeline is not just a way to move the girls, it is a way to reprogram us for what is to come."

She describes Claudia. I haven't seen such a woman aboard, and don't think I'll be able to go hunting for her. No, I'll take Roxana, in the hopes she can help us identify the men she met in Bucharest, because they are running this entire show.

"Okay. Any chance you know how to scuba?"

She shakes her head, a distant look in her eyes now.

"No problem. I'll get you through this. I've staged a rig on the aft deck. We'll get to it. You can breathe from my octopus, it's my spare regulator, it attaches to my tank. We're not going deep. The water is going to be cold without a wetsuit on, but I'll keep my arm around you and we'll stay close together all the way to the shore. We're not very far from—"

"No."

I stop midsentence and shake my head. *Not this again.* "Roxana, no one is going to come after your family. I can protect them."

She speaks flatly now. "I am not leaving the girls below. You have to take us all."

"It's just me. I don't have a boat or a submarine or a dozen Navy SEALs. It's just me. Alone. How am I going to scuba dive with twenty-five women?"

Roxana deflates a little. "The yacht is going to Venice, I know that much. Tomorrow night there is something they call the market. They are going to sell off the women below, plus some more women they are picking up here."

"Sell them to who?"

"Claudia says they'll go to mafia organizations, oil sheiks, high-end prostitution operations around Europe and the Middle East. After tomorrow night in Venice, all these women will be gone, and there will be no way to save them."

I just stare at her and say nothing, because even with this information, I don't know how to save them.

She must see the uncertainty on my face. "You just have to go to the police there, they can find out where—"

I interrupt with, "The cops are useless in this. The pipeline only goes places where they control a section of the police."

This doesn't seem to surprise Roxana much at all. She just nods, looks to the floor. "I'm being taken to the Director. I can lead Talyssa to him. I don't know how. Maybe I can find a phone or a computer or something to communicate with her once I get where I'm going and find out where that is."

She's as brave as her sister but, also like her sister, I'm not sure she fully understands what she's in for. "Do you have any idea what is likely to happen to you between now and then?"

With a nod she says, "Of course. I will be raped. Beaten. I'll be punished for you coming here."

I am thinking the same thing, and I don't know if I can deal with more of what I've been feeling since Mostar. Before I can reply, however, I hear a sound outside the bulkhead.

An outboard motor, increasing in volume.

The tender is returning to the boat.

"Don't let them catch you," she says. "Go."

Telling myself I have a little time, I look away for a moment, and I begin to worry that I don't want to know the answer to the question I'm compelled to ask. But I *have* to know. Turning back to her, I say, "What did they do to you after I left the red room?"

She sits back up on the bed and begins weeping again. "That night, after you left, they took us into the mountains. Raped some of the girls. Maybe most of them. One tried to run . . . she did not get far."

"They killed her?"

In answer she says, "She was only a kid."

I feel nausea coming on. I can put up with so much awful shit in this world, but only when it's not my actions that caused it. This? This child getting murdered, others getting raped?

It's on me.

Guilt can cripple you. Or it can be a driving force. Only your internal strength decides how you respond to your failures.

I fight my stomach into submission with a couple of deep calming breaths. "I'm sorry" is all I can say.

She rubs tears from her eyes as she says, "I'm glad you killed that man.

The Serbians had been raping the girls, anyway. That is not your fault. And the girl ran because she thought she had an opportunity. Who knows? She might be the luckiest one out of all of us."

Once more I try to get her to listen to reason. "Not if you come with me right now. I can protect you, Roxana. Trust me." But I see a resolution in her eyes that is so similar to what I've seen from her sister for the past few days that I know it's futile to fight her.

"Tell Talyssa I love her." She breaks down in fresh tears, and I can read it all on her face. She knows this is her one decent shot at survival, and almost definitely her only chance to get out of this situation without being brutalized by her captors.

But she is steadfast in her decision.

And I know when I'm beat. "I'll tell her. She thinks you blame her for what happened."

Roxana wipes her eyes again, shakes her head. "No. I did this. I did this on my own. And I'm going to continue my mission until I find out where this all leads. I'll contact her, and then she . . . and you . . . can come and tear this whole thing apart."

"That sounds like a good plan." I offer my hand to her and she looks at it. With a beautiful little smile that takes me by surprise, she says, "I haven't had a man want to shake my hand in a while. Other things, yes, but not that."

I feel bad for what I'm about to do, but I do it anyway. She offers me her hand finally and I take it in mine, and as I shake it I say, "I'm going to have to make this look good. You'll thank me later, but probably only *much* later." I add, "I'm sorry."

"Sorry about what?"

I pull her up from the bed towards me and, at the same time, I fire out a left hook to her temple, knocking her out cold, and then I catch her and gently lay her down on the floor in a heap. I tear open her sleeveless blouse and position her next to the bodies.

I couldn't leave her sitting here in this stateroom untouched with two dead guys lying around. Even if I ran around this boat till everyone saw me and all on board knew an assassin had schwacked this perv and his shithead bodyguard, it would look damn suspicious that I didn't at least hurt her in the process. If she looked in any way complicit in what happened, I couldn't imagine what they'd do to her then. And even now, leaving her lying here on the floor feels wrong on every level.

But it was her call to make.

I hear the tender on the port side motor away, probably back to the rear of the vessel so it can be winched out of the water, and this tells me everyone is on board. I head to the door, now wondering if I can even get *myself* out of here before getting killed.

• • •

Jaco Verdoorn climbed up the ladder and stepped onto the deck. Behind him the eight women he and the Greek mafia men picked up on the coast of the Croatian city of Rovinj ascended, one by one, until they all stood there with him, squinting in the bright light.

Though there were eight in this shipment, only seven of them would be generating revenue for the organization. One of them, and Verdoorn eyed her as she climbed aboard, was a special-handling item. A beautiful Hungarian blonde, Cage had seen her at the ballet in Budapest with his wife several months earlier, and he'd demanded she be pulled into the pipeline.

She'd be taken along with Maja to the West Coast, used by Cage and his friends and business partners at Rancho Esmerelda, and then cast away after Cage found a new crop on his future trips abroad.

When all the women stood on the deck, Dr. Riesling gave her little speech to the new arrivals, they were promised food and a shower, and then the guards began leading them into the saloon to go down the stairs to the lower deck.

As they descended, Verdoorn stepped up to Riesling. "Where is Kostopoulos?"

"He had Maja brought up to his room fifteen minutes ago. Honestly, I'm surprised he's lasted this long. Usually he's done with them in ten."

Verdoorn's eyes narrowed, and Riesling added, "Don't worry. I told him, no permanent marks."

One of the Greek guards came out of the saloon, looked around, and then spun away as he spoke into his walkie-talkie. Verdoorn noted the mannerisms of this man, and when a second one of Kostas's force came running up the main deck, himself showing worry and purposefulness, the South African grabbed him by the arm. "What is the problem?"

In English the guard said, "One of our men. We no can find."

Jaco had his pistol out of his coat an instant later, and he looked to Dr. Riesling. "Get the product below! You stay with them!"

The American woman continued ushering the girls into the saloon, but to Verdoorn she said, "What's the matter?"

Verdoorn was already moving into the saloon, his pistol out in front of him, searching the area as he headed for the circular staircase. But he called back behind him in answer to the doctor's question. "The Gray Man . . . he's on board."

"How do you—"

"Because I can feel him!"

THIRTY

I take stairs up to the open sundeck and then, after checking the area below for armed goons, I kick a leg over the rail and slide down the slick white side of the vessel, landing hard but quietly on the main deck. This portion of the boat is well lit, and I see movement up near the bow, but it's only a deckhand facing away from me, far enough forward on the one-hundred-fifty-foot vessel that I'm not worried about him.

My goal is the aft deck and the scuba equipment I've staged there. Once I get it on, I plan on using the sea stairs to make my way into the water silently.

I begin heading aft in a low crouch along the starboard-side main deck.

I don't make it far before a voice comes over the loudspeaker. He's speaking Greek, and he's agitated, shouting commands. I forgo the crouch and haul ass the last twenty-five feet, pretty certain the reason this guy has his panties in a twist is that he just found out some asshole is killing people on his boat.

Sure enough, the man switches to English and says words to that effect. "Alert! Trespasser on board. He is armed! All security to the main deck."

I slow and peek around the corner to the aft deck, and here I see a couple of deckhands winching the tender, along with one guy wearing a dark polo and holding a subgun in one hand and a radio up to his ear in the other. He's facing the saloon, and he's between me and the diving equipment I need.

I think about just pulling the Glock from the pack hanging from my chest and shooting him, but I need a few seconds to get the tank valve opened and to put the equipment on, and even if I put the suppressor on my weapon first, everybody on the deck is still going to hear the gunshot.

So instead I just start walking towards the armed man purposefully but nonthreateningly.

He's twenty feet from me when he lowers the walkie-talkie and looks in my direction. But all he sees is a diver in a wetsuit, his face partially hidden by the hood, heading to the scuba rack. My pack probably looks a little weird; not many people dive with luggage, but he's unsure enough to allow me to close on him.

Another few steps and it won't matter what he does.

The man on the loudspeaker says something else, and the guard in the polo swings his submachine gun towards me, but I'm two steps away now and I cover them faster than he can fire. I knock the weapon away, spear the man in the throat, and slam my knee into his face as he doubles forward.

The deck crew begins shouting; I reach for the guard's weapon, but he crumples to the ground before I can wrench it away.

Giving up on both the gun and stealth, giving up on everything but getting my ass in the water, I lunge for the scuba rig I placed in the corner. Hefting the fifty pounds of gear, I spin back towards the stern. The deckhands look like they want to make trouble, and my hands are full so fighting them is not an option, so I juke to the left and run for the starboard side, and they give chase.

A gunshot cracks on my left as I make it to the starboard deck; I shift my body around as I hit the railing and start to go over, hoping to use the tank as a makeshift bulletproof vest.

Another gunshot rocks the night and I feel the impact as the bullet strikes my tank just as I tumble over the side, falling headfirst with all my gear slung over my shoulder.

Splashing into the cold black water, I realize I'm clear from the immediate threat of guns, but I've landed into a new threat. I'm heavily laden with equipment and weights, and I'm descending quickly.

I could let go of everything, just allow the tank and equipment to drop, but I won't do that because I'm wearing a wetsuit that adds buoyancy to my already buoyant body, so I'll just shoot to the surface.

And the surface is where the jackasses with guns are.

Somehow I have to open the air valve on the tank, get the vest onto my body and buckled in, arrest the descent by adding air to the vest, and then find my regulator and get it into my mouth so I can breathe.

With my eyes closed, because my mask is in the pack on my chest.

All before I drown.

But I'm not thinking about this, I'm doing this. I pull the entire rig off my shoulder and place it in front of me below my pack. Wrapping my legs around the steel tank, I crank open the valve. As my ears scream from my rapid descent, I muscle my way into the BCD, snap one of the three quick-release buckles to keep it on, and whip my hand around wildly for my regulator.

I find the hose and grab the mouthpiece, then pop it into my mouth, inhaling deeply.

Saltwater rushes into my mouth and lungs.

Gagging, I realize the bullet that hit the tank must have ricocheted and damaged the hose to the regulator, so I release it and yank down on the emergency regulator, tucked into my vest, knowing that if the hose on the octopus is also damaged, then I'm a dead man.

The panic welling in my chest now is as painful as the pressure against my eardrums.

I put the octopus in my mouth, push the purge button so I can spit out the seawater, and then I try a shallow breath.

Air has never felt so good going into my body.

Breathing normally now, I continue to sink, so I pump just a little air into my vest to slow my descent, then open my pack to retrieve my mask. I get it over my eyes, and then clear it of water by lifting the bottom of it off my cheeks and breathing out my nose.

Then I pinch my nose through my mask and simulate several sneezes, and this quickly regulates the pressure in my ears and the pounding pain goes away.

I pull my fins out and slip them over my boots, then more securely tighten my BCD to my body. I tie off the regulator hose to slow the loss of air from the tank. It continues to leak—I can feel bubbles brushing against my face—but it's better than it was.

Finally convinced I'm not going to die in the next ten seconds, I look at the illuminated depth gauge and find myself nearly seventy feet below the surface. From the deck of the *Primarosa* it looked like about five hundred yards to the nearest shoreline, and farther to the marina at Rovinj, so with the leak in the hose I don't have any time to wait around.

I add more air to my vest, finally arresting my descent at eighty feet, then pull the red flashlight and turn it on. With it I see I am ten feet above the sandy and rocky ocean floor. I turn off the light and begin kicking to the east, using the illuminated compass on my BCD to guide me.

That went well, I think with no small amount of sarcasm.

· · ·

Jaco Verdoorn leapt off the back of *La Primarosa* and into the tender. Already three Greeks armed with submachine guns and powerful flashlights were on board, and the tender captain fired the engine and spun the craft tightly back around to the east.

"Watch for bubbles!" Verdoorn ordered the men. He snatched a light from the hands of one of the gangsters, knowing his handgun was no more useful than the other weapons on board against a man more than a couple feet below the surface.

He was furious now, wild with rage. This was all bad; the death of the Greek, the poor security of the yacht that allowed the assassin to board, the inevitable questions that would come from Cage about Verdoorn's own actions that did not prevent this . . . but still, Jaco recognized that the prevailing emotion he felt as they shot over the water scanning back and forth with the flashlights was one of incredible excitement. He wondered if he, right now, was closer to killing the infamous Gray Man than any other man had ever been, and he relished this opportunity more than anything he'd ever done in his life.

Jaco was in the zone.

As the Zodiac began weaving left and right, covering virtually the only track the diver below could have reasonably taken to get to land, Verdoorn called into his radio back to *La Primarosa*. "I want three divers suited up and armed with spear guns. Put them in the reserve tender and send them to our position. I saw him when he went in the water and he did not have a spear gun. We're going to kill him right here, right now!"

Seconds later one of the Greeks at the bow shouted. "Bubbles! One o'clock! Twenty meters!"

The tender adjusted course and soon Verdoorn could see the bubbles himself. All the men shined their lights on them, till Verdoorn ordered them to shine straight down. The water reflected the light and they couldn't see any signs of the diver other than the bubbles he made.

Verdoorn, an avid diver himself back in the shark-infested waters of South Africa, regarded the bubbles a moment, and then he smiled. "That's constant. Not just from breathing. Bladdy bastard's sprung a leak!"

He knew he'd hit Gentry's tank as he'd fallen into the water. Apparently, the scuba gear had taken some damage.

Shouting into the radio, he said, "Hurry those divers! He's four hundred meters from land!"

. . .

I keep kicking my freediving fins, using the light as sporadically as possible to make certain I don't slam into a rock wall. I'm fifty feet below the surface now, just a few feet over the bottom as it slowly angles up towards the shoreline.

I check my air and realize the leak in my regulator is worse than I thought. I've expelled almost one third already, and I've only been in the cold water five minutes or so. Normally I could make a tank this size last an hour at this depth with this level of exertion, but now it looks like I have less than fifteen minutes to get where I'm going or I'll have to swim it on the surface.

I see the glow of lights shining down, so I know my bubbles have ratted out my position. There's not much I can do but keep kicking towards the shore, hoping I make it before the tank bleeds dry.

I push this out of my mind as I press on, and I begin thinking about Roxana, about Talyssa, about the younger sister's drive for the acceptance of her older sister and the older sister's drive to assuage her guilt and risk her own life to fix her mistake.

I am amazed by the reserves some people have, and I wonder about the drive inside the bellies of the men in the rubber boat above me, what lengths they will go to in order to kill me tonight.

I hear the faint sound of another tender now, and I have an idea that those above, or at least the ones in charge of them, are more than passionate about seeing to my demise.

I suspect there will be divers in the water now, and my shitty situation has only become more so.

I look down to the air pressure indicator, see that half my air is gone, and I wonder if I'm fucked.

No. I'm not. I tell myself that nobody on or in this water tonight has more drive to execute his mission than I do.

It may not happen tonight, and it sure doesn't look like it right now, but I'm going to find these guys above me, and I'm going to fuck them up.

• • •

The tender with the three divers turned hard to port fifty meters ahead of the northernmost of the trail of bubbles appearing on the gently undulating waves. They were just one hundred fifty meters from the Rovinj marina, but they estimated they were closer to land than their target below.

Verdoorn used his flashlight to indicate a position in the water, and he called out to them from his craft, just ahead and to the right of the telltale trail.

"Right there! I want you all in the water there. Get down and spear the diver. Bring his body up to me!"

The South African wished he'd had time to throw a tank on himself. If he had a scuba rig with him on board he would have donned it right over his clothing and dived in, ready to wring the Gray Man's neck if his hands were the only weapons available to him.

Just as the three divers sat on the gunwale of the smaller tender closer to shore, one of the Greeks on Verdoorn's craft shouted out. "Wait! He's changing directions!"

Verdoorn looked at the surface of the black water and, sure enough, the bubbles had begun trailing from due east to southeast, towards a tiny spit of land far from the marina and only about one hundred meters distant.

The South African said, "That way! He's running out of air and going for the nearest land. Get ahead of him and dive!"

The smaller tender raced off, the divers held on tightly to keep from tipping back and in, and soon it had traveled fifty meters to the southeast.

The dinghy turned sharply to slow, and then the divers rolled backwards into the water, grabbed their spear guns from their hips, and turned on their underwater flashlights. The seafloor was only twenty-five feet below the surface here, but there were rocks and valleys and swim-throughs all the way to the shoreline.

One of the three banged his flashlight on his tank to draw the attention of the others, then used his light to indicate a shallow cavern just off to their left behind them, farther from shore than the divers.

Here a steady stream of bubbles rose swiftly towards the surface, moving along towards the shore.

All three men spread out, keeping their lights on the bubbles and the hidden portion of the seafloor below them, and they converged from the east, west, and south, their spear guns loaded and cocked with enough tension to drive the steel shank straight through a diver's body.

As they arrived above the narrow little chasm, their beams shot back and forth, until the origin of the expelling air became apparent.

All three men held their positions above the source, unsure what they were looking at for a moment, but they finally put it together.

It was a scuba tank with its regulator removed, spewing air from its open valve. The spewing gases propelled the device in the water; the attached buoyancy-control device had just enough air to keep it jetting along slowly but steadily, some dozen feet above the ocean floor.

But there was no diver attached to the equipment.

All three men spun around, back to the north, and they began kicking as hard as they could as they ascended, certain now the Gray Man could only be found at the surface, because he only had the air left in his lungs.

• • •

Two minutes ago I knelt on the ocean floor, thirty-three feet below the gentle waves. Here I took off my BCD vest, turned off the tank, removed the regulator, and then reopened the valve slightly. Sucking in one last mouthful of unpressurized air directly from the tank, I used one hand to reach down to pull two stones from the seafloor, while with the other hand I pointed the bottom of the steel canister towards the south and cranked open the valve the rest of the way.

The entire scuba rig began jetting away like a very slow torpedo, and I turned to the northeast, kicking myself into shallower water while ascending slightly as I swam.

The stones are keeping me from shooting to the surface now, but once I'm halfway up, I drop one of them. I'm not breathing so there are no bubbles; the only trail evident on the water above me should be the air from the tank, now probably fifty yards away or more and heading in the opposite direction.

I'm hoping the tenders take the bait, and by the fact that I can't hear the outboard motors any longer, I feel certain they have.

At five feet below the surface I kick as hard and as fast as I can, until my lungs scream in agony, and then I let the other rock drop from my hands. The only things weighing me down now are the few items in my pack, so I rise easily to the surface.

I don't take my head out of the water, only blow out through the snorkel and then back in, still kicking but making sure to kick in a way that doesn't make a splash or allow my long fins to come out of the water.

God, I love breathing.

Finally, I raise my mask up to get my bearings. The marina at Rovinj is lit with streetlamps, but no one is in sight this late. It's straight ahead, less than fifty yards away, and I cover this distance in under two minutes.

Here I climb ashore, look back out to the bay, and see a pair of little boats racing around, far to my southwest, flashlights whipping in all directions. The near constant voice of a man, shouting what sounds like both orders and admonitions, rolls over the water to me.

Removing my fins and mask, I adjust my pack on my back and start running for the warren of streets that make up the Old Town district of the small city, ready to disappear in an alleyway till the coast is clear. My plan is to call Talyssa to see where she is, then steal yet another car and pick her up.

For now, that's where my plan ends, but I just demonstrated to myself that I'm pretty fucking good on the fly. I accomplished nothing more tonight than finding out the city where the market is being held, but it's enough to move forward.

Still, it's becoming more and more obvious that Talyssa and I aren't going to be able to pull this off on our own, so my thoughts start drifting to a phone call that I really should make, but one that I *really* don't want to make.

THIRTY-ONE

The sleek Gulfstream 650 flew thirty-six thousand feet above northern Illinois, heading east from Van Nuys on its way to Venice, Italy. On board Kenneth Cage sat in the center of the cabin facing forward, and he dined on roast duck, sipping a light pinot noir along with it. He was surrounded in the aircraft by other men, seven in all, but his attention during dinner was on a notebook computer on the tray next to him: more specifically, the spreadsheet reporting this fiscal year's revenue from merchandise trafficked from the East and into Scandinavia. Estonia was producing some excellent product these days, but the real numbers were still coming from Belarus, where the poor economy and difficult conditions made it exponentially easier to dupe young girls into heading west for more opportunity.

The economy in the Baltic had developed greatly, in contrast, and this made it tougher on an enterprise like Cage's. The Consortium preyed on the downtrodden, those who wouldn't be missed or, if they were, would be missed only by those without the means to come looking for them.

Still, Scandinavia was generating tens of millions of euros in revenue, and Cage was happy enough with the reporting.

He was just biting into a forkful of saffron orzo when the phone on the table next to him chirped. He picked it up without looking.

"Yeah?"

. . .

Across from the Director of the Consortium, his chief protection agent, Sean Hall, sat facing aft, also dining on the roast duck. He regarded his boss as he chewed, then looked around the cabin at his full six-man executive protection detail, here to help him ensure Cage's safety on this trip.

Everyone on the team drank either wine or beer, a rare occurrence when around the principal, but for the next ten hours or so they had no duties whatsoever. Once they got where they were going, however, Hall knew they'd be working as hard as any of these men had worked since they'd served in combat or in critical SWAT callouts.

Hall sipped more wine, taking advantage of the rare opportunity, but his thoughts shifted to the job ahead. They would land at Marco Polo Airport in Venice early afternoon local time, and then Cage would be taken in a motorboat out to *La Primarosa*, with Hall and his six men surrounding him.

And then, around eleven p.m., Cage would go to the sale of the women to shake hands with some of his clients, again at the nucleus of a large security operation.

Everything in Hall's training told him this was a bad idea. This entire trip was Cage flexing his muscle to him and Jaco to show he wasn't scared of this Gray Man and wouldn't be ordered around by his subordinates.

Hall thought it to be an asinine risk just so his boss could get some tail that was on its way to him anyway.

The forty-year-old ex–Navy SEAL kept his eyes on the shorter, older American while Cage took the call, only because the two men were facing each other. But when Cage leaned back in his chair with an unmistakable look of exasperation on his face, Hall quickly tried to listen in to the one half of the conversation in his earshot.

"You're kidding. Wait. Tell me you are kidding?" Then, "*Fuck!* This has gotten *completely* out of hand!" Cage shouted into the receiver, drawing the attention of everyone in the cabin. "What the hell am I paying you bastards for?"

Sean Hall's roast duck was forgotten now, as was the wine. From the context of Cage's words, and the expression on his face, he knew this would be Jaco on the line, and Jaco would be telling him that yet something else had happened somewhere along the Balkan pipeline.

This had turned into a security emergency, Hall was certain, and as the head of security he told himself he was now officially back on the clock.

He snapped his fingers at his closest man, who was just bringing his bottle of Stella Artois to his lips. Hall said, "Dude, stop drinking. Pass it along."

Hall called the attractive flight attendant over, handed her his glass of wine, and told her to clean up the glasses and plates on his men's trays. Hall had a bottle of vodka in his kit bag, but right now his alcoholism wasn't a problem because he was more concerned with keeping himself and his principal alive for the next several hours.

He climbed out of his cabin chair and sat down next to his boss, who was still talking on the phone.

Cage said, "You're damn right, I will! Just because you can't do your job doesn't mean I'm not going to do mine. I swear to God, Jaco, you need to get this shit handled or I'll bring people in who can. Am I clear?"

There was another minute of talk, seemingly about one of the girls in the process of being trafficked, and then Cage slammed the phone down, thumped his head back into the leather headrest again, and closed his eyes.

Hall knew better than to speak up right now. He'd only get his head bitten off by the mercurial fifty-four-year-old.

Finally, the Director of the Consortium turned to look at his director of security. "Kostopoulos is dead. Strangled to death on his own yacht."

"*What?*"

"It was the Gray Man."

Sean's heart began to pound. "Verdoorn was on the yacht, wasn't he?"

With a quick nod Cage said, "Jaco says he shot at the fucker as he was making his getaway. Apparently without effect."

"Christ, Ken. If he was on the boat and he got away, then that boat is compromised."

Cage shrugged at this. "Jaco says the girls are going to be moved to shore as soon as they get to Venice. They're already on the way and will arrive in less than three hours. They'll put them up at a private house, and we'll take them to market from there."

Hall took a slow breath, steeling himself for the fight that he knew was to come, then said, "This was already an extremely difficult security equation when you were protected by the yacht and the water around it. We were going to take you to market via a skiff, and you wouldn't have to walk through those narrow pedestrian streets while an assassin targeted you. But now you are telling me that's just *exactly* what we're doing. No offense, Ken, but that's crazy. We need to turn this jet around right now and call it a day."

Cage looked off into space a few seconds. Hall knew all his men were watching this interaction between their boss and their protectee.

Finally the Director of the Consortium said, "Jaco says his men will check out the route, and they'll position themselves accordingly. All you and your boys have to do is catch any bullets that come my way. That doesn't sound too hard, does it, Sean?"

Hall tried another approach. "How about we take you to this private residence, you spend the afternoon and evening there? Meet all the girls. Spend all night with the special-handling merchandise. But don't go to the market. It's just too dangerous."

"Sean, let me explain to you a few things about the responsibilities of being in charge. People will know I'm in Venice, and they will expect me to come for the festivities."

"Not if there is a world-class gunman out there hunting for—"

"I'm going! You and these other guys, Jaco and his shock troops, the local mob who administrates the market . . . all of you just do what I pay you to do and there will be nothing to worry about."

Hall knew that changing his employer's mind was going to be a long shot, and like he'd anticipated, his long shot had failed, so he nodded without speaking and moved to the front bulkhead. Here he called his men up with him, and they sat, stood, or knelt close while their team leader talked about updates to their plans.

And while Hall spoke, he fumed. The ire he felt was not directed towards Cage, or at least the majority of it was not. He was, instead, furious at Jaco Verdoorn, because apparently Jaco had just told his boss that, despite all evidence to the contrary, the situation was under control and it was safe to come to Venice.

But Sean Hall knew something Ken Cage did not. He knew Jaco Verdoorn was as giddy as a schoolgirl at the prospect of going up against the uber assassin Gentry, and he wasn't above using his employer as bait to draw his prey in.

Hall wasn't going to tell Cage his concerns; he knew he didn't have the juice to get into an interoffice political war with Jaco Verdoorn. The South African was higher in the food chain than Hall, and Hall knew Verdoorn would simply turn Cage against him if this morphed into a real fight between them.

No, even though Hall had nothing but misgivings about this operation in Venice, he would do what all good military men and women are taught to do when they don't like an order—salute and draw fire.

He'd do what was asked of him, and he'd find a way to get his employer through the next twenty-four hours.

He thought of his bottle of vodka in his kit bag and wondered if he'd be able to sneak a few swigs before landing.

. . .

Roxana Vaduva lay on the bed in her stateroom on the lower deck, locked in with an armed Greek security man standing right outside the door.

Dr. Claudia sat on the edge of the bed next to her, an ice pack in her hand, and she held it to the young Romanian woman's right temple.

"You are going to be okay, young lady. You are very lucky."

"Lucky? The old man raped me, and then some man in a mask killed him right in front of me, then beat me up. Why don't I feel lucky?"

The truth was Roxana had not, in fact, been raped by Kostopoulos, but she wasn't going to reveal that to the American psychologist.

Claudia said, "Lucky to be alive." She pulled the ice away. "And lucky to be still considered a friend. By me, at least."

"What do you mean?"

"John doesn't believe your story. He finds it suspicious you were only knocked out, and he thinks you might have spoken with the assassin. He thinks the man was here to help you."

Roxana drew on her acting background now. "Then where is the help?"

"We watched the playbacks of cameras around the boat. The assassin was in Kostas's room for almost five minutes before he appeared on the main deck and jumped into the water. Plenty of time for you to talk to him."

"He knocked me out. I don't know what he did in the room while I was unconscious. He didn't kill me, because I wasn't what he was after. It's pretty obvious, even to me, that he came to kill the old man."

Claudia regarded her closely, but Roxana didn't waver.

Finally, the doctor said, "I am inclined to believe you. But John . . . I warned you about him. He will follow the Director's orders, but I'd keep my eyes open if I were you."

"Did you tell the old man to do what he did?"

"Of course not. But these are powerful men with powerful desires. I can't control what they do, and neither can you. Honestly, though, I think what happened to you is for the best."

"For the . . . best?"

"You needed to learn your place in all this. You have to give to get in this world, and you will be getting a lot of good things the moment you do your part.

"I hope this difficult lesson was . . . was beneficial."

Roxana knew she needed to be the best actress she could be now. "I . . . I understand. I don't want that to happen again." She looked down at the floor, then lifted her eyes back to the American woman. "If the Director can protect me, then I will behave."

Claudia smiled. "Very good. I am so pleased the program has helped educate you in all this. And just in time, too. The Director will be here this evening, and he wants to see you."

The young Romanian fought tears until Claudia dabbed her face once more with the ice and then handed it to her. Then the American left the stateroom, and when the door closed, Roxana closed her eyes, holding the ice there on her temple where it throbbed.

Tom was coming here. Her entire objective in staying on the boat had been to learn who he was, where he was, and what was at the end of this entire pipeline. This information she'd have to get to her sister some way, but now that she knew the American Director was coming to her, she wondered how the hell she was supposed to contact her once she had what she needed.

She fought more tears and told herself to be strong. Her resolve had gotten her this far through this mess, and all she could do now was do her best.

· · ·

I pull off the road less than ten kilometers south of Rovinj. My stolen Ford Focus rolls slowly along the rough shoulder as I peer into the darkness, but soon I see what I'm looking for. Talyssa comes out of the brush, waves at me, and then climbs into the passenger seat. She'd taken the boat along the shore, following *La Primarosa* with me on board, until her engine began to sputter, and then she'd beached the little craft and begun walking to the north.

She looks as exhausted as I feel, but her alert, hopeful, and expectant eyes belie all she's been through.

"Are you okay?" she asks as we pull back on the road.

"Yeah." I start to say more, but then I hesitate. I don't know how to tell her what I need to tell her.

"You got on board, obviously."

"I did."

"Well . . . what did you see?"

Looking forward through the windshield as I drive through the morning, I say, "Your sister is alive."

Glancing her way, I see her bring both hands to her mouth, and I can see her face redden, even here in the darkened car.

Finally, she asks, "You saw her?"

"I spoke with her."

"Oh my God."

"She is okay." *For now,* I think, all but certain that things are only going to get worse for Roxana.

"But . . . where is she? I need to see her."

"She's . . . actually, she's still on the yacht."

Out of the corner of my eye I see her lower her hands to her lap. Her tone changes, becoming angry and challenging. "I don't understand. Why didn't you rescue her?"

"I tried. She wouldn't go. They've told her she's being taken to the Director of the Consortium, and she sees this as the best chance to blow the doors wide open on this entire trafficking ring." I add, "She's doing it for you."

This is hard for the Romanian woman to accept; she argues with me for a minute, insinuates that I should have popped her sister on the head and hauled her off the yacht. I don't mention that I *did*, in fact, pop her on the head, and then I left her right there in the clutches of the murderous sex trafficking ring.

Not my finest hour, I'll admit.

She's furious at first, but as I drive north I calm her down, and it's clear Talyssa knows what I know, that Roxana's desire to live up to her sister's expectations was what put her on that boat, not me, and it's also what's keeping her on that boat now.

She asks, "What was she like? Her condition . . . mentally."

"She doesn't blame you for anything. She is as strong as I've seen from someone in this situation."

Talyssa turns to me. "You have seen people in this situation?"

"Similar situations, yes. The trauma bonds can be built quickly, and they can be very powerful. She's a trouper for fighting back the way she is."

"How do you know about trauma bonds?"

With only a little hesitation I say, "I have some training."

"In kidnapping people for slavery?"

"No. In being held hostage. There is a school for it. You learn survival, evasion, resistance, and escape."

"Where is this school?"

"Can't say."

"Of course you can't."

"The point is, you can be taught how to resist your captors, and you can build up a lot of defenses to their techniques. But these young people, snatched off the street, out of nightclubs, picked up through modeling agencies, thrown into this world . . . I can't imagine what they are going through psychologically. Whatever it is, they don't stand a chance."

"But Roxana's tough. She's *really* tough."

"So . . . what is our plan now, Harry? We just leave Roxana with them and wait to hear from her?"

"No. We're going to Venice. They will be there tonight, unless me showing up on *La Primarosa* changed their entire agenda." I can't rule out that possibility, but so far the pipeline seems to have continued on despite my harassment, with only a few diversions.

Talyssa asks, "And when we get to Venice? What will we do there?"

"The other girls will be sold off, and they'll all go to different groups, different countries. If I can't stop it tonight, I'll never get another chance to save those victims I saw in Bosnia."

But I sure as hell can't save those women by myself. I've been trying and failing at this since that night in Mostar when my actions made their awful predicament even more awful.

I know now that I need a hand, and I also know where to go for it.

Maybe.

"This has gotten too big," I say. "We're going to have to try to bring in some help."

"But . . . the police are corrupt."

"I'm not talking about the police."

"Who, then?"

I sigh and then drive in silence for a moment. Only when she asks me a second time do I reply. "Some acquaintances. But you need to understand one thing. They will either make the situation better, or they will make the situation worse. It's only out of desperation that I'm reaching out to them."

"But who are they?"

"I can't tell you," I say, and then I turn back to her. "Trust me."

She nods and looks out the window. Soon she starts to sniff back tears, no doubt thinking about Roxana, somewhere out to sea.

• • •

An hour later we're in the Italian town of Villa Opicina as the sun rises onto a clear morning. Talyssa is sitting on a stone bench in front of a church, and I'm walking around the grounds with my earpiece in. No one is in sight this early save for a couple of nuns who passed me by a minute ago, and they didn't exactly trigger my threat radar, so I feel secure enough for now.

I place a call that I've been considering, but dreading, for days and days now.

It's two a.m. in D.C., which means I'll be waking up someone on the eastern seaboard, but I honestly don't give a shit.

After five rings the call is answered with a sleepy female voice. "Brewer?"

"Hey. It's me."

Suzanne Brewer is my handler at CIA. To say our relationship is difficult would be underselling it significantly. She is not my biggest fan, which is also an understatement. In fact, it is entirely possible, perhaps even probable, that she tried to kill me a couple months ago.

I don't trust her, but right now, I'm out of options.

"Me, *who*?" She's just being difficult. It's par for the course from her.

"It's Violator."

She takes a few more seconds to wake up; I can hear her climbing out of her bed and walking, probably over to a computer in her house.

She says, "Iden code?"

I groan to myself and want to tell her, *For fuck's sake, you know who this is!* But I don't. Not because I'm above that sort of talk, but because I need something from her now.

I answer with a clipped, "Iden to follow: Whiskey, Hotel, Quebec, fiver, two, three, India."

The pause is brief. The voice is annoyed. "Iden confirmed."

I lay on the charm now, as thick as I can. "How's it goin'?"

"It would be 'goin'' better if you were working instead of on another one of your vacations."

I think about the past week and realize how much I wish I could take a vacation from this vacation. But I say, "I'll be back soon. Sooner, actually, if you give me a little help. It's really important."

"You wouldn't be calling if you didn't need help. You wouldn't be calling at this hour if it weren't important. What do you want?"

This is going well, so far. I decide to add to my charm offensive to reel her in.

"You feeling better?"

Suzanne Brewer had been shot a couple of months earlier; she fell into my arms, in fact, and I guess I probably saved her life. That's how I remember it, anyway, although my recollection of the incident is a bit fuzzy.

I hope that's how she remembers it, as well, to earn me a little more respect in her eyes so she'll give me what I need.

But she barks back at me. "I asked you what you wanted."

Nope, the ice queen is as frosty as ever, despite the fact that I stopped her from bleeding out back in the UK.

I reply with, "I need whatever the Agency knows about a sex trafficking ring referred to as the Consortium."

"Perhaps you are confused."

"Confused about what?"

"Let me explain how this is all supposed to function. You work for *this* intelligence agency, Violator. This intelligence agency does not work for *you*."

Yeah, I knew it was going to be like this, though I was hopeful it would be all unicorns and rainbows.

Hope is not a strategy, I tell myself yet again. Then I tell myself, *Screw it.* I turn off my faux charm and let her have it. "Just cut the shit and do this for me! Lives are at stake."

"Lives are at stake all the time, with *everything* we do. Every *single* day you run off to go find yourself, or whatever the hell you do during your hiatuses, lives are threatened. The program you belong to needs you, and you are out there—"

"*Please*, Suzanne. Please get me *something.*"

She stops bitching, which is a first, and then she sighs, which happens all the time. Finally, she says, "I've never heard of the Consortium."

"What about the pipeline?"

"What is that?"

"It's kind of like an underground railroad for the trafficked women. A smuggling circuit the victims are put through by the Consortium."

"No, I've never heard of that, either."

She sounds credible, but again, she also sounded credible when she said she hadn't been trying to shoot me in the head back in Scotland, and I retain doubts about that event.

I say, "Fine. But I bet you are sitting in front of a snazzy computer that has access to all sorts of supersecret files and databases, and you can query those terms in that context, and find out if the Agency has any intel I can use."

"Yes, I do have just such a computer in front of me. But what do *I* get out of this?"

As I walk through the garden of the church in the cool morning, it occurs to me, and not for the first time, that everybody wants something from me.

"What do you *get*? How about my unwavering devotion?"

"I already have a cat, Violator."

Of course you do. "Just tell me what you want from me."

"If I give you this intel, you will come back to D.C.?"

"Not immediately; I need actionable intel so I can *act*. But as soon as I'm done with—"

She interrupts. "Sorry, Violator. I need you. Your country needs you."

"I'll kiss your ass and I'll kiss the flag, probably not in that order, very soon. But for now I need to know about the Consortium. Seems to be run by an American male in his fifties. He used the name Tom, but that's going to be a pseudonym. There's an American female psychologist and a South African involved, as well. A rich Greek dude . . . he's dead. Don't know his name."

"How did he die?" she asks, but the way she asks tells me she has a pretty good suspicion that I killed him.

"Would you believe natural causes?"

Brewer just sighs again.

I continue. "The organization either owns or has access to a megayacht called *La Primarosa*. Right now it's in the northern Adriatic, heading to Venice, unless they changed their plans."

Brewer sounds like she's typing all this into her computer. Then she says, "Fine. Give me an hour and I'll call you back."

This went better than I thought. Momentarily stunned by my powers of persuasion, I can't even speak.

"Violator?"

I do my best to recover. "Uh . . . yeah. That's great. Let me call you, though. One hour."

The line goes dead, and I stand there in the middle of the well-kept church grounds, staring up at the steeple. It's a magnificent sight on this sunny, warm morning, but all I can think about is tonight and the twenty-three women and girls who have been on my mind since Bosnia.

My best chance to save them is a woman who hates my guts, and an organization that regularly uses me, while offering little in return.

But if this doesn't work, another option comes to mind. It chills me to think about employing plan B, but I may just be desperate enough to do so.

THIRTY-TWO

An hour later I'm parked at a gas station near the Italian town of Portogruaro. Talyssa is sitting in the car eating a pastry for breakfast, and I am lying twenty-five yards away in the grass by the parking lot, looking up at the sky. I'm tired as hell again, and I know I'm going to have to find a way to sleep before tonight. But that's not all I need, so I call Suzanne Brewer back.

She answers, and I say, "Violator," and then I play the game by the rules. "Iden code Whiskey, Hotel, Quebec, fiver, two, three, India."

"Confirmed."

"What did you learn?" I ask.

"I'm transferring you."

"*Transferring* me? It's three a.m. there. You're at the office?"

"I am now," she says, her voice no more or less annoyed sounding than usual. She adds, "Hold," and I do.

There is no hold music at CIA, which is too bad, because it's a missed opportunity for them to have fun and play the *Mission: Impossible* theme song or some shit, but nobody at Langley I've ever met has that kind of a sense of humor.

Soon the line clicks. "Hanley."

I launch up to a sitting position on the grass. Matthew Hanley is the deputy director for operations, the top dog in Ops. Brewer somehow got him into the building at three a.m. for this.

Matt and I go way back. He and Brewer are the only two people at Langley who know I'm doing contract work for the Agency, and that's because I'm essentially doing contract work directly for Hanley, with Brewer as the go-between. Still, though Hanley and I have spoken quite a few times over the past couple of years, I was hoping to avoid going all the way up to him in my hunt for intel about an operation I'm running on my own.

But I mask my unease. "Hey, Matt. All good with you?"

"Not so great."

"What's wrong?"

"Well, it's simple. I have three operatives in a special sub rosa unit. One of them is recovering from injury, one of them is a pain in my ass, and the other is AWOL."

I thought I was the pain in his ass until he mentioned AWOL. "I'm coming back. I just got myself involved in something and I need a little intel to wrap it up. Brewer shouldn't have bothered you with this."

Hanley replies to this with "The Consortium. That means nothing to us. There are sex trafficking rings all over. In your area, Albania and Turkey are big players."

I cock my head slightly. "How do you know what area I'm in?"

"Isn't it obvious?"

"How is it—"

"Because of Ratko Babic."

Matt knows I killed the general, or at least he thinks I did and he's trying to get me to confirm it. If it were anyone else, I probably would play stupid, but it's Hanley.

"Right."

He adds, "I wasn't going to ask you if you waxed old Ratko Babic, although from the minute I heard about his death, I knew that you did. Shit . . . everyone knows. But you're basically admitting it, so I'll just go ahead and say it."

"Say what?"

"Nice work. Not perfect . . . you fragged a bunch of Serbian goons who were active-duty members of their intelligence service. They were also Branjevo Partizans, so I'm not going to lose any sleep over that, but our Balkan desk is running interference, insisting to the Serbs that the former asset who became a rogue hit man called the Gray Man was seen in Santiago, Chile, at the same time as the Babic killing."

"If I don't work for the Agency, then why does the Agency give a shit if the Serbs think it was me?"

"We trained you, didn't we? We installed that wacky do-gooder moral compass of yours, didn't we?"

"Yes to the first. No to the second."

"Well, whatever. The Balkan desk will deal with Serbian intelligence. Wasn't exactly like we had a great relationship with Belgrade in the first place."

"Roger that. Back to the Consortium. Nothing? Really?"

"Sex trafficking is the third most profitable criminal enterprise in the world, behind drugs and counterfeiting. It's ahead of the sale of illegal weapons. So, yeah, I'm sure what you're talking about is real, I'm sure the people involved in it are nasty, and I'm sure a lot of poor helpless victims are abused and enslaved by it. But the specifics of what you are telling us . . . the Americans, the South African, the pipeline, this doesn't line up with anything we have."

"Can I get some help from you guys on this? Could you get Brewer to do a little digging?"

Hanley breathes one of his trademark long sighs, and I can picture his huge frame inside his too-large suit puffing up and then shrinking as every ounce of air leaves his lungs. I can also picture what he's about to say before he says it.

I'm about to hear a big fat no.

"No," Hanley says. "You are a hard asset, a denied hard asset at that, unaligned with any existing structure in the Agency. You are *not* a case officer, not an analyst, not chief of any station. You don't have read-ins on anything not directly linked to the work we assign you. You have absolutely no standing to ask for resources."

"I'm not asking because I think I am *owed* resources, I'm asking as a friend. I need some help. This is serious shit."

"You know what else is serious shit?"

Yeah, I do, and again, I know what he's about to say.

"Your fucking job with us! *That's* serious shit. I've got a backlog of work I need you to take care of."

"Get one of the other Poison Apple assets to—"

"They're already out there, Court, in the field, doing what they're told, while you're trying to save the world by yourself. Every day you're not here pulling your weight is another day Romantic and Anthem are under more stress, more risk. Anthem isn't even one hundred percent after what happened to her back in Scotland. You remember that little incident, don't you?"

My voice feels weak in my mouth as I answer back with "Yes, sir."

And then, just to hammer home a point that needed no further hammering, he says, "You're risking your girlfriend's life with all these crusades of yours, don't forget that."

Hanley is referring to Anthem, one of the three Poison Apple assets. She is Zoya Zakharova, former Russian intelligence, and also formerly someone I was in something of a relationship with. The relationship is strained for a couple of reasons right now, not the least of which is that I shot her.

I don't claim to know all the rules of dating, but I'm pretty sure if you shoot someone then you can't really refer to them as your girlfriend, but Hanley is turning the screws on me, because he knows I still care about her.

But Zoya is tough, as tough as or tougher than I am, and as tough as or tougher than the women and girls I'm desperately trying to help.

She can handle herself in the field.

"Sorry, Matt. That shit doesn't work on me. I'll be back with you as soon as I can. First I've got to try to do something."

"What are you going to do?"

"I'm going to Venice, and there I'll talk to somebody who can actually help me." I hang up the phone, knowing that this will piss Hanley off, but I don't really care. He could have lifted a finger to get me some assets directed to this, and he should have done so.

Fuck him. He doesn't know it yet, but he is about to do me a favor, and the thought of how annoyed he'll be when he realizes he did, in fact, help me out makes me smile.

I walk back over to Talyssa, who pulls a hot croissant stuffed with ham and cheese out of a bag and hands it to me, along with a cup of coffee.

"That didn't look like it went well at all."

"Not great, no. But I have someone else I can call."

She cocks her head. "Who?"

I answer with, "If I can't work with the good guys, I'm going to work *for* the bad guys."

The Romanian woman looks at me like I've lost my mind, so I clarify. "Not those bad guys. Some other bad guys."

She has no idea what I'm talking about, and that's for the best.

I send a few texts before we get back on the highway, and then, a little more than an hour later, I get the call approving my request for a face-to-face meeting with a man in Venice.

Talyssa doesn't lift her head out of her computer for the next three hours of our drive. Every now and then she takes a bite out of an apple or sips some bottled water, but she remains completely focused on her work.

Finally, as I'm arriving at the northern outskirts of Treviso, a city not thirty minutes from Venice proper, she leans her head back and groans like some sort of a wounded animal.

"I take it something's wrong."

She ignores me while she rubs her eyes, then takes a long swig of water. Finally she says, "I'm so close, but I can't do anything."

"What do you mean?"

"I've been going back through everything I have on the Consortium, all the relationships between all the companies, all the capital equipment I can trace to them: the plane, the yacht, stuff like that. I've traced bank accounts to the Caymans and the Dominican Republic and Crete and Luxembourg . . . but I'm no closer to finding out who the people are who run this thing."

I was hoping she'd be able to pull a rabbit out of her hat with her research, because I have serious doubts about my plan for tonight. Still, I see that she tried. "Sometimes there is no answer."

"There is an answer, it's just not available to me. If someone could hack into one of the law firms around the world that set up these offshore accounts, then they could swim upstream into the account information."

"You think the name of the Director of the Consortium would be tied to these accounts? I don't know much about money laundering, but I know they keep an air gap between themselves and the illicit money."

"Of course the accounts won't have the names of the people in charge, but they will have information on where the transfers came from: investment firms, hedge funds, real estate brokers. That could . . . no . . . that *would* lead me to the actual men and women who run this whole thing."

Her plan sounds about as likely as mine now. "Yeah, but you can't hack into the law firms. Can you?"

She shakes her head. "No. I can't. I mean, there are people out there who can, but they are criminals, and they sure as hell won't work for me."

"Do you know who they are?"

"Some of them. Europol is involved with investigations around the EU where we have identified hackers."

"Are they in jail?"

She shrugs, rubbing her neck. "Some are. Most aren't. The wheels of justice move very slowly in Europe. It's not like in America, where they put you in the gas chamber the day after they know you did it."

Her English is amazing, but her knowledge of the nation of my birth is lacking.

An idea comes to me slowly, and even as it begins to form, I ask her about it. "These people under investigation. Do they know you are watching them?"

"Well, technically Europol isn't watching them. Their nations' law enforcement entities are. But I do know who some of these people are."

"Where is the closest hacker who has the skills to do what you need?"

She thinks this over carefully. It looks to me like she enjoys the mental exercise of remembering the names and locations.

She says, "There's some good ones in Romania."

"Do they have protection?"

"Well . . . they work with organized crime, but virtually all of the black-hat hackers at this level do."

"Virtually all? Is there someone who isn't tied to any crime syndicate?"

Again she thinks in silence. "Well . . . for what I need, there is one man who has the skills and is not aligned with any known mafia group."

"Where is he?"

"He's in Amsterdam, which, coincidentally, is only an hour or so from my office and home in The Hague. His name is Maarten Meyer. We've been watching him for a while. He used to work in private banking for ING Group, a Dutch multinational, but he was caught embezzling. They fired him but did not prosecute him—they thought they'd lose private clients if they made too much noise about it."

"If they didn't prosecute, how do you even know about him?"

"We only learned of this after he was suspected by Dutch authorities of data theft at ABN AMRO, another large bank in Amsterdam. He was interviewed, he was suspected, but again, he was not prosecuted. There was some question at Europol about whether he was paying off high officials. We never found out, but the investigation into him continues. Interpol is looking into some data thefts in Antigua and Barbuda, and some others in the Caymans. He is highly skilled at picking the cyber locks of banks."

"You think he could get into the bank transfer records you need to identify where the money is coming from?"

Talyssa nods. "I know he can."

I lift up my phone and change my GPS destination. "Here's what I need—"

"You want to go find him, and beat him up until he agrees to do what we need."

"No. Finding out who runs the Consortium might save Roxana, but it won't save the girls we've been chasing. I have to go to Venice to try to find out where they are being sent."

She's confused. "So . . ."

"So," I say, "I need you to go to Amsterdam to convince Maarten Meyer to work with us."

"But . . . even if I could get him to do the hack, that's totally illegal."

"I hate to break it to you, Talyssa, but the 'doing things by the book' ship sailed a long time ago. You're pretty much an international criminal already."

She says nothing, so I finish my thought. "If there is some way to find out that intel, even if it's illegal, we probably should be considering it."

Slowly she nods. "But . . . how do I convince him to help us?"

"Tell him he's under investigation. Tell him you'll tip him off to a raid when it comes if he does what you want him to. Tell him you'll destroy evidence to help his case. Tell him anything to get him on board with us."

"But I . . . I can't do *any* of those things."

"You don't have to *do* anything, you just have to *say* you'll do something to help him."

"What, then we just fuck him over?"

"Pretty much. Look, think about your sister."

Now she looks at me with hard narrow eyes. "Think about my sister? That's all I am doing! I can't think about anything else at all other than what has happened to her, and what will happen to her if I can't get her back! Don't tell me to think about my sister!"

"I'm sorry. That was a stupid thing to say. I just need you to start breaking some dishes here. I need you to go to Amsterdam and convince Maarten Meyer to help us find the money launderers. If I could do it myself I'd put that guy's nuts in a vise and start flaying him, but I have to stay here."

"I am not going to put his nuts in a—"

"You won't have to. You just need to use what you have to get his compliance, and that is information about the international warrant being prepared against him."

I can see she's still pissed at me, but slowly she begins to calm down. "I can do that."

"I know you can. We'll go to the airport, and then you're going to Amsterdam."

THIRTY-THREE

La Primarosa made good speed for Venice, arriving just after eight a.m. Jaco Verdoorn was all but in command on the vessel now; the captain did little more than drive the boat while the big South African organized the quick and efficient disembarkation of the product. He knew he had to get all the merchandise along with all the evidence off in case the Gray Man had resources to have the yacht boarded. The Consortium controlled a portion of local law enforcement here, but it certainly didn't control all law enforcement, so there was a definite threat as long as the yacht was in the area.

By noon Verdoorn had removed his people from this potential compromise, relocating all twenty-three pieces of merchandise shipped on *La Primarosa* to a large private residence in Venice proper, on the Rio della Sensa, a canal on the northern side of the city. The impromptu safe house building was run by the Mala del Brenta, one of the local mafia groups here in northern Italy, and now all items were sequestered in several rooms on the second and third floors while armed Italians guarded them.

As was always the case on market days, the women and girls were well fed and given plenty of time to bathe. Clothing was brought in by stylists, hair and makeup would begin at five p.m., and Dr. Riesling spent the entire day speaking with each one of them privately, checking their mental state for what was to come.

Jaco Verdoorn established a secondary security cordon around the building, positioning most of his White Lion men in the streets and along the canals, eyes open for any hint of Courtland Gentry.

A couple more men had overwatch on the route Cage would take to the safe house, and Verdoorn was in near constant communication with Sean Hall so they could perfectly coordinate the movement of the principal during his short walk.

Verdoorn himself planned on taking an overwatch position, both today for Cage's arrival at the safe house and this evening as Cage and his security men went to the market. The South African had a Belgian FN F2000 rifle with a scope and a laser, and he wished for nothing more in this world than to see Gentry in his sights today or tonight.

He was experienced enough to recognize that there was an extremely low probability of he himself killing the target, but this was his op, these were his men, and they'd received his training, so if any one of his boys took out the American assassin, he'd consider it his kill.

. . .

After dropping Talyssa off at the airport I take the causeway to Venice and park the car at a lot on the western side of the 121 islands that make up the city proper. I climb out, stretching my legs and back. It's just past noon; I have some time before my two p.m. appointment, so I use it to do some shopping and to rent a room for the night. I find a little place in Santa Croce on the Rio de Santa Maria Maggiore, and here I take a shower and then, with scissors and a razor purchased during my stop at a pharmacy, I go to work.

I'm wearing a suit I bought off the rack an hour and a half ago, and cherry wingtip shoes purchased just after that. My face is clean-shaven for the first time in months and my hair is slicked back with product, and although this is hardly my normal look, I've made a career out of blending in with my surroundings, and I am certainly dressed for the part I'm about to play.

Then I go back out onto the street to walk to my nearby meeting.

Venice is a tourist trap; the narrow streets and passages are packed so tightly with foreign travelers that you shuffle along like cattle, restaurants all sell the same food, and gift shops all sell the same few dozen items.

It's the Disney World of Italy.

I've only been here once, doing a job for the Goon Squad a few years back. The Agency was tailing a Tunisian lawyer they thought had ties to Al Qaeda, and my unit of Ground Branch operators was brought in to roll him up, which we did in an alleyway near his flat on a moonless night.

It was a textbook op; we shuffled the guy to a waiting Cessna Citation, and then we watched it climb into the Italian sky.

Never heard what happened to the lawyer, or even if he was, in fact, tied to AQ, but that was standard operating procedure back then. I was a sled dog on a team; nobody told me where we were going, and my job was simply to respond to the crack of the whip.

Now I have authority over my actions, and I have discretion to move forward or to pull back. But Venice seems so much more ominous today, while working on my own, than it did back then as part of a cell of American operatives.

THIRTY-FOUR

At two p.m. I step up to the nondescript door of an equally nondescript building on the Fondamenta Santa Caterina. There is construction going on around this building and those nearby, and I look over some of the workers and wonder if they are really who they purport to be.

I'm guessing not. I'm assuming a lot of them are armed, and I'm pretty sure all of them knew I was coming.

I *really* hate being looked at, but in times like these, it's part of the job.

I'm frisked inside the door by a pair of young guys wearing coveralls. I know for certain they are Italian mafia, and they are just wearing the blue-collar work duds as a cover. They take my phone and wallet, but I've left my pistol and the rest of my gear at the rental unit so as not to get anyone excited. A woman descends a wooden staircase and shakes my hand, then escorts me back up. She's all smiles, but I see the armed goon watching me from the mezzanine and feel the presence of one of the guys I met at the front door looming close behind me now as I ascend.

Soon I enter the library and find myself face-to-face with Giancarlo Ricci, the security chief for the Alfonsi crime family, one of several mafia concerns here in northern Italy. The Alfonsis aren't as connected and don't have as much reach as some of the Sicilian and Calabrian groups, and they are nowhere near as powerful in Venice as the Mala del Brenta organiza-tion, but regionally they are relatively big players.

I've spoken with Ricci before but never in person. I've done work for him, and he's been happy with the service I provided, so as soon as I knew I was heading to Venice without any support from the Agency, I decided to reach out to him.

Still, I'm going to have to do one hell of a dance to get any assistance from the Alfonsi clan. Just like the CIA, the Italian mob doesn't simply hand out favors for the asking.

I'm wearing the suit and I've combed my hair and shaved my face for one reason only. I can't come in here looking like the flailing, scrambling, exhausted, beat-to-shit, lost puppy that I am right now. I need an air of control, a visage of power, and at least a modicum of authority. Ricci would have me tossed out on my ass here if he didn't think I was in a position to do something in exchange for what I am about to request from him.

Giancarlo Ricci stands and shakes my hand, but I can see that his eyes are wary. More than once he flashes a glance in the direction of the two men standing nearby, and their hands are crossed in front of them, where they can quickly reach inside their jackets to pull a weapon.

I wait for Ricci to talk, showing him the respect I imagine he garners from all his subordinates.

When he does talk I'm reminded how good his English is. It's flawless, in fact. He has the look and demeanor of a European who grew up not in his home country but in a Swiss boarding school, where he was no doubt taught five languages.

He doesn't ask me to sit down. Instead he says, "I spoke with the Gray Man over the phone a few times, as I recall. But I've never met him in person, and I've never seen a photograph. How do I know . . . that you . . . are you?"

"I did a job for you three years ago. I can go into detail if that will help."

"No need. Just tell me what I told you when it was done."

"You gave me a warning, in no uncertain terms. Told me not to double-cross you. You said the Alfonsi family wasn't the largest organization around, but you have a lot of friends, and the right kind of friends to settle scores."

"Almost correct. My employer, Luigi Alfonsi, *he* has friends. I myself do not have any." He shrugs. "It comes with this life. You certainly understand that, don't you?"

I don't answer. I am not prepared to agree that his life and my life have any points of connection beyond this meeting.

Instead I say, "Well, since I didn't double-cross your employer, I hope you will consider me a friend now."

With a smile and a dramatic shrug, Ricci says, "I must confess . . . I am confused. They say you are invisible." A pause as he looks me over head to toe. "But I see you."

The man may be a mafia security chief, but he's also hilarious.

I reply, "When I want to be seen, I can make it happen. When I want to disappear, same thing."

Ricci nods again; he appears more relaxed now, and he motions to a chair in front of where he had been sitting when I entered. "*Sí*. Very good."

We both sit while coffee is poured, and I don't hesitate to drink down a hot gulp. Ricci makes no small talk, and I'm glad for this, because I don't have a hell of a lot of time.

I say, "You want to know why I am here, right?"

With another flash to his security men, Ricci says, "I don't think you are here to kill me. Most of the people who want me dead insist on trying to do it themselves. They don't hire someone else. I have that effect on people, for some reason." He smiled, at ease now, considering the situation. "So . . . yes, I want to know why you are here."

"I need something from you."

The man shrugged. "Maybe I need something from you, too."

"Of course you do. I understand how this works, signore. You help me, and I help you. You will have my services at your disposal as soon as I'm done with the project I'm involved in now."

"Who are you working with?"

I sip more coffee, and a man in a fitted blue suit refills my cup. I say, "You wouldn't believe me if I told you."

"People lie to me all the time, so you may be right about that. But tell me anyway."

"I am not working with anyone. I am on my own."

"That seems hard to believe. You are one of the highest-paid assassins in the world."

"I didn't come here to lie to you."

Ironically, that itself is a lie. I've come here to do just exactly that.

The man does not speak for several seconds. "*Bene*. What do you need?"

"A group of trafficked sex slaves is in town. They will be sold at a market tonight. Here, somewhere in Venice. I'd like to know where this is."

Ricci drinks coffee, then raises an inquiring eye to me. "You are speaking of the girls from the pipeline?"

He knows, as I knew he would. Now I can only pray he's not involved with it. If he is I'm diving out the window in front of me, or else I'll go after the closest armed man and fight to get his weapon out of his hand.

But I know both of these options would come with a *very* low probability of success.

Ricci puts his cup down and leans back. "The pipeline. Are you wondering if they are us? They are not. The Consortium is aligned with Mala del Brenta here. Bad men in that organization."

I just nod and say, "I'm not a fan of the MdB."

He says, "They are our competitors. Disrupting their operations, as long as it can't be tied to us, would give us pleasure."

I start to speak again, to tell him I would be happy to fuck with the MdB on my own, if he just gives me the intel I require.

But before I can tell him this, he says, "I'd like to help you, signore, truly. But there is one problem."

"What's that?"

"The Consortium . . . they serve a purpose. They help my firm with . . . how do you say it, *securing* some of our earnings."

Shit. The Consortium launders money for Alfonsi.

"Apparently they are quite good at that part of the equation, too," I remark.

Ricci shrugs. "It's a big business."

I am dead certain Ricci's organization makes a lot of money from prostitution; he and his boss are probably just as bad as the men I'm after. But frankly, I've got a pretty full to-do list right now, so I'm not going to worry about that.

I spend a lot of time with strange bedfellows when I work in the private sector. It's pretty much my modus operandi.

I need to convince him I'm not going to disrupt his organization's money-laundering needs, so I say, "This has nothing to do with the Consortium. This has to do with Mala del Brenta. I figured your boss wouldn't have any problem with my screwing around with them. You and your staff have plausible deniability. I was never here, and I certainly was never working for you."

He regards me a long time before asking, "Why do you want to know where the trade will happen?" When I don't answer immediately, he smiles. "You want to rescue one of the girls, is that it?"

That's a good story, let's go with that. I nod. "For her father. An old friend from my days working in Russia."

Ricci's eyebrows rise again, and I can't tell if he believes me. Finally he says, "If I give you the location of the sale, what will you do with it?"

Holding intense eye contact, I reply, "My plan is to wait for my girl to be sold, then separated from the others. And then I'm going to get her back from the people who bought her. I am assuming security will be easier to manage once she's moved."

"You will act in Venice, or once the girl is taken to her final destination?"

"I will act at first opportunity. No matter where that is."

He takes this in for a minute. I know that telling him I would wait till they were out of the area before I start kicking ass would have earned me more favor, but I'm hoping he regards my comment as honesty, and he'll offer up some brownie points to me for not insulting his intelligence.

Giancarlo says, "So . . . though you may act here in the city, it will only be against the buyer, and only for the purposes of recovering your missing property."

Yeah, he just called the victims property. I'm in bed with a prick, but I knew that going in, and what choice do I have? He's like Vukovic, and probably like all the others involved in human trafficking. The dehumanization of the women and girls is absolute, a necessity for the twisted minds who scout them, take them, smuggle them, and abuse them.

And this motherfucker in the five-thousand-euro suit in front of me is no better.

But I'm in character here. I say, "I'm not trying to make life more difficult here for anyone. I just want the property back."

He presses, "You can assure me there will be no disruption of the Consortium's work itself here in Venice. You have no plans to target the organization, that is what you are saying."

He *wants* to help me, that much is evident.

Without batting an eyelash, I say, "None whatsoever. I just want to bring a nice girl home to her father."

Ricci nods thoughtfully. "If I give you information, you must do a job for me. A difficult job."

And this is, of course, why he wants to help me.

I ask, "Where is this job?"

A pause. "America."

Shit. I don't know the job, the target, the location, or the threat . . . and I certainly have my doubts about the morality. There's no way in hell I'm killing some dude in the United States for the Italian mob.

But I need a break here. I say, "The moment I have the girl back to her father, I will go to the States and do whatever you want me to do."

This is going well, and just as I think this I recognize that Ricci is suspicious of how well it is going. Finishing his coffee and putting the cup down, he says, "The story going around about you, as I'm sure you are aware, is that you double-crossed your masters in the CIA."

I reply flatly, "They started it."

He laughs, surprising me. "Maybe so. Maybe so. But you know my brotherhood is not like the CIA. I will find you if you double-cross me."

"As you've told me before."

"And as I will remind you again. You do *not* want me as an enemy. You do not want Luigi Alfonsi as an enemy. Is that clear?"

I have every intention of double-crossing the man across the table, but I also happen to be a pretty good liar. "You can count on me, sir."

"Well, then." Ricci sticks out a hand and I shake it. "I will give you information."

"Tell me about the market."

"It's held by the Consortium for their best customers. Six times a year or so." He nods. "And you are correct. It is tonight. It begins at midnight."

"The location?"

"It's in a building that adjoins the Casino of Venice. It's invitation only, needless to say, and invitations are scarce and well checked."

"How much security will be there?"

Ricci shrugs. "Mala del Brenta men, two dozen or so the last time I heard. The Consortium will have their own security."

That's a lot of guns, but I imagine that's not all of it. I assume security will be well beefed up after what I did in Bosnia and Croatia and out on the Adriatic Sea.

It sounds like a no-go zone for me, and my heart sinks. His next words do nothing to assuage my frustration.

"It will be incredibly difficult for one man to get inside the event. I can't help you there."

I'm desperately thinking about sewers, air ducts, rooftop access, and the like, and I'm thinking about stealing credentials and uniforms from employees of the venue. Hell, I'm even thinking about finding a way to steal or forge an invitation.

None of it sounds promising, especially because I know the opposition will be checking all these avenues of approach to make sure some jackass isn't trying to slip into their party tonight.

But then Ricci brightens up. "There is a bar, it's two blocks away. I can get you in there. If I remember correctly you'll be able to see the building where the market is being held. You will be an employee, just for tonight. No one will bother you. Just do a little work, then run off and do what you need to do. You won't be able to get close to the casino, but it's along the route anyone leaving the building will take to get to the main street."

This probably looks to Ricci like a completely safe option for me to get some reconnaissance tonight, but I know what he doesn't.

The Consortium is looking for me, and they'll be ready.

Still, I don't see any better opportunity for getting real eyes on and getting pictures of the buyers and sellers.

I stand and extend a hand. "That sounds perfect, signore."

It's not perfect, it's not even close, but it's as good as I'm going to get, and again, I have to look like I know what I'm doing.

THIRTY-FIVE

The pilot of the Dassault Falcon 50 lined its nose up between the runway end identifier lights beaming out of the dusk, checked his adherence to the glide path, and listened while his computer told him he was one thousand feet above the ground.

The pilot worked for Air Branch, the CIA Special Activities Center's air wing, and this meant he was one of the best fliers on Earth.

Before qualifying to fly the relatively sleek and advanced Falcon 50 he'd flown fat and slow Twin Otters off muddy and rocky jungle strips in Central America and Southeast Asia, so big, wide, and flat that runway 04 Right, dead ahead and a half mile out, was a piece of cake.

In the cabin of the aircraft behind him the flight attendant strapped herself into the folding bulkhead seat, and then she rubbed her hands and wrists repeatedly.

This was only Sharon's third Agency flight since she'd been wounded in a tarmac shootout while on board a CIA Gulfstream a couple months earlier. Both her hands still ached where the bullet had smashed into them, but she'd passed her medical requirements a week and a half earlier and had been returned to duty.

Facing aft, she was able to gaze upon the six men seated in the captain's chairs. They were all in their thirties and forties; many wore longer hair and beards. They were quiet and soft-spoken and had been no trouble during the eight-and-a-half-hour flight from Reagan National in D.C.

Sharon had been doing this long enough to recognize a Ground Branch unit when she saw one. These were CIA paramilitary operations officers, among the most highly trained fighters on planet Earth. Individually, they looked normal. They could be oil rig workers or construction workers or any other banal job that required manual labor. But together, to a practiced eye like Sharon's, these were obviously American intelligence commandos.

The Dassault touched down moments later at Aeroporto di Treviso, twenty miles northwest of the city of Venice, and then it taxied to a fixed-base operator on the southwestern side of the airport. Here the plane parked on the ramp, one hundred yards away from the doors to the FBO. The pilot and copilot shut it down while in the back the passengers readied their equipment.

The arrival of the CIA flight had been arranged and approved by Italian officials, who were told these men were NATO forces and tied to the nearby U.S. air base at Aviano. There were no checks of customs or immigration, as this was a "black" flight, allowed by the Italians.

Chris Travers stood in the low cabin and turned back to his team. At thirty-five years old, he was young to be running his own six-man Ground Branch unit, but he'd proven himself in the U.S. Army as a Special Forces officer, as a CIA para unit member, and then, finally, as a second-in-command on a Ground Branch team.

After the death of his team leader and meritorious accolades for Travers's actions during the event where the TL died, Travers himself was promoted to team leader.

Ground Branch reported to the director of the Special Activities Center, who reported directly to the deputy director for operations, but things on tonight's op were a little bit more streamlined than normal, because command authority of the entire operation was not located in Langley.

Tonight command authority rested with the man sitting in the darkness in the back of the cabin. This figure said nothing while Travers gave final instructions to his crew, even though he himself had once run a team not unlike the one sitting in the cabin with him.

Travers said, "Listen up. We have a sixteen-passenger van waiting to take us into the city. As I told you before, our mission this evening is the location and removal of a CIA asset, code named Violator. We have a general understanding of where he will be but no good timeline, so we're heading there now, will remain clandestine, and will use nonlethal means to obtain his compliance with our commands."

One of the older men on the team muttered, "Yeah, right," and others around him chuckled.

Everyone on the team had been around the block enough to know the legend of Violator, aka the Gray Man, but only Chris and the man sitting in the back of the aircraft knew the former CIA employee personally.

Travers addressed his doubtful subordinate directly. "Yeah, I hear you. We all know Violator is a badass, and if we can't talk him into coming along with us, then this will get ugly. But that's our op, so if you don't like it, you can go fuck yourself."

This received a few chuckles, as well, including from the man who'd seemed to doubt the wisdom of taking on Violator in the first place.

The team leader continued. "We know he's worked with the Luigi Alfonsi family in the past. We are going to set up surveillance around the quarter where the Alfonsis are strongest, and if we get more specific location intel, I'll flex you over to those areas as necessary. This might take some time, so be prepared for a long night."

The men hefted packs and filed out of the aircraft in silence. Travers was the last through the hatch, but as he neared the stairs he turned around and looked at the man in darkness in the back.

"Hey. You coming?"

Chris Travers saw the silhouette of the man as he reached for his bottle of Corona and took a slow sip. "Nah. You boys run along. I'm going to hang out here."

Travers shrugged. "Long flight not to get off the plane. Figured you'd want a chance at a little action."

The man chuckled softly, then said, "I might be seeing more action than you tonight, kid."

"Whatever." Travers left the aircraft, then climbed into the van with his men.

. . .

When he was gone, the man in the back of the cabin called up to the front. "Sharon?"

The flight attendant stepped up as the man dialed a number on his phone. "Sir?"

"I'm going to put you on the phone with someone. He's going to give you some direction for this evening."

She cocked her head. "Yes, sir. Can I ask what this is about?"

"Of course. He is going to tell you that you are to do whatever I tell you to do."

"I'm sorry, sir. I don't know who you are, but I am pretty certain I don't work for you."

"No, you don't. But you *do* work for him."

He tapped a button, putting his sat phone on speaker, and then a voice said, "Miss Clarke. This is Matthew Hanley, DDO. I need you to listen very carefully."

The flight attendant sat down in a captain's chair with wide eyes.

"I'm listening, sir."

. . .

I sit in my rented flat on the Ruga Giuffa, watching the last of the day's light fade through the dirty windows. I caught a few hours' sleep and I ate in a restaurant down on the first floor of the building, careful to sit far in the back to avoid any detection from the street.

But it's eight forty-five p.m.; I'm back in the room and it will be full-on dark soon, which means it's almost time for me to leave.

Before I set out I call Talyssa, who should be on the ground in Amsterdam, en route to the home of black-hat hacker Maarten Meyer. She answers on the second ring, which I take as a promising sign.

"Hello?"

"It's Harry. You made it there?"

"I'm outside his house. I don't think he's home."

"That's okay. You knew you might have to wait."

"I don't know if I can do this."

"You can, and you can call me if you need help. Remember, you have your Europol credentials and a lot of information about his crimes and the investigation under way. Come at him hard, threatening even, but then show him a way through the door. You have to make him *want* to work with you so he doesn't end up in prison."

"But . . . what if he says no? What if your plan doesn't work?"

This isn't going to work, I tell myself. Then I tell Talyssa, "It's going to work. Trust me."

After a moment she replies softly, and with no obvious confidence. "All right. I will call you when I have him." Then she says, "While I'm doing this . . . what will you be doing?"

"I'll be doing what I do best."

"Which is?"

"What do you think?"

Talyssa heaves a long sigh. "You are going to try to catch someone and beat information out of them."

"You know me too well."

I am worried about her, just like I was back in Dubrovnik when she had been rolled up by the Albanians. But now I can't do anything to help her. She's on her own.

"Listen," I say. "If it's not working out, if you feel like you might be in any danger, then you need to just pull out of there. I can try later."

"Later all the girls will be gone."

"I know. I just don't want you getting hurt."

She sniffs into the phone. "Thank you, Harry. You be careful, too."

Thirty minutes later I am out on the street, walking east through the artificial lights towards the Casino of Venice.

I begin focusing my attention on my mission this evening. I need to be gray, to blend in with my surroundings, more so with each step as I near my target location.

Talyssa can pull this off, I tell myself. *I can pull this off, too.*

It's an affirmation borne not out of real conviction but rather out of desperation.

We *have* to pull this off.

. . .

Ken Cage stepped out of the bathroom off the foyer of the Mala del Brenta safe house with a long, labored sniff, then he rubbed his eyes and nose.

He grabbed his black suit coat off a leather wingback chair, slipped it on, looked to his bodyguard, and gave him an energetic nod.

Cage knew Sean Hall would understand that this meant he was ready to leave for the auction.

Hall immediately slipped on his own jacket, then radioed his team through his cuff mic. Within moments the six men appeared in the foyer and formed around their boss and their principal.

Hall gave the men last-minute instructions, then radioed Jaco Verdoorn. He had no idea where the South African and his men were stationed outside, but he knew they would be trying to spot Gentry, if he was even in the area at all.

Verdoorn acknowledged Hall's message that the movement was beginning, but he gave the American lead protection agent no more information about his and his team's dispersement around the route to the auction.

With a head bob by Hall in the direction of the exit, the point man on the Cage detail opened the door and the entourage began filing out. It was eleven forty-five p.m., nearly nine hours after they'd arrived at the safe house.

Cage walked along through the surprisingly cool July night, wiping sweat from his forehead with a handkerchief as he did so. He wasn't feeling great right now; he'd done enough Viagra, cocaine, and ecstasy this afternoon and evening to flare up his angina to the point where it felt like a steam hammer was pounding around inside his chest.

For Ken Cage, a full day of sex required no small amount of external assistance, and the side effects of all the stimulants were as wearing on him as the physical activity itself.

He'd slept for a few hours after his exertions; the girls had been moved to the market in the early evening so there was nothing else for him to do, but it was an uncomfortable sleep with the drugs pumping through him.

He put away the handkerchief and, from the same pocket, pulled out a few Valium he'd staged there to calm his heart, swallowing them dry.

Still, despite his chest pain, he felt he'd had a pretty good day. He'd had sex with three of the girls, all of whom would be sold off in the next few hours to Saudi sheiks or Asian billionaires or diamond-level prostitution agencies in Belgium or Holland.

He'd been rough with the merchandise, even rougher than usual, in no small part because he was frustrated by the events of the past few days. In all his working life, this was the first time that some entity seemed to have a personal stake in upsetting one of the most lucrative veins of his wealth. He'd dealt with rival operations, mobsters in competition with mobsters who worked for him, but that was just business.

But this? This uber killer chewing his way along the pipeline? This was something else.

And Cage was angry at his employees like he'd never been in the past. At Hall for showing fear and doubt when up against one lone man, and at Verdoorn for being unable, despite all the resources Cage had afforded him, to find and end this persistent threat.

As the entourage turned down a narrow side street, he looked up to the roofs and immediately saw a man looking down on them. He didn't say anything to Hall, because he knew this would be one of Jaco's guys, and Hall would only freak out until this was confirmed.

He walked on, thinking about the girls who would be sold off tonight. He'd looked over each and every one. He'd also paid a short visit to the cream of the crop here. The two girls he'd ordered sent to Rancho Esmerelda and been waiting to get his hands on both occupied their own quarters on the third floor, and Cage had gone to visit them both. He found Sofia to be compliant, but Dr. Claudia Riesling had told him she'd administered a large amount of Xanax to the eighteen-year-old Hungarian shortly after her arrival because she hadn't had time enough with the girl to bring her into line.

Maja, on the other hand, had not been drugged. Cage found her inquisitive, obstinate, the same free spirit he'd encountered in Bucharest months earlier. She had nothing but questions about where she'd go and who she would be around, and Cage thought, a few minutes into their conversation, that the doctor should have plied her with pills, as well, before he came.

But Maja had not been any real trouble, per se. Claudia had told Cage upon his arrival that she'd worked especially hard with the young Romanian, and she felt that her psychological reprogramming had been successful.

Cage had not laid a finger on either of the Rancho Esmerelda–bound women. There would be time enough for that when they got to Southern California in a couple of days.

Now it was approaching midnight, and the entourage walked through the Calle Larga Vendramin after being dropped off by a pair of eight-meter-long speedboats a couple blocks from the casino. The boats had rumbled away, and everything was perfectly silent around Cage apart from the men's footsteps in the narrow alleyway.

The coke was wearing off; he told himself he'd need one more line when he got to the market.

His phone chirped in his pocket and he answered it loudly and abruptly, showing that perhaps his coke had not, in fact, worn off to the extent he'd first thought.

"Yeah? Who is it?"

"Daddy," a young female voice said, "it's Juliet."

Cage shook his head to clear his mind. He'd been thinking of sex and drugs and hit men and bodyguards, but quickly he had to morph himself back into the family man role he played.

"Hey, honey. How are you?"

"Mom won't let me go over to Madeline's tonight. It's summer. I'm bored here. Can I tell her you said it's okay?"

Cage sighed and continued walking while talking to his twelve-year-old daughter, his voice echoing off the stone buildings all around him.

...

Chris Travers took the call on his sat phone at midnight, just as he found a position on the Rialto Bridge that gave him incredible sight lines along the Grand Canal. The phone was Bluetoothed to his earpiece, so he flipped off the interteam radio and took the call, stepping away from the group of tourists he'd blended with to avoid detection by Gentry. "Zulu Actual."

"Iden, six, six, four, November, Alpha, India."

He recognized the voice of Suzanne Brewer, an operations officer who worked directly for Deputy Director Hanley. He recognized her identity code as well.

"Iden confirmed," Travers said. "My iden is forty-six, Bravo, Sierra, nine, Kilo."

"Roger, Zulu. Be advised, I have new targeting information for you. Target can be located in or around the Casino of Venice, in Carnareggio, two zero, four zero. Be advised that while we believe he is working alone, the area will likely be populated with third-party hostiles, forces from the Mala del Brenta crime organization."

Travers scribbled this all down on a small pad. "Got it. Interrogative: where did we get this information?"

"That's 'need to know' only, Zulu. Just treat the intel as credible."

Need to know? Travers thought. *Why wouldn't the guys on the ground need to know where the hell the CIA was getting intricate location and disposition-of-forces intel?*

He didn't argue, but he did ask another question. "Do we know the time when the target should arrive at this poz?"

"Time, now, Zulu. Get there ASAP."

"Roger that. We're en route."

Suzanne Brewer then said, "As per the DDO, the subject is to be taken alive. Is that clear?"

Travers sighed in disbelief now. Court Gentry was his friend, more or less. At the very least they had fought and bled alongside each other. Travers had been given the rules of engagement already, so he knew Gentry wasn't hostile. Gentry was just being Gentry, doing his own thing, and the DDO wanted his ass dragged back to the East Coast so he could be put back in service.

Yeah, he might not want to go, and he would try to escape and evade. Gentry might even throw a fist or try out some of his whiz-bang judo shit. But neither side was going to pull guns on each other.

Court was a good man in the Ground Branch team leader's book, despite what the Agency brassholes said about him from time to time. There was no way Travers or his team was going to kill him, and Brewer's stressing of the rules of engagement just made him dislike the already dislikable woman even more.

But Travers was a good soldier. He kept his voice much more dispassionate than he felt as he replied, "Alive. Understood and wilco."

He then transmitted on his interteam radio. "Listen up, Zulu. New target coordinates, one klick my poz on foot to the east. Everybody flex over there, and double-time it."

THIRTY-SIX

Here I am, in yet *another* dark room, in yet *another* congested European city, looking out yet *another* dirty window in search of yet *another* group of assholes.

At times like these I can't help but wonder if I should have gone to college.

I've been working at the packed restaurant and nightclub downstairs for the past two hours, carting ice to the bartenders, changing out kegs of beer, and schlepping cases of wine and liquor down two flights of stairs, then schlepping the empty bottles out to a loading dock in the back.

But at a quarter till midnight I slipped away from my assigned duties, picked an office door lock on the second floor, and found an overwatch position above the alleyway that looked directly out towards my objective.

I'm sitting in the dark, staring down on my target location, waiting for something to happen.

The Casino of Venice is in an ornate palace with a simple facade, tucked away in a tiny square surrounded by taller structures. Next door to it is a square building with a pair of large red wooden doors on the other side of a stone forecourt with an impressive iron gate. I see several people milling about inside the gate, all male, all dressed in fine suits. These don't look like security, and they don't look like Italian mafia to me.

So I'm guessing these shitheads are the buyers.

I'm assuming there are more inside, and I'm also assuming the women from Mostar have already been brought in, either via the passageways in front of me and off to my left or else through some sort of back entrance. The building does back up onto a small canal, so I know I may miss some of the comings and goings, but I also know beggars can't be choosers, and this spot gives me a good chance of getting a look at some of the players.

I pull out my camera and begin taking pictures of the men I see, all the while scanning the buildings, windows, and alcoves within sight. I take it to be a one hundred percent chance that the Consortium will be on the lookout for me, and they'd be idiots not to put surveillance at the front entrance to tonight's market. But despite my searching, I don't see any threats except a couple of goons standing at the casino door.

Still, I know they are out here somewhere.

Close to me, hunting me.

I keep shooting images, but soon I hear a voice in the alleyway off to my left. I don't move closer to the window to improve my angle so that I can get a visual on the noise, but instead I patiently wait for whoever is talking to come into view.

Finally a group of seven or eight men, all in business suits, walk together in a tight profile, casting one long shadow as they pass in front of a streetlamp. One of their number is talking loudly, in an animated fashion, as if he is on the phone. I can't make out the words, but I can hear that he's speaking English.

I focus on the middle of the cluster of men as they turn and begin down the alleyway towards the casino entrance. I see the top of a bald head, barely visible among the much taller men around.

I see a phone to his ear and realize he's the one speaking.

Who the hell is this guy?

I don't know why I'm asking myself that, because I know. He's American, short, bald, and obviously important.

This is exactly how Roxana Vaduva described the Director of the Consortium.

Holy shit, I say to myself.

If Roxana was aware that the man she knew as Tom was going to be in Venice tonight, she sure didn't tell me. I saw no signs of her trying to deceive me back on *La Primarosa*, so I'm guessing she had no idea he'd be making an appearance.

This makes me wonder if she was correct about her going to the USA after the sale.

And it also makes me worry, because if the Director is here, it may mean he's already raped her.

I close my eyes and fight to push the thought out as a wave of guilt washes over me. I tell myself I could have found a way to get her off that boat, even if she didn't want to go. I *know* I could have but, if I'm being honest with myself, I know exactly why I didn't do it.

Roxana was absolutely right—she *was* Talyssa's best chance for finding out who was running the Consortium.

I left her there, on the yacht and in mortal danger, because she was our agent in place and, despite the risks to her, we needed her in play.

I'd never tell her sister this in a million years, but it's the truth. Roxana's life was worth risking for me to complete my mission.

And knowing all this does nothing to mitigate the guilt I'm feeling.

I open my eyes, refocus on my objective, and start taking pictures like a madman.

Soon the men enter the tiny square, then step through the iron gate in front of the house next to the casino. They walk through the small forecourt and enter through the red doors.

I don't get a single usable shot of the man in the middle of the security detail.

Son of a bitch.

All I can do now is sit here till they leave and shoot images of anyone else who comes and goes. There are over twenty women who will be lost in the wind forever unless I can ID the shitheads who are taking them.

I settle into place, ready to wait this out.

. . .

Willem Klerk stood inside a well-lit gelato shop on the Rio Tera San Leonardo, biting into a pistachio cone and gazing only intermittently out onto the touristy street, still relatively crowded at half past midnight. He was the only White Lion operative in a three-block radius, and as he listened in to the others reporting from their positions, all closer to the market, he put his own chances for sighting the Gray Man as low.

He ate more of his gelato as his eyes focused on a pair of men walking a meter apart through the crowd. He'd noticed they were moving a little faster than others around them, and this pace set them apart at first.

But that was not all that Klerk found remarkable in the pair. He watched them as they passed, then scanned behind them for signs of others who might be with them. He did see one man who interested him but quickly discounted him when he stopped walking and picked up a menu from a rack in front of a restaurant. Then he brought his hand to his mouth and spoke softly into his cuff mic.

"Lion Actual. Lion Eight. I've got a pair of suspicious characters on the main street up here."

"Describe them."

"Subject one is white, thirties, gray jeans and brown shirt. Subject two is white, forties, off-white shirt and black pants. They have small rucks with them. They are moving with intent in your direction."

Verdoorn replied, "We're looking for one man, not two. Either of them look like the target?"

"Negative. Neither of these blokes is Gentry. But they are *somebody*. Maybe they're confederates."

Verdoorn paused as he thought, then said, "Or maybe they're hunting him, same as us. CIA has been after him for years."

"These two definitely could be from American intelligence."

"If they are, they might be watching you now."

"Negative. Saw one potential follower, a military-aged male with a pack, but he didn't look American. These other boys are Yanks, for sure."

Verdoorn said, "Copy."

Klerk then asked, "What do you want me to do?"

Verdoorn paused a moment, then replied, "Tail 'em. The rest of you stay on mission. Gentry is the primary target. These new fucks are just a curiosity."

Klerk brought his cuff mic down, stepped out onto the street, and continued eating his gelato as he slipped in behind the pair.

. . .

Seventy-five feet behind the South African, a third-generation Mexican American CIA Ground Branch officer named Teddy Gonzalez put the laminated menu he'd been holding back in the rack at the outdoor café, then he brought his own hand to his mouth. "Zulu Four to Zulu Actual."

A second later he heard Travers's voice through his earpiece. "Go for Zulu."

"Be advised, I've got a subject on your six. Looks like he's made you. Can't see him clearly, but don't think it's our target."

"He look like he's carrying?"

"Can confirm he is armed with an ice cream cone. Anything else on him is concealed at my distance."

"Roger that, we'll do an SDR to confirm."

"I'll tail and report."

Gonzalez caught a glimpse of his team leader and Zulu Five as they turned left down Calle Rabbia, a narrow passageway that led to the north, away from the casino area. Their surveillance detection run would lead the potential follower away from the rest of the Ground Branch team, and it would lead them away from their target.

He then began following the unknown subject half the distance away and saw him bring his hand to his mouth. He couldn't tell if the man was transmitting through his cuff mic or just taking a bite from his cone.

A few seconds later the lone man turned north on Calle Rabbia.

"He's still on you, Zulu."

"Roger that. If you're sure, we'll drop the SDR and lose him, head back to the target location. All Zulu elements, run SDRs to see if there are others out there."

Gonzalez rogered up, then said, "I can get ahead of you, check my own six, and then find a route for you guys to slip your tail."

"Do it," Travers said.

Teddy Gonzalez walked past Calle Rabbia, then picked up his pace. He made his own left at Calle Masena, walked through the darkened alley, then stepped into an open rear doorway into the kitchen of a restaurant. Slipping past the cooks hard at work, he made his way to the dining room undetected, then exited the front. Once he saw he could make his way back down to the main street from here, he transmitted to Travers with the location, confident they could lose their one-man tail easily.

• • •

A few minutes later Willem Klerk's frustrated voice came through Jaco Verdoorn's earpiece. "Lion Actual. This is Eight. I've lost the scent."

"Did they shake you, or did you just fook it up?"

"Dunno. They didn't see me, dead certain of that, but I can't say there wasn't someone back behind me I didn't recognize who alerted them."

"All right," Verdoorn replied. "Bring the ring in tighter. If Gentry is here at all, he'll come to the bladdy market. I want all Lions within one hundred meters. If CIA is here, we'll be ready for them, too."

• • •

Kenneth Cage stood in the lobby just off the sales floor of the palace where the market was being held. Behind him, in the darkened great hall, four of the women had already been paraded across a small riser, surrounded by buyers, then sold off, each going for over one million euros. A fifteen-year-old Ukrainian, a twenty-two-year-old Bulgarian, a nineteen-year-old Macedonian, and a sixteen-year-old Romanian were already the property of four different criminal organizations, and would soon be shipped off to Dubai, Frankfurt, Bangkok, and Stockholm, where they'd be condemned to a life of servitude.

There was a break in the action now while the next four were prepared to go on the block, so Cage and some of the buyers from a group of Gulf states stood in the lobby chatting and drinking whiskey.

Hall stood close by his charge, but his attention was partially focused on listening in to Verdoorn's men on his earpiece as they discussed a potential new threat.

During a pause in the conversation in the lobby, he leaned into Cage's ear. "Sir, Jaco's team has identified a pair of unknown men in the area. We need to—"

"Is one of them that Gentry prick?"

"No, sir. But they think—"

With a dismissive wave, he said, "Jaco will handle it. Don't bother me while I'm working again," and returned to his conversation.

Hall knew Cage was coked up, again, and he would be even more intractable than usual, if such a thing was even possible. He did not respond, only focused more carefully on his mission. If there were new unknown actors involved, then it was certainly a security issue, even if they were not related to the Gray Man.

He took a couple steps away from his principal and spoke softly into his radio. "All elements. Keep it tight out there. White Lion thinks there are possible CIA officers hunting for Gentry in the area."

One of his men radioed back. "What are the ROEs?"

Hall felt the stomach acid gurgling inside him. "The rules of engagement are don't engage. We aren't shooting it out with the fucking CIA. They won't be here for the principal, they'll be here for Gentry. Stay out of their way and maybe they'll nab him."

If I could be so lucky, Hall thought.

• • •

Chris Travers moved through the crowded restaurant calmly, as if he were making his way back to his table from the john. Several steps behind him, Ground Branch officer Pete Hume stepped out of the door to the kitchen, moving more quickly. Travers had made it through the kitchen undetected, but Hume was spotted by a cook, who yelled at him but quickly turned his attention back to the chicken marsala he was plating, no doubt annoyed at the tourist who'd taken a wrong turn heading to the bathroom and wandered through the kitchen.

Outside the restaurant both men turned to the south and picked up their pace even more. The SDR had consumed several minutes, and since they had no idea how long their target would be at his location, they knew it was time to haul ass.

. . .

The guy I've pegged as the Director of the Consortium has been inside the building next to the casino for nearly thirty minutes. A couple of guys I take for mafia security men are walking around in front of the gate and the casino next to it, but I haven't detected anyone else from my admittedly limited vantage point here above the nightclub.

I take a few seconds to rub my eyes, then clean off the lenses of my binos. But before I can bring the optics back up to my face I see new movement, close, just outside the window in the alleyway running left to right in front of me.

A pair of men walk below my position, but they don't turn up the passageway towards the casino and the market building. Instead they glance idly in that direction, but continue along the alley that runs from my left to my right.

I make them as suspicious immediately. They are slick enough, not showing any intensity in their actions that make for an easy tip-off, but there is something about their bearing and dress that tells me this isn't a pair of rando tourists who wandered off the main streets and down a quiet alleyway.

Nope, these two are in the game.

I can feel it.

After they pass out of view from the market, one of the men brings his hand up to his mouth and speaks into it.

And now I know that these guys are in comms, which means there will be more out there.

They don't look like the rest of the mob goons, so I'm wondering if these are Consortium operatives sent out into the neighborhood to look for me. There is one other possibility, but I immediately discount it, certain that it can't be.

Can it?

I rise from my position for the first time in an hour, and I move to another room up here on the second floor above the nightclub, on the opposite side of the building. Here I find a window that looks out over a street one block to the west. It is well lit and there are dozens of men and women in view, but after scanning slowly back and forth for a few seconds, my eyes lock onto two men in particular. These aren't the men I just saw passing in front of the casino, but they are cut from the same cloth, moving at a steady pace through the tourists and restaurant patrons walking around.

I bring my binos up to my eyes to focus on them, careful to remain far enough back in the room to where it's unlikely I'll be spotted by someone on the lookout for me.

As I focus the binos, my eyes widen.

And then I lower the optics. I sag back against the wall, sliding down to a seated position.

What . . . the . . . fuck?

I recognize one of the men below me. His name is Chris Travers, he's Ground Branch, and I've spent a lot of time with him in the past year or so while I've been doing contract work for Matt Hanley. Chris works for SAC, formerly the SAD, my old outfit.

The outfit run by Matthew Hanley.

On the one hand, this confirms that Hanley has sent Agency paramilitaries here to drag my ass back home. But I'm not worried about this. No, I expected it. Counted on it, even.

But I *am* worried, because I didn't expect them to show up over here by the casino. I told Hanley I was in town to talk to someone. He would know, no doubt, of my past associations with the Alfonsi crime family, and he would rightly make the connection. But the Alfonsis' headquarters and main turf are centralized a kilometer or more east of here. I am deep in

Mala del Brenta territory now, so how the hell did Travers just happen to wander by my position?

I know the answer. Matt Hanley told him *exactly* where I'd be.

And how would Hanley know where I'd be? I'm certain I'm covert, certain my phone can't compromise me, certain I don't have any tracking device in or on my body, because if I did they would have been able to find me a long time ago.

No, there is only one way Hanley could have known my exact location tonight.

Despite his insistence that he was unaware of the Consortium, I am certain now I've caught him in a lie.

He knew I was targeting them, and he knew they would be right fucking *here*, right fucking *now*, auctioning off their trafficking victims.

I rub my hands through my hair. This isn't the first time in my life I've felt the sinking feeling in my chest when someone I trusted betrays me. It's a palpable hurt, and it sucks, but I guess it toughens me up and teaches me not to trust anyone.

I lower my hands and look up, and my eyes narrow slightly.

Hanley's in on it?

I move back to my original overwatch position and resume scanning the forecourt of the building next to the casino for any new activity while I continue to think over Hanley covering up a multibillion-dollar sex trafficking ring. I can't figure out how that makes any sense, but I don't understand how I could be misreading this.

As soon as I'm settled back in position, my phone buzzes in my pocket, and I touch my earpiece.

"Yeah?"

"Harry?" It's Talyssa, her voice is strained, and I can instantly tell that something's wrong.

THIRTY-SEVEN

One hour earlier, thirty-nine-year-old Maarten Meyer drove his dark gray Porsche Panamera 4S up the driveway to his four-million-euro home in Aerdenhout, a woodsy and ritzy suburb of Amsterdam. He rolled into his garage, and then the door lowered silently behind him.

He'd worked a long day at his posh office in the Museum District of the capital city, and the forty-minute drive home had given him a chance to relax and decompress. Tonight would be a quiet one: thirty minutes on his rowing machine, a home-cooked meal of herring in beetroot and horseradish, halibut with asparagus, and lemon curd for dessert.

Meyer didn't look or act much like a computer hacker, at least not the kind in television and movies. He didn't have advanced degrees in computer science, and though he had a deep knowledge of programming languages and codes, there were millions on Earth better at physical hacking than he was.

What Meyer did have, however, was a deep understanding of international private banking, the processes and the secrets, the systems and the software. And he had incredible powers of social engineering. He could convince people of things, helpful both as a banker and as a black-hat hacker, and he put these skills together, added a dash of moral ambiguity, and used this to earn tens of millions of euros, skimmed off private clients out of their offshore accounts, often without them ever noticing it was gone.

Meyer was good at what he did and he didn't worry much about being caught because he had an incredible team of lawyers, all of whom had their own offshore accounts where he could wire them riches they'd never have to report on their taxes. And he had connections in the federal government that kept all but the most obdurate investigators off his back.

Meyer lived alone now, although he dated a woman in town, and his ex-wife and two children lived not far away in Arnhem. He didn't see the kids much; he hadn't spent the money on his divorce lawyers that he had on his criminal defense attorneys.

Meyer finished his workout, put his halibut in the oven, then stepped into his home office on the second floor of his three-story home. He sat in front of his array of computer monitors and began perusing the markets online.

He'd not been at this for long before he heard the doorbell echo throughout his large modern home. He glanced over at the dedicated monitor for the front-door camera and saw a small woman in a neat black raincoat standing there, a purse over her shoulder, a hand on her hip. A sensible two-door rental was parked in the drive.

Meyer almost reached for his intercom button to ask the visitor who she was and what she wanted, but she couldn't have looked any more harmless or nonthreatening standing there, so he didn't bother. Deciding he wanted a closer look before he turned this stranger away, he stood and walked in his warm-ups and socks through his house, down his stairs, and into the foyer. Here he looked through the glass at the lady, who smiled right back at him.

She was young; she looked like she couldn't be out of college, but her clothing was sophisticated. She had bright red hair, obviously dyed, and narrow features with small brown eyes.

To Meyer she seemed like a little boy in women's clothes.

Instead of opening his door, he just leaned up to the glass.

"Can I help you?" he asked in Dutch.

The reply came in English, which Meyer had spoken fluently since child-hood.

"Maarten Meyer? Hello, my name is Talyssa Corbu."

She fumbled through her purse for a moment, then took out a leather credential folio. Opening it up, she pressed it against the glass, inches from his face.

He read the word in bold aloud. "Europol." Making a face out of annoyance but not out of worry, he said, "All right, Talyssa Corbu, Junior Economic Crimes Analyst . . . what can I do for you?"

"I'd like to talk to you for a moment about a matter of interest to us both."

Meyer looked around. He'd been arrested enough times to know how this worked. Europol didn't send analysts to make arrests; they didn't even send analysts out in the field. He saw no local or federal police, so he imagined this woman did simply want to talk.

Still, he said, "Call my lawyers."

She shook her head, and he thought he noticed a little tremor in her throat. But with a strong enough voice she said, "Ten minutes of your time, and then I'll leave. Trust me, you want to hear this from me, first, like this."

He was intrigued. He let her in, then had her follow him into the kitchen, where he checked on his fish and began whipping up a lobster sauce from last night's leftovers.

"You drove here from Den Hague, did you?"

"Yes, sir," Corbu replied. "Just arrived."

"And what would a junior economic crimes analyst want from me?"

"I want a partnership."

He stopped whisking his eggs and looked up at her quizzically.

"What?"

. . .

The halibut was burned by the time he remembered to take it out fifteen minutes later. He'd spent the intervening period sitting across the kitchen island from the Europol woman sipping wine—he'd offered her some, but she'd declined—and listening to her spiel.

The gist of it was easy to follow. He was under investigation by international law enforcement, his future was bleak, but she could make his problems disappear.

She told him what she would do for him, and she told him what she wanted from him.

As she spoke, he began to see something in the woman. A weakness, or a set of weaknesses. She was terrified to be here in front of him, unable to stop her hands from trembling, fighting to keep authority in her voice that he doubted she really possessed.

With each passing minute this visit became stranger and stranger.

Finally he said, "So . . . you are telling me that in exchange for me breaking into online bank transfer records, illegally, that you will keep me apprised of the investigation into me, and do whatever you can to slow or stop it."

Talyssa nodded but did not speak; he wondered if she was worried her voice might crack.

Meyer hesitated, but not for long. "As I said when you showed up at my door, I want to call my lawyer."

"Sorry, Maarten. If you talk to your lawyer, then this deal is off the table."

He leaned forward, his elbows on the island, his eyes narrowed. "It's *already* off the table, miss. I want no part in whatever criminal activity you are involved in. I am an honest man. All my work is aboveboard."

She just stared at him.

"And," he added, "if you don't leave right now, then I will report you tomorrow morning to the authorities."

She did not get up from her seat.

"Did you hear me?" he said again, his voice louder now. "Get out of my house."

He saw that his powerful voice was taking a toll on her limited reserves. Her lips trembled and her voice cracked now. "I will not leave. You will do what I ask, or I will be forced to—"

She paused an instant, and Meyer took the opportunity to jump in.

"Forced to what?" When she did not answer him, he repeated himself. "Forced . . . to . . . what?"

She looked down at the island, then meekly she replied, "I'll be forced to come back here with a friend and let *him* convince you." Her eyes flashed up to his now. "Believe me, I've seen what he can do, and you *don't* want that."

Maarten told himself this woman was insane; she was threatening him, in his house, telling him she'd be back with a dangerous man to force him to commit a crime.

He looked to his right on the kitchen island, and he saw the knife block. He thought if he could just snatch up one of his large blades and hold it up, then he could threaten her right back. He wouldn't hurt her, he'd never hurt anyone, but he could intimidate her right out the door with a little push. He'd be well within his rights, because he'd asked her to leave many times, and it was obvious she was herself operating illegally.

She wouldn't run to the cops about him pulling out some cutlery on her.

She shouted at him now. "Just do what I ask! *Please!*"

Insane, he told himself again. Maarten Meyer decided to go for the knife, just to intimidate. But as he stood quickly he telegraphed his intentions by locking his eyes onto the block.

Talyssa Corbu was closer, and she launched to her feet herself. She looked down the path of Meyer's gaze. "No!" she shouted in a panic, then reached out for the block and knocked it out of the Dutchman's reach with her forearm, causing it to spill to the floor. All the knives shot across the kitchen, then skittered down into the sunken living room behind her.

All the knives save for one.

A single butcher's knife remained in Talyssa's hand; she'd not even tried to take one as they fell, but she found her fingers wrapped around the hilt and the hardened steel blade pointed up and in the direction of the Dutch black-hat hacker. Meyer looked at her with fear, and then he turned to check behind him for something else to grab. He opened a drawer full of bakeware, then ran his hands across the counter, desperate for a weapon. He knocked over a coffee grinder and a rack of porcelain cups, and jostled a toaster, but he came up empty.

Spinning back around towards the woman with the knife, he found that Corbu had climbed over the island in desperation, and now she was inches away, the blade under his chin.

He froze solid, and she held her position without moving, either.

No one said a word for several seconds; they were both out of breath from the tension and action.

Finally she spoke through her rapid breathing. "We will go into your office and you will sit down."

. . .

Ten minutes later Talyssa Corbu left Meyer affixed to his chair by the legs and arms with the zip ties Harry had directed her to buy once she got to Amsterdam. Facing his monitors and the keyboard on his desk he sat there, staring straight ahead, sweat shining on his brow.

She stepped out of the room, but only into a hallway where she could still see her captive, and here she placed a call to the American who was so much better at this sort of thing than she.

"Harry?" she said as he answered.

"What's wrong?"

"I . . . I have him. He is tied up. But he refuses to help."

She could hear the American breathe a long sigh of relief, and this served as the first and only thing to relax her since she'd first rung Meyer's doorbell thirty minutes earlier.

He then said, "It's okay. You've done well so far. I doubted he'd go for that."

"But you said—"

"I just had to get you this far. We can do it together from here."

"Why are you whispering?"

She heard Harry chuckle a little. "You think *you* have problems?"

"What is happening there?"

"It's fine. Let's focus on Meyer. You are going to have to resort to other measures."

With a tremble in her voice she tried and failed to control, she said, "I . . . I don't think I can do what you are going to ask me to do."

"We have to find answers. Look, I'm not going to get us what we need tonight. There are too many men around. I can't threaten, capture, torture, follow, or kill anybody here tonight. So it's up to you now. *You* have to get us some fresh intelligence."

Talyssa looked at the man in the other room and wondered if she had what it took to go forward. But she lifted her head, brought her chin back, and said, "What do I do?"

"Exactly what I tell you to do, without hesitation. I need you to become me. If I were there I could get that little dipshit hacking into NASA in fifteen minutes, because I would put the fear of God in him."

"Yes. I saw you do it with Niko Vukovic."

"Exactly."

"But I am not you. I am not scary."

"Intimidation is about selling an attitude. The more they believe you will do something, the less you will have to do. I can't give you the ability to snap some bastard's neck, but I can give you the attitude so that he *thinks* you will snap his neck."

"How?"

"Keep your earpiece in. I'll hear him and you, and you will hear me. I can talk you through every single thing to say. But you can't waver."

"Okay," she said after some hesitation.

Harry replied, "But look, Talyssa. This plan is not guaranteed. It may not be pretty. If I tell you to stick an ice pick in that fucker's eye, you're going to make him think you are going to do it."

Her stomach lurched. "An . . . ice pick?"

"I need you to be a heartless, soulless robot for the next few minutes. If you can do that for me, then we can get Meyer to do what we need him to do, and we can find out where they are taking your sister."

"All right."

. . .

I direct her to the kitchen, and I give her a list of items to collect. In the garage she finds a toolbox, and, despite her persistent questioning about what all this is for, she brings all the equipment I've specified upstairs.

Once there, she says, "I have it all. What do I do with it?"

"Put it all down next to him. If it's there where he can see, that will amp up his anxiety."

A minute later she has done what I ask, and then I hear her talk to her prisoner for a few minutes more. I direct her on what to say, but this Maarten Meyer is a hard sell. Other than some "fuck yous," he barely responds.

Finally I say, "Okay, Talyssa. You're going to have to hurt him some. I'm sorry, but you can do it. Pick up the pliers."

I can't see her, I don't know if she does it or not, but I'm assuming she's made no moves towards the tools. I say, "Pick up the fucking *pliers*."

She can't answer me, but I hear slow movement, the shuffling of tools on the table.

Then the noise stops.

Right in front of him she says, "I can't!"

Damn. I say, "It's fine, Talyssa. Put me on your speakerphone."

"Okay." I hear a click, and then I talk. My voice is nothing like Talyssa's, because if I were there I'd tear that piece of shit apart without a moment's thought, and I sound like it.

"Hello, Maarten."

"Who is this?"

"I'm the guy she warned you about."

"You're Europol?"

I laugh. "Do I sound like I'm Europol? I'm not European, so I'm not Euro. I'm not the police, so I'm not pol."

"So you are . . . you are *what*?"

"Right now I am the guy trying to convince the young lady holding you to place that pair of pliers on your nuts and squeeze, but I'm having a hard time getting her on board with that. Some people aren't as crazy as me, I guess."

He barks out a thin laugh. "She won't do it, and you aren't here. You don't scare me. Go fuck yourself, American. You're bluffing."

I turn my attention to Talyssa. "Think of your goal. Just think of your sister. There is one person between her and you right now. The man sitting right there."

It's quiet for a long time. Finally she says, "Yes. I . . . I understand." To my surprise, I hear the sound of metal tools being moved around.

Now Maarten says, "What are you doing?"

I speak in a robotic, dispassionate voice. "Talyssa. Don't wait. He's just trying to buy time. There will be no more delays. We have to begin destroying his will now. To do that we have to destroy his body." This disconnected tone only increases the certitude in the captive that I don't give a shit about what's happening. Like I could torture him to death and then order lunch without a moment's pause. It's psychological warfare, which is effective. Not as effective as actual warfare, but since I'm not there in the room, it's the most powerful tool I have at my disposal at present.

I hear the Dutch hacker begging, and I hear Talyssa's heavy breath. I worry she's about to pass out, but apparently Maarten Meyer worries she's about to start fucking him up with hand tools, because he screams now.

"No! Please! No!"

Talyssa Corbu speaks, and her voice surprises me. Apparently she's found a wellspring of strength. "I've got it from here, Harry. I'll call you back when I have what I need from him."

"Wait, what are you going to do?" shouts Meyer.

Her own tone has become robotic now as she answers him. "I'm going to do to you everything my friend told me to do to you."

I remind her, "We need him alive. Listen to me. You puncture an artery and he's no good to us. We need him—"

"He'll live," she says. And then, "Just."

And then she hangs up on me.

Holy shit.

. . .

"Who is he?" Maarten demanded. "Who is he?" Spittle flew from his mouth, and tears drained freely from his eyes.

Talyssa leaned close to her prisoner, just as she'd seen the intense and frightening American who called himself Harry do in the bunker in Herzegovina. In a soft voice, still bereft of personal connection or passion, she said, "I don't know, exactly. But he is a mass murderer. I've watched him kill in three countries over the past few days. I myself have never done *anything* like this, but unfortunately for you, I have reached my breaking point. I can see myself picking up that ice pick and filling you with little holes. *Also* unfortunately for you, I am not very well versed in human anatomy, so there is a reasonable chance I'll hit one of those arteries he warned me about." She shrugged. "Maybe we will both be lucky tonight. Let's find out."

"I'll do the fucking hack! I'll do the hack!"

"My friend warned me about you stalling, didn't he? I think I better go ahead and show you my conviction to—"

"No stalling! Release my hands right now and I'll get to work. You just tell me what you need."

Talyssa thought it over for a few seconds, the ice pick shaking in front of her face. Finally she said, "I'm going to need to see some very fast progress from you."

"You will get it! You *will*! I'll show you! Just don't hurt me."

Talyssa's heart had never beat so hard in her life, and she wasn't even the one in mortal danger at present. But she cut off his wrist ties with the butcher knife, and she pushed his chair up to the computer.

THIRTY-EIGHT

Jaco Verdoorn stood in a window on the top floor of the Casino of Venice, looking across the passageway in front of him, down to the north-south street a block away. He saw men pass, and he thought they looked suspicious, but like Klerk said before, he didn't see Gentry.

He radioed Hall inside the auction taking place in the next building over. "Hall? Lion Actual. How much longer do you anticipate the market lasting?"

Hall answered in a whispered voice. "I'm guessing no more than a half hour, but you know the boss. He's amped up right now; he might decide to leave at any time."

Verdoorn knew that meant Cage was snorting coke, which was no surprise to the South African, because they traveled together regularly.

Frustrated that he only had a few more minutes to bag Gentry before he'd be on a plane back to LA, he decided to ramp up the pressure.

He then transmitted to his own team. "Lion Actual to all Lions. Everybody pull in tight. If he's here, he's here, and if he's not here, then it doesn't matter."

A minute later he saw the first of his men. Klerk and Van Straaten turned off the road to the alley from opposite directions. They then began walking idly up the slight rise towards the casino.

He watched them for a moment, then scanned all the windows in view. There were dozens, but his eyes kept returning to three windows on three different stories of the building down at the mouth of the alleyway that led to the casino. It was about seventy meters away, and the ground floor and first floor were the rear of a restaurant and nightclub.

Above the establishment, however, the windows were pitch-black.

To himself he said, *Perfect sight line, close enough to see with binos, far enough away for a chance to escape and evade, and easy to get into with the activity of the patrons.*

He nodded.

That's where I'd be.

He lifted his radio to his ear. "Jonker. Duiker. What are your positions?"

A second later the reply came back. "This is Duiker. I'm two blocks north."

"This is Jonker, sir. I'm a block east, in the north-south passage. You want us in tighter?"

"I want you both to go to the building with the club again. Go up to the second and third floors, check out any and all vantage points on my poz. Then go to the attic."

"Right away," Duiker replied, and then Jonker followed suit.

But Verdoorn wasn't satisfied. "Loots. Back them up. Go to the employee entrance and stay outside, ready if anyone tries to leave."

"Roger that," Loots replied. "But be advised, I think I have two more men who don't belong. Down by the canal on the south side of the passageway."

"What are they doing?"

"Just walking around, taking pictures. I'm not buyin' it."

"Got it," Verdoorn said. "Sounding more and more like Agency boys looking for their target. Avoid them."

"Right, boss," Loots replied.

Jaco Verdoorn peered through his Steiner binoculars at the windows, desperate to catch even the slightest sign of movement, still hopeful that the world's greatest assassin was in the area.

. . .

I've spent the last ten minutes thinking about calling Talyssa back, but I decide against it. She sounded like she knew what she was doing, although I can only hope she was playing a bit of theater when it seemed she was about to torture the man to get him to comply. She may have to in the end, but for her sake I hope she doesn't do anything to him that's going to haunt her in the future.

I return my thoughts to my own predicament just in time to notice two men strolling from opposite directions, then turning up the alleyway that leads up to the casino and the building where the auction is taking place. Neither of them looks particularly out of place, but the coincidence of them converging like this causes me to focus on them carefully.

Through the binos I try to make out weapons under their clothes, or shoes or boots or watches that look tactical, or commo gear secreted away.

I see nothing, but somehow my sonar for bad guys keeps pinging.

They aren't Mala del Brenta, and they don't have the look or feel of Italian mob.

And these guys aren't Ground Branch, or I doubt they are, because even if Matt Hanley is involved with the Consortium, the Ground Branch guys aren't, so there's no way he'd send his paramilitaries straight into their hands. Nope, these guys are moving too close to the action to be CIA officers tasked with shanghaiing me back to D.C.

So then maybe these are the dudes I've been looking out for since Dubrovnik. Some sort of security force for the Consortium. They are here for me, and they were out of sight when they kept their distance, but now as these two men step into darkened alcoves on opposite sides of the street and light cigarettes, they've officially been made.

And I know there will be more than two of these fucks out here.

They are tightening the cordon, I guess, which could mean several different things. Maybe they saw the Ground Branch personnel, so they are bringing their men in thinking there will be less chance for an altercation. Maybe they are frustrated because they haven't detected any signs of me, so they are recalling patrolling forces to create a tighter defense for the principal.

And maybe they've seen me, and they are converging for the kill.

I sit here weighing my options. For the last hour I've been fantasizing about taking out the Director when he leaves the auction, but there are a lot of problems with that plan. He moves inside a protective bubble, this I've already seen, so I know I may not get a good sight picture on him from this distance before he passes out of my line of fire. Also, and this is no small thing, me firing on him from this building would send God knows how many armed goons my way, and as I'm already surrounded, it would be damn hard to slip the noose.

I consider trying to involve Ground Branch in the fight, basically finding a way to strike a match so that the two forces can duke it out while I sit up here and watch, and this may even give me an opportunity to make a play for the kidnapping victims in the building seventy yards away from me.

But no, that could lead to a bloodbath, there are still civilians around, and although the Ground Branch dudes are here to fuck up my mission, they are still my brothers, and I'm not going to trick them into a gunfight they had no intention of fighting.

I slowly determine there is nothing else I can do from this vantage point other than take more pictures, so I wait, ready to do just that when the sale is over.

But it's not long before I hear footsteps on the same floor of the building I'm on. Two men, moving slowly and carefully.

Predators.

I have escape routes planned, taking into consideration all the access points to the floor, and since these guys are moving off to my right, I get up, leave the room, and go to the left. I'm careful with my footfalls, and careful to listen for the sounds of anyone else coming this way, but soon I'm at the rear stairs and heading down, towards the nightclub on the second floor of the building.

I arrive seconds later, the place is dull and drab and the music is shit, and I move through it.

On the ground floor I exit the stairs, make my way through an employee-only door to the kitchen of the adjoining restaurant, now closed for the night, and continue through the dark and empty space to the back door. Here, I hesitate; there's no window, so no way to know if something awaits me on the other side, but behind me I think I hear more noise, and I wonder if the Consortium security people have decided to "flood the zone" in the hopes of rooting me out of here.

I look around me, hoping to find a cook's uniform or a waiter's uniform to put on before leaving. I don't see a uniform but hanging with a mop I find a large brown rubber apron like the kind used by dishwashers. I put this on, hoping it makes me look like a late-working restaurant employee heading out for the night, and then I open the door with authority.

It's an alleyway, narrow and high on all sides, and ahead I see a street that runs along a canal. There are boats passing by, both gondolas and powered craft, and I know this is the Grand Canal. It's big and wide and well traveled, there are boats docked up and down the lengths of both sides, and this looks like a suitable escape route.

But only for a moment.

Then, on the street that runs alongside the canal, two men walk into view. They turn to see me, and then they stop.

Then I stop.

One of them is Travers.

We are thirty yards apart, but even from here I can tell he's ID'd me.

I start to turn to run in the opposite direction, but before I can do so, Travers yells at the top of his lungs. "Gentry! Down!"

In the world where Chris and I operate, a shout of "Down!" doesn't mean, *Get down so I can cuff you*. It means, unequivocally, *Get down because somebody's about to shoot you*.

My body reacts to this with instant muscle memory; I'm barely conscious of the fact that I'm dropping like a stone. I land on my chest on the hard surface of the alley.

As I hit the deck I hear the crack of a pistol shot behind me, and then another, and then I begin rolling to my right, both to make myself a moving target and to gain access to the gun on my right hip.

After my second roll I have my weapon in my hand and I continue towards the cover of a cluster of scooters parked together, another dozen feet or so on my left.

Another shot cracks in the night, the pavement sparks a foot from my head and, as I roll, I aim between my legs and return fire—at what, exactly, I have no idea.

Simultaneous to me opening up on the shooter to the north, I hear the snapping of two handguns coming from the south by the canal. This will be Chris and the other SAC guy, engaging the asshole who's shooting at me, and I hope I survive this shit so I can buy them a beer and thank them.

The three men fire at one another; I can't tell if anyone is getting hits.

I chance a look around the scooters and I see a muzzle flash coming from around the corner of the building housing the nightclub. Then, just ahead on my right, the door of the restaurant flies open, and instantly more muzzle flashes crack off. I dive back around just as men begin running into view, crouching down behind scooters on the other side of the alleyway.

It's three on three now, I think, and we all have cover, but from the sound of new booming reports echoing around, one of the bad guys has a rifle.

I look back over my shoulder. Travers and his partner are backed up to the canal, both crouched behind pylons used to tie off boats.

This feels like a stalemate, but I have a strong suspicion that both sides have more men with guns on the way to this fight.

. . .

Chris Travers shot his head around the left side of the iron pylon he was crouched behind, and he spotted Court Gentry about seventy-five feet ahead of him, on his knees by a bunch of scooters in the alleyway.

He touched his push-to-talk button, then said, "Zulu elements, we are two blocks west of the casino, do not know the name of this alley. The

Grand Canal is behind us. Three . . . possibly four hostiles one block to our north. Approach with caution." Then he said, "But get your asses over here!"

He turned to Hume, a few feet away behind another pylon, and watched his teammate reload his Sig pistol.

"You good, Pete?"

"For now, yeah. We might have to jump into this nasty-ass water behind us, though. Not looking forward to that."

Hume fired again, then ducked back down.

Travers heard the tone of his sat phone in the earpiece in his left ear, and he jammed a finger in his right ear to drown out some of the shooting.

"Go for Zulu."

"Status report?" It was Brewer, and to her credit, she wasn't wasting time with the identity check.

"We are in sight of Violator, but we have enemy contact at this time."

"Negative! You are *not* to engage with the hostiles."

"Well, it's a little late for that, ma'am." He leaned out to his right and fired his pistol, and saw a man thirty yards away duck back down behind a row of parked scooters.

Next to him Hume said, "There's more of them."

"Keep your eye on the canal. If these dudes have a boat, we're in trouble."

Brewer spoke again. "Zulu, your orders are to immediately disengage. I want you out of there, now!"

"We don't have Violator. If we leave now, he'll be running for his life."

"And he's damn good at that. Leave him, get back to your staging area in town, and await instructions."

"But—"

"You *can't* be compromised. End of discussion. Brewer out."

"Fuck!" Travers shouted, and then he transmitted to his team again. "All Zulu, belay my last. Move to RP Foxtrot for exfil."

More gunshots rang out from the north.

A Zulu officer replied to Travers's command. "Roger that, but . . . uh, somebody's still in contact."

"No shit, that's us. We're moving off the X now." He turned to Hume. "Bound to my left. I'm right behind you."

Hume took off laterally while Travers emptied his Glock up the street and quickly reloaded. Once Hume arrived at the edge of the building that gave him cover from up the alley, Travers said to himself, "Good luck, Court," then followed his teammate out of the line of fire.

Both men scampered over crates stacked canalside, and Hume lost his footing on stone polished by centuries of foot traffic and fell into the water on his left. Travers stopped and fished him out, and then the two men took off again to the west through a narrow passage.

· · ·

I pause for a second to pound my last mag into the grip of my Glock 19, and this is when I realize I'm the only guy returning fire on the enemy. Looking back over my shoulder, I see Chris Travers disappear around the side of the building that runs along the canal.

Well, shit.

I don't know what's up, but I have a strong suspicion that Brewer is involved.

I'm just about to lean out around the scooters when behind me I hear the wail of a siren. I look back to see a large police speedboat shifting into view; spotlights train on me and up the street at the other shooters.

My gun is low between my knees as I squat, and I don't think the cops could possibly see it, so I drop it on the ground and kick it down a drain next to me. Then I turn, raise my hands, and start screaming like a little bitch.

"Help me! Help me!"

The gunfire to the north stops. I figure the security dudes for the Consortium are unassing the area, and I decide to do the same. I take a deep breath, pray that the Italian cops are either bad shots or slow on the trigger, and then sprint across the alley, back towards the door to the restaurant. It's unlocked, nobody shoots me, and once inside I pull my knife and move carefully through the building, concerned that bad guys might still be close.

But soon enough I'm mixed in with the crowd of clubbers and club employees fleeing the area, and with my leather apron I look like one of the crowd.

We all run together up to San Leonardo, where I drop my apron but keep running.

THIRTY-NINE

Sean Hall raced with his protectee along the bank of the canal, in the opposite direction of the sound of gunfire a hundred yards or so behind them. Only two of the other six guards were shouldered up around the protectee; the rest had been in other parts of the auction site when the shooting began, and they were still catching up.

He'd been told that Riesling and the two girls at the Mala del Brenta safe house, Maja and Sofia, had been sheltered there by mafia men, and the MdB forces there were on high alert.

While Hall ran, his left hand on Cage's shoulder, he shouted into his cuff mic. "I need those boats to pull up on the Grand Canal, two hundred yards from the casino! Principal will be there in forty-five seconds, and we aren't waiting around!"

The driver of one of the two mahogany power boats radioed that they would comply, and soon both Spirit Yacht P40s came into view, racing out of a smaller canal.

Once Cage, Hall, and the others boarded and were speeding over the water, Hall spoke again into his mic. "Lion Actual? You copy?"

"Lion Actual."

"Did you get him?"

There was a long pause. "Negative. We encountered other hostiles. I have one man dead."

Hall put his head in his hands. The organization he worked for had just shot it out with CIA personnel. As bad as things were for him already, he knew they'd just gotten worse.

While still reacting to the worry that he was in even deeper shit if it ever came out that he worked for the Director of the Consortium, he felt a hand squeeze his knee. He looked up to see Cage leaning over from the other side of the boat. Over the sound of the engine and the pounding of the hull against the water, he said, "Thanks, Sean."

The forty-year-old ex-SEAL thought he was going to be sick to his stomach. Distractedly, he said, "You bet."

Cage added, "I want Claudia and the two girls coming to the U.S. brought to the jet, and we'll all go back together."

Hall couldn't believe it. "They are on another flight, tomorrow. You *never* travel with the merchandise."

Cage shook his head. "I want them out of here, now! Make it happen."

Hall angrily brought his cuff mic back to his mouth. His last two men would pick up Dr. Claudia, Maja, and Sofia from the Mala del Brenta safe house and take them to Marco Polo Airport. Then Cage, Verdoorn, the two girls, and God knows who else would climb into the Gulfstream for the flight back to the States.

Hall couldn't wait to be airborne, to get the danger behind him and his protectee, so he could pound vodka when the coast was clear.

．．．

An hour and a half after the gunfight by the Grand Canal, I climb out of a taxi in the city of Treviso, Italy, on the mainland twenty-two miles northwest of the island city. During the drive I called Talyssa, twice. The first time she did not answer, but the second time she picked up, and though there was obvious stress in her voice, she assured me that Maarten Meyer was right in front of her and working his magic to break into the banking records Talyssa had targeted. I ask her for regular updates, and then I tell her I'm going to America.

She is surprised by this, but she shouldn't be. Roxana said she was being taken to the West Coast, and her captor was American. All roads lead west, and I want to be there when Talyssa gives me someone or something to target.

I have the cabdriver take me to a bridge overlooking the Sile River, and when he is out of sight I walk through manicured trees until I reach a dry concrete drainage ditch. On the other side of this I drop to my knees, pull out my binoculars, and train them through openings in the large chain-link fence in front of me.

A hundred meters ahead is a fixed operating base for private jets coming to and leaving from Aeroporto di Treviso. On the far side of the building, I know from experience, will be a hangar and a ramp and, undoubtedly, several high-end corporate aircraft.

I'm hoping that also among them will be a CIA transport jet.

The plane that's been sent to haul me back to the United States.

The plane I plan on hijacking.

I can't see any aircraft from my vantage point here, so I climb the fence, drop to the other side, and begin moving through the parking lot, avoiding any lights.

Three minutes later I'm prone under a commercial truck on the edge of the ramp. I scan the dozen different aircraft in front of me, all corporate-sized jets. There are Bombardiers, Citations, Learjets, Embraers, and Gulfstreams, but my eyes focus on a Dassault Falcon 50. It looks older than most of the other planes around, but in good condition, and what really draws me to it is that, in contrast to every single other aircraft here at this FBO, the Falcon 50 has its stairs down and its rear luggage hatch open, and the APU, the auxiliary power unit, is sitting next to the jet's nose.

Someone either has recently deplaned or is planning on using this aircraft soon.

The cockpit and cabin lights are off, which means departure isn't imminent, but I take this as a good sign.

It will give me time to do what I need to do.

The moment I told Matt Hanley I was headed to Venice, I knew without a doubt he'd send guys to come grab me and drag me back home. And although it's been a long time since I've been here with the Agency, I do remember we landed here at this FBO. I wasn't sure the Agency was still using the same facility, but I figured there was a very good chance they would be.

I needed a lucky break, and I think I just got it.

There was no way I could fly commercial back to the USA; the Agency would pick me up on facial recognition and I'd be grabbed before I left most any airport in Europe, then hauled off to an Agency safe house till I could be ferried home.

And I sure as hell don't have time to get on a freighter and steam all the way to the United States.

So I use the one thing I have at my disposal. An angry CIA DDO who wants me home and working for him again.

I'm going to get on that plane, knowing that when Travers and the others are a half hour out or so, the pilots will climb aboard for preflight. Then we'll take off, leaving the SAC dudes behind. Obviously Travers and the others will notify Langley, and there will be one hell of a welcoming committee wherever this plane is due to land, but I can divert it by having the pilot declare an emergency once we cross over the U.S. border, and I should be able to deplane before Hanley can get any more goons there to take me down.

Yeah, as plans go, this one is out there. I've certainly never hijacked an aircraft before, but I'm a desperate man with few options.

And this shit is what I do.

I have a plan B, in case I'm wrong about this not being a trap, but plan B relies on factors that, so far in my experience, I've not been able to rely on.

I sure as shit do *not* want to rely on plan B, and if I have to pull it out, it's only because it's my very last hope.

I start to crawl out from under the truck to head for the Falcon, but then I stop myself. *When has anything I've done ever been this easy?*

There is nothing in front of me that makes it seem like I might be step-ping into a trap, except my sudden, rare turn of apparent good luck.

But I don't have time to do this the slow and careful way; I have to act.

What the hell, I tell myself, and I begin walking through the night across the ramp.

A minute later I climb the jet stairs. I'm unarmed, for two reasons. One, I only had the Glock, which I kicked into the drain. And two . . . I'm not going to go lethal with anyone in the CIA, and I doubt they'd go lethal against me.

Hanley wants me alive, because I'm useful.

I then look into the darkened cabin. Every last one of the interior lights is off, which is weird, meaning this is a cold aircraft with the hatch open. I start to wonder if the pilots are even on airport grounds, but I know they wouldn't leave the Falcon compromised like this unless they were nearby in the lounge.

Unless . . . of course . . . this *is* a trap.

And then it happens. A light flicks on over a sofa in the rear of the cabin, and I know, without a doubt, what I'm about to see. I turn to the light.

A man sits there, leg crossed over a knee, a cowboy boot on full display, and a cold bottle of Corona in his hand. He's silhouetted by the light be-hind him, but that doesn't matter.

I know who this is before he says a word.

"Howdy, Six. You looking for a lift?"

Shit. I can't see his face well, but I recognize the voice of Zack High-tower, my old team leader from my own Ground Branch days, and cur-rently a denied Agency asset run by Matt Hanley.

Just like me.

In the Goon Squad his call sign was Sierra One, and mine was Sierra Six. He's rarely called me by anything other than Six in the past decade.

I play it as cool as possible as I respond. "I knew Matt would send a plane for me, and I halfway figured you'd be on it."

Zack sips his beer. "You know how it is, bro. He calls me into this shit to serve as your voice of reason. And usually you ignore reason, so I have to do the strong-arm thing." He adds, "Don't make me do the strong-arm thing."

Zack is good at what he does, and I'm pretty sure he's also crazy.

I look around the aircraft a moment to confirm the two of us are, in fact, alone. "How, exactly, are you planning on strong-arming me?"

"Travers and his boys are on the way back to the jet right now. They made a little noise tonight, apparently, so they've been recalled."

"But they aren't here yet."

Zack laughs. He loves it when he's got me where he wants me. "Neither are the pilots, dumbass. You going to fly this yourself all the way back to the States?"

I just look at the cockpit, then look back at him.

He laughs, but I can tell he's suddenly uneasy. "*Hell* no. You can't do that."

"Then call the pilots. Right now."

He cocks his head. "You're hijacking an Agency aircraft?"

"I wouldn't put it like that. I'm just borrowing it."

"And you're planning on flying this jet all the way to the U.S.? By yourself, if I refuse to call the pilots? Seriously? That's your play?"

"I was hoping to avoid that play. But if you don't give me another option, then I'll have to give it a shot. You feeling lucky?"

Zack rolled his eyes. "This isn't some four-seater twin-prop bush plane. This is an elite corporate jet."

I look around a little more. "It's okay. I've seen better."

"You suck as a pilot, dude. You always did."

"Then let the pros come on board and we'll jet off into the sunset together safely."

He drinks down half the beer now, then burps. He's in his early fifties, but apparently no one told him this. Then he looks back to me. "I'm gonna go ahead and call that bluff, Six. Fly this plane back to America. I'll take that ride with you."

Shit.

I can fly a corporate jet this size, but I've never done it transcontinentally, and I imagine that's not something one normally just does on one's own, with no guidance and little sleep.

But what choice do I have? I start for the jet stairs so that I can go out and close the aft hatch. I don't even know if the aircraft is fueled, but I'll figure that out when I get in the cockpit.

But when I step up to the top of the stairs, I see a gun pointed right at me at a range of three feet.

A woman is holding the weapon, a large-framed Sig, and she motions for me to step back into the cabin.

I do so, then sit, and she comes in and turns on all the lights.

Zack says from the back, "The cavalry has arrived. Just as well; I'm guessing you'd have slammed us into a mountain in Iceland."

I look at Zack, thinking about my plan B. While turned away from the woman at the front bulkhead with the gun on me, I hear her speak.

"It's you."

I turn back. *Huh?* There is nothing more disquieting in my life than to be recognized, and at first this fires my defenses up. But quickly I recognize her, too.

The last time I was on an Agency transport, she was the flight attendant.

She and I were also virtually the only survivors of a gunfight on a tarmac in the UK.

"Yeah," I say. "It's me."

She lowers the pistol.

"This is a step down from that Gulfstream you used to ride on."

"I believe that aircraft has been retired from service. Too many holes in it." She smiles. "I'm just glad to be working. I never got a chance to thank you for saving my life."

"Not how I remember it. You took an unlucky hit, I bandaged you up, and then I left. You'd have made it, anyway."

She shakes her head. "But you taxied the jet out of danger and then you—"

In the back of the aircraft Zack says, "Are you fucking kidding me right now? You've charmed the stewardess?"

Now the woman glares at the big man in the cowboy boots. "I'm not a fucking stewardess, asshole!"

This makes me laugh, and I haven't had much reason to laugh tonight.

"Check your loyalties, lady. I'm on an op for the DDO. This dude is freestyling."

She looks at me as she replies to him. "I'm on the same op for the DDO that you're on, Romantic. Doesn't mean I can't say hi to an old friend." She taps her pistol against the side of her leg. "Also doesn't mean I'm going to let him steal my jet."

Right. I turn to Zack. "Call the pilots," I say. "Let's go to Langley."

He looks at his watch. "Travers is thirty minutes away. The pilots will be here in five. We're fueled and ready; they just have to light the fires and kick the tires. When the Ground Branch boys get here, we'll go home. Just as we planned."

I sit back in the cabin chair. Plan B is my only plan now, and I'm wondering if I would have had a better chance trying to fly the Falcon home myself.

I guess I'll never know.

FORTY

Chris Travers is the last of the six CIA operators to board the Falcon, and I'm glad to see they all made it out of the gun battle. They cram into the tight confines of the jet, with Chris sitting in front of me.

Most of the guys look my way like I have a horn sticking out of my forehead, but Travers shakes my hand.

I'm not happy to see him, but I do owe him some thanks. "I appreciate the heads-up back there in the alleyway."

Travers shrugs. "Was supposed to bring you back alive."

"Right. So . . . you're TL now. Congrats."

He shrugs again, then takes a beer passed to him by one of his team-mates. "It's tough barking orders at these degenerates." A couple guys laugh, but most of them are still securing their gear.

Then Travers says, "Quick question. The boys and I have a bet you can settle."

"Okay."

"Did you schwack Ratko Babic last week? I say yes, most of these other dipshits say no."

"No," I reply.

Travers grins, turns to his team. "That means yes!"

One of the other guys says, "It also means no, Chris."

The Falcon 50 begins taxiing towards the runway while the SAC team argues.

Zack is next to me now, and I can see him looking my way, but I avoid his gaze as long as possible. We take off, and an awful smell fills the air.

I look around for its origin for a moment. I'm not sure, but it seems like one of them either jumped or fell into a canal.

Finally, not ten minutes into the flight, Zack leans over to me.

"I'm missing something here, aren't I?"

"What do you mean?"

"I mean . . . you didn't want to come back to Langley. But you showed up here, and you let Travers and his team board. You could have gotten that pistol off Sharon. She wasn't going to shoot you, and you knew that."

"Your point?"

"You've just, basically, shanghaied *yourself*. Now . . . gotta ask, why would you go and do a thing like that?"

"I needed to get to the States."

With a quizzical look he says, "Really? You ready to go back to work?"

I shake my head. "Not to go back to work at Poison Apple. I have to do something else first, and I need your help."

"And Hanley will be cool with it?"

I reach for my beer now. "No, Hanley won't be cool with it at all."

Zack drains the last of his Corona and has another passed down his way. When it arrives without a lime he yells back towards the men sitting near the galley, and Sharon grabs an uncut lime and hands it to a Ground Branch guy I heard called Teddy. Teddy tosses the lime the length of the cabin, and Zack catches it, then pulls a pocketknife and cuts off a chunk. "Now, Six, you know me well enough to know I follow orders. And my orders are to get you back to Matt."

"Well then, I'll just have to appeal to that hard heart of yours." This is my plan B, and if possible, it may have an even lower probability for success than my plan A.

Zack squeezes lime juice into his bottle. "Yeah, well, good luck with that."

"I'm doing the right thing, man. I've uncovered something big, something awful, and it involves Americans. I want to stop it."

Zack replies with one word. "Yawn."

"I'm targeting a massive sex trafficking consortium."

He still looks bored by my spiel as he gulps his Mexican beer. "Sex trafficking."

"I've been working with an analyst from Europol. Her sister's been taken. They run the girls from the east, through the Balkans and then to Italy, where they are sold. We know this particular outfit is making billions of dollars a year, so we estimate they have tens of thousands of victims around the world."

An eyebrow rises on Hightower's otherwise impassive bearded face. "That's bad."

I nod slowly, looking into his eyes. "A lot of them are just kids, Zack."

With this he puts his beer down on the table in front of me, and then he looks away. "That's real bad."

"Damn right it is. Talyssa and I are this close to breaking it wide open. Right now she is getting intel we can use to pinpoint the leadership of the organization, but we already know they are located somewhere on the West Coast."

Zack doesn't respond to this. He's silent for several seconds, in fact, and I think I'm getting through.

But then he says, "I have orders, Six, and when I have orders I don't listen to anything else. Sorry, dude. That's a fucked-up sitrep you just gave me, and your heart's in the right place, as always, but I do what I'm told."

I shake my head. "Not this time. This time you are going to help me."

"You should know better than that by now. Remember when I was tasked with killing you? What did I do?"

"You failed."

He sighs in frustration. "Fair enough, but I did my fucking best, didn't I?"

"And I bet you regret that every day." It was sarcasm, but he doesn't pick up on that.

"Not once, man. Not once. I don't ponder over the wisdom of my orders. I joined up with this outfit knowing it wasn't all about me. You, on the other hand, just go wherever the wind blows you."

"But you aren't an Agency employee anymore. You're a Poison Apple asset, and that means you can, and *should*, think for yourself. I'm not asking you to do one damn thing against Hanley, the Agency, or America. I'm just asking you to do what's fucking right."

He hesitates a moment, but I can tell he's not giving in. "Sorry, man."

I want to hit him in the face, and apparently it registers in my eyes.

"Calm down or I'll get the boys to restrain you."

I control my urges and lean back in the leather chair. It's time to play my next card.

"What if I told you Matt Hanley was in on it?"

Zack pauses, then laughs. "Hanley's a sex trafficker, right." When I don't respond, he says, "C'mon, dude. No fucking chance."

I turn to Travers. "Chris, where did you get the intel that I was near the Casino of Venice tonight at midnight?"

Travers looks to Hightower, not sure if he should tell me. Zack just shrugs like it doesn't make any difference.

Chris says, "Brewer. I asked where it originated from and she said that was 'need to know.'"

I look to Zack, and Zack is confused now. To Chris he says, "You are the TL on the ground. You would need to know the origin of the intel so you could evaluate it."

Travers replies, "That's what I'm sayin'."

"Zack," I interject. "I told Hanley I was going to Venice to get help so I could combat this thing called the Consortium, something he said he knew nothing about. Fourteen hours later Hanley puts Ground Branch right on top of me, in a Mala del Brenta stronghold far away from my known contacts in the city, right when the Consortium is holding a sale of kidnapping victims. How the *fuck* does that happen if he doesn't have knowledge of the Consortium?"

Hightower doesn't have an answer.

I lay it on even thicker now. "If you'd been there with me, in Bosnia, when I saw them. If you had seen them led around like cattle on a yacht in the Adriatic like I did. If you'd heard the stories about what has been done to them like I have. If you'd talked, face-to-face, with two of the victims like I have . . . then I *know* you'd help me out."

Hightower is on the fence, I can see it in his normally confident face. He says, "We'll talk to Matt when we get back. This shit will all get straightened out."

I think about punching him again but this time I mask it better. I take a slow breath and play the last card in my hand. "Zack . . . you told me you had a kid. A daughter."

Zack leans back in his chair dramatically. "Don't you dare fuckin' play the daughter card right now, Six."

"I'll play any card I have in my hand. She's, what? Twelve? Denver, did you say?"

"She's thirteen, you son of a bitch, and I think she's in Boulder but I don't even know because I've never even met her. You need to can this shit, brother, before I—"

I talk over him. "I didn't see any thirteen-year-olds in the dungeon I found in Bosnia. But I was told there were two fourteen-year-olds in the group. Lots of fifteen- and sixteen-year-olds."

Travers is listening in. He mumbles softly. "Bosnia? So then you *did* schwack Babic."

I don't deny it this time. "He was running a way station where the smuggled women were brought along the pipeline to the West. It was a fucking horror show."

"Jesus," Travers says, and then he turns and gives Zack a look like he's an insensitive dick. "You've got a kid? How did I not know that?"

Hightower doesn't answer.

I say, "Zack, a lot of people have died, a lot of people have been abused, and a lot of people have lost their freedom. Every one of those girls has a dad. Their dads can't do shit for them. But *you* can. What the fuck do you stand for if you can't stand against *this*?"

Hightower looks out the portal next to him for a long moment, into nothing but darkness.

But before he says anything, my sat phone buzzes in my pocket.

Instantly I'm terrified something is wrong. I grab it and answer, knowing it's Talyssa. "What's happened?"

In contrast to her last call, this time there is a buoyancy in her voice that I've never heard. "I've got something!"

FORTY-ONE

I can tell by Talyssa's breathless tone that she has somehow found the big break we need, the one I wasn't able to provide by skulking around Venice, taking pictures of billionaire pervs and dodging bullets.

"What is it?"

"The psychologist Roxana told you about on *La Primarosa* is Dr. Claudia Riesling. I found her through an account in Antigua attached to one of the accounts Meyer dug into. Her name wasn't on the account information, but a personal bank account of hers had received monthly transfers from a shell corporation I tied to the Consortium."

I'm beyond impressed. I wonder how many idiots' faces I'd have to bash in to get the same information.

"Where does she live?"

"She has a house in Pacific Palisades, California, and another in the south of France."

"Great. We just have to find out where she is now."

"No, we don't," Talyssa says.

"We don't?"

"No, because we know where she is going to be tomorrow and the day after."

"Where?"

"She booked a room at a luxury hotel in the San Fernando Valley for two nights."

I think about this for a second. "That's not far from her home."

"An hour or so. I had a hunch her hotel stay was work-related, especially right after this trip to pick the women up. I looked at property records around it, ran a scan of ownership of anyplace that seemed large enough to be considered a ranch, and then I looked through the ones set up by corporations and trusts and such."

"Jesus," I say. "How long did that take?"

She says, "Maarten and I did it in a half hour. Anyway, there are a few large ranches nearby, and one of them is owned by one of the one hundred sixty-eight shell corps I've identified as being part of the Consortium. It's a sixty-acre property north of Los Angeles in the San Fernando Valley. Looking at Riesling's credit card purchases, she stays at this nearby hotel every other month, usually for two to five nights at a time."

I wonder if that's how many times they bring trafficking victims in from abroad.

I don't have a computer in front of me, because I'm basically a prisoner on this aircraft, so I can't look up the property. But I get all the information I can from Talyssa and I borrow a pen and pad from Sharon and write it down.

I then say, "You've done incredible work. Now, I need you to be very careful. Get out of there and watch your back; this Meyer guy might see an opportunity and take it."

Talyssa replies, "Maarten and I have an understanding, Harry. He won't be any trouble."

I raise an eyebrow, wondering what she's been doing without me there to guide her. But whatever it is, I can't complain about the results.

"Okay," I say. "Find someplace to hide out. I'll call you when I know more."

"Are you joking? I'm not going to stay over here and hide out."

"I don't need you over here in the middle of—"

"I'll call you when I get to California." And with that the line goes dead.

I look over to Hightower, and I realize he's been listening in on the conversation. Before I can speak, he says, "Let's make a call to the boss."

I nod. "You're doing the right thing, Zack."

FORTY-TWO

We're still five hours from landing when Zack Hightower takes the airphone sitting on the table next to him and punches a couple of buttons. He places the call on the cabin overhead intercom, and then we all sit there silently for half a minute listening to it ring before we hear a *click*.

"Hanley."

I let Zack start things off, which he does with, "Hey, Matt. ID check Whiskey, Yankee—"

"The package is with you?"

Hightower clears his throat. "Yes, sir. You're broadcasting on the intercom."

"The package is listening now?"

"Yes, sir. He wants to speak with you."

"Violator," Hanley says. His voice relays his annoyance, which is cute, because I'm fucking furious right now.

"I have some questions for you," I say.

"Take me off the comms and we can talk."

I shake my head at Zack. "Everybody around me is TS/SCI with all appropriate read-ins, and what I'm about to say is personal, it's not classified in any way, shape, or form. You pull me off comms and you are telegraphing to these seven men and one woman that you're afraid of them hearing our conversation. Is that what you want?"

Another pause; I can feel Hanley's palpable sense of concern about what I will say.

"Go on, then."

"You lied when you told me you didn't know about the Consortium. You were the one who told Brewer where to task Ground Branch, which means you are well aware of their activities. You refused my request for resources in saving two dozen sex trafficking victims, and you sent men to pick me up to stop me from doing anything to the Consortium by myself.

"I'm no detective, but that all tells me you are somehow involved in this international sex trafficking ring, either directly or else you are helping to cover up their activities."

"That's ridiculous, Gentry. You know me."

I say, "Then who's pulling your strings?"

I can hear Matt sigh, which he does with regularity when talking with me. He asks, "What do you know?"

"Not a chance, Matt. Let's hear *you* talk."

Hanley next says, "Court, have I ever lied to you?"

This is rich, coming from him. "Have you ever lied to me? *Fuck*, Matt, you tried to kill me. Does that count?" I glance at Hightower next to me. "Both of you did."

Hanley barks back instantly. "That was under orders!"

And Hightower raises a hand in the air. "Same. Get over it, dude. Move on."

Hanley says, "I did not know about the Consortium. Not by name, anyhow. But when you called Brewer, I looked into it. We know about their operation, and we knew about the meeting tonight in Venice."

"Who is the American who runs it?"

"He's an asshole, apparently. But he's also an asset."

I understand. "He is providing you some sort of intelligence product, and in return you are protecting him. Is that it?"

"That's it."

"So, Matt, when you gave me that impassioned plea for me to drop this pipeline thing and haul ass back home so that Zoya wouldn't die alone in some shit-stained hellhole, it had less to do with Zoya and more to do with you trying to protect international criminals so they could continue to feed you intel product."

"If I say yes, are you going to show up at the foot of my bed in the middle of the night?"

I don't answer him, but I get the reference. I *did* come to him one rainy night for a chat, and it was clear he did not appreciate the intrusion.

After my silence, Hanley adds, "People in the real world aren't like you, Court old buddy. The rest of us, we take orders. We work to the best of our ability to satisfy the wishes of our higher-ups. I've got bosses I listen to and respect, unlike you, out there just winging it, dancing to your own music playing in your goofy head. Music nobody hears but you."

"You're stacking your metaphors, Matt."

"Let me help you understand, then. I'm saying this. I was told the man at the center of this—"

"What's his name?"

"I don't know his name. I just know his code name."

"The DDO doesn't know the name of an intelligence asset? Bullshit."

"He's the one who's kept it hidden. He came to us originally, a walk-in, and he set protocols in place to where we can't easily identify him."

"All right," I say. "People in the Balkan pipeline call him the Director."

"Okay, fine. The Director, he works with us, and the intel product he generates takes precedence over whatever side business he may or may not be involved in."

"Side business? For God's sake, Matt! He's running a massive international sex slavery ring; this isn't a fucking chain of Pinkberrys!"

The rest of the cabin around me is dead silent.

I believe Hanley to be a good man, despite how he treats me sometimes, and he wouldn't want to be part of a scheme to ruin the lives of thousands of young women and girls. But still, his devotion to his duties is stronger than his moral compass, because he says, "I truly hope that sex slavery operation gets shut down. But it can't be shut down by stopping the Director. He's proven himself too important to America's national interests."

"How the fuck so, Matt?"

"He's doing something we need him to keep doing."

I'm not the sharpest tack, but I've been in this game a long time, so I had been suspecting this all along.

"This is about international banking. I know the Consortium has money laundering down to an art form. He's working with other entities. Terror groups, rogue states, weapons proliferators. And he's passing that info on to you."

"Can neither confirm nor deny," he says.

I've known Matt ten years, and when he says this, he is one hundred percent confirming, *not* denying.

I say, "But . . . you *do* understand he's only playing ball so you guys will run interference for him while he conducts criminal activity, right? Every country I've been in over the last week is full of government personnel either working for him outright, supporting his efforts in some way, or covering for him. I'm sure he pays out millions of dollars to those who can be bought off, and he gives vital information to those who cannot."

Hanley sighs again. I imagine he's recirculated more air in whatever room he's in than the HVAC system has in the last ten minutes. He says, "That's how this works. That's how *any* intelligence operation works. Court, you know better than anybody how to play this game! You work with the biggest shitheads on the planet so you can go after some other big shithead. That's *your* own business model, is it not?"

I don't answer this, because I hate it when he's right.

"Isn't it?" he shouts again.

It's quiet for ten seconds, until Zack breaks the still. "Six, I love the sound you make when you shut the fuck up."

Hanley speaks again. "And here you are, telling me the right thing for me to do is to roll up the Director and give up vital national interests: intel on terror groups, opposition dictators, warlords, drug cartels. Sorry,

Court, I love you, man, but you need to get off your goddamned high horse. What the Agency does on a large scale, you do on a small scale."

Again, I sit quietly.

But he keeps going. "That time you dealt with the biggest cartel in Sinaloa . . . Remind me, did you bring them down, or did you use their resources to help you bring down someone else?"

He has a point. A strong point. An unassailable point. But I'm not in a conciliatory mood.

"Look," I say, but he talks over me.

"Just today. Just today, Violator! Who did you meet with in Venice? I bet it was your buddy Luigi Alfonsi, wasn't it?"

He's wrong, I met with Alfonsi's security chief, but I don't quibble.

"You know what they're up to? Gun running, drug running, immigrant running. A boat linked to them just last month sank in the Med; thirty-eight Libyans were on it. They *still* haven't picked all the dead kids out of the water."

Everyone in the Falcon looks towards me, ready for my brilliant rejoinder to Hanley's reasoning. But all I can say is, "Fuck you, Matt."

Matthew Hanley is the deputy director for operations for the CIA; he has every right to hang up the phone in the face of some foul-mouthed and insubordinate contract agent, but he does not.

Not because he loves me or respects me.

But because he needs me. He needs me to come home and work for him and be the best fucking killer of men on the planet.

And I know it, which means I know I can lose the argument on the merits, and win the argument with leverage.

And he knows it, too. He says, "Look, son. I respect you for what you are trying to do. But you will die trying, and you won't fix anything. I can't have you dying. I mean . . . not unless it's on one of my ops."

He snorts out a laugh at the end, but he's not kidding, and I'm not laughing.

Neither are the others on board, because they all know Matt Hanley would sacrifice them for a greater good without a moment's hesitation. We all knew it when we signed up for this shit, but that doesn't necessarily mean we want him joking around about it.

After a few uncomfortable seconds, I say, "There is an American psychologist who works for the Consortium. I know her name. I know where she lives. And I know where she is going to be for the next several days."

The speakers are silent for a moment, and then Hanley says, "Let me just get out ahead of you here. Request denied."

Dick. "This is not a request, Matt."

"Oh, really? So . . . what? This is the point where you take down seven highly trained paramilitaries and an armed flight attendant, all by your lonesome, in the cabin of a midsized executive jet, then hijack the aircraft and fly below the radar around the globe until you land on some out-of-the-way American airstrip? FaceTime me while I get the popcorn, because *this* I've gotta see."

"No, Matt. I'm not fighting anybody. You are going to let me do what I need to do."

"And why would I?"

"You may have me in pocket, but you don't have my associate. I've been working with someone else on this, and even if you have her name, you don't know where she is right now. If I don't contact her in six hours"—I take a quick look at my watch—"sorry, five hours and twelve minutes, then she is going to call your good friend Catherine King at the *Washington Post* and tell her an amazing tale about how the CIA is propping up a sex trafficker."

"We're not propping him up, we're just—"

"We've got the evidence of the relationship, that's all we need. Do you think the *Post* is going to tell your side of it, or are they going to tell the most sensational version they can?"

Hanley doesn't answer me. *He* hates it when *I'm* right.

I continue. "I don't want to do that, and you *know* I don't. But I *will* do it, and you know I will."

Hightower leans over closer to the speakerphone. "Say the word, Matt, and I'll toss this prick out of the plane without a chute."

But Zack winks at me after saying this, letting me know he's just sucking up to his boss.

I'm surrounded by nutjobs.

When Hanley doesn't reply, I say, "My associate has banking records tying Dr. Claudia Riesling to the trafficking ring. There is also one of the heads of the Consortium, a South African. I saw him. His first name might be Jaco, but I can't be certain. He was on the boat that transported a shipment of victims to an auction in Venice, where they were sold off into slavery. My associate knows this, too. Shit, Matt, the *Post* won't write about anything else for a fucking month!"

"What is it you want, son?"

"I want to get off this aircraft in D.C., unmolested. I want to walk away."

Hanley hesitates a long time, but that feels promising to me. His "hell nos" come quickly. His reluctant "yeses" take a minute.

Eventually he says, "Approved, under conditions. Is that it?"

He knows that's not it. "No. I want Hightower, Travers, and four more Ground Branch guys at my disposal for seventy-two hours."

Hanley laughs now, and I worry I just overplayed my hand. "*That* request is denied. They're not your men to use, and you certainly can't use them in the States." He pauses, and I wait him out. Finally, he says, "But I'll talk to Romantic privately. We might be able to throw you a bone. Again, with conditions."

I'm not sure what he means by this, but it sounds like more than I had hoped for originally.

"What are the conditions?" I ask.

"You won't find the Director; this guy is as good as anyone on the planet at insulating himself from his operations. That's why he's been informing on international criminals for ten years and he's not taking a dirt nap in some gully somewhere. And it's why we don't know who he is.

"And if you roll up this psychologist, or this South African asshole, they won't talk. They know the reach the Director has."

"What are the conditions?" I repeat.

"But if I'm wrong. If you *do* somehow find the Director," Hanley says, "then you absolutely cannot kill him, and you cannot have him arrested. He must remain in place. I don't give a shit if you tear down his entire sex trafficking ring, but we need him in play in the international finance world; we need him able to operate a computer and deal with the offshore tax havens and criminal elements. And there can be no comebacks on the Agency. He can't think we sent you."

I don't like this. Not at all. But I tell myself there is more than one way to skin a cat. "Deal. If I find the Director, I will let him live, I won't turn him in, and I won't let him know I spoke with you. What else?"

"I need you to be as discreet as possible. I know what you do, and I know how you do it. You can be deep cover, invisible, stealthy like a fucking greased ninja cat." He pauses, then says, "And you can also shoot up city blocks on live TV like you're Arnold fucking Schwarzenegger. If you are going to operate in the U.S. against an entity you aren't sanctioned to take down, then I need you to be the greased ninja cat and not Rambo. You hear me?"

Arnold wasn't Rambo, but I take his meaning.

"Agreed. What else?"

"What else? Don't die, that's what else. I have work for you."

I bet he does. I say, "I understand and wilco on all, Matt. Thanks."

He doesn't say *You're welcome.* No, he says, "Court, one of these days you are going to be more trouble than you're worth."

"But not today."

Another long sigh. "Not today, no. I need you back here. Do your thing, follow the ROEs I set down, and then get your ass back to work. No more delays, no more excuses, no more rogue do-gooder bullshit."

"Understood, sir."

Hanley tells Hightower to take him off the speaker, and then Zack takes the phone to the front bulkhead and sits there, well out of my earshot. I look at everyone sitting around me, and as one they all relax. I'm no longer their prisoner, I'm no longer a threat. No, now I have sanction, more or less.

I'm back in the game.

FORTY-THREE

The Gulfstream aircraft owned by a shell corporation for the Consortium had taken off from Venice's Marco Polo Airport over an hour before the CIA flight left Treviso, so it was over four hours into its transatlantic crossing now. In the cabin were Cage, Sean Hall, Hall's six men, the two European girls known as Maja and Sofia, Dr. Claudia Riesling, and Jaco Verdoorn.

For the first hour of the flight Verdoorn, Hall, and Cage sat in the back, out of earshot of the rest, and they tried to piece together everything that had happened. Cage was furious at Verdoorn, Hall was furious at Verdoorn, and Verdoorn was furious at his men, especially Loots, who'd had the fucking Gray Man in the sights of his Sig pistol and yet failed to shoot him dead.

And he was furious at Rylond Jonker for getting his stupid ass shot and killed in a Venice alleyway.

Loots and the seven other surviving White Lion men would be taking a different private jet out of Verona, several hours to the west, because of concerns that the police presence would be significantly ramped up at Marco Polo after the shootout in the city proper.

For the second hour of the flight, however, Verdoorn had sat alone up at the front bulkhead, leaning forward and talking into his phone, scrolling through information on a tablet computer on his knees, and taking notes on a pad of paper. Behind him, Claudia Riesling talked to Maja and Sofia nearly constantly, trying to work them harder and harder so that they would accept the fate ahead of them. Sofia was teary eyed, no longer under the influence of drugs, but Maja was essentially impassive. Riesling saw her look over at Cage from time to time, but otherwise she did not show much reaction to anything said. Riesling knew the young woman was still in a state of shock, but at least she was compliant.

She'd be a good pet for Ken Cage, and the Director would appreciate his in-house psychologist for it.

. . .

Kenneth Cage sat next to Sean Hall, who drank vodka on the rocks with a shaky hand. That his bodyguard was shaken up by the events of the evening was not lost on him, but Sean and his boys had done what he paid them to do. He wasn't pissed at Sean; he was pissed at Jaco.

Cage himself was into his third scotch and soda when he saw Jaco at the front of the aircraft turn around and ask Claudia to come sit with him. He wondered about this; he couldn't imagine why the severe South African, after losing a man and his target tonight, needed to confer with the psychologist used to reprogram the merchandise, but he didn't think about it for long, because his eyes moved to Maja.

As Cage drank down more scotch, he fantasized about grabbing the little Romanian by the hair and dragging her to the sofa in the back, clearing out the bodyguards seated there, and then raping her on the spot, in full view of everyone else. The thought gave him a charge, a sexual thrill intermixed with his rage.

He needed someone to take it out on. Who better than the Romanian bitch who'd insulted him and slapped him?

He could see the fear in her eyes each and every time she glanced his way, and he loved it. He'd be home in a few hours; he'd have to spend a day or two with his family, and then he'd drive up to Rancho Esmerelda and he'd begin schooling Maja on how to treat him properly.

And when he was done with her, he'd have Jaco "take her back home," his euphemism for disappearing the girls so they couldn't identify him.

. . .

Dr. Claudia Riesling sat down next to the big man Verdoorn and did her best to hide the intimidation she always felt around him. In an attempt to empathize with him and his terrible night, she said, "How are you feeling, Jaco?"

But he did not answer this question. He said, "I've been making some calls, back to Romania, back to Hungary, back to Belgrade. I'm trying to figure out how the fuck Gentry has been able to stay on our heels like this."

"And you found something?"

"I did."

Riesling was confused. "Well . . . why are you telling me this? You are the operations and security chief. Sean is the Director's lead protection agent. I have nothing to do with—"

"I did some research on the merchandise on board this aircraft."

Riesling said, "Research? What sort of research?"

"Genealogical research."

"I'm sorry. What the hell are you talking about?"

"It turns out Cage's Romanian prize Maja, seated two rows behind us, has herself a sister."

"And?"

"She's the fooking Europol analyst who went to the police in Dubrovnik two days ago."

Riesling sat back in her chair and closed her eyes. When she opened them, she said, "Why is it you are just *now* finding out about this? The recruiters and groomers are supposed to look into the items before they are collected."

"Half sisters. Different last names. Our Romanian recruiter missed it. The way Cage demanded the bitch be slotted into the next shipment meant they were pressed for time." He added, "Our whore is named Roxana Vaduva and the Europol bitch is named Talyssa Corbu."

Riesling said, "And this Corbu, she's working with the assassin that's been chasing us?"

"Unquestionably."

"But Maja can't possibly know what her sister is doing. She's been strip-searched multiple times; she doesn't have a way to communicate."

"She could know what her sister is doing if she talked to Gentry while on board *La Primarosa*."

Riesling blinked hard at this allegation. "What, and then he just beat her up?"

"Was the only way we wouldn't suspect her, wasn't it?"

"But . . . why didn't he take her with him?"

Verdoorn looked out the window. "Either he couldn't pull that off, or she didn't want to go because she's on the job, working for her sister. I don't know which, but either way, she's bloody dangerous."

Riesling looked over her shoulder at Cage, who was openly eyeing Maja right now with a look like a fox staring into a henhouse. She said to Verdoorn, "Why are you telling me? Aren't you going to tell the Director?"

Verdoorn shook his head. "It won't change anything. He wants this one back at the Ranch, more than I've ever seen him want any of the merchandise in the years I've worked for him. Telling him she poses a threat to him will only create more trouble for us. Not for him. Not for her. For *us*."

Riesling said, "I don't really understand your reasoning."

"He'll be pissed we didn't figure out the relationship, he'll be *more* pissed than he already is that we didn't bag Gentry in Venice or Croatia or Bosnia, and he won't dispose of her until he's done what he wants with her."

"So . . . what do we do?"

"I prefer to see this new development as an opportunity."

"To do what?"

Verdoorn pointed to his tablet computer. On it was the LinkedIn profile of Talyssa Corbu, including contact information and a photo of a waifishly thin smiling blonde in business attire. "For me to make contact with my enemy."

Verdoorn grinned, and Riesling saw it as an especially sinister expression on the man's normally cruel and hard face.

• • •

I've caught a couple hours' sleep on the CIA Falcon 50 as we cross the Atlantic, but I wake when my phone begins buzzing in my hand. I look around quickly; it's daylight, and a quick check of the monitor at the front bulkhead tells me we're forty minutes away from landing at Andrews in D.C.

I rub my eyes and snatch up my phone.

"Talyssa? You okay?"

Her voice is unsure. "I'm okay. I'm at the airport. I'll be in Los Angeles in twelve hours."

"I don't want you flying to the—"

"Harry. Listen. Someone called me."

This sounds bad. "Who?"

"He didn't say . . . He wants to talk to someone called Gentry. Is that your last name, Harry?"

And now it sounds worse. I close my eyes and lean my head back. "Let me guess. He's South African."

"I believe that he is. I can transfer him from my phone to yours."

"All right. Do it."

I look around the cabin and see that Sharon is up and moving around, but everyone else is still racked out. Men and women in this line of work become experts at grabbing rest whenever and wherever they can. Hightower's head is hanging back off the side of the couch and he's snoring a snore I spent years listening to almost every night when I served under him in the Goon Squad.

I hear a few clicks over the satellite connection, and then a low, gravelly voice starts up in my ear.

"Well hello there, mate."

"Hello, Jaco." It was an educated guess, but the hesitation on the other end tips me off that I hit the nail on the head.

Finally he says, "Impressive. Bladdy impressive. Should have known you'd be doin' your due diligence. Just like I am."

"What do you want?"

"Two things. One, I wanted to introduce myself, but now I see introductions are unnecessary. And two, I'm just calling to let you know that we've figured out who your informant is."

"My . . . informant?" I say, but the instant Talyssa told me Jaco was on the phone, I knew that *he* knew about Roxana.

"Yes, your informant. The lovely sister of your associate."

I don't speak. I knew it was always possible they could connect these dots, but I hoped they wouldn't. I don't know what this means for Roxana now, but it *can't* be good.

"Don't you worry," Jaco says. "We haven't touched a hair on her head. Yet."

I try to help her situation in the only way I can think of. "I didn't know who she was when I punched her lights out on the boat. Thought she was just some whore. Corbu showed me a picture of her after. We thought she was dead. Corbu's still pissed off I left her there."

"You're trying too hard, mate. I know you and Roxana talked after you killed Kostopoulos."

"Kostopoulos? Oh, yeah. I only knew him as 'the old pervert in the bathrobe.' But no, I didn't talk to her."

Verdoorn sniffs out a laugh. I wait to hear whatever his pitch is.

He says, "You're good, mate. You know you are good."

"And you're bad. You know that, too, right?"

"Guilty as charged. But me and my boys will be around Roxana from here on out, and we can't *wait* for you to come and try again."

I find this intriguing. "So . . . you aren't warning me to back off, you're hoping I'll keep coming."

"That's it. I guess you are used to scaring your enemy so bad they don't put up a fight."

I'm hardly used to that, but far be it from me to dissuade him from thinking I'm a badass.

He keeps talking. "Gentry, I'm not like your average bloke. I'm bladdy looking forward to the day we meet."

"Me, too. Why don't you give me your address? I'll pop right over."

"No such luck. Can't make it too easy, can I? The boss man wouldn't be happy with me. Nah, mate, I'll just do what I do, work within the confines of my job. I'll let Roxana do what she does, or what she'll be forced to do soon enough, which won't be pretty. I'll just wait for the stars to align and for you to show up in front of me."

"Hey," I say. "While I've got you, what's it like knowing you are ruining the lives of tens of thousands of innocent girls? How does that make you feel?"

"How does it make you feel killing loads of people?"

Sharon brings me coffee and I take it, my hand clutching the phone tightly. "Sometimes I feel nothing at all. But sometimes, when it's just the right person . . . I feel fan-fucking-tastic. And I'm really looking forward to that day I show up in front of you."

Jaco laughs hard now. "Likewise, mate. You think you scare me, but ya don't."

"I don't want to scare you. I want your confidence at an all-time high when I drive the blade into your gut. Then you'll get that look of disbelief in your eyes, mixed with fear, mixed with anger. You know the look. You've seen it in your victims, haven't you, Jaco?"

He doesn't reply, and I know I'm in this asshole's head, right where I want to be.

Jaco says, "You think you're some kind of a hero, don't you, mate? I know your type. I bet you think you are going through all this because you care about the poor defenseless little whores. But that's not it at all. I can hear it in your voice. You're the same as me. You do all this not because you want to save people, but because you want to kill people. You *need* to kill people."

He's wrong. Totally wrong. I mean . . . he has to be. I don't kill because of blood lust, I kill because of the situations I find myself in.

Or . . . *put* myself in, I guess.

Does this motherfucker have a point?

Pushing my own motivations out of my mind for now, I say, "Well, it's been a blast catching up. Looking forward to our next encounter."

"You and me both, mate."

I hang up the phone, figuring doing so will piss him off a little. I thought about appealing to him to leave Roxana out of this, but I don't want to do anything more to make him think he has that leverage over me with her.

Sharon brings the coffeepot back to refill me, but I haven't taken a sip yet. She says, "Landing in a half hour."

"Thanks."

Zack is awake now, and he moves over next to me. Softly he says, "I talked to Matt while you were racked out. We have an idea that might help you a little."

I'm suspicious, despite Hanley's limited sanction. "Why is Matt helping me with something he doesn't even want me doing?"

"Hanley doesn't want you dying for another cause, he wants you dying for him."

It's fucked up, but I know Hanley well enough to know it's true.

I say, "Okay, so why are *you* helping me?"

"Me?" Zack looks uncomfortable now, weird on the face of a man normally so cocky and self-assured. After a time, he says, "I have my reasons."

I know his reason. His *one* reason. "You're thinking about who I'm trying to help, and you're thinking about your *own* kid, aren't you?"

"My daughter. She lives in Boulder. That's not a guess. I found out last spring. She and her mom are in wit-pro, long story, but I got a guy at the Bureau to find out about her."

I know how hard it is to find someone in Witness Protection, so I recognize the lengths Zack must have gone to. "Why did you seek her out after all these years?"

Now Zack looks almost sick. He isn't the emotional type, so when his eyes glass up and redden, it's awkward as fuck for us both. He says, "I'm not gonna live forever. Hell, I might not live till Tuesday." He sniffs back congestion; there are no tears, but he's close. He says, "Stacy. That's her name. Her mom named her. She probably told her I died in the war or some shit." After another sniff he says, "She's got another dad. A firefighter. I dug into him hard." After a pause he says, "He's a good dude. A saint." He shakes his head. "Fucking bastard."

"You want your kid being raised by a good man, don't you?"

He nods. "Of course I do. But I wish *I* were that good man. I haven't done one thing for her but stay away. That used to be enough for me. But it's not anymore."

Zack clears his head with a hard shake. "Anyway. These girls in the pipeline. I hope you can help them out."

I'm almost certain the ones I saw in Mostar, with the exception of Liliana, are all but doomed. But maybe there is still hope for Roxana. "What is it you are offering?"

"Wish I could go with you, but Hanley would kick me in the dick meat if I tried. I do know a guy you might want to talk to, though."

"Who?"

Zack turns and faces me directly. "Like Hanley said, you've got no problem working with some shady fuckers if it helps you achieve your mission. That's right, isn't it?"

I don't hesitate an instant. "I'd work with Satan himself to help these victims, Zack."

Hightower nods. "There's a former Unit guy." He's talking about Delta Force, and I know them to be among the best shooters on the planet. "He transitioned to Ground Branch. He left the Agency, started a company a few years back in the Philippines, raiding brothels and rescuing kids being abused by foreign tourists. The sickest of the sick fuckers out there. International agencies hired him and his team after they did the prep work. He and his six teammates kicked the doors, Delta style, went in and took down johns and traffickers. Zip-tied the perpetrators and left them for the cops, then got the kids out of there and into shelters.

"This guy saw a lot of action in three years of doing this."

I say, "He doesn't sound like Satan to me. Still, I don't see how some dude in the Philippines is going to be any help to—"

"He lives in Vegas now," Hightower continues. "His company is defunct." Almost nonchalantly he adds, "He and his boys straight-up murdered a bunch of dudes."

I cock my head. "They did *what*?"

"A British national in Manila, they walked in on him raping a little kid. I don't know how little, and I don't want to know, but with all the shit these guys had seen, whatever they saw in *that* room, they absolutely snapped. My buddy grabbed the British sex tourist by the throat and squeezed, didn't stop squeezing till he ripped the motherfucker's windpipe out. Dude bled out right there. Filipinos working at the house stormed in, unarmed, and the Americans opened fire on every last one of them. Thirteen dead in all. A damn bloodbath, right in the center of the capital."

"That's not Satan's work," I counter. "That's God's work."

"Yeah, no shit. But the Philippine government didn't agree. Bad for tourism. Sex tourism, which they tolerate, but also tourism in general. They arrested the seven Americans, held them in some Manila shithole for ten months, then extradited them to the U.S. Due to their ties with the Agency, they weren't prosecuted here. They were just ordered to keep their heads low and stop doing what they were doing."

"But . . ." I say. "You think there's a chance they might do what they were doing again, if I just ask."

Zack shrugs. "I don't know. Neither does Hanley. But they were good shooters, and you can't second-guess their motivation for one second. They lived for this shit before they got popped in Asia and sent home.

"You tell them what you told me . . . you might get yourself some backup."

It's worth a shot. "Who is this guy? Your friend."

"Shep Duvall. Solid dude, or he was when I knew him, anyway."

Upon hearing the name, I close my eyes.

"What?" Zack asks.

I say, "I know that asshole."

"Yeah? Well, beggars can't be choosers, Six."

I open my eyes and say, "True, but beggars *can* be beggars. Any chance I can borrow a gun?"

Hightower makes a face of annoyance, but says, "When we land, when we're off the aircraft, I'll get a piece off one of Travers's boys. That's the best I can do."

"Thanks, Zack."

He nods at me, then gives me a little wink. "Go get 'em, Six."

FORTY-FOUR

The girl called Sofia and the girl called Maja were ushered out of the private plane and marched across the tarmac, far from the small terminal and into a waiting black Mercedes G-Class SUV. Dr. Claudia climbed in behind them.

From the backseat of the Navigator, Roxana saw the Director deplane, climb down the stairs, and look her way briefly as he climbed into the back of an identical Mercedes SUV, with his bodyguard Sean at his side.

Roxana was desperate to find some hint of where she was right now. She didn't know how she could possibly communicate her location to her sister, but it was a moot point until she actually knew it herself.

She'd looked around for an airport sign, but she saw nothing.

The ocean was on her left as they drove away from the city, and although she'd been no geography wiz in school back in Bucharest, she knew this meant they were heading north if they were, in fact, on the West Coast. There were hills, canyons, and lots and lots of businesses and homes, then they drove away from much of the development and into more sparsely populated arid hills.

Minutes later Roxana Vaduva squinted into the sunshine, looking through the windshield of the van as it rolled through the iron-gated entrance of a large ranch. They rumbled up a paved driveway, past a pair of small, squat stucco buildings, and past four young men. The men eyed the vehicle as it drove by, and she looked through the heavily tinted windows at them, saw the big guns hanging from their chests. The vehicle rolled on; Roxana noted the trees and plants around her and she realized she had never been anywhere in her life that looked anything like this place, but it felt to her like movies she had seen about Mexico.

There was a low rise and once the G-Wagen crested it, she peered through the front windshield and saw a massive stucco house, the biggest home she'd ever laid eyes on in her life. It was clearly Hispanic architecture, and when they pulled to a stop in front of it, she saw more Latino men in suits standing around carrying guns.

She and the Hungarian girl followed Dr. Claudia up the steps and through the massive double-door entrance to the building. Inside it was cool and dark, and Roxana saw a beautiful young redhead wearing a low-cut evening dress standing there, a glass of champagne in her hand. Roxana was certain it was morning still, and she couldn't fathom why the girl would dress in this manner so early in the day.

Claudia led the women up two flights of stairs and down a hallway. As they walked they passed other girls, all young, some *very* young, and all dressed exotically in one form or another. None of the girls talked to Roxana or Sofia; some did greet Claudia, but others just looked away.

Roxana was certain that most, if not all, of these girls had been drugged. She could see the distant eyes and slow movement, and she assumed it was more of the Xanax she'd been given sporadically throughout this ordeal.

Sofia spoke up as they neared a door at the end of an ornate hall. "Dr. Claudia? How many girls are kept here?"

Claudia answered, "No one is *kept* here, they all want to be here."

"How many women want to be here?" Sofia asked.

"At any one time, twenty or so. I don't know what the occupancy is now."

They passed a window and Roxana slowed and looked out, again searching in vain for clues as to their location.

Soon Claudia led them into a bedroom, with an adjoining door to the next bedroom. "Maja, you will be in here, and Sofia, just through that door is your room."

Roxana found the space to be beautiful, large, and well-appointed with antique furniture. A four-poster bed, a makeup vanity and a chest of drawers, a sitting area, and a massive oak wardrobe accented the room. She followed Sofia into her bedroom and found it similar but not identical, with a different color scheme. Claudia directed them to their closets, which were full of clothes, including expensive-looking evening gowns along with more revealing attire.

Roxana could see Sofia's eyes light up upon seeing the clothes, upon taking in her new living space. The American psychologist had done a good job brainwashing her, Roxana determined.

After the women were settled in, Claudia said someone would be by shortly to take them on a tour of the house. She explained that although they were not allowed to go outside without permission, the building itself was theirs to roam if they wanted to.

Soon the door was closed between Roxana and Sofia's rooms. Roxana and Claudia stood by her new bed, and the Romanian woman could feel the eyes of the American peering into hers, trying desperately, Roxana imagined, to see if her compliance was genuine.

Roxana masked her true intentions, of course. She was here to help her sister, just like she'd been from the beginning, although right now she had no idea how to be any use to her at all. There were no phones in the room, she'd passed none walking through the house, and, anyway, she didn't know where the fuck she was.

Finally Claudia looked away from Roxana and at her watch as she said, "I have sessions with some other residents. I will be back here to see you each day for the next five days. You will have good days and bad; that is to be expected. I want to make sure you are settling in."

Roxana was confused. "You don't stay here at the property?"

Claudia shook her head. "No. I am not a part of what happens here. I am a part of the process that prepares you for it. I do not stay overnight. I will be back, and I will do what I can to help you."

Gone was her unbridled optimism about Roxana's time here on the West Coast. Now she seemed more sanguine, less upbeat.

Roxana decided to take a chance. "Where are we? What is this place?"

Claudia did not answer; she just stared again into the younger woman's eyes for a long time. Eventually she said, "You should know . . . Jaco is onto you."

"What do you mean by that?"

"I mean, he knows about your sister."

Roxana's heart sank and she lowered onto the bed. She didn't know what this meant for herself or for her sister, but panic welled within her.

She tried to play dumb. "What about my sister?"

But to this the psychologist just made a face of disappointment. "You should be proud of yourself for successfully pulling the wool over my eyes for a time. We've never had an infiltrator before, so I didn't properly evaluate you. But now I see through you."

"What is it that you see?"

"You don't yet accept the fact that your fate is sealed, but you will soon, and as soon as you do, you will realize that your fate is what you make of it. Infiltrator or not, you can have a good time while you are here, if you just let it happen."

Roxana didn't understand this at all, but she was certain this doctor was pure evil, just as bad as the rest of them. She lay back on the bed without another word, and Claudia left the room, shutting the heavy door behind her.

. . .

Fifty-six-year-old Michael "Shep" Duvall slipped his reading glasses off, then put down his Bible. Sitting up from his worn recliner, he looked around the dark living room of his North Las Vegas bungalow.

Something was wrong, but he couldn't say what.

He scratched at his gray beard, then stood, looked at the little plastic cuckoo clock on the wall, and saw that it was twenty-two hundred hours. He hadn't read a clock in anything other than military time since he was eighteen years old and would need a second to realize that civilians would refer to the current time as ten p.m.

The dark house was empty and still; he lived alone, so this was no surprise, but *something* had alerted him, he was sure of it.

He soon pinpointed the source of his disquiet.

Where the hell was his dog?

Duvall's four-year-old lab, Monkey, had access to the fenced-in front yard facing two-lane Hickey Avenue by means of a doggie door in the kitchen. She was in and out all evening, every evening, but by this late at night she could always be found on the threadbare brown love seat next to Duvall's reading chair, either sleeping or just looking lovingly at her master, waiting to follow him to the bedroom for the night.

But the dog wasn't on the love seat, and she wasn't in the living room or in the little attached kitchen by her water bowl.

"Monkey?" he called out, half expecting the big black dog to shoot through the rubber-curtained doggie door from the outside, although it would be rare for her to be out so late.

But she did not come.

Duvall put on the glasses he wore for distance, and he hefted his Wilson Combat 1911 .45 caliber pistol off the end table next to him. He was not a tall man, but he was broad-chested and possessed a dominating persona when necessary. He could intimidate now, even in his mid-fifties, and even with the paunch that had grown around his midsection since he'd left the Agency.

And the big, stainless steel .45 only added to his intimidation factor.

He called for Monkey one more time, then flipped off the light next to his recliner and stepped to his kitchen door. Quietly he opened it; the business end of the pistol led the way outside, and he carefully walked the chain-link perimeter fence of his tiny property, looking for any sign of his companion.

Monkey was nowhere to be found; the rickety driveway gate was closed and locked.

Worried, but knowing he needed to check his bedroom and his tiny home office, he headed back into the house. He'd just moved through the kitchen for the back hall, had just slipped the Wilson Combat into his drawstring warm-up pants, when the light he'd flipped off by his recliner snapped back on.

Duvall didn't scare, and he didn't startle. His body had been through too much to react any way but efficiently when surprised. He turned to the light and saw a man seated there in his reading chair, one leg crossed over the other.

The man said, "Leave the hand cannon where it is and your mitts where I can see them."

Duvall knew he didn't have a play for his gun. In the seated man's hand was a black Glock 19, wearing a silencer and resting easily on his knee, pointed in Duvall's direction.

Duvall said, "Mister, if you're after money, then this is going to be one hell of a disappointing night for you."

To his surprise, the man said, "Take a closer look, Shep."

Duvall slowly moved a hand to adjust his glasses. After several seconds he said, "Gentry."

"Yep."

"You're alive?"

"That's a rhetorical question, I guess."

"I'm surprised."

"You and me both," Gentry said. "Sit down. I'm here to talk, but if you go for the gun, we won't have much left to talk about."

"I ain't goin' for the gun." Duvall sat down on the vinyl sofa. "What the hell did you do to my dog?"

"I gave her a steak. Four-ounce filet mignon. Very rare. Raw, as a matter of fact."

Duvall cocked his head. "And . . . did that juicy steak happen to be spiked with ketamine?"

"Valium. She's fine." A pause. "She's great, as a matter of fact. Lying in the storeroom by your carport, dreaming of more choice cuts flying over the fence and into her mouth, I'd imagine."

Duvall nodded now. "So . . . this is just a social call?"

"What do you think?"

Duvall leaned back on the vinyl, his hands far out to his side. "I'm gonna guess not."

. . .

Shep Duvall is old as dirt, and this disappoints me. He's overweight and his eyeglasses are so thick they look bulletproof. His hair is thin and gray on his head and thick and gray on his face. But I know the man, mostly by reputation. And I know that not too terribly long ago, he was a stone-cold skullfucker. As a Delta master sergeant, he'd been deployed countless times in the war on terror, and in the CIA he ran one of the best teams in Ground Branch.

I knew of him at the Agency, after his nearly two decades in the Unit. He ran another task force when I was on Golf Sierra with Hightower, and I worked under him once when the Goon Squad was non-operational, when Zack was out with a back injury.

I never had a problem with Duvall.

But that was seven or eight years ago. I thought he was old then, and it appears the intervening years have been rough on Shep.

He breaks the uncomfortable silence. "You may not know it, Violator, but I was tasked with killing you a few years ago."

I did know this, and *that* is why I think he's an asshole.

Still, I say, "You and everybody else."

He snorts out a little laugh. "Well . . . it appears I and everybody else failed, because here you are. Is the Agency still after you?"

"Sort of," I say. Then, "Not really." I wrap it up with a little shrug. "It's complicated."

"Right," he replies. Then, "So . . . other than roofing innocent dogs, what are you doing these days?"

"I'm working. Same as ever."

"Private job?"

"Sort of. It's more like . . . humanitarian work."

"I don't follow."

"I need your help." He isn't the type of man to beat around the bush, so I say, "I need you to strap a gun on, and to get some friends with guns. And I need you all to come with me."

"To do what?"

"I expect we're gonna stack some bodies before it's all through."

"You're the world's greatest killer, or some shit. Aren't you?"

I don't answer.

He looks around. "Why me? Why does this feel like a setup?" He shakes his head. "Gentry, I got troubles of my own. I want you out of here. Either shoot or scoot. If you aren't going to shoot me, I'm going to pick up my phone. One call to Matthew Hanley and I can have a team of Agency shitbirds crashing through the skylights."

I look up at the ceiling of his modest house; there are no skylights, and I am reassured he is speaking metaphorically. I say, "Duvall, one call to Matt Hanley will get you a grouchy dude in a bad suit hanging up in your face. Who do you think sent me to you?"

Shep thinks this over. "I'm out. I left four years ago."

"I know."

He eyes me suspiciously. "What else do you know?"

"I know about Manila."

"Yeah," he said. "That was a mistake. Not for killing those monsters, but for getting rolled up by the local five-oh after the fact."

"Yeah. Still . . . you did the right thing."

"Fuck you, Gentry," Shep barks. "That's my cross to bear and I don't need you breaking into my house to try to make me feel better. Make your pitch for whatever you want so you can get the fuck out of here and I can scoop my dog up and put her to bed."

"Here's my pitch, then. I need some shooters. You and your old team from Manila, if you can get them. Solid guys, guys who know how to run together."

"What for?"

"To stop a human trafficking ring."

He just looks at me in the low light of the tiny ranch-style house. "I'm not going to make any sudden moves to the fridge, so you better get us some beers. I'll let you pull my pistol as you go."

I step up to him and he stands and turns, his hands away from his body. I disarm him, then walk into the kitchen, keeping him in view, while I pull a couple of cold bottles of Pacifico out of the refrigerator. After popping off the tops, I walk one over to Duvall, and we sit back down.

Over the next fifteen minutes I tell him about the Consortium. My story would blow a lot of people away: the killing, the rape, the kidnapping, the Serbian general and the Greek mobster and the Italian street battle.

But not Duvall. He's a guy who's seen it *all* before. He sits there impassively, he doesn't interrupt, and he nods knowingly now and again.

And then I finish with the fact that the entire international organization is being run by a man on the West Coast, and we think we've pinpointed a location where trafficked women are being kept.

Slowly Duvall's posture changes. This isn't a tale of remote horrors, the likes of which he's heard more times than he can count. No, now this is about women and girls being brutalized just a few hours away by an animal, and one who is living quite well under the protection of the United States.

I can see it in his posture. He's already in.

"What's the target location?" he asks. "Specifically."

"A sixty-acre ranch an hour north of LA. I assume the victims are held there to be abused and the people who run the entire worldwide enterprise go there to party. I'm going to crash that fucking party."

"The layout of the ranch? Where are the victims kept? Where are the guards and guns?"

"I don't have that information. From Google Maps I see one large structure. Smaller outbuildings a half mile away that look like barracks for the security force. If I had a UAV or some more dudes I could get a better picture. For now, though, it looks like we'll have to just hit it all."

"Oppo?"

"The opposition is unknown. Substantial, I'd be willing to bet."

Duvall rubs his face hard. I see frustration in his movements. "You've got this operation of yours locked down, don't you, Violator?" He mocks my voice now. "'I need you to hook me up with some of your friends to help me go up against I don't know exactly how many of I don't know exactly who in a sixty-acre property where friend and foe are positioned I don't know exactly where.' That it?"

"That's about the size of it, yeah," I say. "I've got a clock ticking on my ass, too. I do this now, or it doesn't happen."

"What kind of clock?"

"You pick. There's the woman being held there I'm trying to save before anything even worse happens to her, there are the women and girls sold off in Venice that I'd like to recover before it's too late, and then there's Matt Hanley."

"What does the DDO want?"

"He wants *me*, Shep."

"He made a deal with you in exchange for me and a chance to go after the Consortium?"

"You got it."

Duvall finishes his beer and stands up quickly.

I reach for the pistol on my hip but don't draw it. "Shep!"

He just chuckles, completely unafraid. "You ain't gonna shoot," he says. "Who'd shoot a man who's about to bring him another cerveza?"

I relax, take my hand away from my waistband. "Not me."

As the big man walks to the little open kitchen, just steps away, he says, "So you need men like me and my associates from Manila. Men you know who will lay down their lives for something like this if it comes to that."

"That's it. As causes go, you have to admit this is a good one."

Duvall passes me another Pacifico and takes a swig from his own new bottle. "Okay, Violator. I like it. I don't really like you, I don't like the weak intel, and I don't like the fact that we'll be acting on U.S. soil. But I like it, just the same. I've spent the last year thinking about Manila. Not sobbin' for the motherfuckers we slayed, but pissed off I couldn't go out and slay some other motherfuckers."

"You're in?" I ask.

"You knew I was in before you got here."

I smile a little. "I was cautiously optimistic. What about your mates? You have a six-man team, I'm told."

Shep shakes his head. "Did have a six-man team. Scott Camp shot himself in the mouth with a twelve-gauge up in Utah a few months ago. His demons got the best of him."

I close my eyes and think of my own demons. I say, "The others?"

"You can pitch it to them like you pitched it to me. Let them decide."

"How far away are they?"

"For an asshole as unlucky as you, you got pretty lucky. We were primarily West Coast based when we worked in hostage rescue in Asia, and the boys grew roots in that area. One of my guys is in LA, one's in Bakersfield. Another in Lodi, another here in Vegas. I can get them together quickly."

I look at a map of Southern California on my phone. "Bakersfield is closest to the target. We'll meet there."

He nods and I tip my drink towards him. Then I say, "I do need one other thing."

"Shit, Violator, what else?"

"That ranch. I've looked at the sat map. It's a big property, flat, arid, and open."

Shep gets it. "They'll see us coming."

I nod. "I need a helicopter, flown by someone who can follow orders, and someone who can put skids anywhere I need them, possibly even under fire."

"And you think I just happen to know a guy with a helo willing to fly into gunfire?"

With a shrug, I say, "You've been around a long time, no offense. Hightower said you know everybody."

To this Duvall leans his head back on the sofa. "Hightower. What's that son of a bitch up to these days?"

"I can't tell you."

He raises an eyebrow. I just tipped him off that Zack was back with the Agency, which is sort of true, but I don't care. I need this guy's compliance, and I'll do whatever I have to do to establish my bona fides.

"A pilot and a helo. You don't ask for much, do you?"

I smile. "You want to pull this op off as much as I do."

After a pause he says, "Zack's right. I know just the guy for you, Violator, and he's right here in town. As good a helo driver as you'll find in the area, and he'd probably pay you for the chance to get some action."

Cocking my head, I ask, "What's he doing here in Vegas?"

"Let's just say he's in the sunset of his career. Like me, I guess."

Great.

"But older. A lot older."

Jesus Christ.

Shep looks at his watch. "Rack out here tonight. I'll call the boys now, call the pilot first thing in the morning."

"Why not now?"

"No use. He takes his hearing aids out when he sleeps."

I blow out a long sigh. "Of course he does."

FORTY-FIVE

Talyssa Corbu had traveled all over Europe, she'd even been to the Caribbean, but she'd never visited the United States before she deplaned at LAX and went through customs and immigration. Once clear on the other side, she rented a car and drove to a mall, where she began buying clothes, a suitcase, and other items she hadn't bothered with in her rush to get on a plane for America.

As soon as she was equipped, she called Gentry and he answered on the first ring. When she told him she was in LA, he begged her to sit tight, not to get a hotel room in her name because she was compromised to the enemy, and he promised to call her back with a plan.

Thirty minutes later he did so, and he gave her an address in Receda.

When she got there, a woman let her in and put her in a little guest room. Talyssa called Gentry back and he promised to keep her apprised of everything, but if and only if she stayed away from Rancho Esmerelda.

She knew where Rancho Esmerelda was, not far away at all; she considered driving there right then. But she did not, because she *also* knew Roxana's chances were better with Harry than they were with her. She thought it unlikely that her sister would be able to live up to her promise to call her with information on her location, but if her guess was correct about the ranch east of the San Fernando Valley, then they wouldn't need Roxana's help in finding her.

She wished she could liaise in some way with the police department here, but her experience told her she needed to stay away from them. Further, Gentry had intimated that he'd learned that the U.S. government had an interest in the operation, and while he didn't think they were actively supporting the sex trafficking ring, he thought it possible, likely even, that they were protecting the Director in exchange for intelligence he was providing them.

America was just as dirty as the other countries the pipeline ran through.

Talyssa pushed this depressing fact out of her mind and tried to think optimistically.

She sat on her bed in her little room and told herself it wouldn't be long now.

She'd see her sister again, and then she'd spend the rest of her life putting things right with her.

• • •

This house is a shit box. I'm in Bakersfield, sitting in a small living room full of car parts, empty beer bottles, and dirty clothes. If the four men sitting across from me now were fresh-faced kids in their early twenties, I would take this for a frat house that lost its house mom.

But these aren't kids. Not even close.

The men are all in their late forties. Rodney and Stu are white, A.J. is Latino, and Kareem is African American. They all have beards, they all wear glasses, and they all look like they could stand to drop thirty pounds.

They're younger and fitter than Duvall, true, but that's not saying much.

This isn't exactly the A-Team.

Duvall isn't here; he's on his way from Vegas after arranging the helo he promised to acquire. But he's called his old team from Southeast Asia and arranged for them to meet me at the home of one of them, and he just texted me to tell me to get started without him.

He also hooked me up with a place in LA to stash Talyssa: at the home of the sister of one of the guys here with me, although I don't even know which one.

There are five surviving members of the Manila team in addition to Duvall, but one of their number told Shep that due to a recent hip replacement, he'd be more hindrance than help.

The four men with me have agreed to nothing; they don't even know the target or the mission, but they are here, waiting to hear my spiel, and I take that to be a good sign.

Kareem, the African American, opens the discussion: "We all talked to Papa."

"Papa?"

"Duvall. His call sign is Papa."

"Makes sense."

"He tells us you're legit, your mission is righteous, and it's time sensitive. But we have some questions."

"Fair enough. Shep tells me you four are as good as they come."

Rodney, the homeowner, eyes me suspiciously. "Then that makes me wonder if the shit he said about you was BS, too, because we sure as hell ain't exactly at our peak."

A.J., the one I take for Latino, says, "Speak for yourself. I've got my shit squared away."

But the one calling himself Stu replies, "Rodney's right. Shep didn't tell you that."

I've oversold the platitudes. Dumb. Quickly I backpedal. "Okay, he didn't say that, exactly, but he said you guys were solid. Together you ran missions in the Third World rescuing kids caught up in human trafficking."

"And *then* what did he tell you?" Kareem asks.

"I heard about Manila."

The tension in the room increases a little, but no one blinks.

Stu says, "Well, if you did, then you know we've been blackballed by the community. No one is going to send us back out anywhere."

"I'll send you out."

It's quiet in the room for several seconds. I register the hopeful looks on the men's faces. Yeah, they want back in the fight just as much as their leader does.

"So . . ." Rodney says, "you are Agency?"

"I'm not going to be able to answer that."

Kareem mutters, half under his breath. "He's Agency."

A.J. turns to him. "How can you tell?"

"Look at him."

"He doesn't look CIA to me."

Exactly.

It's a good thing I don't need Kareem for his grasp of logic.

They are still sizing me up, despite the fact that Duvall vouched for me. Kareem says, "So you want to lead us into certain death?"

"Don't be so dramatic. Probable death."

"Oh . . . terrific."

Rodney speaks up now. "Tell us about your target."

"It's called Rancho Esmerelda. It's the end of the line of something called the pipeline, a sex trafficking network that brings women and girls over from Eastern Europe and Asia to serve wealthy men here in the States."

Kareem says, "Women and . . . and girls. You mean underage girls?"

"Yeah."

"How many?"

"I don't know how many end up in SoCal, but this is a transcontinental organization that makes billions a year."

Rodney speaks with a whisper. "Thousands of victims, then."

I just nod.

"Americans do this?" A.J. seems surprised, but Rodney notices this and says what I'm thinking.

"You don't think we can be just as big pieces of shit as people from other countries?"

Stu adds, "We can be worse if we put our minds to it."

A.J. nods slowly now. "Yeah, guess so."

The men look at one another, and A.J. says, "If you know women and girls are being abused right here, why don't you just go to the cops?"

"Because the cops have been tainted everywhere I've been along the smuggling pipeline. I can all but guarantee there are some bad ones here, protecting this operation." I hesitate, then say, "The guy who runs the whole thing . . . I don't know his identity, but I have been told he enjoys some federal protection, as well."

"Shit," Kareem says; all four stare at me, and the scrutiny makes me uncomfortable. Finally Rodney declares what the others are obviously thinking. "I'm not killing a cop. Not even a dirty cop."

A.J. adds, "That's right. Doesn't matter how dirty he is. The second he's killed in the line he turns into Eliot Ness. A hero. White as the driven snow."

"That's right," echo the others on the sofa.

"I'm not killing a cop, either." This is bullshit, and I feel bad about lying to these guys, but I'm not going into detail about all the dirty cops I've fragged around this planet. They deserved what was coming to them, and my conscience, such as it is, is clear. I add, "But I'll expose a dirty one, and we can bring these guys to justice. Shit, if we do this right, we might really make a difference."

A.J. stares me down now. "I don't know you, bro, but I know your type. Don't start getting too rah-rah, there. You're here because you want to hurt people and break shit. That you're doing it for a good cause doesn't change your underlying motivations."

Hurting people and breaking things *are* both at the top of my to-do list, so there is no sense in arguing with the man, but I'm starting to wonder if either I'm wearing a T-shirt that says "Psycho Killer" or if I'm just that transparent to others, when I myself don't see it.

I let it go.

We hear the sound of a car pulling to a stop out front, and all four men produce handguns from under their shirts. Rodney takes a moment to look down at his phone at a text message. "Papa's here."

Shep Duvall enters a minute later, along with a man who looks every minute of seventy-five years old. He's short and wiry with a patchwork of silver hair and bald spots all over the top of his head, along with a deep-set tan. He moves surprisingly fast for a guy his age, and he steps around the mess in the filthy room and shakes everyone's hands, introducing himself as Carl as he does so.

This is going to be our pilot, obviously, and I am worried that when the other guys here learn that, it will negatively impact the effect of the sales pitch I'm in the middle of delivering.

Shep and Carl pull rickety aluminum chairs from the kitchenette and drag them ten feet to the living room. Sitting down in front of us, Shep says, "Carl will fly us into the target."

A.J. says, "In what? A Sopwith Camel?"

I fight a smile. Carl, on the other hand, does not.

"Screw you, kid. I've got a Eurocopter AS350 on the ramp at Bakersfield right now. But I can fly anything with wings or rotors, tires, floats, or skids."

Stu looks the man over now. "I'm gonna go out on a limb here. You were in Nam."

Carl is obviously the right age. Hell, his skin makes it appear he ate Agent Orange on his breakfast cereal for most of his life.

"Damn right. Two tours flying Huey gunships and transports in Nam and Laos, and then several more years in Air America."

Air America was an airline set up by the CIA in Southeast Asia to deliver men and equipment in support of covert operations. It employed the best pilots in the world, in extremely dangerous conditions.

Despite Carl's advanced age, the men are impressed now. Kareem says, "Air America. That was some wild shit."

"How the fuck would you know?"

Kareem shrugs. "Movies, I guess."

"You went Agency after that?" Rodney asks.

"None of your goddamned business, meathead." Carl looks at the men like they are all children, though not one of them is under forty-five.

A.J. says, "That's badass and all, gramps, but that was then. How long ago did you retire?"

The older man shrugs. "I may be retired, but I ain't expired. I can deliver you boys on a dime in a hurricane if that's what it takes."

Shep speaks up now, looking at his four former teammates across from him. "Carl is solid. Harry is solid. What say you guys?"

It's quiet a moment, and then suddenly the man called Stu stands and looks not at me, but instead at his former teammates. "Gentlemen, you know I'd walk through fire with you guys. Shit, we've done it enough times, right? But I got a kid on the way, and I can't end up dead or in some prison. Not even a cushy American one. I'm sorry, but my days of running and gunning are behind me."

The other men stand and shake his hand, slap him on the back, and assure him they understand. Personally, I'm pissed; I need every gun I can get. But I get it. If I had something to live for, I probably wouldn't be slinging myself around like this, either. I shake his hand, too, and then he leaves without another word.

We all sit back down, and I ask a question that I have to ask, although I know I'm going to get reamed for it.

Looking at Shep, I say, "That going to be a problem? This guy knows our op and he just walks off?"

Shep Duvall shakes his head, and the other three men all grumble at me, angry that I'm unaware what an honorable man I had just been in the presence of. I let it go and so do they.

Rodney next asks, "When are you wanting to do this thing?"

I look to Shep, then say, "Duvall and I will drive down today, get eyes on the location. We'll get as much intel as possible. We'll come back in the morning and meet here and work up a plan together. Then, tomorrow night—say midnight—we hit it."

Kareem says, "Thirty-three hours from now. You ain't messin' around, are ya, bro?"

"Every hour we wait . . ." My voice trails off.

A.J. says, "Yeah. Copy that. If we'd hit that flophouse in Manila an hour earlier . . . who knows?"

I still don't want to know what these men saw over there.

Rodney stands up. "I'm in. Not like I'm doing anything else. Killing some kid-fuckers sounds like time well spent." Both A.J. and Kareem nod along to this.

Shep says, "Okay, Harry. You've got yourself a crew."

"Thanks, guys."

Shep added, "So you've got a pilot, a small team of shooters, a target, and a timeline. Guess you just need a plan. And weapons. Did you bring any weapons?"

"We'll work on the plan together," I say. "As for weapons . . . I was hoping you guys could bring along your own."

This is unprofessional, and the men waste no time in letting me know.

"What kind of bullshit op is this?" A.J. asks.

I heave a sigh. If they thought *that* was unprofessional, they're about to really flip their lids. "And, do any of you gents have an extra rifle you can lend me?"

They bitch, but nobody climbs to their feet to leave the room, so I call that a win.

Rodney, the homeowner, finally says, "I've got guns, Harry. You can pick what you want, but only if you promise not to bleed all over them."

"I sure promise to try."

. . .

Rodney's house might be a shit box, but he has a gun safe in a back room that looks like it cost more than the property itself. It's six feet tall and five feet wide, and when he opens it, I see something like a dozen long rifles and shotguns, as well as a dozen more pistols, and several knives.

There are AKs, ARs, an Israeli X-95, and even a big Belgian FN FAL. He has a pair of sniper rifles; one is a Knight's Armament SR-25 semiautomatic and the other an old bolt-action Remington 700. Both look useful for tonight's mission, but I grab an AK with an underfolding wire stock.

Rodney says, "Got crates of ammo in the storage room out back."

"You allowed to own this stuff in California?" I ask as I adjust the rifle's sling to my frame.

"Nope. Not allowed to shoot people, either, but I figure that's probably on the agenda tomorrow night."

"Good point."

I pull a Walther P22 pistol out of the safe and pick up the .22 caliber silencer lying next to it. "Mind if I grab this one, too?"

Rodney looks at me quizzically. "Sure. But I've got other pistols with threaded barrels. You don't need to take that little peashooter."

I put the Walther and the silencer into my canvas backpack. "You never know when you might need to shoot a pea."

He looks at me like I'm nuts, then hooks me up with the rest of the gear I need.

Seeing the impressive size of his cache, I say, "You guys are supposedly retired. Why are you hanging on to so much weaponry?"

I expect him to say he's just a gun collector or a firearms aficionado, but instead he verifies what I have been assuming all along.

"We're always looking for the next thing we can't stay away from. We're out of the fight after Manila, but we've all wanted to get back into it. Even Stu, until his wife got pregnant. The rest of us? The shit we've seen? Damn, dude. I'm going to be going out hunting traffickers and abusers till I take my last fucking breath. Same goes for the other boys, Papa included."

"Works for me," I say, and then I head out to the driveway to climb into Duvall's pickup for the drive down for our recon on Rancho Esmerelda.

FORTY-SIX

Shep and I drive south for an hour and a half, most of it through canyoned scrubland, finally arriving at our destination at four in the afternoon. He parks his F-350 on the gravel side of Lake Hughes Road; we both pull packs out of the bed and begin hiking through hills. After thirty minutes of this we crest a rise and then drop to our bellies.

We are most of a mile north of Rancho Esmerelda, just south of San Francisquito Canyon Road, and with the maps on our phones and the GPS on Shep's watch we've picked this particular site as a good overwatch position for our evening of reconnaissance. We pull binoculars for a quick look, then unpack a high-end spotting scope Duvall brought along to get a better picture of the property.

Spotting scopes suck in the night, but the buildings around Rancho Esmerelda are lit up and the moon is nearly full. These conditions help us this evening, although Shep and I both know they will hinder us tomorrow when we have to try to get as close to that target as possible without being seen.

After looking through the optics for just seconds we realize we are facing a large and formidable property. The sixty-power scope Shep brought along helps identify the main guard force to be, as near as we can tell, Mexican or perhaps even Salvadoran gangsters. If experience is any guide, these men will be trained in the use of their weapons but not overly organized as a cohesive fighting force. They are carrying what appear to be civilian AR-15s and shotguns, mostly, and they amble about on foot, drive patrols over the sixty rolling acres in four-wheelers, or sit in covered fixed positions around the property.

We don't see any women milling about outside, but that's no surprise. Still, we quickly get an idea about where the victims are being held. The guard force is centralized around the main building, a luxurious three-story ranch house we estimate to be somewhere around fifteen thousand square feet. While there are other outbuildings around the ranch, sheds and warehouses and a barn and a couple of cabins, from the disposition of external security we determine that the girls are located in the big house.

The bunkhouses are to the east on the far edge of the property, but there are vehicles parked behind them and a halfway decent road through the undulating landscape to the big stucco house, a half mile to the west.

Just after nine p.m., a pair of high-end SUVs turn off the main road, roll up the drive, and stop at a guard position. A minute later they continue forward, until they finally stop again in front of the main house.

The drivers open the rear doors in both vehicles, and four men climb out and head up the steps to the front door. They disappear inside a moment later.

Shep says what I'm thinking. "Johns."

"Yeah." If I had a sniper rifle on me I'd be inclined to open up on these bastards, so it's a good thing I don't.

I speak softly, knowing how voices can travel on a quiet night. "We'll do a helo infiltration, concentrate forces on the main building. We secure hostages, and then, hopefully, fight our way back out."

"Hopefully," Shep mutters.

"Yeah, I know. Hope isn't a strategy. But tomorrow night it will definitely have to serve as a tactic."

Shep nods. "We need two outside to keep the responding forces occupied. I'm old, my knees are pretty shot, but I can snipe. I'll fly shotgun in the helo and provide air cover; me and Carl will circle the target during the raid. And A.J. can knock the stink off a gnat's ass from a thousand yards. We'll put him on that hillock over there on the other side of the canyon; he'll do his best to keep the guys in the bunkhouse busy."

I laugh in the dark. "We make it sound so easy."

Shep spits into the dirt in front of him. "Getting in . . . not easy, but doable. Getting out . . . I don't know."

"One problem at a time," I say. Then I ask, "You're sure Carl can handle this?"

Without hesitation, he says, "He'll be fine."

"You met him at the Agency?"

"Nah, he's been retired since, like forever. He flies that helo at a two-hundred-fifty-acre gun range north of Las Vegas. Weekend warriors go there to shoot targets from the air, and he gives them the ride of their lives."

"He knows he's gonna get shot at tomorrow, right?"

Duvall nods. "He knows the mission. Look, you've got five guys willing to face death to help save those girls and frag any of those fuckers holding them who try to stop us. Don't look too deep into the motivations of any one of us, and we'll try not to think too hard about yours."

"Fair enough. Have you seen his helo?"

"Sure. Decent little four-seater."

I take my eye out of the scope and look at Shep. "A four-seater?"

"Yep."

Confused, I point out the obvious. "You, me, Rodney, Kareem, and A.J. Plus the pilot. That's six."

"Doesn't matter."

"Why doesn't it matter?"

"Because you, A.J., Kareem, and Rodney are riding the skids."

Shit, I think. *What have I gotten myself into?* "Says who?"

Shep shrugs. "Carl in the right seat, me in the left. You guys outboard. When we're about one and a half klicks out, Carl will drop A.J. off, he'll set up a sniper position, and the rest of us continue on to the target. You can get off those skids faster than you can get out of the cabin of the helo, and the insertion has to be fast and smooth for us to be able to pull this off."

He's right, but now I add falling off the side of a helicopter to my death to my long list of things to worry about.

And with that we settle in for another hour or two of recon before returning to Bakersfield.

. . .

Ken Cage worked in his home office all morning, beginning at seven, well before his normal start time of nine. Heather was annoyed, but she read his mood, and didn't push things. She only peeked in once to see if he needed more coffee, and the kids didn't come in at all.

But by ten a.m. Cage realized that he couldn't stay on task today. No, there was too much on his mind.

He didn't know how close he'd come to getting killed the night before last, certainly closer than he'd ever been in his life.

White Lion had never had a serious injury in the five years they had been protecting and overseeing the pipeline, but now they had a man dead.

Sean Hall was scared, Kostopoulos was dead, the way station in Bosnia had been closed, and the Serbians, the Albanians, the Greeks, and the Italians were all freaking out about this new danger to the Consortium.

Verdoorn and Hall were both here at the Hollywood Hills mansion today: Hall was outside the office in the living room, working in his close-protection role, his six men patrolling the grounds. Verdoorn was camped in a guest room on the third floor, using it both as a residence and as an office. His men, the eight of them still alive, were up at Rancho Esmerelda, although Cage didn't exactly know why.

In all the years he'd run the Consortium, Cage had never felt himself on shakier ground. He knew he had to be the leader now, he had to show strength, and for this reason he called in Hall and Verdoorn for a conference in his home office.

The billionaire financier turned up the ambient sound, had Hall lock the door, and then the three men sat together in chairs in front of Cage's desk.

Cage looked to the South African first. "Any danger your dead guy in Italy is going to get traced back to you?"

"None. All my men have their own offshore corps set up; there's nothing to trace them to White Lion, any other corporations involved in the Consortium, or you."

Cage next turned to Hall. "I'm going to Esmerelda tonight. That going to be a problem?"

Sean Hall looked to Verdoorn, then back to his boss. He was obviously less sure of himself than Jaco. "We have no intelligence that says Gentry is in America, or that he even knows your identity. But he's managed to show up at location after location along the pipeline. I know we're in America, and that may mean he's less likely to present himself, but still . . . I think it would be best if you laid low for a couple of weeks, just until Jaco and his men get this situation handled."

The South African spoke up immediately. "I disagree. As Hall said, we've got nothing to say he's here, he's coming here, or he even knows about here."

Cage replied coolly. "You said that in Italy. How did that work out?"

To this Verdoorn shrugged. "Look how bladdy close we got to the prick."

"How should I know how close you got?" Cage snapped. "Sean and his boys had to rescue me before the Gray Man got within striking distance."

Verdoorn's eyes narrowed, but only for an instant. "We were close, sir. We've got feelers out for him here, too. If he arrives, we'll know, and we'll put a stop to him. I've got my men at Rancho Esmerelda, supporting the guard force there. We'll get him this time, should he come.

"You've said yourself a dozen times there is nothing in the paperwork that ties you to the ranch. Even if he does go there, even if he comes with federal cops, you are safe."

Hall shouted now, the first time Cage had ever heard him doing so. "Not if he's there on the property when they come!"

To this Cage said, "Calm down, Sean. Look, the feds can't touch me, we all know that. I'm too important to them. I want to go to the property tonight. Jesus, after what I went through a couple of nights ago, I *need* it. Your men, Jaco's men, the Mexicans at the ranch, you'll all keep me safe." Cage smiled a little. "Won't you?"

Hall said nothing; he only looked at Jaco.

"*Won't* you?" Cage demanded.

"Of course, sir," Hall replied.

. . .

Sean Hall pulled the icy-cold bottle of Grey Goose from his freezer, yanked off the lid, then took one long, hard swig. Wincing with the sting of the alcohol, he walked to the front window of his residence and looked outside at Cage's mansion, just seventy-five feet away across the pool.

This is bullshit, he told himself.

He looked down at his phone for a moment, saw he'd gotten a text from Cage's oldest daughter, Charlotte. The two of them had planned to go surfing the following morning, but she'd backed out in favor of spending a couple of days with friends at Lake Arrowhead. He started to read her text, but movement on the patio diverted his attention.

Jaco Verdoorn walked in Sean's direction, through the manicured gardens, and then across the patio.

"Bullshit," he said aloud now, and he put his phone back in his pocket, then swigged more of the frigid alcohol.

He let Jaco in a moment later, still holding the bottle, and this wasn't lost on Verdoorn.

"Drinkin' by noon? On the job, aren't you?"

"Fuck you." Hall took another swig.

Verdoorn sighed. "Look. You're right. Gentry will find the ranch. But that's a good thing. I can end this, once and for all, as soon as he shows. But to do that without risking Cage, I need you watching over him, and supporting my mission."

"What are you talking about?"

Verdoorn said one word. "Maja."

Hall cocked his head. "The Romanian? What about her?"

"Gentry is after her. This entire fookin' thing, all the fighting and dying and burned-down way stations, it's all about that one little bitch."

Hall was confused. "How . . . how do you know this?"

"I know," Verdoorn replied, but said nothing else.

Now the American security agent sat down on his sofa, his eyes distant. "Does Ken know this?"

"No, and you're not going to tell him."

"Why not?"

"Because I'll look bad. And if you make me look bad, I've got more than enough on you to make you look *very* bad."

Hall just stared up at the bald South African.

Verdoorn continued, "You accused me of using the Director as bait over in Italy. Maybe I'm guilty of that, but it was a reasoned calculation that you could protect him while I killed off Gentry. My boys didn't get the job done there, so now we're here. This time, Maja is the bait. I've got my men at the ranch, surrounding her. I'm going there myself, and we'll be lying in wait. When Gentry comes . . . we'll be ready."

Hall looked down at the rug between his feet.

"Why not tell Cage to stay away until that happens?"

"Because I'll have to tell him why. If Cage finds out Maja's radioactive, he'll have me kill her, and then who knows if the Gray Man will continue the hunt? No, she has to stay alive, for now."

"And after?"

"After? After, I'll tell Cage myself that she was the one who caused all this shit. Make it look like I just found out. Don't worry about anyone else comin' lookin' for that little whore. When Gentry is dead, when she's dead, then this little problem will be sorted."

Hall put the lid back on the bottle, then he nodded slowly. This was Verdoorn's operation, Verdoorn's mess.

He shook away the cobwebs the vodka was laying in his brain and stood up. "Fucking kill this guy, Jaco."

Verdoorn nodded curtly, turned, and left the pool house.

FORTY-SEVEN

Roxana Vaduva sat on a small love seat in her room as the light faded outside, and she stared down at her hands. She was alone now, but an hour before an Asian woman who either spoke no English or else pretended like she didn't arrived without warning and painted Roxana's fingernails and toenails in fire-engine red. This came after evening wear had been selected for her, after she'd been told to bathe thoroughly, and after a stylist had arrived to straighten her brown hair.

This was Roxana's second day at the ranch. The evening before she'd remained in her room because Dr. Claudia had told her that while she was free to roam the interior of the house during the day, she would not have any duties herself on her first night, so she should stay away from the guests.

Duties and guests. Roxana had thought at the time the words to be sickeningly euphemistic. *Duties and guests.*

Tonight's attention, the nails and the makeup and the clothing and the hairstylist, she took to be a very bad sign. Last night Roxana had taken her dinner in her room, but still she heard men arrive, usually in groups of two to four, for hours and hours. She pictured the other women and girls on the property, imagined they were all dressed up like she herself was now, and she had no doubts at all about what had happened on the other side of her closed door.

There were no clocks in the building that she had seen during the early afternoon today when she'd spent a half hour walking around, looking out the windows, trying desperately to figure out where, exactly, she was. She'd made some light conversation with a few of the girls, as well as a woman Claudia had introduced who called herself Patty. Claudia said Patty was the coordinator, and Roxana took this to mean she was the madam, here to make sure the men who arrived to be serviced by the girls got what they came for.

The guards around the building were mostly Latino, and while they eyed the girls up and down, they did not speak to them directly. There were also several well-dressed Caucasian men she took for South African here, and one or two of them she remembered from the night she was transported to the yacht that took her to Venice. She had yet to see the man called Jaco since she'd gotten off the Gulfstream the day before, but she could feel his ominous presence in the other men, all of whom had hard edges to them.

Dr. Claudia entered Roxana's room just after eight in the evening. She was dressed in a business suit, not like the gown Roxana was wearing or those she'd seen on the other women.

She spoke in a calm voice, the words coming out through her practiced smile. "Tonight is the night, Maja."

"Meaning?"

"The Director is coming up this evening, just to see you. You should feel very honored."

The twenty-three-year-old Romanian nodded absently.

"Remember," Claudia said, "Jaco is watching you very carefully. Don't cross the Director, and don't cross Jaco, and all the good things that I've been promising you for the last several days will be yours."

The doctor left the room.

Roxana's heart began to pound in fear, but she also saw this as an opportunity. If the Director was coming here, into her room, then there was a good chance his phone would be with him. And even if she didn't know where she was, she could call her sister, make some sort of contact, and describe everything she knew about this property and the people around her. She could describe the little part of the airport property she saw and the drive north and the ocean and the landscape and maybe, just maybe, it would be enough to help.

She knew Tom's arrival would present an opportunity, but that wasn't the chief emotion she was feeling right now. No, it was fear. Abject, un-adulterated terror. She knew she was going to be raped. She could fight it, but she'd seen over a dozen armed men in the house so far, and she had no doubt they all worked for the Director. If he attacked her tonight, he would have all the reinforcements he needed to exert his will.

And how could she sneak his phone if she was in hand-to-hand combat with him around the room?

The thought of killing herself returned for a brief moment, but she knew that wasn't going to happen. Part of her preferred death to what she knew was soon to occur, but another part of her wanted the pipeline ex-posed, no matter the personal cost. She wanted the Director and Claudia and Jaco stopped, and she knew that she, her sister, and the killer working with her sister were the best chances to make this happen.

The makeup artist entered the room and put her cases on the vanity next to her.

Roxana did not speak to the woman; she did her best to hold in her fear, to concentrate on her task, and to try to get herself mentally prepared for the hell, and for the opportunity, that were both sure to come.

. . .

I spend part of the day running simulated room-clearing drills with Rod-ney and Kareem, the two men who will hit the house with me. Then the entire team, Carl included, sits with me in the little house in Bakersfield and pores over online overhead imagery of the property. We work out a myriad of different issues, and by midafternoon we have a plan detailing everyone's duties and responsibilities.

It's a good team and our confidence is high, even though we don't have anything resembling a solid exfiltration plan. I'm confident that we can overpower the opposition long enough for us to secure the hostages and grab some vehicles, but my confidence rests on Carl's flying skills and his ability to keep himself and Shep in the air, raining down merciless aggression on anyone who opposes us.

It's nine p.m. when we load up Shep's F-350 and Rodney's Ford Bronco, and then we head off towards the airport.

It would be a pain in the ass getting onto the airport grounds in Bakersfield with all our weaponry, so instead we drop Carl off at the front gate of the fixed operating base where his Eurocopter is parked, so he can preflight the helo while the rest of us drive south.

By ten we're on the Golden State Highway, still wargaming different scenarios that may come up. I can tell these men have raided a lot of structures together over the years. They are cool and professional and, while they may not be in their prime from the standpoint of their physical ability, mentally they are rock solid, and I know Hanley and Hightower hooked me up with the right group.

I just wish there were two dozen more of them, but when hitting a fifteen-thousand-square-foot building with an unknown number of hostiles inside and an unknown hostage disposition, I can get a little greedy.

But, despite the small force at my disposal, I'll take these guys into battle, and together we'll do our best.

. . .

At eleven forty-five the four of us are sitting in the bed of Shep's truck, looking at the cloudless sky, when A.J. points out a speck of light approaching from the north. It takes minutes before we hear it, but by the time Carl brings the bird on final approach, we're all out of the truck, laden down with our guns and rucks.

The helicopter lands in a field fifty yards away, and we start humping over to it.

The four of us tasked with riding on the outside of the helo make uncomfortable eye contact. Carl is going to fly lights-out to mask us visually, and low so we won't be heard from as great a distance. He's told us about his flight plan and the tactics he will employ, and none of us are thrilled about the prospect of racing ten feet over the Earth at ninety miles an hour, in the dark, hooked to the outside of a helicopter flown by a guy who realistically should be home watching TV and thinking of his glory days.

But at this point, for all our reasons, we're pretty much committed to seeing this through.

As promised, Carl has rigged four thick ropes, hooking them with carabiners to fixed points inside the cabin. The carabiner on the other end we each hook onto our utility belts, then we check one another to make sure we didn't fuck it up.

The doors have been removed from the helo and our lifelines offer us just enough slack to stand on the skids and hold on to the door frames. If we fall from the skids we won't drop to our deaths, but we will find ourselves dangling along, bouncing up against the fuselage of the helicopter, and praying Carl didn't go cheap and buy the rope holding us up at some dollar store in East Bakersfield.

I push this out of my mind and notice four other ropes coiled on the floor inside the cabin. They're each thirty feet long and they'll be tossed out before we get to our target so we can fast-rope down, just a couple dozen yards from the rear entrance.

We considered a roof insertion of the property; the roof of the hacienda is flat enough, but we're worried about squirters, enemy slipping out of the property, while we make our way down three stories, so we'll hit from the back lawn, clear together to the top, and kill anyone who opposes us.

That's the plan, anyway.

I hook on to the front port side, positioning myself right behind Shep and his SCAR 16S rifle in the front left seat. While the other men climb into position, I check my gear once more. I've got a nicely souped-up yet simple AK-47-pattern semiautomatic rifle. It's a big gun for close-quarters work, but it's proven itself over many decades of fighting around the world, and I know how to run it effectively with my eyes closed.

I have four extra magazines in a rack on my chest, giving me 150 rounds total.

The other guys are wearing body armor, but there weren't any extra plates for me. I'm wearing my pistol in a drop leg holster, and there is a trauma kit and a long fixed-blade Benchmade knife in a sheath on my belt. Rodney gave me one smoke grenade and one flash bang grenade, and they're both hanging from my chest, and I'm wearing borrowed ear protection over my interteam radio headset, and ballistic goggles.

I don't have a helmet. Rodney was fresh out of helmets, too.

In a small backpack I have extra pistol mags along with the Walther P22 pistol and an attached suppressor, though I'm not sure how covert I'm going to need to be considering we are flying right up to the target in a helicopter. Still, you never know how tonight is going to shake out, so I like the versatility of a low-decibel firearm on my person, just in case.

At midnight Carl applies maximum power and the rotors battle the air a moment, and then we lift off the field for our twenty-minute flight to the target, surrounded by a swirling cloud of dust.

Instantly my goggles are covered in the dust, and when I wipe it off I see that the Vietnam vet pilot has already turned off all the lights on the aircraft. I look inside the open hatch and see him there, his craggy face glowing with the green light of the instruments in front of him. He doesn't have night vision goggles, he's just flying along low to the ground, picking up speed, and peering into the darkness ahead.

Holy shit.

I catch myself pining for the relative safety of the shootout at the other end of this flight. Surely it won't be as dangerous as the next twenty minutes.

. . .

Ken Cage lay on the bed, his eyes on the ceiling, and he wiped sweat from his brow with a hairy forearm.

His heart pounded in his chest; the angina burned, but he was used to this after sex.

Next to him, his newest victim lay facing away from him, her naked body exposed, and he heard her soft sobs, like a punished child.

This made him smile a little. He lay without moving for several seconds, then reached over and grabbed her by her hair, pulled her head back to him. She screamed in surprise, and their eyes met in the low light, inches apart. "Just so you know . . . I was easy on you tonight. Next time, you'll get to see my wild side."

He rolled off the bed, pulled on his shorts, and headed for the door. "No, you didn't get the high-octane version of me, because I saved my energy for the other new girl." He smiled again. "You can thank her in the morning."

The Director left the room without another word.

The Hungarian girl called Sofia gazed blankly at the wall through tear-filled eyes.

She'd been raped, and she'd been helpless during, and now that it was over, she felt just as helpless.

She looked at a bar glass the Director had left on the nightstand, half full of some brown liquid, and she wondered if she had the mental strength to shatter it in the bathroom and then to slit her wrists.

But she made no move towards it. No, she just lay there and wept.

FORTY-EIGHT

Jaco Verdoorn had taken off his suit jacket and his tie, but his shoulder holster was in place over his dusty blue dress shirt, and his SIG Sauer pistol was snapped into it and ready for instant access. His feet were on an ottoman and he reclined in a chair; at nearly midnight he'd only just fallen asleep here in the library on the ground floor of the massive ranch house.

He'd spent the evening positioning his own men as well as the Mexicans who were the regular security force here at Esmerelda. Everyone had been warned there were special threats here, and everyone seemed as ready as they could be. Mexican cartel soldiers were positioned on the large, almost flat roof of the hacienda-style building, as well as on the property all around, with many more on reserve, a half mile away at the eastern edge of the property.

Verdoorn's own men were here inside the home with him, and he had them in cover. All eight were dressed like the wealthy johns allowed access to Rancho Esmerelda; they wore nice suits, expensive polos, or other casual clothing, and they bunked in a couple of the dozen or so rooms on the second and third floors normally used by the johns and the whores.

His boys wouldn't like this environment at all. They weren't security guards; they weren't here to police the johns. They were hunters, enforcers for the Consortium. But their ill ease was good, as far as Jaco was concerned.

He didn't want them happy—he wanted them ready.

Verdoorn had steered clear of Sean Hall and his team of six security officers since they'd arrived here with Cage an hour earlier. They were all up on the third floor, in or around Cage's private apartment on the eastern side of the house, or else positioned around whatever room Cage was in, either enjoying one of his new arrivals or relaxing in the lounge off the entry hall, eating, drinking, and snorting lines.

Jaco dozed a little, but he'd spent the entire time here tonight wishing Gentry would just get on with it. He'd studied the way the assassin had ingressed to target on the few of his missions about which such details were known. He liked to move silently, with stealth, cunning, and the tradecraft of the most elite assassin in the world.

The South African fully expected Gentry to try to slip into this building unnoticed, and Verdoorn and his men would be here to greet him, and then the Mexicans outside would close off any chance he had to escape.

And Cage? As far as Verdoorn was concerned, Ken Cage was Sean Hall's problem.

Court Gentry was the real VIP.

. . .

I try not to puke as our helicopter lurches up and down in the dark. Hanging on to the edge of the open hatch, I tell myself the fast-food tacos we all ate on the drive down from Bakersfield were a bad idea, and A.J. is an asshole for suggesting them.

But Carl, on the other hand, is a damn fine pilot, and I can feel his skill in the movements of the helo; he has a deft touch to his pedal controls and his cyclic, and I know this flight, as jarring as it is, could be a hell of a lot worse.

Eventually I hear the power come off and then the aircraft slows quickly and pulls into a hover, yanking me and the other outboard guys forward. Then Carl descends the few feet to the Earth, and the skids touch down. Dust swirls all around the darkness, so I can't see a thing, but I know A.J. is unhooking his carabiner and leaping from the skid on the starboard side of the aircraft, dropping down to quickly set up a shooting position, more than a half mile from the rear of the property.

I know with our low flight and our distance that we still should be silent to our enemy, but once we get back up into the air and move forward a few hundred yards, that will no longer be the case.

We're banking on the opposition not expecting us to hit tonight, via air, and with such force.

If we're wrong, then we'll probably get blasted out of the sky before this party even starts, so I try not to think about that.

I brush dust off my goggles again, and I look back inside the hatch towards the two men in the front seats. I can only see the back of Shep's head; he's leaning into the scope of his rifle, searching for targets on the roof of the distant building.

Carl's wrinkled face, all the more wrinkled with the intensity of his focus on his windscreen and on the controls, is a mask of experience and determination. I recognize instantly that he is exactly where he wants to be, doing exactly what he wants, *needs*, to be doing.

For a brief second I feel the same, but then my mind shifts back into game mode. As I watch, Carl looks back over his shoulder, takes his hand off his collective, and holds a single gloved finger up into the air.

His voice crackles over the radio and into my ears.

"One minute out!"

The entire team repeats the call into our mics, and then we bring our weapons to our shoulders and scan forward in the darkness as best we can.

Here we go.

• • •

Ken Cage stood in the bedroom, still in his boxers, still half-covered with the sheen of sweat from his attack on the Hungarian girl five minutes before. In front of him, Maja stood nervously, her back to the wall, the black cocktail dress perfectly fitted to her perfect body.

He'd done nothing to calm her nerves.

"Take it off," he demanded.

The Romanian hesitated, then said, "Look, sir, I am—"

"Take it off!" he shouted now.

She did as she was told, stood naked before him, her jaw quivering but her eyes remaining on his. Fixed. Proud. Afraid but resolute.

Cage said, "I'll finish the job Claudia couldn't manage on her own."

Maja asked, "What job?"

The American smiled. Dropped his boxers, the Viagra he took hours before still on duty.

He looked her up and down and said, "I'll wipe all that delicious defiance right out of your soul." He moved towards her with aggression, his eyes wild with intensity, and he shoved her back against the wall. Pressing his body against hers, he slipped a hand over her face and covered her mouth and nose.

Behind Cage the door flew open and Sean Hall rushed in, a walkie-talkie in his hand and an intense look on his face. He wore a white tank top undershirt and jeans, sandals on his feet, and his pistol was jammed into his waistband.

Cage spun around, making no attempt to cover his manhood. "What the *fuck*, Sean?"

Hall raced forward, pulled a robe off the footstool at the end of the bed, and handed it to his boss. He grabbed Cage by the arm, pulling him naked towards the door to the hall while a nude Maja spun away and raced for the bathroom.

The bodyguard explained as the two men rushed into the hall. "External security says there's a helicopter inbound, flying over the rear of the property with no lights. Until it's ID'd, I'm moving you to a secure position!"

Cage wasn't happy, at all, but he knew it was best to comply. Hall tended to exaggerate threats, but Ken knew that bitching about it after the fact was the way to go. Fighting with him now would only delay the process and cause everyone more agitation, Cage included.

As they ran, Cage threw his robe on and cinched the belt tight, and Hall brought his walkie-talkie back up to his mouth.

But before he did so, the unmistakable booms of gunfire erupted just above their heads, on the roof of the ranch house.

More rifles outside at ground level rocked off fully automatic a second later.

Hall kept Cage's pace up by squeezing his hand on his shoulder as they ran towards the stairs. While doing so, he said, "That's outgoing. That's our Mexicans. They've identified the helo as a threat! Move!"

"Where's Jaco?"

Hall didn't answer. Instead he shouted over his walkie-talkie to his men. "We are leaving. Get in the G-Wagens!"

Cage ran along, enraged that, for the second time in three days, he found himself fleeing for his life with a frantic bodyguard's hands all over him.

. . .

"We're taking fire!" Shep said, and I hear him through the radio, but I also hear the supersonic crack of bullets zipping by the helicopter.

Shep leans out of the opening next to him, his SCAR rifle positioned on a cable running midway across the hatch to serve as a shooting platform. "I've got targets on the roof!" he says, then begins firing slow, controlled shots.

I can't see any targets yet, or even the target building, but A.J. speaks up over the radio from his sniper's hide behind us. "Overwatch has targets on the property, east side, ground level. Engaging now."

I can't hear A.J.'s sniper rifle, but I trust he's dropping some of the sons of bitches who are shooting at the aircraft I'm clinging to.

I'm still scanning for something to kill; I don't have any targets from my vantage point because Shep and his weapon are blocking my view in front of me. But I keep searching, hoping to see the telltale sparkle of a muzzle flash somewhere out there in the dark.

Carl speaks up again. "Too much fire to land on the back lawn! I'm going over the target; we'll come back around and try it from the front."

I finally see a muzzle flash near a small pond behind the house now, and I fire a few rounds out of my AK towards the source. Then I say, "Negative! Negative! Put Kareem and Rodney down on the roof."

"What about you?" Shep asks.

"Carl, can you throw me through a window on the third floor?"

There is a pause; through it I hear Kareem firing on the other side of the helo.

Carl replies, "You want me to do *what*?"

I sling the AK to the side, muzzle down, and I throw out my rappelling line. "Fly exactly thirty feet above any top-floor window on this side of the property. I'll lower down the rope, and you fly me right through the glass. I'll link up with the other two as able."

Carl answers me back quickly as he slows the helicopter. "How do I know exactly thirty feet?"

"You'll get me close enough."

I hear him sigh through the radio. "I can do that, but *you've* only got fifteen seconds to get in position!"

"Copy!" I shout, and then I unfasten my carabiner with my left hand, grab the rappelling line with both arms and legs, and begin sliding down, almost uncontrollably fast.

More gunfire, both incoming and outgoing, hammers the air around me, and then I hear a new sound—a pounding, jarring series of thuds.

Carl says, "Taking hits!" And then, "We're continuing!"

Shep's rifle booms and booms above me.

I draw the Glock from its drop leg holster, sight it on the window not thirty feet in front of me now, and, while still trying to slide down the rope, I fire two rounds into the upper portion of the glass. It's at a small upwards angle so I'm not worried about shooting a hostage, and breaking the glass is worth any small risk, because solid windows aren't much fun to dive through.

I know this from experience, of course.

Two seconds later I let go of the rope, curl myself into a ball, and impact the damaged window at twenty-five knots, because Carl has slowed to land on the roof. I fly in surrounded by shattered glass and shredded curtains, my hearing protection and goggles fly off, and I tumble through the air. I tuck in tight, expecting a jarring crash onto the floor, but instead I bounce on something soft, roll end over end, my rifle's polymer buttstock knocking me in my mouth as I tumble.

And then, somehow, I end up on my boots in an uncontrolled run.

Above me the helicopter hovers over the roof, and gunfire continues all around.

I stumble across a room and finally do bounce against a wall, slamming my shoulder hard and dropping the Glock. I miraculously keep my feet, then turn back around and heft my rifle on its sling.

Yeah, I do all my own stunts.

I see what happened immediately. I came through the window, hit a king-sized bed in a large bedroom, and then momentum shot me back up and all the way to the far wall. As I look around I see the bed is unmade and there is a smell of candles in the air, and once I realize there are no threats present, I pick up the pistol and slip it back in its holster.

Stealth mode, I tell myself, has been disengaged, since I alerted anyone in the area by crashing through the glass.

Moving to the door I'm slightly dazed, and I feel blood on my lips, but it's nothing I'm not used to. I'm operational as long as I have breath in my lungs and brain function, and I'm trained not to slow down for injuries that aren't disabling.

Before I get to the door I hear running just outside. I step behind the door as it flies open, and I see a man with dark curly hair enter with a black AR-15 up at his shoulder.

He scans the room, and I wait patiently behind him, wondering if he has any buddies following, but when I don't hear other footsteps after a moment and the man begins to turn back around, I fire once into the side of his head.

Blood ejects out his temple and he drops ten feet away from me. I fire once more into him as I spin out of the room, into the hallway.

Rodney's voice is on the radio now, just audible through the gunfire raging outside. "All hostiles on the roof are down; we're entering via the stairwell, west side of property."

A.J. speaks up next. "I've got inbound forces, two vics, leaving the bunkhouse. Unknown number of hostiles; they loaded up the trucks out of my field of vision. They'll be on your poz in under a minute unless I can slow them down. Will advise."

Shep transmits, the thumping rotor pounding through my earpiece. "Harry? You inside, or did you hit the wall?"

I respond softly, not sure what threats lie ahead. "I'm in. Keep up that air cover as long as you can."

"Roger that," Shep says.

I call to A.J. "Overwatch, I need you to buy us some time with the hostile QRF. It's gonna take a while for three dudes to clear this place and organize the hostages."

A.J. replies coolly, "I'll see what I can do. Targeting the engine blocks on the trucks."

I push the worry about the enemy outside of the house from my mind, and I focus on the enemy inside with me now. Moving up the well-lit passage with my rifle optic up to my eyes, I see door after door in front of me, like a hotel hallway. The door just ahead on my right opens and, without a moment's hesitation, I lunge at it, impact the person on the other side, and push them up to a wall.

It's a young woman with blue eyes filled with terror. I hold my gloved left hand over her mouth while she deals with the shock of everything that's happening around her.

She's wearing a T-shirt and panties, her sandy brown hair is pulled back in a ponytail, and it appears as if she's just taken a shower.

It's not Roxana, and I have no idea if I saw this woman in Mostar or not.

Leaning close to her, I say, "English?"

When she nods, I ask, "How many guards?"

I take away the hand, and she speaks with a pronounced accent, which I take to be Czech.

"I, I don't know. Many. And new men here. White men. Maybe seven, eight? They have guns. They dressed like johns."

"How many johns are here now?"

Again, she says, "I don't know. Not many. Maybe five?"

I transmit quickly to Kareem and Rodney. "Be advised. Enemy personnel mixed in with the johns. Treat every male you see as potentially hostile."

Rodney responds, "This ain't our first rodeo, Harry."

These are the guys who gunned down over a dozen traffickers in Manila; they don't need me telling them to keep their weapons at the ready.

I stop transmitting and try to extract more target intelligence from the woman in front of me. "How many females here now?"

"Nine," she says, and then she shakes her head. "No. Two came yesterday. Eleven. Eleven now."

"Where are they?"

"Most are on second or third floor, but some of the johns take the girls to the grotto on the ground floor. It's on the other side. There might be girls there."

"I need you to get dressed, then climb into the bathtub and wait for someone to come collect you."

"Where are we going?" Her voice cracks with fear.

"*You* are going home."

She looks at me with bewilderment. "You are . . . you are the good guys?"

To this I only shrug as I turn away. "We're more like the 'slightly better than them' guys."

I leave the room to the sound of her running on bare feet, deeper into the room and, hopefully, to her clothes and shoes.

Telling this girl I was going to get her home might have been a bit ambitious on my part, since me and my mates are probably outnumbered four or five to one right now, but hopefully it will have the effect of getting her moving.

FORTY-NINE

Roxana Vaduva had run naked into the bathroom, and here she quickly dressed in warm-ups and a pullover that she'd left lying over the edge of the bathtub. When the gunfire began she dove to the floor and covered her head, and then a helicopter chopped the night air right outside the bathroom window. She crawled to the door and locked it, but only seconds later she heard a man's voice. "Maja! Get out here!"

It was Jaco; he sounded breathless, excited, but not afraid.

She looked at the locked door but didn't move towards it, hoping he'd go away.

The South African's voice rang out again, but this time he was right outside the bathroom. "Open it now or I'll kick the bladdy thing down and wring your neck!"

She unlocked the latch and opened the door.

Jaco reached in and took her by the arm, then yanked her out of the bathroom, out of the bedroom, and into the hall. The two entered the stairwell, and Roxana struggled to keep up with the tall bald-headed man.

The gunfire outside was mixed in with the sound of the helicopter receding.

"Where are we going?" she demanded.

He kept rushing down the stairs, her wrist tight in his hand, and he said, "Not a word out of you or I'll break your jaw."

Roxana said nothing else.

Jaco took a radio off his belt as they reached the ground floor and began running through a large entry hall towards the front door of the house. "Lion One is exiting."

"Roger," came a reply from one of his men. "The heli flew off to the north, I think he landed. Can't see him."

"Good," Jaco said, "because we're goin' south."

Sean Hall's voice came over the radio now. "I've got the Director in one of the G-Wagens. We're outta here!"

"Wait!" Jaco demanded, then ran out the back door of the building with the girl in his grasp, a pistol high in front of him.

. . .

Carl banked sharply over the property to the east of the mansion, and Shep hung his upper torso out of the helicopter to line up his optics on a man racing up the drive on a four-wheeler with a rifle on his back. He took the shot, hit the four-wheeler but not the man, then told himself he needed to concentrate his fire on a larger group of hostiles moving in from the east, because there certainly were plenty of targets.

A.J. came over the headset now. "Papa, the two QRF trucks are down. I put rounds through both engines, but the men are out and moving on foot. Twenty of them, easy. I've lost them behind a hillock between me and them. You'll have to try and rake them before they get to the house."

Shep acknowledged, then spoke to Carl. The two men were sitting just feet apart in the helicopter, but the incredible noise of the machine meant they needed radio headsets to communicate.

"Take us back to the west, low, slow pass."

Carl said, "I'll give you low or I'll give you slow, but you can't have both. We'll be a sitting duck."

"Low and fast, then. I've got to thin that herd!"

"Roger that. Hang on for a yank and bank!"

Carl pulled the stick hard and the Eurocopter swung violently to the left.

Shep aimed in on a group of flashes right where A.J. directed him, and he squeezed off a single round, killing a cartel soldier with a shot through the stomach. He shifted fire to the right and sent another round into the foot of a second enemy, taking the man out of the fight.

He poured rounds into the group as they flew fifty feet above the men, the sound of incoming gunfire cracking through the outgoing and the AS350's engine and rotors.

Shep transmitted as he aimed on another cluster, moving through thick brush off the dirt road. "Harry, be advised. Me and A.J. are giving this QRF a bloody nose, but you'll still have a dozen or more men at the house in under two mikes. There's too many of them and—"

Just then accurate automatic weapons fire from the ground pounded the nose of the helo.

"Pulling out!" Carl shouted as glass and metal sprayed around the cockpit. He yanked the stick hard to the right now, sending the Eurocopter into another hard turn. Shep lurched to his right and then slumped back in his seat, his head down.

The Vietnam veteran at the controls nosed his aircraft down to build speed and to flee the gunfire and, as he concentrated on the dark landscape feet under his skids, he called out over the radio. "Papa is hit! Papa is hit."

Only when he leveled off did he look over to the big man next to him. Shep had taken a rifle round through the throat, and blood spurted out over the controls on his side of the dash. He was ashen and his eyes were closed, his arms at his sides as his lifeblood poured from him.

"Shep! Shep!" Carl tried in vain to get a response from the big man. Rodney and Kareem called over the radio, desperate for an update on their leader, but the pilot ignored them, because now his oil light flashed on his instrument panel.

He had to land, but he also knew he needed to create more distance from the enemy before doing so.

"Report status of Papa," A.J. demanded now.

"KIA," Carl replied. And then, "Sorry, boys. And you've lost your air cover for now. A.J., I'm putting down about two hundred yards west of you to check this out. You've got the fight on the outside now."

"Roger that," A.J. replied, before adding, "Harry, Kareem, and Rodney, the fuckers from the bunkhouse are heading your way."

• • •

Jaco Verdoorn made it to the row of three black Mercedes G-Class SUVs already idling in front of the house. Cage and Hall were in the second vehicle, with three of Hall's six men in the driver's seats of the impromptu motorcade, and one more in the front passenger side of each vehicle.

Verdoorn opened the back door next to Cage, who was seated next to Hall. The South African all but threw Maja inside across from them.

"What the hell is she doing here?" Cage screamed. Cage was panicking and, to Verdoorn, Sean didn't look much cooler. "Let's move it!"

Verdoorn didn't respond to his boss. Instead he looked to Hall. "Remember. She's the key."

"She's the *what*?" Cage shouted.

Hall nodded to Verdoorn, then turned to his protectee. "Sir, we'll talk about it on the drive. We have to get out of here before that helo circles back."

Verdoorn began closing the door, but Cage put his foot out to stop him. "Wait. You aren't coming?"

Jaco turned around and looked at the house. "Gentry's here, boss. This is where I belong."

He shut the door to the G-Wagen and ran back towards the front door of the home.

• • •

I link up with Kareem and Rodney on the second-floor landing in the center of the building. Both men report shooting two guards, meaning we've dropped five in total, and together we've found six women and girls, all of whom we've asked to shelter in place while we clear the area.

The raid has been going on no more than a minute and a half, but I can see that both my teammates are gassed. Rodney puts his hand out on a wall for a breather, and Kareem is wincing with each step.

"You hit?"

"Hit by time, bro. Bad back."

Christ.

He sees my concern as he begins reloading his rifle. "It's all about adrenaline now, anyway." He snaps a fresh mag in and drops the bolt release. "Let's rock."

Rodney gets off the wall and we stack up in a three-man train, then begin heading down to the first floor, but before we make it more than a couple of steps, a group of three armed Latino males spin into view below us. They are looking for threats, but they hesitate an instant as they size us up as targets.

Kareem, Rodney, and I each fire a controlled double-tap, two into each man, and all three tumble back down to the ground floor, dead.

We start down again, but Kareem grabs me by the shoulder just as Rodney tosses a flash bang grenade past my ear. All three of us turn away as it detonates below us in the entry hall of the ranch house.

We descend the rest of the way, where we stumble upon two white men in plain clothing on their hands and knees, disoriented from the banger. Kareem knocks them both flat to the floor while Rodney and I cover back up the stairs as well as the ground-floor hallways leading into both the east and west wings, and a doorway from the entry hall into the kitchen.

The first man on the floor who Kareem checks is unarmed, but the other is lying next to a Heckler & Koch semiautomatic pistol, and under his coat we can see the telltale imprint of a radio on his belt.

Kareem says, "He's hostile. What do I do with—"

Without speaking, I shift my AK and shoot the man once in the back of the head.

"We don't have time to give quarter to these motherfuckers."

Kareem, who is now kneeling on a dead body, just says, "Works for me," and then he rises and drops back down over to the unarmed man, wincing with back pain as he does so.

This civilian is in the fetal position; he's pissed his pants and he's crying like a baby. He's obviously expecting to lose his life, just like the man on the floor six feet away has.

He is a john, a rapist, likely a pedophile, and my first inclination is to kill him. But he's not a threat to me. Kareem obviously gets it, because he leans into the man's ear. "You lay yo' ass right the fuck here, facedown, and you don't move till you see daylight through that window. You feel me?"

The man turns and presses his face into the floor, and he continues crying uncontrollably.

The front door to the building flies open now and the three of us find ourselves twenty feet away from multiple armed men. We shift aim to the doorway and open up in bursts, and the attackers dive from view. I don't know if we made any hits, but I'm pretty sure they weren't expecting to get shot at the instant they opened the front door, just a couple of minutes after we inserted on the roof and the third floor. They can't possibly know how many of us are in the building, so I expect they'll take a minute or two to reassess the situation before making a second breach attempt.

Rodney runs to the door, shuts and locks it, then reloads while Kareem and I cover the entire area.

Another plainclothed Caucasian, this one young and very fit looking, steps into the entry hall from the kitchen on our right, and he raises his empty hands upon seeing us. "Shit! Don't shoot! Please don't shoot!"

Kareem speaks softly to me. "That ain't no john."

Before either of us can react, however, the man drops hard to the wooden floor. Behind him, two more men, one Caucasian and one black, spin into view with HK MP-7 Personal Defense Weapons at their shoulders.

I fire as Rodney dives for cover behind a massive planter by the front door. Kareem and I shoot the armed men, but both of our rifles run dry simultaneously.

As we transition to our pistols, the man on the floor draws from his hip and aims our way.

He gets off a single shot before Rodney rolls out from behind the planter and dumps a dozen rounds from his SCAR into the prone attacker, killing him instantly.

I look next to me and see that Kareem is hit. His right shoulder glistens red, and he stumbles back a step but does not fall.

He looks down at the wound. "Dammit!" he shouts, in anger, but not in pain.

I've been shot before. Pain comes later.

I reach for the medical kit on his chest rig to patch him up, but he just shakes his head. "I'm good to go. First things first; we ain't got much time till those cartel boys bust back in. Rodney and I will get the girls together upstairs; you go check out that grotto."

"Roger." I sprint off to the west side of the building, my rifle in front of me, as the two other men make their way back up the stairs.

FIFTY

Jaco Verdoorn, White Lion One, and Duncan Duiker, White Lion Seven, knelt in the kitchen with pistols pointed towards the doorway to the hall. They'd just seen three of their colleagues killed right in front of them, and the kitchen shot up around them, bullets from the entry hall tearing through everything in sight.

They couldn't see the shooters from here because of the angle. Verdoorn imagined the Gray Man and his cohorts were no more than fifty feet away from him now, but he wasn't racing into the "fatal funnel" of the doorway to find out.

Duiker turned to Lion One. "We thought he'd sneak in low profile, but he came in a fookin' helicopter and he brought a platoon of men with him. Who does he think he is?"

Verdoorn boiled, angry at Gentry, angry at himself. He'd misjudged the American assassin, took his previous stealthy modus operandi as a predictor of his future actions, and now Jaco realized he'd pay a terrible price for it. He couldn't raise any of his men on the radio, and it now seemed likely that he, Duiker, and Loots, who had driven off with Cage, were all that remained of the original ten White Lion men.

Verdoorn made a decision while still squatting behind the table. "We're gettin' out of here before the police come. We have to get the Director out of the country till the heat from all this recedes."

"What about the Mexicans on the property?"

"What about them? There's twenty-five of the bastards, or there were, anyway. Let them take their best shot at Gentry and his mates."

The two South Africans backed out of the kitchen, their pistols still pointed at the doorway to the entry hall, and then they sprinted for the row of luxury cars outside driven here from LA by the guests.

. . .

I find three young women in the grotto hiding behind a faux waterfall, one no older than sixteen. Four johns, all of them unarmed, are with them. They're hiding, too, and even more terrified than the hostages. I search the men quickly, then leave them behind as I lead the women to the main stairs.

I don't like going back in the entryway; there are a lot of entrances to cover, but I don't see that I have any choice.

As I advance carefully up the east wing hallway, one of the girls grabs me by the arm.

"What?" I ask, annoyed.

"Where are we going?"

"Upstairs."

"Wouldn't the back staircase be safer?"

I spin around and reverse my direction. "A hell of a lot safer. Show me where."

We encounter one more hostile on the rear stairs, and I dump a half dozen rounds of 7.62 into his back before he sees me. A minute after this we are back on the second-floor landing, looking down the main staircase at the entry hall and the front doors. Kareem and Rodney are with us now, along with all the hostages they've rounded up.

Roxana is not here. I call out to the group. "Who knows Maja?"

One girl says, "The Romanian. I know her. I came with her yesterday."

"What's your name?"

"Sofia." She shakes her head, then says, "Nora. My real name is Nora."

"Where is Maja now?"

The hostages confer a moment, and then the young girl from the grotto says, "The tall bald man from South Africa dragged her downstairs and outside. Just after the Director left. I don't know where they went. I ran into the grotto."

Shit. Jaco must have fled with Roxana so he could use her as a bargaining chip.

I start to turn away but then spin back to her. "Wait. The Director? He was *here*?"

Nora says, "He's been here all night. They just drove away."

Un-fucking-real. It's just like Venice. I've missed this asshole once again.

I fight away the frustration and think about my predicament. The large enemy quick reaction force hasn't attempted another breach of the building, but I know it's just a matter of minutes before they do.

I hit the transmit key for my radio. "A.J. What do you see out there?"

The team sniper responds quickly. "I can only see the back of the property. The QRF went around to the front three minutes ago."

I tap the push-to-talk button again. "Carl, say status."

"Oil leak is dealt with. Not too bad. This bird will fly, but I won't want to do much in the way of acrobatics."

Rodney says what I'm thinking now. "Harry, there are a lot of ways into this building. If fifteen or twenty guys hit in a coordinated fashion, the three of us are gonna get our asses overrun."

He's right, of course. We can't hold back that entire force if they come hard from different directions.

I decide to call Talyssa to tell her that finding Roxana and the Director is her responsibility, because I'm not making it out of here alive.

But before I do, a statuesque blond woman in an evening gown pulls on the torn arm of my tunic. "You think you men are the only ones who can fight?"

I don't have time for this. "What are you talking about?"

"I can fight, too."

She looks like a twenty-year-old fashion model, and I discount her immediately. "I love the spirit, miss, but those guys out there are gonna be Mexican cartel, and they know how to handle their weapons."

"So do I."

Incredulous, I say, "You can shoot an M4?"

"I've never tried."

I start to turn away. "Yeah, let us handle—"

"But I can shoot your AK. I spent two years in the Ukrainian army."

I turn back to her, astonishment evident on my face. "Doing what?"

"Infantry."

Kareem hears this. "No shit?"

She looks into my eyes and lifts her chin. "I can handle that rifle on your chest, but you won't let me because you men are too proud to—"

I pull the sling over my head, removing the Kalashnikov from my body. "You've got me all wrong, sister. I couldn't be happier you want to fight. Hell, I'll let you run this shit." I hand the weapon to her.

She takes it, slings it around her neck, drops the mag to check the ammo, and then clicks it back into place. I look around to the nine other women up here at the top of the stairs. "You guys got any handy skills?"

Three hands rise. A woman tells me she spent two years in the Polish air force, where she learned basic firearms handling. Another, the sixteen-year-old I found hiding in the grotto, says her father is Bulgarian police and she's probably shot a pistol as much as I have.

She's wrong, but her attitude is right, so I pass her my Glock.

Other women head off to pick up weapons and ammo from dead men on this floor, and soon one brings me an AR-15 along with two extra magazines to replace the weapon I handed off to the tall Ukrainian. Rodney and I position our four new shooters behind cover facing both wings, and Kareem shows a few more how to handle guns while the first three keep watch down the stairs.

The rest drag furniture out of bedrooms, sliding it across the floor. A dresser, a table, a TV stand: it's more concealment than it is cover, but it's something, and Rodney helps them line it all up on the stairs to provide cover from below.

I radio A.J. and tell him I have nine guns in the fight now, and he responds by letting me know he's moving to Carl and the helo. It's the right call to shut down the sniper's hide at the back of the property, and for the two of them to link up. We won't be flying thirteen people out of here with a four-seater helicopter, but when the time comes, one more low-and-fast pass with the helo and a rifle may help disrupt the enemy attack.

It takes the cartel boys a few minutes to plan their second wave, but they do a decent job of it. First the power goes out on the property, and then the front door opens again, while the shooting simultaneously begins from both hallways.

But the enemy's advantage is greatly decreased by the fact that they have three narrow attack points, and we have three weapons pointed at each one. All nine of us fire like mad, dumping so many rounds downrange that it overwhelms the two or three men who can fit abreast at each attack vector.

It's too dark to see who's getting hit, but our outgoing fire is awesome to behold. I lost my ear protection when I crashed through the window, so I doubt the girls and I will be hearing much for the rest of the night.

None of the armed women will probably win any marksmanship awards, but they all seem to be able to dump rounds in the dark just about as well as me and my two teammates. The three with experience reload, the others run dry, and then, after I rock off my second full magazine and reload with a third, Rodney calls a cease-fire.

Shell casings trickle down the stairs for several seconds, but no more enemy contact returns.

Just then, Carl transmits over the radio. "All call signs, I've got multiple pax fleeing on foot to the south. I'm not going to pursue. I've got this bird flying, and I don't wanna fuck it up by catching more lead."

Kareem rogers up, and we begin getting the women ready to move.

Now I hear a shriek behind me, and I spin around as Rodney actuates his weapon light, shining it on the floor in the direction of the noise. The tall Ukrainian who'd fielded my Kalashnikov lies on her back, her irises rolled back in her open eyes, a pair of bloody bullet holes in the center of her gown.

One of the other hostages, a small Asian woman who doesn't seem to understand English, has been shot just below her right knee, and a red-headed girl in her twenties looks like she took a ricochet to her left hip. Kareem drops to the floor next to the Asian, along with several other women, and they all work together to treat her, while Rodney pulls out his medical kit and bandages the redhead.

One of the hostages is dead, and two are wounded. Anger threatens my mission, so I force myself to take a deep breath. "We're going to go for a couple of those SUVs out on the driveway. We'll either find the keys or we'll hot-wire the things, I don't give a shit which. Everybody is coming, we'll carry the wounded."

. . .

It seems like a thousand police lights flash in the darkness just a mile or so behind us as we race overland in a convoy of two silver Cadillac Escalades. Our headlights are off and I'm glad I'm not behind the wheel, but soon enough Kareem and Rodney find a back road that leads off the sixty-acre ranch and we drive it to the highway, then turn to the south, heading to Calabasas to drop the injured women off at the hospital.

I make contact with Talyssa and tell her what happened at Rancho Esmerelda. I hate letting her know that her sister was hauled away during the fight by Jaco and the Director, but I do so. I tell her to stay put down in LA, ask her to watch as much news as she can about the shootout and to see if she learns anything of note that might help us find out the identity of the Director.

She doesn't like being sidelined like this, but I finally convince her that I don't have any other plans on how to move forward, so it's not like she's missing out on anything.

I've got a vague idea about going after this psychologist Talyssa has identified, but in the short term it doesn't sound that promising. Even though we didn't see her tonight, we can be sure she is aware that I am here, and that makes it pretty unlikely she'll just be sitting around the house waiting for me to show up.

Sooner or later, yeah, Dr. Riesling might show herself, but I don't have that kind of time. Hanley is going to send Travers and his boys to LA the minute he hears about the battle in the San Fernando Valley, and I'm going to get yanked back into service for the CIA.

Whatever I'm going to do on this op, I figure I have about twelve hours to get it done before I'll be ducking Ground Branch.

The two Escalades drive on through the early morning: me, two other men, and nine women, with not one of us knowing what the hell happens next.

. . .

Ken Cage sat in the back of the Mercedes SUV, his heart sending sharp pains through his chest as he worried about everything that was falling apart around him.

He held a phone to his ear and it rang and rang. Cage cursed at the delay, until finally a sleepy woman's voice answered.

"Ken?"

"Listen to me, Heather. I need you to wake up."

"Wha—what time is it?"

"Don't ask any questions, please. I need you to get the kids and get out of the house. Now. There's a little mix-up and it won't be for long, but Sean feels it's safer if—"

"What's going on?"

Cage looked across the vehicle at Maja, who just stared back at him with blank eyes. He wanted to move to her and choke the life from her, but Jaco had stopped him from doing so once already, insisting that she was important leverage to use against the Gray Man.

So Cage refocused his attention on his wife. "Heather," he continued. "I'll have to explain everything later, but—"

"What have you done?"

"*Done?* I haven't done—"

Heather was fully awake now, and she screamed—in anger, not in panic. "What . . . have . . . you . . . done?"

He answered her in a meek voice. "Nothing. I didn't do anything."

"I don't know what you do and I don't know who you do it with, and I really don't care. But you and I have built something, and you are *not* going to fuck it up!"

"It's just work, babe. It's not—"

"Bullshit!" Cage's wife screamed. "You are a criminal, and I'm not talking about cooking the books. You've been doing that for twenty years. But whatever you're into now, it's changed you. Look, you can be gone as long as you want, you can fuck whoever or whatever you want while you're gone, I can't stop you. But you keep that shit away from me and the kids, and you keep us in the life you've given us. You are *not* going to take that away. *Nobody* is going to take that away from us. Do you understand me?"

Cage bit his lower lip, thought about his next words carefully. "I am doing my best to keep you out of any danger. Sean wants you to leave the house, just for a day or two, while he and Jaco take care of things. *Please* do this for me, honey."

Heather Cage breathed into the phone for a few seconds, and Ken sat there listening, his eyes closed. "Charlotte isn't here. She's up in Arrowhead at the Ambertons' lake house."

"Call her. Tell her to stay right there."

"She's not going to answer her phone in the middle of the night, Ken."

"Call her anyway. Do that, then take Justin and Juliet, and go."

"Go *where?* The beach house?"

"No! Don't go to one of our properties." He thought a moment. "It's almost one in the morning. Just go get a hotel. I don't care where, but text me when you know where you'll be. This will all be over and I'll come—"

Heather hung up the phone.

Cage handed the device back to Sean. "They're leaving."

Sean had been listening in to the conversation. "Charlotte's in Arrowhead, right?"

"Yeah. She's fine."

Cage then looked again to the girl he first met a month ago in a nightclub in Bucharest. He said, "So . . . all this is about you. Doesn't that make you feel special?"

She turned away from him, gazed out the window.

His voice turned both sinister and sexual. "You thought things were tough before? Now I'm *really* going to punish you, and I'm going to love every second of it." He smiled. "Jaco says we have to keep you alive. Anything else that happens to you is at my discretion, and you'll pay dearly for this shit."

The Romanian woman said nothing.

Cage leaned forward, close to her face. "I will fuck you up, and I'll start today. By the time I'm finished with you, you won't want to go home. You'll want Jaco to fucking kill you to make the nightmares stop."

"You are the devil," Maja said.

"You bet I am, little girl." Cage reached out, took her by the throat, and squeezed.

Sean Hall sat in the row in front of Cage and Maja, but he was still turned back in their direction. He grabbed his employer's arm and pulled it away. "Keep your head in the game, Ken. We have to leave her in one piece to use her as insurance. She's important."

Cage shrugged away from his bodyguard's grip, but he kept his malevolent eyes on the kidnapped woman, a cruel sneer of a smile on his face. "You just wait, bitch. You just wait."

FIFTY-ONE

Carl and A.J. land, refuel, and patch up the helicopter on a darkened tarmac at Bakersfield Municipal Airport. They roll Shep Duvall's corpse into a couple of thick contractor bags and tape them together, creating a poor man's body bag, and then A.J. takes a cab back to the house to retrieve his truck. He returns with it, loads Shep's lifeless body into the back, and then drives it to the parking lot of a hospital. Here he gently lays it under a tree at the edge of the lot, in sight of the emergency room.

After a prayer over his fallen friend, he drives back to the airport, where he and Carl drink coffee and wait, hoping like hell for another chance to go after the Director.

The rest of us make it back to Rodney's place in Bakersfield at three thirty a.m.; we've treated Kareem's shoulder, and he's doing okay but bitching constantly about letting the mastermind of the entire Consortium get away.

It's annoying, but I get it. I am bitching just as much as he is, and I didn't even get shot.

The hostages are racked out on the floor all over the place. Most are still in a state of shock, but every one of them seems happy to be free from captivity, which is a relief, because I thought it possible, even after all the horrors these girls have undoubtedly suffered, that a few of them, at least, would side with their captors.

Some demand to speak to their embassy, but most understand that they are in the middle of a very fluid, if very low-rent, operation, and they calm the most anxious down. They all promise to sit tight, and we promise them we will help them get where they need to go soon.

Me and the boys grab more ammo and smoke grenades from Rodney's garage, and we're in the process of cleaning our weapons when Talyssa calls me from down in LA. I step into the backyard for some privacy, thinking she's going to light into me about failing again to rescue her sister, probably because it's all I'm thinking about right now, myself.

But instead she says, "Gentry, the Director will wonder how we found out about the ranch. He'll be worried, at least for a few days, that we can trace the property directly to him somehow."

I hope she's right about this. "Suits me if he's running scared."

"Men like this," she says. "Wealthy, powerful men. They have a lot of places they can flee to in times of danger."

"Sure." I've known a few powerful assholes myself, and she's correct about their modus operandi when dealing with trouble.

She says, "If I knew about other properties he owned, we might have something to go on, but Rancho Esmerelda was so well insulated in its corporate ownership that I can't tie any person to it."

I know all this already. "What's your point?"

"My point is, he is going to leave the area. Soon. If he hasn't already."

"Yeah, of course. Dr. Riesling, as well. But what can we do about it? There are a lot of airports here, we can't just go—"

"Where do you think the Director lives?"

This question surprises me. "I have no idea."

"You know it's within driving distance to the ranch, because he brought my sister all the way here from Romania for himself."

"Right, but ten million people live within two hours of that location."

"The Director doesn't live like ten million people."

This is true. "But still, lots of enclaves for the wealthy around here. Not just in LA, but in towns up the coast, as well."

Talyssa says, "He's a businessman. A financier. He won't be in some beach town hours away from Los Angeles. He's got to be in the city. He meets clients for lunch, he needs the convenience of LA."

I don't have a clue where she's going with this. "Okay. He's in LA, some ritzy part of it. What? Do we go door to door and knock?"

"Of course not. But you and your team shouldn't sit up there in a house in Bakersfield, either. Come down here. If my sister is able to alert me some way, if she is even still alive and still with the Director, then you will be much closer when it happens."

It's a lot of "ifs," but Talyssa is right. LA is the most high-probability location for the Director, and if we head down in that direction now, we will be able to act faster if, by some miracle, Roxana is able to get a message out.

Twenty minutes later, Kareem, Rodney, A.J., and I have left the kidnapping victims alone at Rodney's place, and we drive in A.J.'s truck to the south.

Carl is still at the airport with his helicopter, but when we tell him what we're doing he decides to fly it to Van Nuys Airport in the San Fernando Valley. That will put him just minutes' flying time from anywhere in LA and it also gives the rest of us a place to position ourselves.

This may not be much, but it feels like forward momentum to me, if only incremental forward momentum.

But one thing feels certain. I got us to Venice, and Talyssa got us to Rancho Esmerelda. But if we're going to find our way to the top of this evil organization in the next twelve hours, it's up to Roxana.

. . .

Roxana Vaduva drank the tepid vodka straight out of the little bottle while the men around her discussed whether to kill her.

Three men held her fate in their hands, and all three of them were aware of who she was and what she had done. They knew she'd been sent by her sister to meet the Director, and then, once she'd been taken, she'd communicated with her sister's colleague on the yacht, no doubt giving him the information that led him to Italy.

So now she sat quietly, took a last gulp to finish the bottle, and awaited their decision.

The man she knew as the Director stormed around the massive penthouse hotel suite, hands on his hips, a bathrobe covering his small frame. The tall, bald-headed man named Jaco sat on a sofa in the opposite corner, making phone call after phone call. And Sean, the Director's bodyguard, sat quietly on the kitchen counter, just feet from Roxana.

She'd seen him sneak an airplane vodka bottle out of the minibar for himself.

He was clearly scared. He wasn't as scared as Roxana—no, she didn't think anyone on Earth was as scared as she was right now—but she could tell he wanted nothing more to do with this entire affair, and the one shot of vodka she'd seen him down so far would help him no more than the one she just drank would aid in getting *her* out of this mess.

Dr. Claudia was also in the penthouse now. The older American woman's normally calm exterior had given way to an intense look of concern, nail biting, and chain smoking.

Whoever it was who had shown up at the ranch in a helicopter, they had certainly rattled the top of the Consortium.

It had to have been the assassin from the yacht, although he certainly must have brought more forces along with him.

She hoped like hell her sister had been nowhere near all that fighting. She assumed Talyssa was still in Europe, directing the actions of the American killer from there.

Roxana looked at Jaco now, and he at her. His eyes frightened her, and she turned away, wondering if he might just draw the gun out from under his jacket and shoot her in the head.

That was, ultimately, the Director's call, she was certain, and this terrified her more. If she was the most afraid in the room, the small bald-headed man was the angriest. His pacing, his yelling at his subordinates, his taking of pills, and his occasional bouts of brooding silence had made the last few hours a terrifying roller-coaster ride for the young Romanian.

The Director stormed around now, and she focused on him. She thought, at first, that he looked like Napoleon at Waterloo, but after watching him for a while, she found him to be less like the embattled general and more like a spoiled kid, furious things weren't going his way.

She tried to put the terror out of her mind and think of the positives. It had been a horrific night, but there *was* something positive in all this.

She knew exactly where she was. Los Angeles. On the drive in she'd seen the interstate signs giving directions to Hollywood, and then, after they got off the interstate, the street signs told her she was in Beverly Hills.

When they'd pulled up to this building she saw one last sign before she'd been whisked inside.

The Four Seasons Hotel.

If she could just find access to a phone or get online somehow, she could contact her sister and tell her the Director was right here with her.

It was too late to save her, Roxana was certain. They would kill her soon enough, no matter what she did. But if she could only get the information out before she was murdered, she might be able to help all the other women held in bondage by this horrible organization.

The Director stopped pacing and looked out the window a moment, then his plaintive voice kicked up again at something Jaco said that Roxana could not hear.

The American said, "I'm not leaving the U.S.! Why the hell should I? The government is watching out for me here, and I don't have a single personal tie to what happened at Rancho Esmerelda."

Jaco replied in a strikingly calmer manner. "A week, Ken. Two, maybe. We go down to Antigua, or to Costa Rica, work from your property there, make sure that everything here is cleaned up and this fookin' Gentry bloke is dealt with."

Sean started to second Jaco's proposal, but Cage shouted over him.

"How's that going to happen? You've lost all your men but two, and you haven't put a scratch on him as near as I can tell. There were thirty cartel soldiers on that property. *Thirty!* And still we hear that the men who attacked escaped in their helicopter. Along with the merchandise, I might add. *Expensive* fucking merchandise, each one of whom has seen very important faces around here. Do you have any idea what this will do to every man who's gone to Esmerelda? They're all gonna come at me now! Studio heads, financiers, high-profile lawyers. I don't have to remind you the power of our clientele, do I?"

"All the more reason for you to get out of the country while we get to work cleaning this up! Look, the American government is actively trying to kill the Gray Man. He's in the U.S., they know it, and now they will know what area he's in. That aspect of this problem will clean itself up in short order. Either he runs away, or they get him. You just have to be clear of the area until one of those two things happens."

The Director sat down now, the first time Roxana had seen him do so since his arrival here at the Four Seasons.

He closed his eyes and rubbed them with his hands, his elbows on his knees, the cuffs of his blue bathrobe drooping, exposing his hairy forearms. "I've got so much shit at the house that I can't leave without. Bearer bonds, hard drives. Physical stuff."

"I'll send Sean and his men to get it all."

Sean began to protest this; Roxana knew he'd refuse to leave his boss's side, but Cage said, "If I'm leaving the country, then I'm going by the house first. Sean's not getting in my safe; only *I* go in my safe."

Jaco stood now, looked out over the balcony at the morning. "How much time will you need?"

This time Sean did break into the conversation. "Wait. You aren't suggesting he actually go to his residence. We don't know if Gentry and his people know his address, his name. Shit, I'm not sending him into—"

Jaco pointed at the American bodyguard. "You'll do your job!" He turned to Ken now. "How much time, boss?"

"I need two hours, and I need Sean's men to help me load up cars. If I tell my wife we're leaving the country and she can't go home first, she's going to do more damage to me than Court Gentry." He leaned back on the sofa. "Shit! Heads are going to roll when this is over, I swear to you both!"

Jaco spoke to Sean. "Two hours? The seven of you can watch him.

Me, Loots, and Duiker, too. That's ten armed men there. Claudia can help, as well."

Sean looked defeated to Roxana, but he didn't give in completely. "One hour. We go in hard and fast, all of us, together, and my men are on watch while me and the four of you help the boss get what he needs."

Claudia had not said a single word, but now she spoke up. "I can pack Heather's clothes, get the kids' stuff, while you are dealing with potential evidence."

Ken just nodded and rubbed his eyes some more, then took his hands away and again looked right at Roxana. "What about her?"

Jaco didn't hesitate. "She comes with us. If Gentry and his mates arrive, I'll have a knife at her neck to slow them while you get away. If he makes contact with us, we'll use her to bargain, or as bait."

Roxana's teeth chattered, but through the fear she recognized that she was about to go to the home of the Director. Ground zero of the Consortium.

She didn't see this as yet a new danger.

No, this was her chance, her *last* chance, and she knew it.

FIFTY-TWO

Sixteen-year-old Charlotte Cage stepped out of the kitchen door of her girl-friend's house in Bel Air, then walked down the driveway as the gate opened automatically in front of her, thumbing open her phone's screen along the way. With a couple of clicks she ordered an Uber Lux to take her to her home in the Hollywood Hills, fifteen minutes away in morning traffic.

She wasn't supposed to be here. Her mom routinely disallowed her daughter from overnighting with her eighteen-year-old friend, thinking Clara to be a bad influence, so Charlotte had quit asking permission. Instead she told her mom she was spending a couple of days at Lake Arrowhead with a friend her own age whom her mom trusted. This wasn't the first time this summer she'd pulled this off, and she hoped it wouldn't be the last.

As Charlotte stood there waiting for her ride, she noticed she'd missed a text message and a phone call. The text was from her mom, and it was demonstrative and unusual, but not particularly worrisome.

Call me as soon as you get this. Do not, under any circumstances, go to the house.

She didn't bother listening to the voice mail.

As she climbed into the back of the BMW 5 Series that arrived to pick her up, Charlotte considered calling to see what was going on, but she decided against it. She also decided against complying with her mother's wishes. She was only leaving the house so early this morning because she was meeting Sean for a surfing lesson. Sean didn't work Wednesday mornings, and they'd made plans the week before.

She hadn't said anything to him about Arrowhead, knowing all the time she'd be in town and excited to go surfing.

Charlotte told herself she'd wait to reach out to her mom till she and Sean got to Santa Monica with their surfboards, and she'd tell her she'd caught a ride from Arrowhead early this morning.

As the Uber drove through the narrow, winding streets in the Hollywood Hills, she told the driver to drop her off at the house next door to hers, not wanting her mom or dad to see her. From there she walked to a locked gate in the fence around her two-acre property, punched in the code, and let herself in. Closing it behind her, she headed down the steeply graded drive, then turned and moved across the sloping landscaped yard on the offhand chance her mom was standing at the living room window that overlooked the driveway.

She made her way around to the back of the property right at seven a.m., hoping no one in the house could see her as she rapped on the door to the pool house, but when Sean didn't answer immediately, she began to worry that her mom could be standing in the kitchen dining area that overlooked the back patio. She tapped the code to the pool house into the keypad alongside the door, then stepped in when it unlocked.

"Sean?" she called out through the den and then again up the stairs. It was weird he wasn't up, but she knew her dad gave him Wednesdays and Sundays off; it was Wednesday, so she figured he was just sleeping in.

Charlotte didn't go upstairs to where Sean slept; that would be weird, she decided, so she texted him that she was here, then headed through the pool house to the storage room in the back. There she quietly dressed in her wetsuit, picked out a surfboard for today's excursion, and began collecting other odds and ends she'd need for a morning at the beach.

. . .

Three Mercedes-Benz G550 SUVs rolled down the driveway in front of Kenneth Cage's Hollywood Hills mansion, then parked in a line in front of the house. A pair of Sean Hall's men climbed out of the first vehicle, unlocked the door, and, while keeping their hands over the pistols secreted under their polo shirts and light sport coats, they scanned the area.

Seconds later one of them called into his radio, and all the doors to all the SUVs opened as one. Eight other men and two women, Roxana Vaduva and Dr. Claudia Riesling, climbed out and headed inside.

Everyone in the entourage had a mission this morning, and Jaco had tasked one of Hall's men, much to Hall's disapproval, to be in charge of Maja. He took her by the arm into the large kitchen at the rear of the house and sat her down at a table in front of the sliding glass door overlooking the pool and rear gardens, while he went looking for some cordage to tie her with.

He bound her tightly with an electrical extension cord but didn't bother securing her to the chair because he didn't want to deal with untying her from an object if they had to make haste to the SUVs.

Still, the girl he only knew as Maja was utterly compliant, so he wasn't worried about her running off.

Sean Hall's six security men took up positions around the home, their eyes cast out on the sharp hills and massive homes all around. Hall started to run over to his pool house for a change of clothes; he was still wearing an undershirt and jeans, but he'd only made it into the kitchen before Cage yelled from the living room, demanding that Hall, Verdoorn, and Loots follow him into his office to begin removing incriminating files and computer drives.

Sean turned to comply with his boss's wishes, but on his way out of the kitchen he called across the room to his subordinate. "Don't just sit there, Scott. Make us a pot of coffee."

Claudia headed to the kids' rooms after Cage directed her to a stack of suitcases in a hall closet.

Within five minutes of arrival, the Director and his people were all over the house, hurrying through their assignments, while a few miles away the pilots of the Gulfstream waited at LAX after filing a flight plan for San Jose, Costa Rica.

. . .

It's just after seven a.m. when we park next to an unused warehouse just outside the fenced-in grounds of Van Nuys Airport. We sit down at picnic tables along a chain-link fence, just twenty-five yards from where Carl's bullet-pocked helicopter is parked on a pad at the end of the runway.

We drink coffee and clean and rebandage Kareem's arm wound, in that order. Carl and A.J. talk about Shep's dog, agree to share custody and take care of her now that her master isn't able to do so.

And then we sit around, just hoping for a bolt out of the blue.

We know we can't count on Roxana, so our only fallback plan is to scan the news on a couple of the guys' mobile phones, reading updates about the gun battle a few hours earlier a half hour's drive to the north of our position. We're hoping against hope that the media will be able to tie someone to the property or to one of the dead there, as much of a long shot as that seems.

We also pull out binos and scan the airport grounds, on the off chance the Director is flying out of this airport. It's a hundred-to-one shot, which demonstrates how desperate we are.

My phone rings and I answer it in my earpiece. "Talyssa?"

The Romanian Europol analyst's voice conveys a sense of dread. "Harry . . . it's him. He's on the line. He says he will kill Roxana."

"Patch him through."

I hear some clicks, and then I say, "That you, Jaco?"

His dark voice replies, "Nice work last night."

I laugh. It's phony, but I want to appear relaxed and in control. "You like that shit, do you?"

"Love it. I thought you'd sneak in, your standard operating procedure. Figured you'd kill a couple Mexicans with a stiletto before my guys came across you and did you in. But no, you went big, didn't you? Made a lot of noise, broke a lot of things, killed some people who didn't matter."

"We slayed a lot of your boys, didn't we?"

"Maybe. But what did you get out of all that?"

"I recovered a house full of sex trafficking victims, all of whom can identify the people who—"

"Nobody's identifying a bladdy thing, mate. Those whores will be useless to you. We're protected at the highest levels. You're pissin' into the fookin' wind."

I don't respond.

He then says, "I was just telling your girlfriend on the phone that I've got her little sis here with me, in the next room. I'm thinking about walking over there and sticking my knife through her heart. What's the Gray Man going to do about that?"

"I don't have to do anything about that, because you aren't going to touch her."

He laughs. "Oh yeah? Why's that?"

"Because the only reason you took her away from the ranch last night was that you know she's your fail-safe, your last chance to bargain to save yourself, save your boss."

He pauses for a long time, and then he says, "Gentry . . . I'm going to tell you something about me."

I sigh. "Knock yourself out."

"I was South African military, Fourth Special Forces Regiment. As a recce I saw action in the Congo and the Central African Republic, plus some other shit I'm not talking about."

"Good. Because I couldn't care less."

Jaco sniffs out a short laugh. "My point is, when I left the military, I went into intelligence. For three years I chased down every Gray Man sighting or potential Gray Man sighting in Africa. A couple hunts in the Middle East, others on the Indian subcontinent. Hell, I even went to Bangladesh on a lead."

"Yeah," I say. "Never been to Bangladesh."

He acts like he doesn't hear me. "But intel work was a fookin' bore. No Gray Man, no action, no test of the mettle like I'd gotten in my twenties as a recce."

To this I say, "Any chance I could get you to tell me why you called?"

Another laugh from the South African, but I can tell in his voice he's stressed. He ignores me again and keeps up his story. "No other options for a bloke like me but to go into corporate security. I thought it would be tiresome and monotonous, but it was even so much worse than that. So when my company was contacted by a corporation in the Consortium, when I started gettin' the full picture of what this is all about, when me and my boys started working tough, demanding jobs to keep this entire bladdy enterprise afloat . . . I was like, 'Yeah. That's more like it.'"

"You're a piece of shit. You know that, right?"

He ignores the comment and continues. "I love my job, Gentry, is what I'm saying. But now . . . now I'm up against you, the one prize I've wanted for years and years. Can't believe how lucky I am that you got drawn into this whole thing."

I shake my head at this. "I bet Kostopoulos and Babic wouldn't consider themselves lucky. Does the Director know you see my arrival in California as a positive turn of events?"

Now Jaco laughs maniacally into the phone. "I see the glass as half-full. The Director wouldn't get it, he's not like us, not a huntsman. He likes his food caught and cleaned and carved and served to him on a china plate. You and me, on the other hand, we don't care about the dish. We only care about the art of the pursuit, the thrill of the kill."

"You're right about that. So why don't you let Roxana go, and then you and I can hunt each other into oblivion."

"Nice try, but if you got your girl back, I can't be sure you wouldn't just slip away, Gray Man style. No, mate. I need the lamb on the stake for the lion to come for it."

"You've told your boss she's a bargaining chip, but that's not it, is it? You are holding on to her so that I keep coming for you."

Jaco says, "Bingo."

A.J. hands me a cup of coffee from the McDonald's on the corner, and I take a swig. Normally I would benefit from the caffeine almost immediately, but this asshole has me so amped I have plenty of energy. I say, "I'm going to be on top of you, soon. My face in your face, while your life is leaving you through a hole in your chest. And, as you're bleeding out, I'm going to ask if you're still so happy to have me chasing you."

"Keep tellin' yourself that, Gentry. It will bring us closer." Almost to himself he says, "I love my job."

I'm tired of this testosterone-infused back-and-forth, but I'm trying to get something out of him I can use. He seems to think I'm going to appear in front of him any minute, but the truth is I've only got his boss narrowed down to an area some hundred miles in diameter.

But before I can try to pull intel out of him, he says, "Until that day, Court." And then the line goes dead.

Shit.

. . .

As the bodyguard worked on pulling coffee mugs out of a cabinet and pouring milk into them, Roxana looked out the window at the back of the property and thought it looked like images she'd seen of Versailles. The pool, the marble deck, the foliage and setting: it was idyllic.

9102 Jovenita Canyon Drive. *What a strange place for the devil to live,* she thought.

She'd seen the address on the way in; all she had done as they drove was try to find street signs, notable buildings, and other things that would help her direct her sister to her, should the opportunity arise. But while pulling into the drive they stopped a moment for the gate to open, and right in front of her she saw the street address on the massive mailbox.

If she had harbored any lingering doubts that she would be killed by her captors, they disappeared when she realized no one around her had any qualms about her knowing exactly where the Director lived.

She knew she was a dead woman now, there was not a shred of doubt about it, but she still held out faint hope that she could reach out to her sister before she died.

On the walls around her in the kitchen she saw pictures of the Director, a man she now knew was named Ken, and his family. A girl of about fifteen stood with her younger brother and sister in one; they all held oars and life preservers in front of a swiftly moving mountain stream as they smiled at the camera. In another, the same kids—younger—stood lined up back to front on skis with an impossibly gorgeous snowcapped mountain chain in the background.

Her eyes drifted back out to the rear of the property, and she was surprised by a hint of movement through the sliding glass doors to her right. There, on the first story of a detached white two-story building covered in vines next to the pool, she saw a brown-haired girl pass in front of a window. Not once, not twice, but repeatedly. The girl seemed to be carrying items back and forth, appearing and then disappearing from view.

She was the right age to be one of the girls Roxana had seen along the pipeline over the past two weeks, but this one didn't look familiar to her.

The foreign man watching over her poured coffee in cups and insulated tumblers, draining the pot. As he finished, one of the South Africans entered the kitchen.

"We don't have time for that, mate."

"Your boss isn't my boss, and my boss says to get some coffee in his men. Watch the merch while I pass these around the house."

The man Roxana had heard referred to as Lion Two sighed. "Got any left for me?"

"Be my guest." The bodyguard grabbed four mugs and started out of the kitchen. On his way into the living room, he looked back to the South African. "She's tied up. Just don't let her go anywhere."

"Hurry it up, then."

The bodyguard left the room, and the White Lion operative grabbed himself a cup, then began to take a sip.

Just then, Verdoorn came out of the library, hanging up his phone. He had a smile on his face. "Where's the guard?"

Loots rolled his eyes as he said, "Delivering coffee to Hall and Cage."

Verdoorn asked, "Is she tied?" referring to Maja across the room at the table, her hands behind her.

"Yeah, boss," Loots said.

"Okay, come with me. We'll start hauling shit to the cars."

"You gonna be a good girl and sit right there?" he asked Roxana as he walked.

She nodded without speaking, and he left the kitchen.

As soon as they disappeared, Roxana looked around frantically for a telephone, and she found one across the kitchen on a cradle. This gave her a moment of optimism, though she had no idea how the hell she could possibly dial her sister's number, country code and all, with her hands tied behind her back.

But then she turned her attention to the pool house, where she'd caught glimpses of what she took as a young trafficking victim through the window. That girl had clearly not been bound, and Roxana wondered if she could make it out the back screen door, across the pool deck, and inside the pool house without being detected.

She knew she had to try.

She looked quickly back over her shoulder to make sure no one was approaching from behind, then she rose, shot across the kitchen, spun around, and used her hands behind her back to unlock and slide open the glass door. She shut it behind her, then ran as fast as she could in her stocking feet to the pool house. Once there, she turned around again, felt blindly until she grasped the door latch, opened the unlocked door, and stepped inside.

On her left she saw the open kitchen, so she stepped to a counter, found a paring knife on a cutting board, and carefully cut the ties lashing her wrists together.

When this was done, she looked down at the knife in her hand. It was a weapon, but she knew she couldn't fight her way out of here.

She thought about using it to kill herself, but only for a moment.

No, she wasn't doing that. Roxana was on a mission, and the mission was to find a damn phone.

A noise startled her, and she looked up to find the girl she'd seen through the window, now walking through the living room. She wore a purple wetsuit, unzipped at the waist with the arms hanging down by her legs. On her body she wore a black long-sleeved rash guard, and she had handmade bracelets on both wrists.

Roxana had seen dozens of sex trafficking victims; none of them dressed like this.

The girl saw her, stopped, and stared, obviously confused.

"Do you speak English?" Roxana asked breathlessly.

"Uhh . . . yeah. Who are you?" The girl spoke with an American accent, and this Roxana found bizarre. There had been no American slaves at the ranch, and certainly none in the pipeline.

Roxana began to answer her, but the American asked, "Are you a friend of Sean's?"

Roxana just looked at her before saying, "He brought me here. My name is Roxana."

"Hi," the girl said awkwardly.

In the quiet that followed, Roxana suddenly realized she'd seen this girl before. Moments ago, in the photos in the kitchen of the Director's house. She had been younger then, but she was the oldest of the three kids pictured on the ski slope.

"What is your name?" Roxana asked in disbelief.

"Charlotte Cage."

"You are Ken's daughter?"

The young girl nodded nervously, like she'd been caught doing something wrong. She said, "Sean and I were supposed to go surfing this morning. I guess he forgot. Look, I'm not supposed to be here. I mean, I'm supposed to meet Sean, but my mom told me not to come home. Will you do me a favor and—"

"I won't say anything, but your father is over there in the house right now."

Charlotte looked out the window. "Shit," she said again.

"Stay here; I'll tell Sean where you are, and when they are finished with what they are doing, you guys can go surfing."

Charlotte looked relieved. "Thank you. Please don't tell my mom and dad."

Roxana looked at her a moment more, then asked, "You wouldn't happen to have a phone I can borrow, would you? I need to send a quick text."

Charlotte cocked her head. "Who doesn't have a phone?" She reached into the waistband of her wetsuit and pulled out an iPhone.

Sixty seconds later Roxana moved back up the pool area, rewrapping the loose cord around her wrists behind her back as she did so, and tucking the ends in so it looked like she was still bound. She'd just finished when the sliding door opened and the American guard who'd stepped away with the coffee lurched out, grabbed her by her throat, and yanked her back into the kitchen, leaning into her ear as he did so. Softly, so no one else in the house could hear, he said, "Where the fuck did you go, you bitch?"

Roxana stared back at him, and she answered in a low tone herself. "I was looking for a bathroom."

"Outside?"

"Yeah, outside. I thought there would be one in the pool house and I could get some privacy. But the front door was locked."

"You weren't out here a second ago."

"I tried going around back but couldn't get in. My hands are tied up, remember?"

The bodyguard stared at the pool house a moment, then shoved her back down into her chair. He searched her thoroughly, but she had done a good job with the cord so he didn't pick up on the fact she was no longer securely tied.

He began pacing around the kitchen in a panic, but said nothing until the South African who'd been watching her passed by in the hall with a load of files in his hands.

Quietly, but with unmistakable anger, the American said, "Hey! You were supposed to watch her. She went outside."

The White Lion operative looked at Roxana, then back at the body-guard. "No, mate, you were supposed to watch her. I thought you had her lashed to the bladdy chair."

"But—"

"Did you search her when you got her back?"

"Yes. She's clean."

"Then what's your worry?" He started moving off, then looked back to her. "We'll keep this to ourselves; we'd both get an ass kicking."

The American nodded. "Right. Okay."

The South African disappeared on his way to the SUVs parked out front.

As he paced back and forth, the protection officer tasked with watch-ing Roxana raised his hand to strike her twice, but both times he lowered it before hitting her. Finally, he just sat down in front of her, his hand fin-gering the butt of the pistol in his shoulder holster, and he stared at her with pure malevolence.

But Roxana didn't care. She felt better now. Yes, she would probably die today, but it didn't matter now, because before she left Charlotte Cage hid-ing in the pool house, Roxana had used the teen's phone to send a very short but very informative text to her sister.

9102 Jovenita Canyon Drive. Director is Ken Cage. Ten men with guns here. Whatever happens—I love you. Do not reply.

And then she'd returned to the main house.

Roxana knew that if she escaped, Cage and the others would flee the property immediately. No, she had to wait, to buy time for Talyssa, even if waiting meant dying.

FIFTY-THREE

I disconnect the call with Talyssa, repeat the address she just gave me out loud, and then Rodney types it into Google Maps on his phone. Even before it comes up he says, "Jovenita Canyon? That's up in the Hollywood Hills."

We look at the satellite map, zoom in on the place, and see a large Italianate mansion that looks like it must be worth fifty million bucks. The property is positioned on a steep hill, the grounds around it are meticulously sculptured, and a detached pool house looks like it's twice the size of the home I grew up in.

A.J. says, "We're really gonna hit a mansion in Hollywood? Cops will be all over the place. If the bad guys don't get us, then five-oh will."

Carl adds, "LAPD helicopters fill the skies down there. I can insert you boys, but it will be a one-way trip for all of us."

Both men are right, of course. With a shrug, I say, "I'm going in, with or without you guys."

Kareem chuckles a little as he fingers the bloody bandage on his shoulder. "Settle down, hero. You ain't the only dude here that wants to do the right thing." He looks at Carl and his two surviving teammates. "For Shep, we're gonna see this to the end."

Carl, A.J., and Rodney agree.

The wiry Vietnam vet starts walking over towards the helicopter now. "We're skids up in three minutes, fellas."

A.J., Rodney, Kareem, and I turn back to the satellite image, and we all get to work on making a hasty plan to hit the mansion.

. . .

Fourteen minutes later the last of the bags were loaded into the Mercedes SUVs. Cage grabbed a small framed photo of him and his entire family off his desk and carried it in his hands through the expansive foyer towards the front door. Both Jaco Verdoorn and Claudia Riesling moved along with him, and Sean Hall walked just a couple steps behind, next to Maja, who was being led by one of his men.

Hall pulled his phone out and checked the time, and when he did so he realized he'd missed a text from Charlotte. In a sudden panic he remembered he'd agreed to take her surfing this morning, but quickly he relaxed, knowing that her mom had told her to stay well clear of the house.

But when he tapped the text to look at it, the panic returned.

"Oh, shit," he said, and he slowed, then stopped. Charlotte was waiting for him right now back at the pool house.

Cage kept walking with the rest of the group nearing the front door.

Hall started to call out to his employer, but then he turned his head at a faint noise.

Helicopters are common in the skies over Los Angeles, so no one in the entourage had paid any attention to the thumping rotor sound till it echoed louder than usual along Jovenita Canyon Drive, bouncing off the higher hills in front of the house and rolling in from all directions.

Cage stopped at the front door, Hall's men around him, Jaco standing at the Director's side.

Sean was frozen in place in the grand entry hall of the mansion, recognizing that the helo was low, it was racing closer, and it was right now shooting over the rear of the property.

Then the helicopter flew over the mansion itself, towards the front of the home, its rotor noise vibrating paintings on the walls.

Verdoorn reached out and grabbed Cage by the shoulder and brought him back away from the door, then leaned back out and looked for the source of the thunderous noise. There was nothing in front of him but Hollywood Hills and megamansions, but then a red helicopter suddenly shot over his head, not fifty feet in the air.

He'd not seen the aircraft that attacked the night before at Rancho Esmerelda, but this one sounded identical to him.

He reached for his waistband, and as he pulled out his HK pistol, several small objects, each the size of a soup can, bounced right in front of him on the drive between the front door and the row of Mercedes SUVs.

Red smoke poured from the canisters as they bounced on the stone drive, billowing quickly in all directions.

Verdoorn started shouting orders, Cage's men began rushing forward, and Sean watched twenty-five feet away through the growing cloud of red smoke while the helo pulled up steeply and transitioned to a hover over the steep front drive. Bodyguards and White Lion men raised weapons to shoot at it, but rifles began barking from inside the helicopter, so the men abandoned their counterattack and sought cover.

One of Sean's men was already outside the home, on the other side of the row of three Mercedes; he fired on the threat with his handgun but was cut down by rifle fire before he got a second shot off.

And then the smoke became too thick to see the chopper hovering over the driveway.

Verdoorn yanked Cage down onto his back in the foyer and rolled him away, while Duiker, one of Verdoorn's two surviving operatives, took a round through the forearm and tumbled back, writhing in agony as blood spurted from him.

Sean and his men had pistols and submachine guns. Loots had a rifle, but no one dared return to the doorway. Instead some men took up positions in windows in the front room and the library, eyes peering around walls, searching for a target in the impenetrable red smoke, while Hall and others ran forward to get to Cage so they could move him to safety.

. . .

Two minutes ago Carl dove his AS350 towards sea-level Hollywood, then turned the nose away from the downtown LA skyline and back towards the Hollywood Hills. He followed the incline, low and fast, towards the rear of Cage's mansion on Jovenita Canyon Drive.

A.J. and I stood outside the cabin on the starboard side, with Rodney and Kareem opposite us on the port-side skids.

Carl nearly caught a set of power lines with the skids on the ingress, and a few seconds after this I was certain we were going to plow into a glass-and-steel luxury home. We missed the flat roof by five feet, and then I saw the target location right in front of us, higher on the hill. I reached into the cabin of the helo with both hands, letting my rope lifeline hold me there, my boots on the skids. From a cardboard box I retrieved a pair of M-18 smoke grenades and pulled the pins one by one, and thick red smoke burst from the bottom of each.

Seconds later we rocketed over Cage's infinity pool, and I dropped both M-18s as close as I could to the back door of the home before flying over the roof.

I didn't look to see where they landed because I was already reaching back into the helo, as were all four men on the skids, and we quickly pulled out one more grenade each, yanked pins, and dropped them at the very front of the house as we passed above it.

No more than a second or two after releasing, Carl spun the helicopter violently on its axis 180 degrees, then lowered us down closer to the driveway.

We looked towards the front door and saw men there; both A.J. and I were on the side of the helo with a sightline towards our enemy, so both of us fired a few rounds at targets. A.J. dropped an armed man in a polo standing next to three black Mercedes G-Wagens, and I think I hit a man pointing a weapon at me in the doorway before the targets disappeared.

Carl was pulling off a tricky maneuver getting us so close to the Earth due to the steep downgrade of the driveway. We knew from the first glance on Google Maps that he wouldn't be able to land without striking a rotor against the cement, but he hovered about four feet aboveground, his eyes locked on to his outboard rearview mirror, his spinning rotor within a foot of striking, which would cause it to disintegrate and, no doubt, kill all of us.

The other three men unfastened their carabiners and dropped the last few feet, blunting their impacts by collapsing on their legs when they landed. I know their ankles and knees and hips and backs will have something to say about their decision soon enough, but I was relieved to see all three men adjust their packs and their rifles and begin moving, albeit slowly and uncomfortably, forward towards the Mercedes SUVs.

Now the Eurocopter launches higher into the air as it spins to the right, then begins shooting back towards the house. I'm still outboard on the skid, but I reach for my carabiner and hold it with my left hand while my right keeps my Kalashnikov on my shoulder.

Opening the fastener, I unhook myself from my lifeline but grab hold of the strap so I don't slip and fall.

A few seconds later Carl dips down lower on the far side of the house, flying through the thick red smoke. Once we break through, I step off the skid while the aircraft streaks along twenty-five feet aboveground at forty miles an hour.

Falling through the air, I hold my rifle close to my body and tuck in my legs, saying a prayer that this next stage of my plan works as well as the last one.

. . .

Sean Hall ran over to Ken Cage, lying on the floor near the open front door, and helped him back to his feet. As the two men began running for the rear of the property, Hall shouted into his walkie-talkie. "Scott and Randy, on me! The rest of you, buy us some time till the cops get here! I'm going to get the principal into Citadel Two. Collapse on that location as you fall back."

"Citadel Two" was Hall's code name for the second floor of the pool house, a fallback position he'd set up in case of an attack on the principal or his family at home.

Hall knew Charlotte was in the pool house, so it wasn't an optimal destination, but he also knew it was the last place the men attacking from the front of the property would be able to check.

It was all about delaying now, delaying Gentry and his crew from getting to the boss.

Hall had been in the LAPD, and he knew they'd be surrounding this place in moments, and he assumed Gentry didn't want to get rolled up by local cops, so his helicopter would have to come back to pick him up in a matter of moments.

This was going to be a waiting game, and Hall thought getting Cage as far from Gentry as possible was his best course of action.

"Take Maja!" Verdoorn shouted from behind him. "Maja stays with Cage!"

Roxana Vaduva was grabbed roughly by one of Hall's men and dragged through the house. She dropped the cord she'd cut earlier from around her wrists, then began pulling and swinging at the man forcing her back through the house. She slowed him, and this slowed the entire entourage, but within twenty seconds they were at the back door.

Sean Hall was surprised to see a dense cloud of red smoke on the patio, partially obscuring his view. He took this to mean that attackers were coming from that direction, too, but he kept advancing, knowing that turning around and running back towards the stairs, towards the source of incoming gunfire, would be a bad idea, and hunkering down here on the ground floor would only help Gentry locate Cage sooner. No, he would try to use the smoke to stay hidden from anyone out here, and he'd shoot anything that moved.

Cage, on the other hand, stopped his forward advance in the kitchen when he saw the red cloud at the sliding glass door. Hall screamed at him, pulled on him, just like his men did to Maja ten feet behind. Soon they were all in the smoke, running across the patio, turning right so they didn't stumble into the pool, finally bursting out into clear air by the two rectangular koi ponds.

They ran on. Hall was first to the door to the pool house; he pushed Cage into his living room and kept his gun up high as they raced upstairs.

. . .

I kneel in the shallow end of the pool now, my eyes and the top of my head the only parts of me visible while I watch Cage, Roxana, and three other men enter the pool house, fifty feet away. They're facing away from me, they have no idea I've just dropped from the sky into the swimming pool, and they also have no idea that they've been spotted.

The pool jump seemed like a good idea when we drew it up, but when I crashed into the water, the weight of my gear sent me to the bottom of the deep end. I was aiming for the shallow end, naturally, but mistimed my jump because of the smoke, so I shot right to the bottom and remained there. Movement of any kind was nearly impossible, but I had been prepared to dump equipment if necessary, so I quickly removed my AK and my chest rig, leaving on my utility belt and my small canvas hip pack.

Now I'm armed only with my Glock 19 pistol and the suppressed .22 caliber Walther pistol. I have a spare mag for the Glock, and a fixed-blade knife.

I wipe water from my eyes and speak into my mic, which, thankfully, is fully waterproof. "You guys breached yet?"

"Negative," Rodney says. "We're at the front door now, about to flash-bang our way in."

"Roger that," I say. "Primary target has retreated into the pool house with three hostiles and one friendly."

"Understood; we'll link up with you when able."

I hear the flash bangs go off in the house, and then I hear an unreal amount of gunfire. I don't know how long it will take my crew to make their way back here, so I decide I'll have to hit the pool house alone.

I stand up fully in the pool, pull a smoke grenade from my belt, yank the pin, and hurl it closer to the pool house, hoping to cover my approach in more of the red obscurant.

And then I begin wading forward. I'm down a gun, I'm alone, I'm outnumbered, and I know the cops are closing in. Nothing about this is optimal, but time is not on my side, so I'll have to make it work.

. . .

Sean Hall left his two men behind him covering Maja and the Director while he cleared the upstairs. He had them stop and wait on the landing between the floors while he moved up, checking the two bedrooms, his small office, and two bathrooms, along with the larger of the closets.

Only once he was certain no one was lying in wait up there did he call down to his men for his boss and the hostage to be brought up.

Cage was hyperventilating, the terror evident from his breathing, his wild eyes, and the sweat that covered his pink bald head. Hall rushed him into the back corner of the rear bedroom.

"You stay in here with Maja," Hall said. He normally was deferential to his boss, but now that Cage's life as well as his own was on the line, Hall was the alpha.

The former Navy SEAL felt all the terror right now that his protectee's face displayed; this Gray Man seemed to be some sort of unstoppable force, and unlike Verdoorn, Hall had no wish to get a closer look at him. But his military training had taught him how to compartmentalize his fear and to remain on task, so he was all business now.

"Where are you going?" Cage asked nervously as Hall started for the door.

"Not far. I'll be at the top of the stairs with my men. We just have to hold Gentry and the others back."

"How long will it take for the cops to get here?"

Sean knew beat cops would already be swarming over the lower part of the Hollywood Hills, converging on the gunfire, and he could hear air cover overhead. But as for when SWAT would actually hit the property, he couldn't be sure.

"It might be a half hour; they'll want to know what they're getting into. But Gentry won't want to get caught in the cordon already sealing off the streets. If he doesn't find you in the big house, he'll probably bug out. We delay him until that happens."

Hall hoped this all to be true, but he wasn't certain. He pushed Maja to Cage, and the shorter man took her in his grasp, wrapping an arm around her neck.

"Give me a gun!" the Director demanded now.

Hall had one firearm on him, just like his two other security men. He wasn't giving Cage his gun. Instead he reached into his pocket and pulled out a folding knife with a four-inch blade. He opened it and handed it to his boss.

Then he turned and left the room, heading back for the hallway near the stairs. His two men, Scott and Randy, were there and covering down the stairs. Randy had been shot, apparently back at the front entrance to the house, but his arm wound looked manageable.

Hall pulled his walkie-talkie, unsure how many of his men or Verdoorn's men were left.

"Principal is secure at secondary citadel."

He then clipped the radio back on his belt and grabbed his phone from his pocket. At the top of the stairs he typed a short text to Charlotte.

Wherever you are—find cover. It will be over soon.

. . .

Charlotte Cage was on the ground floor of the pool house, hiding in the utility room, right below her father. She lay flat on her stomach behind three surfboards propped against the wall, and she tried not to scream in terror as gunfire echoed around the entire property.

She had no idea what was going on here, but she was too scared to run for the back door, and she didn't know where she would go if she did.

She held her phone in her hands and saw the text from Sean when it lit up the screen. She struggled to type out a reply, but she finally managed to do so.

I'm in the utility room hiding. Please help!

Charlotte put the phone on the floor by her face, then closed her eyes tight, willing this to end.

. . .

Dr. Claudia Riesling ran through Juliet's bedroom on the second floor, because she'd seen a window there that overlooked thick hillside foliage. Her plan was to climb down into the bushes and escape the property before it was too late. If she could just get to the street, she told herself she could call an Uber and, with luck, she could get the hell out of here before the police stopped her to see how she was involved in all this.

She knew the threat anyone around would face when the police rained down on this property. The Consortium would be uncovered and, if she was here at the time, she'd be tied to it.

This event would be too high profile for Cage's people to cover up, of this she felt certain. Anyone involved here who survived the attack of the Gray Man would be heading to prison.

She had a plan, of sorts; she would leave the country. Riesling held bank accounts in Panama and Antigua and Malta, and she knew which countries would and would not extradite her back to the United States.

Fleeing America would not be ideal for her, but she knew the Consortium itself would live on after this, even without Cage and his minions here.

It was just too large, there was too much money to be made.

And they would always need someone with her skills.

The American woman dropped to the ground from the second-story window, turning her ankle slightly when she landed. She limped along the western side of the property, holding on to branches to keep from tumbling down the steep decline. She made her way to the six-foot-high stone fence surrounding the two acres, and then she began climbing.

. . .

Jaco Verdoorn moved backwards through the kitchen, firing round after round from his HK back into the entry hall as he retreated. Loots was with him, firing his rifle, and Duiker staggered along, as well, though the vicious and bloody wound to his arm was occupying most of his attention.

Another of Hall's men had been killed, but one made it upstairs, and from the sound of gunfire it seemed to Jaco like one of the raiders had gone up there to root him out. That left at least two enemy down here, and Verdoorn found himself still hoping to get Gentry in his sights.

A man with a rifle spun into the doorway from the dining room to the kitchen and Jaco fired over and over, hitting his target in the upper chest and head. The man dropped flat onto the tile floor, but a second attacker appeared behind him, and he shot Duiker in the stomach at a range of twenty feet. Duiker dropped dead in the kitchen, and Loots returned fire, sending the enemy to cover.

Jaco dumped rounds from his VP9 until he ran dry, then reloaded his empty pistol. As he did this he screamed to Loots, "Lead them through the house. You need to keep them occupied until LAPD breaches. I'm heading to the citadel."

"Right, sir!" Loots said, and as he took off for the hall to the rear of the home, Verdoorn ran for the back door. Like Hall, the South African was surprised to see the smoke here, but he didn't expect to find any opposition, because Hall had just radioed that he and the others had made it to the pool house.

. . .

I'm out of the swimming pool now, water rushing from my boots as I begin moving across the patio, stepping into the smoke with my pistol out in front of me.

I make it no more than a few steps before I hear Kareem through my earpiece.

"A.J. is dead. Repeat, A.J. is KIA."

Shit.

The gunfire from the house behind me continues and I don't know how many enemy are still fighting there, but I try to push everything out of my mind so I can focus on my objective.

The slight morning breeze has moved the smoke in all directions; I can't see my hand in front of my face. Behind me I hear a cacophony of police sirens, but I'm not overly worried about being caught by the cops just yet. There is no way in hell the LAPD is going to race into this maelstrom without knowing what the hell they're up against. They'll block roads, they'll fly helicopters overhead, they'll do what they can to get civilians out of the line of fire. SWAT trucks will arrive and a plan will be drawn up, and only then will they begin rooting out the shooters.

No, I'm not worried about the cops. The bad guys with guns here on the property are so much more concerning right now.

I start to emerge from the thick obscurant, and I catch a glimpse of a pair of rectangular pools in the patio in front of me before more smoke whirls across my face.

I try to pick up my pace but only go a pair of steps before I feel an incredible impact on my right side. It's a body; someone running has slammed into me at speed, and I go airborne, my weapon tumbling from my hands. I hit the cut stone patio surface, knocking the wind out of me, and I try to reach to my pack behind me to retrieve the backup pistol I have there.

But before I do, I feel a hand grab me by the leg. I kick free but realize the man who crashed into me is on the ground in the smoke close by.

And then I see the knife. A glint of steel shining through a break in the red cloud, slashing in my direction.

He misses, but he has the advantage.

This man has speed, violence of action; there's a weapon in his hand while I'm still fumbling with my backpack.

In my world we call my situation a deficit of initiative, but that's just a fancy way of saying this asshole got the drop on me so now I'm fucked.

I sense more than see him lunging at me through the thick cloud, and I roll out of the way. The blade strikes the stone, and I launch up to my waterlogged boots.

The man disappears in the red cloud, then reappears just as suddenly. He's on me again as I pull the fixed-blade knife from my belt. He slashes to the right, cuts into my tunic at my rib cage, and I feel a hot sting.

I retreat back a few steps and lose sight of him again.

I'm bleeding. The cut feels long but not deep.

Knife fights on TV are a joke. In the real world there is no dancing around, swinging the blade left and right, or stabbing straight down from the sky. Not by anyone who knows what the hell they are doing. The knife fights *I've* been in are a horror show. A combatant diving forward and jabbing straight out towards the midsection, over and over, three or four times a second if he's fast. The attacks are difficult to defend against; the person defending does what he can to scramble back, falling backwards or juking to the side, but it's not like Hollywood, where the guy on the receiving end has time to parry with a thoughtful move and then counter-attack.

If you fight with a knife, you are going to get cut. By your enemy, or by yourself, you are *going* to get cut. More than once.

I get cut more than once.

I see his arm thrust out again through the cloud, and this time the blade nicks me on the right forearm. I feel a second hot sting and hear the blade tip slicing the flesh. The cut is two inches from the muscles that make some of my fingers work, so it's very nearly a debilitating wound, but his awkward jab presents me with an opportunity.

I lunge low with my own knife, hitting him in the back of the hand and slicing it open with a four-inch gash.

He screams, steps back, and we lose each other in the swirling cloud for a moment again. Smoke wafts over from the back doors of the mansion and spews from the grenade between the koi ponds, and the breeze seems to churn it around us.

I'm breathing hard, not moving, my back to the shallow end of the swimming pool behind me.

Where is he?

From somewhere in the red cloud around me I hear him. "I bladdy love my job, Gentry!"

Fucking *Jaco.*

He appears on my right, closing fast, and, in a desperate attempt to avoid getting slashed, I fall backwards onto the stone. He lands on me, and we're wrestling and swinging and ducking now. Two desperate men using all their strength, all their training and cunning, to try both to kill the other and to avoid being killed.

I'm on my back when I drive a knee up into his crotch and jab with my knife, stabbing him in the right forearm, then I roll again as he dives down towards me, smoke swirling around his now-visible form.

Soon we find ourselves with me holding the wrist that's holding his knife, and him holding the wrist that's holding my knife.

I roll to my right with all my strength, and we tumble together into the shallow end of the swimming pool. I land on my back on the upper step, only a foot deep. But Jaco's on top of me, he still has my knife hand tight at the wrist, his knife is pointed right over my heart, and I use all the strength in my body to keep it from plunging straight down.

By being above me, with the weight of his body over his knife hand, I realize that he has leverage I don't possess.

"Got you, Gentry!" he shouts, and I think he may be right. The knife tip disappears into the water, inches from my heart now.

Smoke wafts over us, obscuring my view of the bald-headed man leaning over me, lying on his knife to drive it down while I hold it up with a weakening left arm.

I find myself hoping Kareem and Rodney will appear over us and save me, but not for long.

I need a new strategy, and hope definitely isn't it.

I realize what I have to do now, and I don't love it, but it's my only play. I drop my knife in my right hand, surprising him, then I spin my wrist down, deeper into the water on my right, whipping out of his grasp. The hand is unarmed now, but I bring it up to grab the knife above my heart. With my left hand I let go now, reach down to my left side, and fumble with my pack there. Jaco senses that I'm making some sort of a move, so he throws his entire body onto the arm holding the knife.

I'm about to get stabbed and I know it.

I shift my body to the right, just a few inches, and Jaco's cold steel connects with the skin on my left shoulder, just below the clavicle. The blade plunges into me, hilt deep, and I scream in pain.

And then I swivel my left hand out of the pack and shoot him on the right side of his midsection, at contact distance, with my suppressed Walther .22.

He lurches back in surprise, and I take the opportunity to scramble back myself. His knife is still stuck all the way into my shoulder, so I disarmed him, but I paid one hell of a price to do so.

My left arm hangs low to my side now; I can't lift it to fire the pistol again.

The bullet I shot him with is small and slow, one of the least powerful rounds one can use. I haven't killed him, but I'm sure I've hurt him and put a tiny bit of lead a few inches into his intestines. He starts to stand, and I try to do the same, but my left arm still won't cooperate.

But my right arm is fine. I reach down one more step into the pool, retrieve the knife I dropped there seconds ago, heft it as I launch to my feet out of the water, and dive on him at the edge of the pool.

I land on him fully and the knife sinks into his chest, hilt deep.

I push myself off him and sit on the top step. The smoke blows away enough to see him there on the patio, his legs dangling down into the water, his face ashen and his eyes wide with bewilderment. He just lies on his back, staring skyward.

"Still love your job, Jaco?"

He coughs up blood that stains his face, then runs down to his white shirt and crimson tie, trickles into the pool, and reddens the water around him much like the last wisps of the smoke grenades redden the air around us.

He dies lying next to me without saying a word, and I pull myself up to my feet and step out of the pool. I walk over to him and kick him over towards the edge, and he falls into the water and begins floating away, facedown.

The smoke clears finally, and I regard the knife sticking out of my shoulder.

I have to leave it there for now; otherwise it will only bleed more.

I switch the Walther to my right hand and begin again for the pool house.

Suddenly I'm aware that the gunfire from the main house has stopped. "Rodney? Report status?"

"House is clear. I'm hit. Not life threatening. I've linked up with Kareem. We're coming over to the pool house."

The door is just feet in front of me now. "Remain outside. Watch for squirters."

"No reason for you to breach alone, Harry."

But he's wrong. There *is* a reason. "Say again, hold positions on the patio and provide cover."

Rodney is obviously confused by this, but he's a good soldier. "Understood. Be careful in there."

. . .

Dr. Claudia Riesling had called the Uber when she was still hidden in the trees on the hillside, and then she'd waited until the app told her it was less than a minute away before struggling over a fence and out onto the street.

The road in front of her was empty other than parked cars. Police sirens wailed lower on the hill, but she didn't think there was any law enforcement presence up here just yet.

There was an LAPD helicopter nearby; she was very familiar with the sound, and farther away she heard what might have been a news chopper. She didn't see either of the aircraft directly above her, so she straightened out her clothes, put her phone in her purse, and walked out into the winding two-lane road, just as a gray Toyota Camry pulled around a tight hillside turn and stopped twenty feet in front of her.

A woman sat behind the wheel; Riesling hadn't bothered to look on the app to see the driver or the car, but she stepped to the back door, opened it, and climbed in.

The woman just turned back to her and stared.

Riesling said, "The Four Seasons, Beverly Hills. You got that, right?"

"What's your name?" the woman asked, her voice accented, like many Uber drivers here in LA.

"Claudia. Let's go."

The woman behind the wheel reached for her purse, fumbled in it a moment.

"Don't you hear the shooting going on down the street? I said, let's go!" Riesling demanded.

Soon the red-haired woman began driving forward, towards the sound of gunfire, not away from it.

"Turn around! What the hell are you doing?" Riesling asked. "You know, forget it, I'll walk. Pull over, now!"

But the Camry only picked up speed on the winding road.

Dr. Riesling shouted with all the authority she could muster. "Pull over!"

She reached for the door handle, but the driver slammed hard on the brakes, sending the psychologist forward. Claudia's face smacked the headrest in front of her, hard.

Dazed, she held her hand to her bloody nose and started cursing her driver, but only until the back door opened next to her.

The driver reached in, grabbed Dr. Claudia Riesling by her sweater, and shoved her down onto her back. Riesling brought her hands up to protect her face, but a large kitchen knife was pressed against her throat.

The younger woman leaned over her through the open door. In an accent Claudia suddenly realized was Central European, perhaps Romanian, she said, "You're not going anywhere, bitch."

Talyssa Corbu pulled the woman she recognized from the LinkedIn page of Dr. Claudia Riesling out of the car, and soon both women walked down the hill along Jovenita Canyon Drive.

. . .

I clear the downstairs of the pool house and find a young girl hiding on the ground floor in the back. She's terrified, crying, and dressed in a wetsuit, which seems like a very strange thing for a young sex trafficking victim to be wearing.

I say nothing to her at first, only help her up to her feet and walk her back down the hall towards the living room and the staircase there, because I know now Cage and the others are on the second floor.

I motion to the front door with my head, my gun still pointed at the staircase.

When she doesn't move, I say, "Do you speak English?"

She nods, her voice is meek. Staring at the dagger hilt jutting from my blood-drenched left shoulder, she says, "Yes, sir."

She's clearly American, probably fifteen or sixteen, and this confuses me. "What are you doing here?"

"I live here." Then she says, "Are you going to kill my dad?"

Cage's child? She's so like the girls I saw along the pipeline that I can't even process it. How could these people, Cage and the others in the Consortium, be so unspeakably evil when they themselves have children?

I don't ponder this for long. Instead I answer the girl as truthfully as I can. "I'm just here to make things better."

That's true, isn't it?

"Please," she implores. "Don't hurt him."

I smile a little, but I guess it must look sinister to her, seeing who I am and what I'm smack-dab in the middle of. My smile fades as this occurs to me, and then I say, "I need you to run out that front door. There is no one out there who will hurt you, I promise."

Into my earpiece I say, "I got one, green, coming out the front."

A green is a noncombatant. Not a friendly, a blue, or an enemy, a red.

I wait for the reply from Rodney. "Understood, one green out the front door of the pool house. Do we detain?"

"Negative. Just make sure she gets clear."

"Roger that."

Rodney will probably think this little girl is another sex slave, like the hundreds he's rescued in his life. This realization only serves to make me want to kill her daddy so much more.

But I can't. *Can I?*

"Go ahead," I say to her. "Out the door."

Fresh tears fill her eyes, and I know she'll never be the same. It's a shame, but her tears aren't going to stop me from doing what I came here to do to her father.

"Why?" she asks, now watching blood drip from my left fingertips, onto the floor.

She thinks I'm a monster. I see that in her eyes. She doesn't know that her own father is the monster. Maybe she will soon, or maybe this will all be swept under the rug somehow. But I don't have time to walk her through Kenneth Cage's crimes, so I don't answer.

I swing my gun towards her now, shifting it towards the front door, and soon she leaves, sobbing all the way.

When the door closes behind her, I turn my attention to the staircase.

Cage is up there, I can feel it; he's with Roxana, and it all ends here.

With my Walther aimed up the stairs, I begin ascending. There is a mirror on the landing that gives me a narrow view to the second floor, and my eyes are on it, but I can't see anyone above.

I only make it halfway to the landing when I hear a man up there speak. "Gentry?"

I stop, take a few steps backwards till I'm on the ground floor again.

I don't recognize the voice. "Who's that?"

"I'm Cage's bodyguard."

I sniff out a little laugh. "I hope you've updated your résumé." I resume my climb, slowly and carefully, my weapon high in front of me.

"Look, man," he says from above, and I stop again. "There's three of us up here, all armed and well trained."

"Thanks for the heads-up. I'm liking my odds, though."

"And we're all ready for you. You can turn around now, get out of here, and we won't come looking."

"If you were ready for me, you wouldn't be giving me that option, would you?"

I hear the man sigh all the way down here. Then he says, "Look, bro. I've had enough. I don't want to die for this shit. Let's just call a truce. We stay up here, you leave. I can send the girl down to you. Unharmed."

Roxana isn't unharmed, of this I'm certain. Before I respond I hear a man shout out from another room upstairs. "What the fuck are you doing, Sean?"

I don't recognize this voice, either, but I know exactly who it is. "Hi, Ken. Just met your daughter. She's going to miss you."

There is no response.

"I met your man Jaco, too. By the way, you might want to get that pool out there professionally cleaned."

The bodyguard shouts down again. "If you won't knock it off, Gentry, we *will* kill you."

I back off the stairs, my right hand holding the Walther because of the knife still sticking out of my left shoulder. Through a grimace of pain I say, "I love your optimism, Sean."

"It's desperation, dude," and that's exactly what I hear in his voice now. Then he screams out, plaintive and terrified. "What *are* you? A hero? A fucking saint? We aren't all like that, you know? Some of us out here are just trying to make a living."

I kneel down, searching for a target in the mirror's reflection. While doing this, I say, "I had a mentor, and he had a thing he used to tell me. 'Every saint has a past, and every sinner has a future.'"

For several seconds I hear nothing, nor do I see anything through the reflection.

Softly, Sean says, "I like that."

I think he's right above me, so I can fire into the ceiling and, with a little luck, get some .22 rounds on this guy, but I don't know where Roxana is, so I decide that I'll have to ascend the stairs to verify my targets.

But just as I begin to move, he says, "Look. What do you say I tell my guys to toss their weapons, I do the same, and you let us all walk out of here?"

I'd like to shoot this guy. I imagine that the remorse he seems to be feeling now only comes after getting busted protecting an evil man, and I don't have any respect for that type of self-development.

But three armed men on the second floor are slowing down my approach to my target.

"Anybody else up there? Other than Cage and Maja?"

"No, sir. I swear to God."

"Is Cage armed?"

"A little folding knife. That's it."

"All right. You boys come down, slowly, and nobody will fire on you."

After a pause the man says, "I'm trusting you to do the right thing here, Gentry."

"Ditto. You step onto that landing empty-handed, or I drop you where you stand, got it?"

I hear the other man again, the one I take for Cage. "Sean! I'll double your salary! I'll double it! And no hard feelings, swear to God. Just hold out till the cops come, do your job protecting me, and I'll double . . . fuck it, I'll triple your salary! Permanently."

Hall speaks to me, not to Cage. He just says, "This fuckin' guy. Right?"

But I respond, "That's a lot of dough, Sean. It's gotta be tempting. It's your call."

The squadron of LAPD helicopters flying overhead nearly drowns out his soft response. "I'm just a surfer, bro. I don't need much. But I need my life."

Cage shouts, "Sean! Sean!"

I hear Sean's weapon thud on the carpeted floor right above my head, and then he steps in front of the mirror. He's directly above me, but I don't shoot the ceiling. Two more men come into view, their hands raised. One has blood smeared on his face, and more blood stains the sleeve of tats on his right arm.

All three men walk downstairs, past my position. Sean, the last of the three, looks at me as he passes. He nods in cool appreciation, then forces a smile as he says, "Maybe we grab a beer when you're done."

I look away, back to the staircase. "Why would I do that? You're still a piece of shit. I'd love to be your karma, but I know it will catch up to you someday."

Sean looks downcast, and then he turns away and walks towards the door behind his men.

I call over the radio. "Three coming out. Don't fire unless they pose a threat."

Rodney says, "Roger. Be advised, cops have blocked off the roads out front, but they haven't moved on the property. Helos in the air all around. Got a call from Carl. He was forced to land at a heliport in Hollywood. The LAPD will have him in custody by now."

"Okay," I say. "You boys try to get clear. I'll wrap up here."

Kareem answers now. "We're not going anywhere, Harry. We've got your back."

"Sean?" Cage calls out again from upstairs. "C'mon, Sean."

But I am the one who answers. "He's gone. It's alone time for you and me, Kenny."

"Look, Gentry! I can—"

"Yeah, yeah," I interrupt. "You can make me a rich man, I know. But I don't need money. I just need Roxana. If you don't hurt her, I'll let you live."

He doesn't respond. I step over to the kitchen, open the freezer, and retrieve a massive frosty bottle of Grey Goose vodka. I bite the glass-and-cork lid off, then pour some on my bloody shoulder, coating my wet tunic, my wound, and the hilt of the dagger protruding there. Vodka runs down my arm and drips with blood from my fingertips. Then I recap the bottle with my mouth and head up the stairs, the pistol in front of me and the vodka down to the side now in my nearly noncompliant left hand.

On the second floor I see blood on the carpet, obviously where the wounded bodyguard had been standing. Cage's voice came from a back room, so I walk up the hall, push in the door slowly, and find him standing there, with Roxana tight against his chest.

There's a knife to her throat.

I look at her. The veins in her throat pulsate; her breathing is fast and shallow. "It's going to be okay," I say, and I actually believe it now.

She doesn't respond.

I point the Walther at Cage's face with my right hand. My bloody left shoulder is screaming at me now. I say, "Let her go, or you will die right now." He holds the knife against her carotid, but I just aim in carefully. "Dude, you are a dozen feet away. Do you *really* think I can't put a bullet in your eye socket if I want?"

"I'll kill her!"

"Nope, you'll drop like a sack of wet sand."

Cage gets it. The only chance he has is to comply. He lowers the knife and lets it fall to the floor. He raises his hands slowly into the air.

"Roxana," I say, "there are men outside. They'll help you. Go to them."

She seems utterly bewildered to be alive as she heads for the stairs, still in shock. As she passes, she stares at the knife sticking out of me, and the left half of my body, which by now is all covered in blood.

With my pistol on Cage's face, I transmit to the guys. "Blue coming out. Talyssa's sister. Protect her."

"Hell, fuckin' yeah!" Rodney says.

Cage looks at me, at the gun, at the massive bottle of Grey Goose swinging from my left hand. He says, "You're after the wrong guy."

I raise an eyebrow. "This ought to be good."

"I help the process, obviously, but I don't do it myself. Jaco was the brains. I just do the financing. Stuff like that."

"So what you are saying is, you are the money guy for a massive consortium of sex traffickers. *That's* your defense?"

"You promised you wouldn't kill me."

I laugh a little, but say nothing.

He continues. "Last year we grossed ten point three billion. Sounds like a lot, but this is a one-hundred-fifty-billion-dollar-a-year industry. I'm just a small player. But I know names, Gentry. I know names and locations. I can get you steered towards the big fish. You want that, right? This wasn't just about Maja. This was about you ending this whole thing. Wasn't it?"

I say nothing, just glance out a second-story window. I see Roxana run past Rodney and then Kareem appears, limping, and he wraps an arm around her and begins escorting her up the driveway. Within seconds he's leaning on her, and she is the one helping him along.

Both surviving members of the Manila team are hurt now, but the aches and pains that come from doing this kind of shit at their age are going to only get worse.

Cage keeps talking. "I can help you. I feel terrible about what we've done. I *always* have. Always wanted out of it. It's just . . . shit just got out of hand. Believe me, Gentry, I'm so sorry."

I sigh a little, and I force my left hand up to my face so I can bite the lid off the vodka bottle. I take a swig of the alcohol; it's ice-cold, and it's good going down. I say, "One thing I've noticed in this line of work. Nobody is sorry when they are doing what they do. But everyone seems so fucking sorry when I show up to make them pay for it. What do you suppose that's about, Kenny?"

He knows there's nothing he can say that will stop me from doing whatever it is I want to do. But he tries, anyway. "Listen. I have an arrangement with the government. I help them. Intel on terrorists, mostly. I've saved a lot of lives. Just right now I'm working on something, something that's going to be huge."

I sigh a little. "And that's my dilemma, Ken. If I kill you, then I am going to make some enemies that I can't afford to make. I'll be hunted down and assassinated by the American government."

A slight look of surprise flickers on his face. "Then . . . then you'll let me go?" he asks.

I nod. "I will. Not because I want to, but because I have to."

I'm egging him on now, hoping to get more bravado out of him.

He nods up and down vehemently. "So you know. You understand. I do a hell of a lot of good for this country. I'm a patriot."

I feel my jaw clench, and then I say, "Like I said, I can't kill you, because then they would kill me." I give him a little wink. "But I bet they'd only get really mad at me if I fucked you up for life." With a smile I say, "And I'm used to them being mad at me."

Cage's bravado is slow to drift away, but it drains from his face finally and he stammers. "Wha . . . what?"

I aim quickly and fire. I'm not fucking around. And I shoot Cage in the testicles, so that he's not fucking around, either.

He screams bloody murder, even more than I'd expected, and then he drops and flails on the floor in shock and agony.

I walk over to him and pour Grey Goose over the hands covering his bloody crotch. Then I drop the bottle on the floor next to him. Vodka pours from it.

"Put that on your junk."

It takes Cage another five seconds before he takes the bottle, and then he rolls over onto his stomach, writhing around on the cold glass like he's humping it.

"Kill me! Just kill me!" he screams.

I kneel next to him and speak in a slow and measured tone. "The people you assist in the government. They are the ones who saved your miserable life today. You need to go back to work for them with the exact same intensity and effort as before . . . or you know what will happen."

"Kill me now, you sick son of a bitch!"

"I'll never kill you. I'll just return and take away more of what you hold dear. This time it's your manhood. Next time . . ." I see a framed portrait of Cage with his family in the bedroom. It's lying on the floor, the glass broken. I set it up next to where he's writhing.

"Next time . . . who knows what I'll take from you."

I'm bluffing. His wife is probably in on it, but I'm not a detective, so I don't know, and I would never harm anyone's kids.

And now, when I look into Cage's eyes, I realize he believes I will do what I say I'll do.

He'll comply, he'll keep working for the Agency, with or without functioning balls.

I rise to my feet again. "Keep the vodka on your nuts till the paramedics come. It will slow the bleeding."

I turn and head for the stairs. Into my mic I say, "I'm coming out the front."

"Roger that," Rodney responds.

A few seconds later I meet him by the pool. He's been shot through the thigh; the round went through and through, but he's already bandaged it tightly.

He looks me over. "Dude. Your shoulder."

I turn and stare at the knife there. "I hadn't noticed."

Rodney laughs. "Better leave it in till you get to a hospital."

"What happened in there?" Kareem asks.

"I let Cage live."

"Why would you leave him alive?"

"Trust me, I took all the fun out of it for him."

Kareem sits on a planter by the back door. "Wish the cops would hurry the hell up."

Rodney lowers to the ground next to him. Both men look utterly smoked. But I don't sit. "Guys, I've got to try and run."

Both older men nod, but Rodney says, "Get out of here, brother. Good fighting with you. We'll see you around."

Kareem adds, "Yeah, in the yard at Pelican Bay."

All three of us laugh at this.

It's the only supermax prison in California, and the only reason we're laughing is that, right now, none of us really gives a shit. We did our jobs today, and we know what we did was righteous.

"When LAPD gets here," I say, "tell them to send a paramedic to the second floor of the pool house. There's a wounded man, an innocent, and he needs help."

"What the hell do you mean, 'innocent'?"

I shrug. "I don't make the rules. I just follow them." I pause, then say, "Sometimes."

. . .

Three minutes after this I'm climbing up a steep incline to a street a block north and a hundred feet higher up the hill, my left arm useless at my side. I've pulled my mask down over my face, so if I run into anyone dumb enough to be out on the street I'm going to look pretty scary, but at least the TV choppers above won't show my mug on the evening news.

I make a turn and see a gaggle of police cars, twenty-five yards ahead. I can just make out Roxana there, standing next to a squad car with two other women. I recognize Talyssa by her bright red hair, and by the fact that she and her sister embrace so hard it looks like they are trying to crush each other. I don't know who the other woman is, but after several seconds Roxana turns to her and punches her in the face, dropping her to the ground.

I suddenly have no doubts about her identity.

A cop on a bullhorn tells me to drop to my knees on the street, but I just turn away from the roadblock and begin walking back down the hill.

The guy keeps shouting at me, but I'm unconcerned.

I guess it's possible I'll be arrested by the local five-oh, but I have a sinking suspicion I won't.

You're the Gray Man, you can just slip away, I tell myself.

But I'm wrong.

A pair of vans appears around a turn below me on the road, and I'm sure they've already crossed a police line to make it this high up on the hill. As they approach, I stop, look at a densely wooded property next to me, and consider making a run for it.

But I don't. Instead I just let out a long, tired sigh.

The vans stop alongside me and the side door of the closest one slides open.

Zack Hightower looks me over, up and down. "You look like shit, kid." He sees the hilt protruding from just below my collarbone. "But on the bright side, looks like you won a free knife."

I don't speak, I just climb into the back of the van and it begins rolling off. Armed men all around search and cuff me while Zack looks on. When they're finished, he reaches over to me and puts his hand around my back. Hightower knows I keep a handcuff key secreted under a belt loop, so he grabs it, then tosses it out of the van.

He pulls out his phone as we start driving off.

"Sir? I've got him. No trouble, but half of Hollywood is on fire." He waits a moment then says, "Yes, sir."

Zack holds the phone to my ear. I know it's Hanley.

I'm right. He says, "Subtle, Violator. Real subtle."

I just look out the window.

He adds, "I want to break your fucking neck."

"Get in line, boss."

"Is he alive?"

"He is."

"Okay." I think that's the end of it, but what he says next surprises me. "Court, here's what I'm prepared to do. This isn't a negotiation; this is *not* my opening offer. You get what you get, and what you get is *all* you get."

"I'm listening."

"We'll reach out, quietly, to all the federal law enforcement agencies along the route of the pipeline. Not the state or regional or municipal agencies, but the big guys. At the highest level."

I start to speak but he cuts me off.

"We'll pass on any information Talyssa Corbu gives us, and then we'll tell these agencies that we'll be checking back to see if the pipeline is shut down and the women safely recovered."

I think there's more coming, but when he says nothing, I reply with, "That's it?"

"That's it. You are too precious a commodity for me to let you run around the world saving individual girls. The next job I have for you . . . frankly, kid . . . it's bigger than that."

"What about Kareem and Rodney and Carl?"

"I assume those are the men who helped you and survived."

"Yeah."

"The Agency will assist them. We'll get them out of custody." He adds, "Eventually. Quietly."

Hanley ends the call before I can put up any fight, and Hightower takes the phone from my ear, disconnects it, and drops it back in his bag.

The Ground Branch guy called Teddy pulls the knife out of me; I scream in agony, but he knows what he's doing, and instantly he's cleaning and then bandaging my shoulder, while another guy pours antiseptic on my arm and rib wounds. Chris Travers reaches out from behind me and gives me a squeeze on my good shoulder, then leans forward. "We gotta stop meeting like this, bro."

I don't reply.

We pass through a police line unmolested, then leave the Hollywood Hills a few minutes later.

Soon I can tell we're heading towards the airport. "What's our destination, Zack?"

"There's an Agency Citation waiting for us at LAX. We'll land at Andrews around twenty-one hundred hours. Hanley's going to want you wheels up pretty shortly after that, so you'll need to be treated on the way. Something big's brewing."

I'd put my head in my hands if my hands weren't cuffed behind my back. Instead I just let my head hang down to my chest.

To the other guys it may look like it's exhaustion, frustration, disappointment. They'd be right about that; I am feeling all these things.

But they'd be wrong if they thought it was a sign I was giving up.

Fuck no. I'm just getting started.

Zack misinterprets my demeanor. "It's all right, kid. You kicked ass." He slaps me on the back, and I hate when he does this. "You'll be off killin' bozos again before you know it."

I'm too tired to give Zack a "fuck you," so I just sit here, and I think about this entire damn thing.

I hope Kareem and Rodney and Carl are taken care of by the Agency. I hope Talyssa and Roxana and the other girls from the ranch can all go back to their lives, putting this behind them. I hope Liliana made it back to Moldova safely, and I hope the twenty-two women and girls sold into bondage in Italy can be found and rescued.

All these people need so much help, but I can't help them. I can't help any of them.

All I can do is hope.

I close my eyes and lean my head back now. Men continue to treat my wounds as I sit there.

Hope isn't a strategy, but sometimes it's all you've got.

ABOUT THE AUTHOR

Mark Greaney has a degree in international relations and political science. In his research for the Gray Man novels, including *One Minute Out*, *Mission Critical*, *Agent in Place*, *Gunmetal Gray*, *Back Blast*, *Dead Eye*, *Ballistic*, *On Target*, and *The Gray Man*, he traveled to more than fifteen countries and trained alongside military and law enforcement in the use of firearms, battlefield medicine, and close-range combative tactics. He is also the author of the *New York Times* bestsellers *Tom Clancy Support and Defend*, *Tom Clancy Full Force and Effect*, *Tom Clancy Commander in Chief*, and *Tom Clancy True Faith and Allegiance*. With Tom Clancy, he coauthored *Locked On*, *Threat Vector*, and *Command Authority*.

CONNECT ONLINE

MarkGreaneyBooks.com

⬛ MarkGreaneyBooks

🐦 MarkGreaneyBook